THE
THIRD
TRUMPET

MRDS

Holly —

Thank you for your
support

+ Larry D.

THE THIRD TRUMPET

The Last Eulogy Series Book Two

A Novel by

ANTHONY R. DIVERNIERO

gatekeeper press

Columbus, Ohio

This book is a work of fiction. The names, characters and events in this book are the products of the author's imagination or are used fictitiously. Any similarity to real persons living or dead is coincidental and not intended by the author.

The Third Trumpet

Published by Gatekeeper Press
2167 Stringtown Rd, Suite 109
Columbus, OH 43123-2989
www.GatekeeperPress.com

Author can be reached at tdproph20@gmail.com.
www.anthonydbooks.com

Edited by Alice Peck
Copyedited/proofread by Ruth Mullin
Cover design by Duane Stapp

ISBN (hardcover): 9781642374087
ISBN (paperback): 9781642374070
eISBN: 9781642374063

Printed in the United States of America

To my mom and dad, Lucille and Dominic.

*Thank you for your love, kindness,
and support throughout my life.*

Acknowledgements

FIRST AND FOREMOST, to all the readers of my first novel, *Messenger From God*. Thank you! Thank you! I hope you enjoy *The Third Trumpet*.

Thank you to my editor, Alice Peck, a true wordsmith. Thank you for your guidance.

Thank you, Duane Stapp, for the cover design and your patience.

Thank you, Ruth Mullen, my copy editor. Your inputs are invaluable.

Special thank you to my Barnes and Noble family in North Haven: Frank, Ellen, Marjorie, Clive, Diana, John, and Emily. I so enjoy the mornings when we are all together. To the marvelous employees who allow me to spend countless hours writing and drinking espressos, especially Jean-Marcel, Noelle, Lisa, Nye, Michelle, Robert, Jaylyn, Rachel, Paul, Holly, Jay, Nyzae, and Anna.

To my longtime childhood friends Lisa, Bunny, and Janet. Thank you for reading the manuscript and giving your input. I hope the final version doesn't disappoint.

Debbie Abrams and the book club babes Diane DuPont, Cindy Gilhuly, Nancy Labanara, SueCroce, Susi Zuse, Carol Cusano, Kathy Mitchell, and Gina Hart

Thank you, Sharon and Joe, for your resounding wows.

Monte Cassino, Italy, 1510

A priest sat at a wooden desk. He read the yellowed scroll, written in AD 34. The Benedictine translated the Hebrew words on the papyrus into Latin: *From the ancient village will arise a family from an orphaned child.*

He was interrupted by the call for afternoon prayers and would return to his translation the following morning.

The last page of the hidden journal read:

There are three absolutes to our world: we are born; we live; we die. We have no choice when, how, or where. In our youth, we are dependent on others to mold our minds. What we see, what we hear, what we are taught, and how we are treated shape who we become. These events form our perceptions and ideals. Objectivity is swayed by the truths and lies of the era we live in. We all meet the same demise, whether young or old—our life span is a miniscule fraction of eternity.

A time of deep spiritual deception summons us. The reality of life is distorted. We believed in the good that we accomplished but failed to recognize the injustice we caused. Those who shone like bright stars were the ones who tried to help us understand the power of evil, but the light of their souls was often obscured by the pervasive darkness of humanity. In our ignorance and pride, we failed to follow their example. Our hearts hardened; we grew deaf. Humankind rationalized the truth to further its agenda. We were absorbed in ourselves, in the complexity of our existence.

When we study the tapestry of life, we see the prejudices we created. The choices we made and assumed correct were, in fact, wrong. We did not follow the blueprint bequeathed to us.

The war between good and evil, the battle within the mystical world, will deceive the religious as the secular powers gain momentum in these final days—the end of an era begins. The confrontation I speak of started with a mere aberration of the truth—a tiny lie—our unwillingness to live a simple life.

The deceivers are in your midst; their actions, coupled with the world's ignorance, will culminate in a thunderous crescendo. Many will be misled. The evil tentacle will grasp the souls, minds, and hearts of all humankind.

The governments will be brought to trial for their injustice, for over the centuries, the deception stayed hidden within all humanity, deep within the fabric of our beings. Truth is truth and can never be changed, no matter how we rationalize. Remember, Ishmael's descendants became the fathers of Islam, while Isaac's offspring became the fathers of the Hebrews and Christianity. All were created by the same true God.

The time has come to make amends for our actions. First, the prophecy of old must come to fruition.

—Paolo DeLaurentis
November 11, 2001

Chapter 1

July, Four Months before the American Presidential Election

"THANK YOU, ETEN. I agree. We need to ally ourselves in the fight against financial inequity. I'll be in touch."

Rio DeLaurentis ended the phone conversation with the president of the European Union. She had been in Washington, DC, for four days. As the founder of the three-year-old American Party, a bipartisan congressional committee subpoenaed her. Republicans and Democrats joined forces to discredit her leadership. Today, the contentious battle of ideologies would strengthen the resolve of those who wished to destroy her. The media labeled Rio a "legal revolutionary." The established parties had another name for her—*traitor*. As she put it, the American Party was, "a true political organization that would transform America."

She leaned against the window of her hotel room and undid the top button of her white silk blouse under her gray Armani jacket. A pigeon landed on the sill, and the movement of the bird's wings focused her attention outside. She took in the sights of the city. To her right, bright orange fencing surrounded the toppled Washington Monument, the lawn still speckled with spots of burned grass. Climate prognosticators had been correct; the summer was the hottest and driest in a hundred years.

The thirty-nine-year-old attorney known for her philanthropic activities had grown tired of a government that refused to help the poor, so she focused her energies on the American people. She became a patriot who helped the multitudes who didn't have the resources to protect themselves. The United States had become a two-class society, a schism perpetuated by a president who manipulated the system. Troubled by a divided country, Rio believed there had to be a better way. At least her influence helped defeat a debtor's prison law Congress tried to pass in 2018.

Her thoughts were interrupted when her cell phone rang. "Hello? Yes . . . I'll be right there."

Rio was disappointed it wasn't Dean Essex confirming their dinner plan for tonight before she returned to New Haven. Her fortieth birthday was less than a year away, and she felt motherhood beckoning. Although she dated, she had never found the one man to make her heart pound with awe—like the love her father had for Sydney. Maybe today was the day. Maybe Dean was the one.

*   *   *

A black SUV pulled up to the Capitol.

"Thanks for the lift, Danny." As he was about to close the door, Giacomo added, "Good sparring match today. Thanks for the workout."

"No problem. We'll talk soon."

"Will do." Giacomo DeLaurentis jumped out of the vehicle as a similar one parked behind him. The chauffeur exited the car as the rear passenger door opened. Giacomo walked the short distance to meet his twin sister, Rio.

"Day three. Are you ready, little sister?"

"I am, big brother."

The two hugged. Born less than four minutes apart, they often joked about their age difference.

"When did you arrive?" Rio asked.

"Landed an hour ago. Your news groupies are circling."

"Please . . . just what I need. Ignore them."

"Miss DeLaurentis!" someone shouted.

"Rio, can you answer . . ."

"What's it like to be attacked by the Senate?"

That question made Rio stop. Her face flushed with anger as she turned to the cameras. Ten reporters shoved their microphones at her.

"I don't care." The lines of tension at the corners of her eyes told a different story. "Let me say this: they attack me because I represent the poor, the downtrodden people of our country. They malign me because I'm not influenced by their greed or power. It annoys the hell out of them that I can't be bought. They badger me because they can't face the truth. They betrayed the citizens of our country. *They* are the traitors, not I."

"We heard that kind of talk in the past from President Waldron, but he failed. What makes you different?" another reporter asked.

"I'm not a man. And I don't lie."

Rio took her brother's arm, and they climbed the steps of the Capitol. "Rio, be careful what you say today," Giacomo cautioned.

"If I don't tell the truth, who will?"

"I understand. But remember who you're talking to."

The congressional hearing room overflowed with reporters. American flags hung on either side of the grand dais. Perched high on their throne-like chairs, the ad hoc committee consisted of leaders of both the Senate and the House. These political elites were surrounded by fourteen bipartisan representatives who would question Rio. As she adjusted her seat, she eyed her inquisitors with malice. Cameras flashed, and a screech from Senator Rawlings's microphone opened the proceedings.

"Good morning, Miss DeLaurentis."

"Senator."

The political leader shifted his papers and skipped the formalities. "Miss DeLaurentis, why do you wish to subvert the US government?"

"I take offense at your statement."

"Answer the question."

"Can you be more specific, Senator?"

An aide whispered in the senator's ear and presented him with a sheet of paper.

"You own a house in Italy?"

"Yes, I do."

"Do you have ties to the Italian government?"

"No."

"No, Miss DeLaurentis? What is your relationship with Sergio Esposto?"

"He's a close family friend."

"Was he not the prime minister of Italy?"

"Yes, he was."

The craggy senator blew his nose into a white monogrammed handkerchief. He sniffed as he continued. "Is the ex-prime minister a business partner of your brother, retired Colonel Giacomo DeLaurentis?"

"Yes."

"Are you familiar with your brother's company . . . um . . ." The senator fumbled with his notes. "Remote, LLC?"

"No, I am not."

Giacomo was unfazed by the interrogation. As ex-commander of the Black Operations Elite Team—BOET—he'd been through worse. He just hoped Rio would stay calm.

"No further questions, Mr. Chairman."

Senator Esther Boyle was next. Chair of the Energy and Natural Resources Committee, she served the constituents of Texas. In her twenty-four years in office, the career politician had held the top positions on the Foreign Relations and Intelligence Committees. Her peers referred to her as "the bitch of the Senate" because she was not afraid to clash with the legislative body. Half Cherokee Indian, she had overcome prejudices by touting herself as the only real American in politics. A proud woman, it was her way or no way. Now she had the task of defeating the American Party.

"Ms. DeLaurentis, once again I would like to thank you for your concern for the poor."

"You're welcome, Senator Boyle."

"You made the following statement. I quote, 'The time has arrived when we the people must rise up and take a stand against our government.' Those are treasonous words, Ms. DeLaurentis."

"Your point, Senator?"

"I'm saying, Ms. DeLaurentis, it sounds like you have a problem with our government."

"I do. What's your point?"

Ignoring the question, Boyle continued, "Are you familiar with the militant group called the Fighters for Freedom Brigade, or FFB?"

In May 2004, the FBI warned the director of Homeland Security of the threat to the country from the militant group. To the dismay of both directors, the congressional Intelligence Oversight Committees terminated the investigation. FFB leaders planted their followers in the southwest and northwest parts of the nation, establishing homegrown American terrorist cells.

"I am. I disagree with their philosophy of violence."

"Do you or the American Party support them financially?"

Rio's anger swelled. *How dare she ask me a question like that.* She could see how Boyle earned her nickname. "No! Don't be absurd. But let me warn you: given the chance, the FFB will attack us."

Composed of a cross section of disgruntled Democrats, Republicans, and political independents who wanted their country back, the FFB believed the democratic system had failed to enforce the constitutional rights of the people. Their desire for revolutionary change was precipitated by the fierce battle over gun control, the intrusion of the Internal Revenue Service, spying on private citizens, censorship of the news media, and a decline in moral attitudes. The 120,437-member militia waited in abeyance for their opportunity to attack.

"How do you know?" the senator demanded to know.

"Because my father said it would happen."

"Oh, yes, your father? The famous Paolo DeLaurentis? The man who could tell the future." Boyle snickered.

"Ms. Boyle, my father's words were truthful. The events he foretold came to be." Rio's voice flowed louder and stronger. "His words could unite a broken society, an injured people, and most of all, bring peace to our world."

Giacomo tried to catch her eye as he shook his head. *Please, Rio, stop. Keep your mouth shut. They didn't listen to Dad then. They won't now.* As the interrogation droned on, Giacomo recalled that day.

It was October 28, nine months after their father's death. A beam of sunlight streamed through the big window. Giacomo and Rio sat on a couch in the corner of what had been their father's study. Not much had changed. There was a new Oriental rug, and law journals had replaced the various business books. Paolo's old desk was still cluttered with papers. Pictures of the twins and their parents were scattered throughout the room.

"How are you feeling, older brother?"

"Better now that I'm out of the hospital."

"Tell me about it. Mom and I were so worried. I can't believe your fever got that high."

"Yeah, the doctors were puzzled."

"Sounds like the story Dad told us about when he was a boy. Did a white light surround you?"

"No, no white lights." Giacomo changed the subject. "Do you have the key?"

"Yeah. Came yesterday by FedEx. I found the box hidden under the floorboards over there by the window. I'm surprised we received the package, considering how much damage Hurricane Adam caused."

"Did you see the news footage of Florida? Totally devastated. How are they going to recover? Not to mention, how is the government going to pay for it?"

Rio wiped a tear from her eye. "Those poor people. This is unbelievable; our world is going to hell. The coastline flooded to Lake Okeechobee, and hundreds of thousands are homeless. I don't understand how a flood could be that bad."

"The president told me this morning the satellite pictures show a tsunami hitting the coast. They estimated the first wave at over one hundred fifty feet. Thank God most people were evacuated—Adam was a category 5 when it slammed into the shoreline."

"Unbelievable." She shook her head and handed the key to Giacomo. He opened the box. Inside was a note attached to a journal. They read the pages together.

My dear children, if you are reading this I am dead. I always wanted to say that.

Giacomo and Rio laughed.

I hope you are both well. I am sure you are. Attached is my journal containing all the visions I had. I give this to both of you. Giacomo, with your contacts, and Rio, with your legal mind, and with all your financial resources, maybe the two of you can do better than I did. I love you both. What you hold in your hands is a burden, I know—I lived with it for many years. Giacomo, if you and your sister feel the burden is too great, you have my permission to give the journal to the president. Whatever you do will be the right thing—there is no wrong decision.

I love you,
Dad

Brother and sister leaned back on the leather couch, tears in their eyes. Rio reached over to the coffee table and picked up the journal. She sat close to her twin and opened the prophetic book. Together they read the first page.

When Adam, the giant hurricane, hits the coast of Florida and Lake Okeechobee becomes part of the Atlantic Ocean, humankind will enter an era when the earth will shudder and quake. The meteorological events will tax the economies of the world, igniting a maelstrom of want and greed. The nations will rise against each other as foretold, until a new era of peace, a new dawn awakens humankind . . .

"Holy shit, Giacomo! This is unbelievable."

"What the hell do we do with this?"

"Shit if I know." Rio thumbed through the ink-covered pages. "Listen to this!" She read it aloud:

Within six months, there will be three earthquakes successively escalating in intensity. The first will measure 8 in magnitude; the second 8.5; the third will be beyond comprehension. This last one will affect the economy so severely that the Eagle will borrow with no success. A man who is no stranger will arise from the East with a false economy that many countries will embrace. Major cities throughout the world will be destroyed, and millions will die.

"What does this mean?" she asked.

"The Eagle represents the United States, but other than that, your guess is as good as mine."

Rio fanned the pages of the journal and chose another paragraph at random:

When the lost brothers hug, peace will reign for a short time. Then the last pontiff will awaken and rise, and a false sense of peace will rest in the hearts of humanity. The prophecy of old will come to fruition, and the earth and its people will shake with fright and dread as an era of dystopia takes hold.

Giacomo took the journal from his sister and flipped through it. "Look at this, Rio. The last couple of pages were torn out!"

"What do you think it means?"

"Not a clue, but I'm sure we'll find out."

"You've got that right, brother."

The words "You're an ass" snapped Giacomo out of his daydream.

"Order, order," the chair of the committee repeated, sending a harsh glare at Senator Boyle. "Miss DeLaurentis, I do not wish to hold you in contempt. Please, let's move forward."

"Are you in contact with the FFB?" Boyle repeated.

"No, I am not. To my question, what's your point?"

"My point, Miss DeLaurentis, is that we don't need people like you stirring the pot."

"*Stirring the pot?* Are you serious? Let me explain the problem to you, Ms. Boyle. While you moronic a-holes sit—"

"Order, order." The gavel sounded. "Miss DeLaurentis, may I remind you of where you are?"

"I know damn well where I am. I'm sitting in front of a pack of baboons whose only interest is their own agenda, not the American people. If I were you, I'd resign before it's too late. Yes, I want a revolution, but my revolution will abide by the Constitution. We'll vote you jackasses out of office."

Everyone in the crowded room rose in applause. The gavel continued to bang as the chair of the committee struggled to restore order.

"I'm tired of you losers," Rio said as she stood and marched down the aisle, cameras flashing and whizzing.

Giacomo shook his head.

His sister noticed the fury in his eyes and whispered, "Big brother is not happy. Oh well, it is what it is."

Two Capitol police officers guarded the doorway. Her glaring eyes said it all: *Out of my way.* One cop leaned toward her as she passed by. "Nice job, Miss DeLaurentis."

Chapter 2

Two Weeks Later

"Hello."

"Good morning, *principessa*."

"Sergio, how are you?" The familiar voice of her father's old friend, the former prime minister of Italy, made Rio smile. When he spoke in Italian, the words flowed with the harmony of musical notes.

"*Bene, bene*—good, good. Your brother told me you're traveling to Ottati next week."

"Yes. I can't wait, landing in Salerno. Should be cooler in the mountains. August is a good month—no tourists. Besides, I need to leave the States for a while."

"I understand. I saw the news reports."

Rio ignored the comment. "How are you?"

"Quite well. I received a letter today from your father."

"Dad?"

"Yes, a sealed envelope to be opened when you arrive."

"Damn! Another one of his secrets," she mumbled.

"I'm sorry, Rio, what did you say?"

"Dad had a habit of leaving us hidden notes to find after he died."

"Me as well."

"Really?"

"Your father was a gift to those who listened to him."

"Yes, he was. Still more to happen, I'm afraid."

"You should forget your American Party and move here."

"I wish. My father always said to live a simple life—but I'm in too deep." Rio changed the subject. "Why didn't you call Giacomo?"

"I haven't spoken with you in a while—thought I'd try you first."

"You're so kind, Sergio."

"What day will you be arriving in Salerno? I'll meet the airplane."

"Tuesday. Sergio, I'll tell Giacomo, if you don't mind?"

"Not at all, *principessa*. Ciao."

"Ciao."

Rio hung up the phone. Through the window of her study, she watched two deer as they drank from the lake. She enjoyed the views of the twenty-two-acre Brewster Estate. The history of the property dated back to the mid-1800s when local industrialist James Brewster acquired the land. At that time, there were rolling hills, a manmade lake, and Brewster's thirty-room mansion surrounded by a ten-foot-high, three-foot-wide stone wall encompassing three city blocks. Servants' quarters flanked the two entrances. Except for the house, the structures remained.

In the reading of her dad's will, Rio discovered her father had given the money to his best friends, Tony and Steve, to buy the land on his behalf, enabling him to keep his privacy. The reluctant tycoon bequeathed each of his children $100 million, and his instructions to invest in gold had paid off—their combined wealth now exceeded $1 billion. They followed their father's example and donated much of their money. He had often told his children it's best to stay under the radar, and, like him, they tried to keep a low profile.

An old maple clock with a drawer built into its base chimed the hour. The three-hundred-year-old Swiss timepiece had been a gift to her father, but Rio couldn't recall the origin. From her workspace cluttered with law journals and family pictures, she picked up a photo of her dad.

"What surprise do you have for us now, Pops?"

Rio took a navy-blue Mont Blanc pen from the holder and wrote herself a note to call Sergio with her arrival time in Salerno. She had not spoken with her brother since she'd returned from Washington, figuring he was still angry about her outburst at the hearing. She dialed his number.

"Hello."

"Morning, Colonel. I hope I didn't interrupt your morning workout?"

"No. Finished about an hour ago. What's going on, little sister? Long time."

"Well, I figured you didn't want to talk to me."

Giacomo ignored the comment.

"Are you ready for this one?" she asked.

"Shoot."

"Sergio called. He received a letter from Dad."

"Are you shittin' me?"

"Nope."

"What did it say?"

"'To be opened when we arrive in Italy.'"

"Damn. How many notes did he send us? Three?"

"Yes. One, a year after he died, the other two on our thirty-fifth birthdays."

"How did he do that? I mean, who's mailing these letters?"

"Dad had secrets and a lot of money. When you're that wealthy, you can do anything."

"I guess so. Everything he wrote in the journal happened, but nobody listened."

"Whatcha gonna do, Giacomo? We did what Dad said. We gave it to the president. It's not our fault his administration did nothing."

"What about Waldron? He didn't do anything either. Maybe we should've been more proactive."

"Too late now. We gotta move forward."

"Yep. I can tell you, whatever Dad's message is, I will handle it."

"Be careful, Giacomo. Mom told me Emily is pregnant. What great news! I'm so excited."

"Yeah, I'm going to be a dad. You're going to be an aunt."

"Me an aunt—God help us."

They laughed in harmony.

"When's the due date?"

"January."

"Boy or girl?"

"Patience, my little sister."

"Are you and Emily still going to Paris?"

"Yeah, we're meeting Emily's father there. She doesn't want to go."

"How come?"

"Remember the story Dad told us—how he met her father when she was kidnapped?"

"Yes."

"Well, she still has nightmares."

"Wow."

"Yeah. Are we set for our trip to Italy?"

"Sure are. I spoke with Tony D; his new Gulfstream G750 will be waiting for me on the sixteenth. We'll pick you two up in Paris and then head to Salerno. I called Sabatino—the house will be ready."

"Excellent."

"How are you getting to Paris?"

"Air France."

"Still leaving in two days?"

"Three to be exact."

Rio glanced at the clock on her desk. "I gotta go—have a lunch date."

"Oh . . . anyone I know?"

"Nope, just business."

"Well, have fun."

"Will do."

"Oh, sis?"

"Yes."

"Even though I disagreed with how you did it, I'm proud of you."

"Thanks, big brother."

Chapter 3

Four Days Later

RIO PLACED HER suitcase in the trunk of her car. She got into the electric hybrid with a quick glance in the rearview mirror. As she pushed the start button, the vehicle awoke. It was an unusually cool, zero-humidity August day marked by bright blue skies and green trees. An occasional white birch tree broke up the landscape. She drove out of the estate's gate and turned left on Cliff Street and then right on Whitney Avenue. She needed to stop at her office to sign checks.

"Hello?" She answered the cell phone using the car's speaker.

"Hi, Rio."

"Dean."

"I'm in town. Would you like to meet for coffee?"

"I'd love to—what a pleasant surprise. Where?"

It would be Rio's third date with Dean Essex. The second had been at a Japanese restaurant in Washington, DC. For the last couple of weeks, he'd called her every other day. She could feel romance blossoming.

"How about the Omni Hotel?"

"I'll be there in twenty minutes. Why didn't you tell me you were coming?"

"I wanted to surprise you."

"You're so sweet. I'm on my way."

Rio entered the café. Her outfit was casual—a pair of jeans, a loose-fitting tan satin blouse, and brown shoes. Still beautiful, she enjoyed the complimentary glances she received from passersby when her shoulder-length mahogany hair shone in the morning sun. Rio found Dean in the furthermost corner of the café.

Dean was attractive—not necessarily handsome but not ugly either. Dressed in a dark navy-blue suit, white shirt, and red tie, he was exactly her height. His dirty blond hair had been combed back with styling gel, and he wore tortoiseshell glasses with round lenses. When he spotted Rio, he placed his copy of the *New Haven Register* on a side chair—its headline read "FFB Threatens Militant Action."

He rose to meet Rio, and they embraced. He kissed her on the lips. Rio welcomed the softness of his touch.

"Wow—you're a good kisser."

"Thank you. I got you a black coffee and a cinnamon scone."

"I love their scones."

They sat opposite each other. Legs crossed, Rio leaned forward, her hands wrapped around the green mug. "How's Washington?"

"Not bad. Hopefully I'll be working with Tom Maro."

"Excellent. I've spoken with him a couple of times."

"You've talked to him?"

"Yeah, nice man. We discussed policy issues."

"Interesting."

"He'll be a respectable president. Waldron will lose. The people are tired of his lies."

"I hope you're correct. I'll be in the chief of staff's office."

"You mean you have the job?"

"Not quite, but after today, I will."

"Congrats."

"Thanks. He'll definitely win."

She reached for his hand. Rio enjoyed his smile at her advance. "So, why are you here?"

"I wanted to say goodbye." His eyes darted back and forth as he rubbed his left ear.

"What's wrong?"

"Nothing."

"You seem preoccupied."

"No—not when you're in front of me."

"Wow, kind of deep in here." She chuckled.

"No. I . . . I . . ."

"Yes?"

"I care for you, Rio. I enjoy your company."

"Are you blushing?"

"Boy, you're tough."

"I'm sorry—it's the lawyer in me. My brother says the same thing."

"Is Giacomo going with you to Italy?"

"No. He and his wife will meet me at the Salerno airport."

"He's not traveling with you?"

"No, he's going commercial. I'm flying on a private jet."

"Wow."

"A family friend is going to Positano; he asked if I wanted a ride."

"Nice."

"Yeah, sure beats the TSA lines."

"Out of New Haven?"

"No, Oxford."

They talked for over an hour. Rio glanced at her cell phone. "Sorry, Dean. I have an eleven o'clock appointment."

"I understand. My flight to DC departs in ninety minutes. I should leave as well."

They exited the coffee shop.

"This is mine." Rio opened her car door.

Dean reached into his coat pocket and pulled out a white envelope and a blue velvet case. "This is for you." He opened the case. Inside was a gold heart pendant with a small diamond in its center.

"Dean, you shouldn't have."

"I don't want you to forget me while you're away."

"How sweet." Rio took the gold chain in her hands, placing the strand around her neck. She turned, saying, "Can you clasp this for me?"

He fumbled with the locket for a moment. "There you go." He kissed the nape of her neck.

She touched the charm. "Thank you."

"Promise me you'll read this on the airplane."

"I will. What is it?"

"You can't tell?"

"A card? I love cards!"

"Maybe."

"I need to go."

"Have a safe trip. Call me when you can."

"I will. I promise. Thank you."

Dean took her hand. "Rio?"

"Yes."

He took her other hand. Their eyes met as they embraced and then kissed.

Rio patted him on his lapels as she gazed into his eyes. "I'll call you from Italy."

As she drove away, she looked into the side mirror and saw her new boyfriend answer his phone.

Chapter 4

THAT EVENING, RIO arrived at the Key Air hangar. She pressed the intercom button, her identity was verified, and the gate to the ramp lifted. On the tarmac sat Tony's new Gulfstream G750. The plane was equipped with the latest technology—the first corporate jet to fly faster than the speed of sound. Flight time to Salerno, Italy: four-plus hours. In honor of her father, Tony kept the registration number N7PD on the tail of the plane—Paolo DeLaurentis.

The lineman opened her car door.

"Tommy. How are you today?"

"I'm good, Miss DeLaurentis, and you?"

"Wonderful. How's Laura?"

"My wife is well. Thanks for asking."

As Rio boarded the private airplane, she felt the stares of the ground personnel. *I still got it.* She approached her seat, appreciating the interior—plush and expensive; the cabinetry made from cherry and maple wood. The aircraft sat nineteen, slept nine. Each passenger had their own monitor, loaded with a library of over fifteen hundred movies.

"Hello, Tony."

Tony's eyes brightened when his childhood friend's daughter arrived. "Rio . . . Rio. I'm happy you're here."

Tony, now in his sixties, his hair almost gray, had a small paunch. An author, his twentieth novel had been published the previous

November. He was unscathed by the world's economic turmoil because he too had taken Paolo's advice, and prudent gold investments had made him a wealthy man. A humanitarian, he helped Rio's causes as well as those stricken with cancer.

Rio settled across from Tony in the oversized tan leather seat. The stairs tucked into the plane, and the jet engines roared to life.

"I understand our route changed."

"Yes—no, Paris. Giacomo and Emily will meet us in Salerno. They're in Positano. They had dinner with Arnaud and then left."

"Damn! They could've stayed at my house."

"I guess it was a quick decision. How long are you staying in Italy?"

"Don't know yet. Depends on the airplane's schedule."

Tony donated the plane to terminally ill patients. The stateroom had been equipped with the required medical equipment for care during passage. His pilots transported the sick to treatment centers throughout the world. In most cases, he paid the hospital bills.

"How old?"

"Fifteen-year-old girl from Iraq, stage 4 lung cancer."

"Are you taking her to Smilow?" Yale University's research hospital was ranked first in the country.

"Yes. They've made great strides—88 percent recovery rate."

"Fantastic."

He nodded. "Is Cardinal Andrew still spending the weekend with you and Giacomo in Ottati?"

"Yes. I so love talking with him. He said he needed time away from the Vatican. You know he's working on the reunification of the churches?"

"Yes, I read that in the *Times*. He's a good man." Tony opened his briefcase. "This is for you."

"Your new novel?"

"Sure is."

"I can't wait to read it. Did you catch me on TV?"

"I did—the entire world saw you. You pissed off a lot of people."

A chime echoed through the cabin, signaling the impending takeoff. Rio placed the manuscript to the side.

"I don't care, Tony. When are these stupid politicians gonna realize *we* are the people—we voted them in, we can vote them out. They destroyed our country with greed and indifference. I shouldn't say they destroyed—but they *allowed* it. So many people barely subsist; they muddle through life with no hope of change. Those senseless ass bureaucrats can't get out of their own way. We need a president the people can trust, not a demagogue. Now the imbecilic morons want to collude with Trivette."

"You don't like Trivette?"

"No, not really. We've had several conversations. In fact, we spoke two weeks ago. I have a bad feeling about that man, but what he's done with the European Union is astonishing. There's more to him than we understand. Besides, we don't have to get in bed with him. We could do something similar—it's our government that won't let us." Her hands animated, she pointed her finger at Tony. "The government can't help those families affected by the natural disasters that pummeled us in February." She shook her head in disgust. "The politicians are more concerned with themselves than with the citizens. How many homeless—two hundred thousand? Shit, they're all jackasses. We are on the precipice of another economic collapse and a revolution—please . . ." She scowled and continued the rant. "They didn't even learn from their mistakes—the people are disgusted with politicians. The issue is not only the presidency; it's the other five hundred *gimokes* on the Hill."

"I understand what you're saying, Rio. However, you're not making any friends when you tell our enemies in Congress to resign. Then, to top it off, you called them moronic a-holes in front of the world press. The news media characterized your remarks as inflammatory and embarrassing to the United States. You're *hurting* the American Party."

Rio said nothing.

"You're an internet sensation. You went viral on YouTube—over fifty million hits in one day. Euro News branded you 'the revolutionary.' So much for staying under the radar."

"My Italian temper got the best of me. Tony, they should resign.

So many of our people live in poverty. There is no middle class. As my father said, the failure of our government to end the two-class society will cause a revolution. You wanna know the real issue?"

"Sure."

"This fight is the government against the people—the conspiracy theorists are in their glory. Believe me when I tell you we're facing a genuine uprising. A downright bloody face-to-face battle. Rumor has it the brigades are preparing."

Tony raised an eyebrow.

"Don't worry, Tony. I'm not stupid enough to back the FFB. My point is my father will be right once again."

"Not everybody believed the words in his journal—especially President Stalworth and now Waldron. Remember, Rio, we're part of the rich."

"I'm well aware. We have to gather the wealthy like ourselves to pool our resources. We need to help the poor, begin a real revolution—a legal revolt—by voting out the Democrats and Republicans in Congress and replacing them with the American Party. We are the people, damn it. One victorious sweep to rid the current politicians. Tony—we can do it. By the next presidential election, we'll have enough support for the party. We'll abolish the establishment; they will be humiliated into oblivion. They should've heeded my father's warnings. In their arrogance, they let the country fall apart. All he wrote came true. We were fools to give Dad's journal to the administration." Rio's eyes welled.

Tony listened and nodded as she continued.

"What I said to the leaders of the House, well . . ." She hesitated and allowed herself to relax.

"At least you had the guts to tell them. You were the topic of conversation at Katz's."

"Katz's—you guys from the old days still meet there on Tuesdays?"

"We sure do, now that we're retired. Warren's pig roast is next month. He'll be expecting you and your brother."

"I'll be there. Can't speak for Giacomo."

The flight attendant came down the aisle; a pretty woman with auburn hair that fell below her shoulders, a bright smile, and beautiful brown eyes.

"Tony, when would you like to eat?"

"Whenever you're ready, Sharon."

"Half hour?"

"Sounds good."

"What's on the menu?" Rio asked her.

"Veal marsala, green beans, and garlic mashed potatoes."

"Excellent. How about a Pepsi with dinner? Rio?"

"Please."

Rio grabbed the manuscript and leafed through the typed pages. "A murder mystery?"

"No, a love story—about your father."

"Dad?"

"Yeah. Read chapter 42. Tell me what you think."

Rio pushed the recline button on the armrest. A motor hummed as the seat tilted back. She opened the manuscript to chapter 42 . . .

The day after Sydney arrived in Ottati, the two reunited lovers sat on the portico. Below them, a valley of colors. Green trees and golden meadows sprinkled the mountains. The midmorning autumn day was warm and bright with the fragrance of fall. Italian music serenaded them. Giacomo, Rio, Arnaud, and his daughter Emily sat inside at the kitchen table. Their smiles were radiant as they watched Paolo with the love of his life, Sydney Hill.

"Syd, I can't believe you're alive." Tears welled in his eyes. Paolo gently touched her face. "Life has a new meaning today."

"I don't understand." Sydney held his hand.

"Everything we've been through, and now I'm on death's doorstep. God brought us back together for what purpose? I say that as a question, but I know the answer."

"What's that, my love?"

"I came to realize life is how we love one another—in our struggles, in our hurt, in our tragedies as well as our joys. Without the essence of love within ourselves, we're nothing but flesh and bones. Our legacy to each other is the love within hearts that we hold dear to ourselves. I sit here with no misgivings of loving you and the love I have for you. I'm grateful I am here today."

"That's beautiful, but I'm sorry for—"

"Sydney, be joyful. Qualms only get in the way; there is no longer time for uncertainties. Life continues."

"But, Paolo, what I did—"

"Sydney, stop. You're here now." He reached up and wiped the tear that trickled down her face.

"Thank you, Paolo. Do you mind if we stay here for a couple of days?"

"No, not at all. It would make my heart happy."

"I'll be right back."

Sydney kissed the dying man on the cheek and walked into the house. She passed Giacomo, who was speaking with Emily, and went to whisper something in Rio's ear. Paolo stood by the black wrought iron railing and gazed out over the orange roofs of his village, Ottati. The pain in his head diminished as joy overcame him.

"Paolo?"

He turned. Sydney held an object in her hand. Behind her in the doorway were Giacomo, Rio, and Sydney's children—Andrew and Lisa.

"What are Andrew and Lisa doing here?"

"Paolo DeLaurentis, will you marry me?"

"What?"

"Will you marry me?" She held a miniature replica of the Eiffel Tower. "Will you marry me?"

Paolo was speechless as his eyes welled. "Yes, yes, yes." With a broad smile on his face, he asked, "Would you care to dance?"

Paolo embraced Sydney, and as the two danced, he repeated, "How I love this woman . . . how I love this woman."

The next afternoon, they were married in the Church of St. Biaggio, surrounded by their children and friends. Piazza

Umberto filled with guests, music, food, and laughter. Two days later, they returned to the States where, after three months, Paolo lost his battle with brain cancer. He passed away in his sleep on January 23, 2004, with his wife, Sydney DeLaurentis, holding his hand.

"Tony, this is beautiful. I remember the day. The smile on Dad's face . . ."

"It's a wonderful story."

Sharon entered the passenger cabin with their meals. "After you eat, I'll prepare your beds?"

"Yes, thank you."

Tony and Rio dined in companionable silence.

"The food's delicious. Tell you what, Tony—I'm exhausted."

"Go to sleep. Sharon will wake you up a half hour out."

"I only need a couple of hours."

Rio closed the sliding doors; the stateroom partitioned from the rest of the plane. She lay in bed reminiscing about her coffee with Dean that morning. She reached inside her purse, pulling out the envelope he gave her. She opened it. A picture of two young children dressed as adults had been printed on the front of the card. The little boy held a bouquet of roses behind his back as he leaned forward to kiss the girl. The inside was blank except for the words "I'm falling in love with you—Dean."

Rio unclasped the heart-shaped charm around her neck and placed the jewelry in the cupholder next to the bed. She fell asleep smiling.

Chapter 5

RIO AWOKE, STRETCHED her legs, and went to the bathroom to brush her teeth. Refreshed, she entered the cabin. Tony was drinking an espresso and writing on a yellow pad.

"Morning."

"Morning. How did you sleep?"

"Excellent. The bed is comfortable."

"It better be—for what I paid for this thing."

The pocket door that separated the passengers from the cockpit, galley, and crew quarters slid open, and Sharon appeared. "Rio, care for a coffee or espresso?"

"Yes, coffee please." She sat in the seat next to Tony. "Starting a new book?"

"Yeah, seeing where my mind takes me. By the way, we need to call Giacomo and tell him we're ahead of schedule."

"I'll give him a ring."

Tony opened a leather compartment and withdrew a satellite phone. "Here—you can use this."

The captain's voice came over the intercom. "Tony, we're approaching Corsica and Sardinia."

"What a beautiful sight. Have you ever been to Corsica?"

"Yes, the island is gorgeous."

Rio dialed her brother's cell phone as they approached the Amalfi coastline. She squinted out the oval window as she listened to the distinct ring. In the distance, she saw an odd flash—before she could register what it was, a rush of air screamed into the cabin. As she grabbed the armrests, she noticed a hole in the side of the aircraft.

"Tony!"

"Holy shit, Rio!"

An alarm sounded, followed by the pilot's instruction to prepare for an emergency landing. As the crew struggled to keep the crippled plane in flight, Pontecagnano—a village on the shoreline—grew closer. Not able to reach their destination, the captain announced their decision to ditch in the Bay of Salerno. While they coordinated the rescue with air traffic control, Sharon prepared Rio and Tony for the controlled crash.

The skilled pilots set the Gulfstream on the water five hundred feet from the shore. The tail pointed precipitously toward the sky as the nose of the plane tilted downward in the ocean waves. Within seconds, rescue motorboats surrounded them.

Chapter 6

GIACOMO AND EMILY DeLaurentis sat on the breakfast terrace at Le Sirenuse in Positano, Italy. The rays of the morning sun highlighted the tiled dome of the church of Santa Maria Assunta shimmering purple, gold, and blue as the day began to warm the chilly air. The fifty-eight-room hotel had spectacular views of the village that scaled the mountainous Amalfi coastline. By midday, the stone-cobbled stairways would fill with tourists.

Giacomo read a report from his Italian business partner. Retired from the army, he owned a private security firm that provided aerial surveillance for American corporations and the governments of the United States, Italy, and France. The company was a hobby—Giacomo didn't need the money. He employed over a hundred personnel stationed throughout the world. Remote, LLC operated fifty high-tech drones that patrolled the skies. The precision-guided cameras downloaded images to the contracted agencies.

Emily taught French Studies at Yale University. Her father, Arnaud Chambery, a longtime friend of her father-in-law, Paolo, now headed the French DGSE—the intelligence agency akin to the CIA. The thirty-eight-year-old mother-to-be wore an above-the-knee white summer dress. The V-neck accentuated her breasts, and a simple gold cross hung around her neck. Giacomo and Emily were an attractive pair. No longer sporting a military haircut, Giacomo—his brown hair loosely styled—wore jeans and a green short-sleeved polo shirt.

Emily's Parisian accent intrigued those who met her. The sound of his wife's voice was one of the many attributes—besides her beautiful face—that had attracted Giacomo. "*Mon ami*—my love."

"Oui, mon ami." Giacomo rested his hand on hers. They were both fluent in English, French, and Italian.

"What time are we meeting Tony's plane?"

Giacomo put the report about the clandestine search for a man named Sharif on the chair next to him and glanced at the clock. "They should land in a couple of hours."

A waiter approached with a carafe of Italian coffee and a basket of breads and pastries. He placed them on the violet-colored tablecloth. The view of the bay of Positano and the islands of Capri and Li Galli added to the ambiance.

"Grazie," Giacomo said. He picked up Emily's hand. "You're radiant today."

"Merci, mon ami."

"What a great visit with your father. Did you see his face light up when you told him?"

The pregnant woman placed her hand on her stomach. "What about when I said we're having twins? I thought he'd faint. Then when I told him 'boys,' . . . jeez." They both laughed.

"Cardinal Andrew will be excited when he hears the news."

"He will. He's going to meet us in Ottati."

"Do you think he can be a godfather to one of the boys?" Emily asked.

Giacomo's cell phone rang. He answered to the sound of a whoosh, then silence on the other end of the line. Fear gripped his body and almost caused him to vomit as he felt the blood drain from his face.

"Giacomo, who was on the phone? Is everything . . ."

He shook off the sick feeling. "Must've been a wrong number. What did you ask?"

"Do you think Andrew could be a godfather to one of the boys?"

Giacomo was flustered as he replied, "Sure . . . why not? We'll ask him this weekend."

Chapter 7

CARDINAL ANDREW ANGELONI sat in his Vatican office behind a cluttered, seventeenth-century dark oak desk. In one corner were two pictures: The first, his stepbrother and father, the young boy in the photo twenty years his junior. The second, him with his mother and father as they posed with Mickey Mouse at Disney World. He was eighteen years old when he stood between his parents. The vacation would be their last, his mother dying of pancreatic cancer. That year—1975—influenced the rest of the cardinal's life.

Born in the small town of Bethlehem, Connecticut, the only child of Frank and Maria Angeloni, Andrew was an average American boy, with typical adolescent tendencies. There was nothing to set him apart from his peers. He and his girlfriend, Carla, had dated for two years, experiencing love to a point but keeping their virginity. In the summer before his final year of high school, they went their separate ways.

Bethlehem is Connecticut's Christmas town. Each year during the holiday season, the post office is inundated with thousands of holiday cards from around the world seeking the Bethlehem postmark. The municipality was the site of the first theological seminary in the country. In 1947, a group of Benedictine nuns established the Abbey of Regina Laudis. Andrew worked in the abbey's mailroom during the Christmas season and did chores at the convent during the spring and summer months. The sisters adopted him and prayed for him daily.

Andrew would never forget the day he traipsed through the door of his parents' center-hall colonial home. A senior, he enjoyed privileges and was free to leave the school premises as long as he had no classes. That day, he was going home for lunch, then off to the abbey.

"Mom, I'm home." The tall, lanky, long-haired teenager entered the kitchen and opened the refrigerator. He grabbed the Genoa salami and sharp provolone cheese and made a sandwich. With his mouth full, he called for his mother again.

"Andrew, Mom and I are up here," his father's voice boomed.

With lunch in hand, Andrew climbed the stairs. In the master bedroom suite, his mother sat on the sofa, her eyes red. His father gazed out the window.

"What's going on?"

"Nothing good," his father quipped.

"Mom?"

The words couldn't escape her mouth. She sobbed.

"Your mother has cancer."

"*Cancer?*" Stunned, Andrew turned toward his mother. "Mom?"

The tissue in her hand had deteriorated with her tears. Maria nodded.

"Dad?"

His father turned. "I'm sorry, son."

Andrew cried. "I, I don't understand. You look healthy."

Maria took a deep breath and spoke softly. "I haven't been feeling well for a while. Always tired—I didn't think it was anything."

"You should've gone to the doctors when I told you."

"I'm sorry, Frank."

"Yeah, yeah, yeah." Frank stormed out of the room.

Perplexed, Andrew asked, "Mom, why is Dad so mad?" He sat next to her.

"Because . . ." She placed her hand on her son's leg and bowed her head. "Because I'm terminal—I'm going to die."

"What? No . . . that can't be."

"I'm sorry, Andy."

"Did you get a second opinion?"

"Yes, we've done that, honey."

"Oh."

Andrew tried to come to grips with the upsetting news. The young man leaned forward, placing his head in his hands. His mother rubbed his back to comfort him.

"How much time?" His voice trailed.

"Doctors said six months."

"Six months?" *Shit.*

Frank returned to the room and stood in front of his wife and son. "I'm sorry, Maria. I didn't mean to yell."

Maria died in her sleep six weeks after watching her son receive his high school diploma with honors.

* * *

A few months passed. Andrew prepared to leave for St. Anselm's College in New Hampshire. With a recommendation from the prioress of the Abbey Regina Laudis, he had received a full scholarship to the Benedictine school.

"You're packed."

"Almost, Dad. Were you at the cemetery?"

"Yeah. Mom's headstone arrived." He shook his head. "All those prayers those stupid nuns said did nothing to save your mother. No, he took her away from me. There is no God."

"Dad, you're just mad. Don't say things like that."

"Yeah, you're right—I am angry. My life is ruined. Now you're going to a dumbass Catholic school. You could go to Cornell—I have the money. You could get a good education. No, instead you listened to those senseless nuns."

"*Dad.*"

"Don't 'Dad' me, Andrew—I'm your father!"

"Dad."

"Do what you want—it's your freakin' life. By the way, I'm selling the house."

A pang of hurt swept through Andrew. "You want to move up to New Hampshire with me?"

"Thanks, son, but no. I'm moving to Manhattan. No sense in commuting anymore with you away at school. Too many memories . . ."

"I understand."

"I checked the oil in your car. You're set to go. Can I take that downstairs for you?" He pointed to a suitcase.

Andrew's black Chevy Malibu was jam-packed with clothes and books, the rear seat filled with his personal possessions.

"I guess I should be leaving." Andrew entered the car.

"Yeah. Andrew?"

"Dad?"

Andrew got back out of the vehicle and rested his arm on the door. "I'm sorry."

"Don't worry, Dad. We'll survive."

Andrew's father extended his arms, pulling his son close. "I love you, son. Time will heal our pain."

"I love you too, Dad."

* * *

Andrew settled into the quiet, peaceful campus of St. Anselm's. Drawn into the Benedictine community, he quickly made friends. In his sophomore year, he felt the call of the priesthood touch his heart. His father had no time for Andrew's Catholic God. The two seldom talked, and eventually his father remarried—a much younger woman. By the time Andrew was twenty, he had a stepbrother.

Accepted to the Pontifical North American College in Rome, where Andrew received his master of divinity. He was ordained in St. Peter's by the pontiff. He pursued his doctorate of religious studies at the American College in Leuven, Belgium. His thesis was titled "The Reunification of the Christian Churches."

The acclaimed 377-page doctoral dissertation made its way to the pope. Asked to return to Rome, Andrew respectfully asked to continue his studies at Yale Divinity School. He believed in the necessity of understanding the current Christian philosophies outside of the Catholic doctrine. After he'd served at the Vatican for six months, his request was granted.

Andrew studied Protestant dogma for two years. His arguments for balance and synergy between the churches influenced Yale to offer him a professorship. Rome approved the appeal without hesitation. When not in class or lecturing, Andrew performed his priestly duties at St. Mary's Church on Hillhouse Avenue in New Haven. Eventually, he resigned his teaching post in favor of contemplative prayer and ministry to the parish, which was where he was stationed when Paolo died.

*   *   *

"We are gathered here this day to honor a man whom people say saw the world through God's eyes. There are those who said he spoke the words of God. One thing is sure—he understood the nature of humankind. His remarkable gift of unconditional love for people can only be given by God. Through his adversity and pain, Paolo witnessed the love of God for others. He was a good man, and his death only solidified God's love for his people. I pray that all will heed the words he wrote about the need for and importance of love."

Giacomo and Emily were next to Father Andrew in the vestibule of the 120-year-old church. As the congregation exited the Gothic structure, one after another they paid their respects to the children of Paolo DeLaurentis.

"Father Andrew, thank you so much."

"My pleasure, Colonel DeLaurentis."

"We've known each other for a year. Please, Father—Giacomo."

"I don't often have the opportunity to rib the military elite, my friend."

One of the youngest colonels in American history at twenty-six and the commander of Black Operations Elite Team, or BOET, Giacomo reported to one person—the president of the United States. Giacomo was credited with the capture of the American traitor Dr. Colin Payne. Payne, a member of the NSC, was responsible for the atomic detonation in the Ural Mountains of Russia and the placement of a nuclear bomb in Detroit. Giacomo DeLaurentis never asked for fame, but many in the armed services still considered it unjust that he rose through the ranks as fast as he did.

"How long are you here for?"

"Two days. Then I head back to DC. I'll be here for Sunday Mass."

"I read your father's journal—a modern-day Nostradamus. The poems regarding his love for his wife are beautiful. The hand of God undoubtedly touched your dad."

"Why don't you come over for dinner so we can discuss the journal?"

"Yes, Father. You must, I'm cooking coq au vin," Emily said.

"Sounds delicious. We can celebrate my news."

"What news?" Giacomo asked.

"I'm headed back to the Vatican. I've been asked to lead an exploratory committee to unify the churches."

"Congratulations, Andrew! Next they'll make you a bishop." Giacomo smiled at his friend. "Tonight, we will celebrate."

"And when are we going to celebrate you two having children?" The priest's eyebrows arched.

"Not until I retire. A soldier's life is no way to bring up children."

Rio walked through the large wooden door into the vestibule, her face stained with tears. "Children? Emily, you're pregnant!"

"No, no, no." Emily blushed.

"Oh. That would've been news to brighten up the day. Thank you, Father, for saying Mass."

"You're welcome, Rio. I wish I had met your dad. I understand he donated copious sums of money to the Catholic Church?"

"Copious, really?"

Emily backhanded Giacomo on the chest and mouthed "stop." Giacomo shrugged.

"Yes, we never realized how wealthy our dad was." Rio touched the priest's red robes as she glanced at his face. "In his writings, he mentioned you several times. Yet you two never met?"

"No, never. I told your brother your father's donations ensured my placement here at St. Mary's."

"You mean he paid off the pope."

"*Giacomo!* I'm sorry, Father—my husband speaks before he thinks."

"Quite all right, Emily. It was funny."

"I'm funny." He put his arm around his wife and kissed her on the head. "Rio, Andrew's going back to the Vatican."

"Andrew—when?"

"Next month."

"I'm so happy for you, Father." She kissed the priest on the cheek.

Chapter 8

"**Y**OUR EMINENCE."

"Marcello, please come in." Cardinal Andrew Angeloni waved the man into the office. "What can I do for you?" he asked as he placed his pen on the desk and sat back in his chair. Half-rimmed glasses rested on the tip of his nose. His once-brown hair was now gray at the temples. The sixty-three-year-old had a few wrinkles around his eyes.

"I'm sorry to bother you."

"No, not at all. I can use a break. Do me a favor and adjust the air-conditioning—too warm in here."

The young priest did as asked and then spoke. "I want to review your calendar before I leave for vacation."

"Sure. Please sit." He pointed to one of the two chairs opposite his desk. "What's the schedule?" The American cardinal leaned forward as he listened.

"On Thursday, you meet with the Greek, Russian, and Serbian Orthodox Church representatives. That will begin at nine at the Rome Marriott. Friday, you travel to the mountain village of Ottati to be with the DeLaurentis family. You'll celebrate Mass at St. Biaggio on Sunday morning. You return to Rome on Monday for a meeting with the Holy Father on Tuesday to discuss the reunification. On Wednesday, you meet with the representative of the Egyptian Coptic Church here at the Vatican. I'll be back on Friday."

"A busy week."

"Yes, Your Eminence."

"Marcello, you can call me Andrew. I go to the bathroom the same way you do. I am no different."

"Yes, Your Em—Andrew." Marcello chuckled.

"What's so funny?"

"The bathroom."

"Well, I do. Don't I? I stand to pee just like you."

They were both laughing as the cardinal's phone rang. Marcello jumped to answer it.

"Marcello, relax." Andrew put out his hand and answered, "Hello. Cardinal Angeloni."

"*Andrew?*" The voice was somber.

"Giacomo, you sound terrible. What's the matter?"

"Is there a TV in your office?"

"Yes." The cardinal motioned to Marcello to turn it on. "What's wrong?"

"Rio's plane crashed as it approached the Italian coastline."

"May God have mercy on us!" He signaled to his assistant. "Marcello, switch to the news station."

"Yes, Your Eminence."

The headline scrolled across the bottom of the screen—"American revolutionary killed in terrorist attack"—as the announcer spoke: "American revolutionary Rio DeLaurentis is believed to have died today in a missile attack on the private plane she traveled in. A staunch advocate for the people and protector of the poor, DeLaurentis fought for the rights of Americans against the injustices of the United States government. The leader of the American Party, she lambasted the political status quo . . ." Video played of Rio calling for the resignation of the leaders of the House and Senate. Her now-famous tirade in which she called the legislators "moronic a-holes" had garnered international attention.

"Giacomo, this is terrible. Did Rio die? Where are you?"

"No, she didn't. I'm in Pontecagnano with Emily and Sergio. Everyone's rescued, alive with minor bruises, except for Rio."

"What's the matter with Rio?"

"She's . . . in a coma."

"A coma?"

"Yes. And, Andrew, I need a favor."

Chapter 9

"THE MISSILE PASSED through the fuselage without exploding. Last report said four of the five occupants survived, DeLaurentis died."

The transmission ended. Winston Tarmac, the United States ambassador to the United Nations, walked over to his secretary's desk. A stout man, Tarmac was as tall as he was round and deserving of his nickname: Santa Claus. The gray-haired sixty-one-year-old reached for the pink sheets of paper with his telephone messages. He scanned and memorized them.

Ruth looked up, shaking her head.

"I know it would be easier if you emailed me the messages." The ambassador was not a fan of electronic communication.

"Easy day, Mr. Ambassador—lunch at La Mela, then a two o'clock meeting with the staff."

"Cancel the staff meeting."

"Do you want to reschedule?"

He paused for a moment. "No. Make sure my car is here by eleven thirty."

"Yes, Mr. Ambassador."

Tarmac waddled back to his office. A friend of Vice President Jerry Richardson, he had easily won Senate confirmation of his appointment. Not President Waldron's first choice, but an agreement was an agreement. Favors done and favors repaid.

"Ruth, get me the vice president on the phone."

"Yes, Mr. Ambassador."

A moment later, "Winston, how the hell are you?"

"Fine, Jerry. You?"

"Same ol' stuff. Cleaning up Waldron's messes."

"I understand. Do you think we'll still be working in January?"

"I doubt it. But you never know."

"Come on, Jer. He's so far behind in the polls—no way he'll be reelected."

"Only if something earth-shattering occurs."

"You got that right. I take it you heard the news coming out of Italy?"

"Yeah, what a shame."

"Do I detect sarcasm in your voice?"

"Me? Sarcasm? This good ol' boy from Georgia—sarcastic?"

"How stupid of me. I'm sure your friend Boyle is happy."

"That bitch. She's no friend of mine."

The ambassador swiveled his black leather chair around and gazed out on the Turtle Bay neighborhood of Manhattan. The view of the East River from the twenty-fourth floor was spectacular. Gray clouds hid the sun, a hint of imminent rain.

"At least the next presidential election is looking better for you. We don't need DeLaurentis around. Do you think she was really connected to the FFB?"

"No way. She was out there in la-la land, but she wouldn't back them."

"I have news—your line secure?"

"Of course."

"I have a lunch meeting today that promises to be enlightening."

"What do you mean?"

"I've been promised information on goody-two-shoes president-wannabe Maro."

"What kind of information?"

"The kind that will make sure you and I are still employed come inauguration day."

"Really?"
"Really."

*   *   *

Neither man noticed the third phone disconnect. Two women sat by a speakerphone. The one with a long face and disproportionately tiny nose leaned back in her chair. The other with midnight-black hair removed her finger from the disconnect button and adjusted the window shade to obscure the view of the crumbled Washington Monument in the distance. Senator Boyle turned to her companion and said, "You understand what needs to be done. The helicopter will take you to Manhattan."

Chapter 10

THE BLACK SUV with diplomatic plates turned on Mulberry Street and stopped at La Mela Italian restaurant. It was one of Tarmac's favorite eateries.

"Hello, Mr. Ambassador. Your table is ready."

"Hello, Anthony."

Due to the ambassador's girth, Anthony seated him near the door where there was ample room.

"Ambassador Tarmac, your usual scotch?"

"Hello, Dominique. Yes, please. My guest should be here shortly."

"Yes, sir."

Tarmac pulled his black-onyx-cufflinked left shirtsleeve up and gawked at his gold and diamond bezel Rolex. A half hour passed, two scotches down, and no guest. Dominique approached the table.

"Would you like to order lunch, Mr. Ambassador? Or continue to wait?"

"Lunch. Screw them—their loss."

"Gnocchi and meatballs?"

"Yeah." He lifted his scotch, swirled the ice. "Another one of these, please."

He finished his lunch with an espresso and a slice of New York cheesecake. Dominique brought the check. The round ambassador exited the eatery. His driver held the limo's door open as a casually dressed woman moved toward Tarmac.

"Mr. Ambassador?"

"Yes?"

He couldn't help but stare at her long and disproportionate face as her eyes held his gaze. Transfixed, he waited for her to speak.

"My client apologizes for not being here today. This is for you."

Tarmac smiled. He grabbed the white envelope and entered the car with a huff. Handkerchief in hand, he wiped the perspiration from his forehead. The vehicle drove up Mulberry, took a right on Bond, then a left on First Avenue. Tarmac tore the envelope, anxious to see the contents. He read the note in shock—the message spoke of the vice president in derogatory terms that caused him to panic.

When they stopped on the corner of Thirty-Ninth Street, a motorcycle squeezed next to the automobile. The rider placed a device on the car's hood—the clanking sound reverberated through the limo.

"What was that?" the ambassador asked.

"Don't know, sir."

Tarmac reached for the secure satellite phone.

"Ambassador Tarmac here. I need to speak with the president right away."

As they passed through the intersection of First Avenue and Fortieth Street, Tarmac's limo exploded. It was obliterated, along with twelve innocent victims.

Chapter 11

IN HIS HOME on a side street off historic Charles Street in Baltimore, Republican presidential nominee Thomas Maro rose from his prayer mat and went to sit at his desk. Secret Service agents were stationed outside the building in the exclusive neighborhood, keeping his family secure.

The red-pink, brick, six-thousand-square-foot house had been a gift from his mother's second husband, his stepfather. Maro's birth father died when he was five years old. His only memory was from a picture of himself and his dad outside their house. When he was ten, his mother, a Muslim, married Selah Maro, a Coptic Christian. A year after Tom graduated from the Wharton School of Business, his mother and adoptive father perished in a car crash. An only child, he took over his father's Oriental rug business. Over fifteen years, the small company became a corporation—the largest importer of handcrafted Persian quilted carpets in the US. The presidential nominee sold the business in 2008, just before the economic collapse. A discreet philanthropist, he was known for his national television ads and his conviction that he was destined to be the next commander in chief of the United States.

Thomas Maro's beliefs were tempered by Christianity and Islam. Fluent in four languages—Farsi, Hebrew, Spanish, and English—he had faith that Jesus was the Messiah and the writings of Mohammad had meaning. Never forced to choose, he found comfort in the Bible as well as the Qur'an. A private man when it came to his faith, Maro never discussed the subject. This almost became an issue during the primaries and the early days after his nomination. He squashed the religious critics with one statement: "I believe in God." The country was in such peril that religion was the furthest thought from the American people's minds.

"Come in," he responded to a knock. The solid oak pocket doors slid open. "Hello, Sal."

Sal walked into the library, grabbed the television remote, and turned on the news.

"What's going on?" Maro glanced at his watch—3:35 p.m.

"Winston Tarmac is dead."

"What?"

"Assassinated, in Manhattan."

"By whom?"

"No idea."

"The talk on the Hill was he'd be Richardson's running mate in the next presidential election. What's happening to this world, Sal? It grows worse every day. First the death of Rio DeLaurentis, and now this." He shook his head.

"Yeah, that crackpot—we don't need her around."

"Cousin, those are harsh words. Rio was a fighter for the people, and she believed in our country."

"*Our* country? We are here by the grace of Allah and a long way from our homeland, my cousin."

Maro's face turned red. "Saleem, you speak like an ass. We are Americans. This country gave us the opportunity to live free. Damn, Sal, I could be the next president of the United States. This cannot be tolerated. We've talked about it before—I'm tired of your rhetoric! If you are to be my chief of staff, you'd better keep your comments to yourself. I mean it, Sal . . . it's got to stop."

"I'm sorry, Tom."

Agitated, Maro rubbed his face and changed the subject. "How's DC this morning? You said you had a doctor's appointment?"

"Everything checked out fine. I waited two hours before I saw a doctor. When you become president, do me a favor."

"Yes, Sal—I'm gonna fix the health care issue. I'd better, or I'll have a short tenure."

"No." Sal had a disgusted expression on his face.

"Oh, I'm sorry. What is it?"

"That phallic symbol—the Washington Monument. Gotta go. Only a quarter of it is standing, the rest crumbled on the ground."

"Phallic symbol? Remind me not to let you talk to the press. What a shame it won't be rebuilt."

"Are you serious? Unemployment is in double digits, gas is seven fifty a gallon, and a loaf of bread is over five dollars. The world is in shambles, and this damn country is a piece of shit."

"Sal, what the hell is going on with you?"

"Sorry, Tom . . . I'm sorry . . ."

"I don't need this right now. Take a couple of days off. Leave my house and come back when your sanity returns. Think hard about whether you want to be my chief of staff . . . because right now I'm having doubts.

"Sorry, Tom."

"Yeah."

Sal left the office and slid the doors closed.

What the hell is wrong with him? Maro picked up a document of the campaign promises he'd made to the American people. *How will I carry out what needs to be done when the country is rife with discontent?* Never in history had Americans been at such odds with their political system. Democrats and Republicans spewed hate-filled rhetoric: the only unity they enjoyed was the bipartisan attack on a third political party. *Was Rio DeLaurentis right?*

His cell phone rang.

"Hello."

"Please hold for the president."

"Tom?"

"Arthur, how are you?"

"Good. Dinner tonight?"

"Sure. My house at seven?"

"I'll be there."

Arthur Waldron and Thomas Maro were friends. Over the course of the campaign, they met in secret to discuss world politics. They publicly refused to attack one another. They shared an agenda—a better America. No longer a popularity contest, the election was about survival—the continued existence of the United States. Both nominees agreed their campaign focus would be on how to fix the government—a promise Arthur had made four years earlier but failed to deliver on because of his own self-righteousness.

During his first candidacy, Waldron used his inflated bravado to strike a chord with the people. He spoke to their fears of a declining America. On Election Day, he won the popular vote but lost the Electoral College by three votes. His followers were incensed, driven to find a way to overturn the election. Within days, an anonymous video was released of the soon-to-be-sworn-in president-elect in a compromising sexual act with his aide.

Waldron took to the airwaves with a pompous moral message and promised to fight for the constitutional freedoms of the people. On December 21, for the first time in American history, Congress did not certify the results; instead, by a margin of fifty votes, it elected the populist Arthur Waldron as president.

It took two years in office to humble Waldron. His continued failure to keep his promises, thanks to a fractured legislative branch, eroded his authority, and his staunch advocates distanced themselves. The citizens wanted change; they were tired of the two-class society burdened with governmental regulations. A civil war brewed as people prepared to take matters into their own hands.

Waldron tried to change the minds of the bureaucrats, with little success. The government's policies continued to degrade the people. Fueled by a propaganda campaign sponsored by the FFB, workers engaged in mass demonstrations, and strikes pummeled the economy. Self-interest and corruption clouded the minds of the ruling elite, 508 men and women who were convinced they knew best for the people. No longer a military superpower, the nation relied on its secured borders and a failed wall. Oil was now $405 a barrel, and the price of gold had skyrocketed to over $3,500 an ounce. Investors in precious metals became wealthy.

The United States was on the precipice of a revolution, fueled in part by a dystopian fear. The misguided policies of the Waldron administration had imploded and only powered the malcontent. Discouraged by his failures, Waldron *hoped* he would lose the election.

Chapter 12

SALEEM NASIR STOPPED his new forest-green Jeep Cherokee at the end of the driveway and nodded to acknowledge the Secret Service agents. He drove right on Charles toward the city of Baltimore.

Sal had graduated from Harvard School of Law in 1996 in the top tenth percentile of his class. A New York law firm hired him, not only for his intellect but also for his ability to speak French and Farsi.

The son of Duman and Maria Nasir, born in Fairfax, Virginia, his mother was American, his father from Riyadh, Saudi Arabia. Maria was the sister of Eman Maro, the mother of presidential candidate Tom Maro. After his parents' separation, Sal was kidnapped by his father when he was two years old and taken to Saudi Arabia. Maria was devastated and tried to use diplomatic channels to bring her son home. Nine years passed before Duman called Selah Maro, Maria's brother. Two weeks and half a million dollars later, Saleem was reunited with his mother. At first the relationship was tenuous, until little Saleem realized he would no longer be beaten—then it was paradise.

His cell phone rang to the ring tone of a Top 40 hit. The caller ID showed a private number.

"Saleem, *as-salāmu ʿalaykum.*"

Saleem shook his head in disgust. *What have I done?* "Peace be upon you as well."

"Not bad for a Boston girl."

Saleem said nothing.

"Sal—are you there?"

"Yes, I'm listening."

"What's the matter? You seem upset."

Her sarcasm and demeaning manner grated on Sal's nerves. Bile started to rise up his esophagus. The acid burned his throat.

"You knew I'd call. Time to repay your debt, my friend." The smug voice continued, "All you need to do is listen. Will that make you feel better? Now then, my little Muslim friend, outside of an assassination, Tommy-boy will be the commander in chief. As his chief of staff, you will . . ."

Sal stopped the car, rolled down the window, and vomited in the street.

"Sal, did you puke? What—you don't like the sound of my voice? I love this new technology. I can watch every move you make. Don't forget to wipe the corner of your mouth . . ."

"*Bitch.*"

"Sal, Sal, Sal . . . is that any way to talk to a lady?"

"Lady, you're a bitch."

"Tsk-tsk . . . such words. Shut the hell up and listen. As I was saying, when your cousin is elected, you will hire one of our associates to help in the transition of the government. Then in January, that person will become your assistant, but in reality, you will report to him. Do you understand?"

"I hear you," Sal said as he approached a red light on East Pratt and South Street.

"Do I need to remind you of the information we have on your dead father that will destroy your cousin's chances of winning the election?"

"No." Saleem's father had been an associate of Dr. Colin Payne, the American traitor who masterminded the nuclear detonation in the Urals in 2003. Duman, responsible for the acquisition of the two nuclear bombs (one of which never exploded), later died of radiation poisoning in a chateau in France.

"I'm glad we reached an understanding. Sharif will be pleased."

"What the—" A man on a bicycle stopped in front of Sal's Jeep and banged on the hood with his right hand, then sped away. "What was that?"

"Sal! Get out of the car—oh, sorry, too late . . . see you in hell." She gazed at her computer screen, grabbed a tissue, and wiped her tiny nose as the car exploded in a fireball of molten metal and human remains.

"I can't believe you killed him, Sharif! Oh well. Another one bites the dust."

Chapter 13

THE MEDIA REPORTED that Saleem Nasir, Ambassador Tarmac, and Rio DeLaurentis had been killed, along with fourteen innocent bystanders. No one came forward to take responsibility.

Within the fortress of Vatican City, protected by the Swiss Guard and an elaborate security system, Giacomo and Sergio sat by Rio's bedside in a yellow-walled room. Eyes closed, she lay peacefully at rest, a bluish-purple bruise on her chin where a breathing tube had recently been removed. Bags of intravenous fluid hung on poles to nourish her body. A monitor displayed the rhythm of her heartbeat punctuated by an annoying beep.

A crucifix hung on one wall, opposite a painting of Jesus holding a baby lamb in his arms. Two extra chairs had been placed on either side of a six-drawer dresser across from the window next to the door. The curtains were closed, blocking the view of the Vatican Gardens. A gentle knock disturbed the silence.

"*Pronto*—come in," Giacomo said. "Andrew." The men rose from their seats to meet the cardinal. Giacomo walked over to his friend, and they hugged. Cardinal Andrew Angeloni was now a papal nuncio—a representative of the pope. He continued to spearhead the campaign to unify the Christian churches. Men being men, there were those in the College of Cardinals who believed the idea foolish.

"I'm so sorry, Giacomo. At least she's breathing on her own."

"Yes, thank God."

"Sergio, it's a pleasure to see you again."

"Your Eminence." The two men shook hands.

"Come, Andrew, sit. I cannot express how grateful I am."

"Please don't say anything. The Holy Father said it's the least we can do for the daughter of our major benefactor. She'll be safe here. What are the doctors saying?"

"Nothing much—no internal or brain injuries."

"Your sister's a fighter—soon she'll awaken. Did you tell your mother?"

"Yes. Thank you for the diplomatic pouch. I couldn't take the risk of telling her over the phone that Rio had survived."

"She must've been devastated."

"Yes. Horrific—never want to do that again."

"Have you talked to her since?"

"Yes."

"How did that go?"

"She's pissed but happy her daughter is alive."

"Why must the world think she's dead?"

"She's a newsmaker with a lot of enemies."

"Enemies?"

"Political . . ."

"Oh—her comments to Congress?"

"Yep. I'm gonna need confession when this is all over."

"I'm sure God will forgive you. Tony and the rest of the crew, how are they?"

"Uninjured. Tony's at his home in Positano; the pilots are back in the States."

"Giacomo, do you think the assassinations in New York and Washington are related to the attack on Rio?"

"Too much of a coincidence not to be. The Italian government is furious; they've vowed to apprehend those involved. My sister . . . she infuriated quite a few people this past month. Tarmac, Nasir, and Rio? No idea what those three have in common."

"I saw the news. Giacomo—Rio's right, although, she could've toned it down a little. Your wife, Emily—where is she?"

"At our house in Ottati, with Italian bodyguards. I'm going there today. I forgot to tell you—Em is pregnant."

"She is? About time."

Giacomo touched Rio's arm. A bittersweet moment: new life approached as his sister lay on death's doorstep.

"She's protected here, Giacomo. Our medical staff will care for her. A Franciscan nun will be by her bedside always. Nobody will harm your sister while she's here."

"I believe that."

"Peace, my friend. May God's spirit be with you. Our security detail will take you to the heliport."

"Thanks again, Andrew." The two men embraced.

"My regards to His Holiness, Your Eminence."

"I will tell him, and, Sergio, please call me Andrew."

Giacomo leaned over his sister and kissed her forehead. Sergio did the same. While Giacomo was escorted to a helicopter pad in the far corner of the city, Andrew stayed at her bedside. With holy oil in his hand, he performed the rite of the anointing the sick as he prayed for her soul.

* * *

As they headed to the heliport, Giacomo reflected on the day's events. He was grateful that Andrew offered a safe haven for Rio. He felt awe as he looked at his surroundings. Vatican City was in the heart of Rome—a sovereign nation of eight hundred inhabitants within the republic of Italy. The walled-in state was the home of the Holy Father—the pope—and the spiritual headquarters for two billion Catholics who considered it the one true universal church. Its power touched every government in the world. The pontiff, its supreme leader, walked in the footsteps of the apostle Peter as he dedicated his life to God and His people. Through the centuries, the church had been plagued with problems, schisms, scandals, and defiance.

The hierarchy managed to make the wrongs right as it evolved into the image of Christ. Still, humans were human and could not escape their sinful nature.

The whooping sound of the rotor blades increased as the helicopter lifted off the ground. Giacomo and Sergio put the soundproof headsets on to lessen the annoying reverberation.

Airborne, Sergio reached inside his jacket pocket and pulled out an envelope addressed to Giacomo. On it were the words *Open when in the helicopter flying to Ottati*. Stamped along the seal was a date: *March 19, 1998*. Written across the flap was a signature: *Paolo DeLaurentis*.

"Damn. He wrote this twenty-two years ago."

"Your father was an incredible man."

"Yes, he was. Dad told me he felt like a freak—nowhere to go with his words. Even after he died, no one believed his writings, except for the president."

"Until Stalworth came to office."

"True."

"Didn't he threaten you with treason?"

"Yeah, if I discussed the journal with anybody. Said he lost it. I offered him another copy. Next thing you know, I'm sitting at a desk in the Pentagon. When Waldron came into office, I retired. We made a mistake turning it over to the government. Now I don't care. Rio is right—our country has been decimated by the politicians' agendas. They forgot the American people."

Giacomo opened the sealed envelope and pulled out the white sheet of paper.

I'm sure you're perplexed by the recent events and have plenty of questions. Giacomo, you will endure hard choices and sacrifices as a time of discontent infects humanity. Every decision will open a door and lead you on a different path. The outcome will be the same. Trust your instincts; they will not fail you. Just as there is good in the world, there is also evil—seen and unseen. The good can be bad, and the bad can become good.

The misdirected will try to break you and steer you in a direction that would thwart the good. Be careful of whom you trust.

I have hidden a second journal in my study under the fourth floorboard from the window. The writings are significant. The coming Passover holiday will have a new meaning for the entire world. The governments will shake with fright.

Time continues, not like a clock that can stop—time will reveal the prophecy. When the key finds its rightful place, the third trumpet will protect the angels born of man.

Giacomo handed the note to Sergio, who read the words penned by his late friend.

"Sergio, why the riddle? Why couldn't he just tell me?"

"I'm sure he had a reason."

Giacomo reached forward, grabbed his sports jacket from the empty seat, and tucked the letter into the inside pocket.

Chapter 14

A DARK BLUE FIAT Panda waited as the helicopter touched down in the field by the Church of the Madonna del Cardoneto. Giacomo shook hands with Sergio. He picked up his coat and gave it to the pilot who held the door.

"I will bring your suitcase," the captain said.

"I can take it."

"No, no, senor. Go to your wife."

Giacomo shrugged in acceptance.

He trotted the three hundred feet to Emily, who leaned against their four-door compact car. Polizia guarded the perimeter, scanning the surroundings for anything out of the ordinary. Above the valley, nestled into the mountainside, was the village of Ottati.

"Mon ami."

"Mi amore!" Giacomo gave Emily a hug followed by a kiss as he rubbed her belly.

The pilot opened the trunk and stowed the suitcases. He handed Giacomo his jacket.

"Grazie." Giacomo tipped him a hundred-euro note.

"Grazie, senor."

The captain turned toward the helicopter and signaled for the copilot to start the engines. The blast from the rotor wash hurried the couple into the car.

"How are the boys?" Giacomo asked, patting her belly again.

"Fine. How's Rio?"

"The same. At least she's breathing on her own."

Giacomo shoved the leather-wrapped stick shift into first gear. The vehicle hugged the right side of the narrow road. As he sped past a farmer riding a tractor, he reached for Emily's hand. They traversed the ancient streets of the mountain village of Ottati. Giacomo downshifted, stepped on the brake, and turned into the Piazza Umberto. They parked and strolled to their three-story, white stucco, red-orange-roofed house.

Giacomo and Rio had inherited the property from Paolo. They spent half of the year in the town he adored. Giacomo, although he loved his country, welcomed the time when he would retire to this village.

When they entered the floral-tiled foyer, Emily said, "I'll be right back. Meet you on the patio."

"Sure."

"I'll only be a few."

Giacomo's eyes scanned the valley of colors. He had put his concern about Rio out of his mind for the moment, his worry consumed by the knowledge of a second journal.

"Nice to be here again," Emily said. She wrapped her arms around her husband and leaned her head on his back.

"Yes, seventeen wonderful years."

"I'll never forget your father's face when he saw Sydney."

"Yeah, a beautiful moment," Giacomo said.

"If it wasn't for your father, I might not be here."

"But you are, *mi amore*, you are." He turned to face Emily and kissed her passionately. They walked back into the house. "Sergio gave me the envelope from Dad."

"What did your father say?"

"Why don't we go to Maria's for dinner? I'll let you read the letter there."

"Sounds good. I'm starving. The boys are sapping all my energy."

"Then we'd better hurry. Do you mind if we stop by the cemetery tomorrow? The caretaker repaired my father's headstone. I need to pay him."

"You amaze me. With all the money we have, why didn't you mail a check?"

"Because it's my dad, and I want to thank Giovanni personally. Money has nothing to do with . . ." Giacomo spotted the mischievous grin on his wife's face. "You think you're funny, don't you?"

"Sometimes, Giacomo . . ."

"What?"

"Why would I mind?"

"Thanks, honey."

The sun began to set as the two made their way to Maria's restaurant in the Piazza Umberto. A slight breeze swirled a piece of paper as they entered. Inside, a couple sat chatting with Maria's daughter, Claudia.

"Giacomo, I'm so sorry. Rio was such a beautiful woman." He noticed the tears in Maria's eyes as she took them to their table.

"Thank you, Maria."

"How long will you be here?"

"About a week. Then we head back to the States for the memorial."

Maria hugged him before she left to welcome another guest.

"I feel bad lying to her."

"Why can't you tell the truth?"

"I don't know who I can trust."

"Really?" Emily said with a tone of skepticism.

"What would you like to eat, Giacomo?"

Giacomo diverted his eyes from his wife. "Claudia, how are you?"

"*Bene*—good. I'm sorry, Giacomo. Rio . . . she was always very kind to me."

"Thank you." He changed the subject to avoid the lie. "What specials do you have tonight?"

"Dad made a pork roast with roasted potatoes."

"Sounds good to me. And you, honey?"

"The same—with pasta, please?"

"Pasta for me too. I love your mother's sauce."

"Two Pepsis?"

"How about water with lemons on the side, please. Thanks, Claudia."

"Can I read the letter?"

"Of course."

Giacomo reached inside his jacket, then checked his other pockets. "Shit . . . shit . . ."

"What's the matter?"

"I can't find Dad's note. I put the damn thing in my inside pocket."

"Did you leave it in the helicopter?"

"I hope not—damn."

"Maybe you left the note at the house, honey?"

"No." He checked every pocket of his jacket.

"Did you give it to Sergio?"

"No."

"Why don't you give him a call?"

"Yeah, you're right—these last couple of days have been kind of crazy. Besides, if anybody found the message, they wouldn't understand it."

They ate as Giacomo summarized his father's words for his wife.

Chapter 15

CARRYING A COMPUTER tablet and a wooden box, the bearded physician entered the operating room. Greeted by two nurses, he walked to the gurney. He plucked his suspenders as he studied his patient. For the second straight night, he would practice his skills.

"Any problems getting her here?"

"No, Doctor."

"Is the MRI ready?"

"Yes, Doctor."

"Any problems with the arterial catheterization?"

"No, Doctor. The catheter is stable and positioned in the internal carotid artery."

"Good. This procedure will provide us with better results. The cranial insertions are too risky."

"Yes, Doctor."

The patient's head was secured in a three-point apparatus that prevented involuntary movement. He lowered the volume to the heart monitor. Rio stirred. Her eyes opened. She tried to speak as the doctor placed his forefinger on her lips. "Don't try to talk. Go back to sleep, my dear. Too bad we don't have your father's second journal. Oh well—at least you won't die."

He unlatched the six-by-nine-inch brown wooden box. In the purple, velvet-lined container were two vials, labeled DNA and Stem Cells. He felt Rio's hand on his sleeve. "Everything will be all right, young lady. This will make you sleep." The doctor looked to the ceiling, then nodded to the nurse and said, "Let's begin."

Through an IV port in Rio's hand, the nurse injected a cloudy mixture that would place Rio in a medically induced coma. The doctor pushed a button on the side of the machine, and the patient table slid into the cylinder.

"Bring up the MRI photos."

"Yes, Doctor."

An image of Rio's skull overlaid with dashed lines showed the neural activity in different areas of her brain.

He grabbed the empty syringe and inserted the tip into each vial, withdrawing four cc's of liquid. He placed a sound-suppressing headset on and instructed the other nurse to start the MRI. Rapid pinging and banging filled the room.

"This will not hurt you, my dear." He attached the syringe to the femoral arterial line and pressed the plunger. The genetically engineered concoction made its way to the brain. On the monitor, the temporal lobe that controlled memory, understanding, and language glowed a vibrant yellow. Rio's body temperature increased by two degrees.

He continued to watch the monitor. The frontal lobe—the center that regulated emotions, personality, behavioral, thinking, and planning—radiated a bright red. "This is excellent," he said. Three minutes passed as a cascading aura of blue hues highlighted the parietal lobe, the part of the brain responsible for perception and making sense.

Rio's temperature soared to 104 degrees. Her heart rate was 173 beats per minute. The nurse placed a cold compress on her brow.

Two hours passed, and she stabilized. The doctor leaned over Rio, kissed her forehead, and said, "The prophecy—Et Tu Spiritu Sanctus."

The sun rose as he left the Vatican palace with a Swiss Guard.

Chapter 16

GIACOMO AND EMILY arrived back in Connecticut on Monday. Giacomo had purchased his childhood home from his mother—an English Tudor built in the 1920s that had been renovated many times. Once settled, Giacomo went to his father's old study. He removed the floorboard. *Damn—nothing. Dad must have meant his study at the Brewster Estate.* He turned on the TV and clicked the remote to a news channel.

The newscasters sat next to one another, handsome and pretty. The broadcasting corporations made every effort to win the ratings war by hiring the beautiful. At least these two were competent. Within the last four years, the media had come under attack for false, misleading news. Boosted by social media, the facts became distorted. The reality was no one knew what the truth was or wasn't. People relied on their own perceptions and ideologies.

"With three months until the presidential elections, the country faces an economic collapse as it looks to the European Union for help, but first the story of the recent deaths of . . ."

Giacomo turned up the volume.

"By all reports, the only connection between the deaths of Winston Tarmac, Sal Nasir, and Rio DeLaurentis was their individual relationships to the government. Anonymous sources in the FBI have told us Tarmac and Nasir were more than likely assassinated by the same terrorist group. As for Rio DeLaurentis . . ." A video clip of her admonishing Boyle played in the corner of the screen. "One can only say she was in the wrong place at the wrong time. Italian authorities are following up on leads and are tight-lipped with their investigation. Ms. DeLaurentis, the daughter of the late philanthropist Paolo DeLaurentis, will be buried Wednesday in a private ceremony in Connecticut."

"Jonathan, is there any theory that could tie the deaths together?"

"Not at this time, Megan."

"When we come back, our interview with the European Union's Eten Trivette."

Giacomo's cell phone rang. He muted the TV.

"Yes. What? I'm on my way." *Shit.* "Emily!" he yelled.

She ran to the doorway. "What's the matter?"

"Rio's house was broken into."

"When?"

"This morning. I'll be back as soon as I can."

"I'm going with you."

"Em, you're pregnant. It could be dangerous."

"Giacomo, please. The police are there—it can't be that dangerous."

"All right, let's go."

They ran to the garage and jumped into their dark blue Range Rover. Giacomo pushed the button on the visor. The door opened, as did the gate to the driveway. He stepped on the gas pedal and took a left at the corner of Elm and Whitney.

"Slow down, Giacomo. Remember, I'm pregnant."

"Sorry, honey."

They turned left on Cliff Street. A squad car was parked at the gated entrance. An officer leaned against the vehicle as he talked into his two-way radio. Giacomo rolled the window down. "I'm Colonel Giacomo DeLaurentis, the brother of Rio DeLaurentis."

"Our detective team is waiting for you at the house, sir."

"Thanks." Giacomo avoided using the private entrance.

The lieutenant of the robbery division met him. "Colonel DeLaurentis?"

"Yes."

"Lieutenant May." He saluted the colonel. "I'm sorry, sir. Your sister was a stand-up person."

"Thank you, Lieutenant. This is my wife, Emily."

"Hello, ma'am."

"Hello."

"Can we go in?"

"Yes, sir. The house is in shambles."

"Let me ask you a question, Lieutenant—"

"You can call me Bill."

"Was a floorboard missing from the study?"

"Yes."

"Damn it." Giacomo felt his face contort in anger.

"Did he have a floor safe?"

"Yep. Did you examine the surveillance video?"

"No."

"My father was a security nut, loved technology. We can access it on my sister's computer."

The townhouse was in shambles. Broken chairs, plates, papers, graffiti on the walls. "They did a good job." Giacomo shook his head. "How long did it take you guys to respond?"

"By the time we got the call—fifteen minutes. We figure they were in here for a half hour."

"Why the delay?"

"Problems at the alarm company."

"What do you mean?"

"They lost electrical power."

"Interesting."

They walked into Rio's study. Her law books were strewn on the floor, her desk toppled over, the room disheveled.

"What a mess. Any fingerprints?"

"No, sir."

Emily leaned over and picked up one of the items.

"Giacomo, they broke your father's clock." She handed it to him.

"It can be fixed. Honey, leave that stuff alone for forensics. We'll clean up later."

"Lieutenant, is it all right for me to walk around the house?"

"Yes, ma'am."

"Bill, help me with the desk, will you?"

"Sure."

Giacomo picked up the computer, set it on the desk, and then pushed a button. He thought for a moment before he typed in a string of commands. The monitor came alive as the screen divided into four images. Giacomo recognized the faces of the intruders.

Chapter 17

The Next Day

THE AIR WAS filled with the fading scent of summer. The afternoon sun highlighted the multicolored rose bushes bordered by Japanese maple trees. Thomas Maro stood on the steps of his redbrick house framed between two white pillars. He was tall, youthful at forty-five. He exuded a presidential quality. Abby Lamberti, his wife of ten years, stood by his side. Photographers clicked away as they recorded his every move. Television cameras whirred as they zoomed in and out.

"Mr. Maro, did you find a replacement for your chief of staff?" the correspondent from NBC asked.

"The family will take some time to grieve, and then I'll begin reviewing résumés. I should have an announcement next week." He pointed to another. "Yes, Elizabeth?"

"Sir, do you believe that your life is in danger after the assassination of your cousin?"

"No."

A journalist from CNN chimed in. "Mr. Maro, if elected, you said you would not entertain Trivette's European Union agenda on financial reform. Can you tell us why?"

Irritated, Maro replied, "We are the United States of America—we stand for freedom and democracy. For almost two hundred years, our country was an economic superpower. Our financial influence saved Europe in World War II. It was our technology, our innovation, our people who flourished—we taught the world. We've made mistakes. Greed and power have become the norm. Now we, the American citizens, need to come together as a people of righteousness. We are a country of peace, the land of democracy. We must lead ourselves and not rely on anyone else. In the long term, the EU policy is not helpful for the people. We as a nation have overcome adversity. We will do so again under my administration. Do you understand it now, Mr. Franklyn?" An uncomfortable silence ensued as the CNN reporter averted his eyes at the admonishment.

"Mr. Maro! Mr. Maro!" a woman's voice yelled from the group.

He scanned the crowd and pointed to a lady with a tiny nose. "Yes."

"Sir, Marie Greenway from the *Boston Herald.*"

"Yes, Marie."

A Secret Service agent whispered in the candidate's ear. He nodded. Maro's slate-blue eyes locked on the reporter. Two agents moved forward from the street.

The Massachusetts accent was unmistakable. "Is it true you are a Muslim?"

"I am neither Muslim, Jew, nor Christian. I believe in the one true God of Abraham." The cameras ignited in a maelstrom of clicks.

"Your cousin Saleem—was he a Muslim?"

Maro's heartbeat increased; he could feel the pounding in his chest. *Tell the truth. Who is this woman?* "Yes, but our work relationship was not based on our religious beliefs."

"Interesting." Her tone was unabashedly sarcastic. "Are you familiar with your cousin's father?"

Where is this going? "No, I am not." Saleem refused to discuss his deceased father when asked. Maro never wanted to intrude. He did remember a conversation his father had with Saleem's mother but couldn't remember the details.

"You have no knowledge that his father was associated with the traitor Dr. Colin Payne?"

Silence. Maro froze, stunned by the question.

The reporters pelted him. "Is this true?" "Do you think you'll lose the election?" "How could you not tell the American people?"

Maro motioned to calm the crowd.

"Please, please." A deep wind rustled, and a single maple leaf floated aimlessly. The crackle of a reporter stepping on a twig broke the stillness.

"No, Miss . . . Greenway, I did not know this." The shock on his face was a testament to his truth. "Why don't you tell us who you are? You're not with the *Boston Herald*." His voice was calm.

Suddenly, a woman screamed, and the scene erupted into mayhem. The reporters scattered as Secret Service agents grabbed Thomas Maro. With great force, they hauled him into the house. Maro was pushed to the foyer floor as his wife was hustled to a nearby safe room. Within minutes, police and FBI surrounded the property.

Outside, "Marie Greenway" lay on the front lawn, a bullet hole through her heart.

Chapter 18

GIACOMO AND RIO'S mother had aged gracefully. Victoria had remarried four years after the death of Paolo. Her husband, John, treated her like a queen. Content, she lived a joyful life.

"Tell me about Rio. Don't leave anything out," Victoria said.

"Rio is stable, breathing on her own, still in a coma. She'll get well, Mom." Giacomo's firm voice reassured his mother. They sat at her round kitchen table with John. Emily placed espresso cups in front of the two men and a plate of chocolate-chip biscotti on the lazy Susan.

"Is she gonna die?"

"No, Mom. Come on. She's surrounded by priests and nuns. Plus, the pope lives next door." He tried to ease his mother's mind.

Victoria wept as John wrapped his arms around her. "She'll recover, Vic. She's a fighter."

"That she is. Listen, Mom. After the funeral tomorrow, we're flying you both to Rome. You'll be safe there with Rio."

"What do you mean, 'safe'? What's going on, Giacomo?"

Giacomo shook his head. Emily held his hand. They glanced at each other.

"What are you not telling me?"

"Rio's house was broken into."

"What? Why? Damn it. Is it because of what she said? Her Italian temper . . ." Victoria's words trailed off. She bowed her head. "Giacomo, is what they're saying on the news correct? Is this related to the other assassinations?"

"I'm not sure." Giacomo rubbed his left ear as he told her some of what he knew.

"It was the *helicopter pilot*?"

"Yes, I recognized him from the surveillance video."

"Do they know Rio is alive?"

"Probably not. Still, we don't want to take any chances." Giacomo's cell phone rang. "Hello. *What?* Are you kidding me? Em—turn on the television."

"Why? What happened?"

"A reporter was shot in front of Tom Maro's house."

Chapter 19

The Next Morning

GIACOMO SAT ON a love seat and enjoyed the simple task of putting on his socks. When he had renovated his childhood home, he'd converted the au pair apartment into the master bedroom. Decorated in light earthtones, the area was comfortable and pleasant.

Emily walked in from the bathroom, dressed in black. Giacomo gazed at his wife. "You're gorgeous."

"I don't feel gorgeous. This morning sickness is a killer."

"I'm sorry, honey."

"Not your fault."

"Well, kinda is."

"Nice grin. Fine—it's your fault."

"I thought you'd be better after your first trimester."

"Me too."

"Did you see the reports on Maro's cousin? The media is crucifying our next president. They say he should have known about his uncle— whom, by the way, he never met."

"Our next president?"

"Yeah, he'll win the election." Giacomo hesitated. "That's strange . . ."

"What do you mean?"

"Thomas Maro will be the next commander in chief. I sense it—I *know* . . ."

"Oh boy. Spooky—I hope you're not getting like your father."

"God forbid . . . please."

"Giacomo, the limo is here," his mother's voice echoed through the intercom.

*   *   *

The feigned funeral was private; only family members were allowed into St. Thomas More Chapel at Yale. It didn't stop the paparazzi from taking pictures. The ride to St. Lawrence Cemetery was eerie. Rio was in a coma—not dead but not alive. Would there be a real funeral in the near future?

New Haven and West Haven police blocked the entranceways. No one could enter except for the DeLaurentis family. Parked to the side was a black SUV with government license plates. Rio's empty casket would be buried in the family plot. The pallbearers escorted the coffin to the gravesite, which was surrounded by floral arrangements. The bereaved exited their limos and, stepping with careful purpose, began the quiet trek across the green grass. The doors of the SUV swung open. Two well-dressed passengers exited the vehicle, followed by two men from the Secret Service.

The warmth of the morning sun broke through the scattered clouds. A dove cooed in the distance. This was more difficult for Giacomo than he'd thought it would be. His sister was breathing, yet the reality was that she might die. The priest raised his eyes from the prayer book as he said the final blessing. He stopped midsentence when he saw President Arthur Waldron and Thomas Maro standing behind the attendees.

Giacomo turned. He was not surprised that the two politicians were present. When the service was over, President Waldron gave his condolences to Victoria and then to Giacomo, as did Maro. A slight hum of a drone echoed overhead. Relatives said their goodbyes and departed, leaving Giacomo, Emily, Victoria, and John talking to the candidates.

"Giacomo," the president said. "Can we speak in private?"

"Honey, why don't you, Mom, and John wait in the limo for me?"

Emily leaned forward and kissed her husband. "Don't take too long?"

He rolled his eyes. The three men strolled to the SUV, their bodyguards close behind.

"When is she due?" Maro asked.

"Middle of January."

"May God bless your child."

"Thank you. I'm sorry to hear about your cousin."

"Thank *you*."

Giacomo sat opposite the two men in the modified presidential SUV.

The commander in chief spoke first. "Colonel . . . you don't mind if I call you Colonel?"

"No, sir."

Waldron reached inside his jacket pocket and pulled out a sheet of paper—one side torn.

"Best if I let you read this first."

Dear Mr. President and Mr. Maro,

This past week has not been kind to us. The attempt on my daughter's life and the assassinations of the ambassador and Tom's cousin inflict us with deep pain. Our people are confused as they wonder what will happen to America. The upcoming attack on our infrastructure and financial institutions will cause many citizens to question the strength and resolve of the current administration. It will galvanize those who want to overthrow our government. We stand on the precipice of a rebellion that will be instigated by an allied aggression on Iran. My journal has been whisked away. Its contents were not heeded, written off as a fluke. Ego and pride were more important than saving lives. The people who read the words knew they were true. They manipulated the outcomes of the future events to benefit their greed and thirst for power.

A civil war will arise on two fronts—the people versus the rich, the citizens opposing the government. This is the beginning of a coup to abolish our American way of life, to change the rules of freedom, to prevent the truth from reaching the people. We need to go no further than look within our own country and government, for the misguided are led by sources outside of our borders. They are the ones who want to destroy the fabric of democracy. The enemy is divided among themselves, which will allow our victory. Our shining moment is before us. In the months and years to come, America will become the bright star of the world once again—but at a cost. Be vigilant, my friends. The journey is difficult, filled with heartaches and joys.

Paolo DeLaurentis
April 5, 2000

P.S. Hello, Giacomo. Remember: what is hidden will be revealed in *time*.

Giacomo handed the paper back to Waldron, who shook his head. "Why is the word 'time' emphasized?" Giacomo whispered to himself.

"What?"

"My father emphasized 'time,' and I'm wondering why."

The men glanced at each other and shrugged.

"Is that your father's handwriting?"

"Yes, Mr. Maro."

"How . . . ?"

Giacomo explained to them how he and Rio had received the first letter a year after Paolo died and then three subsequent envelopes.

"Do you think there could be more?" the president asked.

"I hope not."

The men were silent for a moment.

Waldron spoke first. "Colonel, I remember the day when your father addressed the world's leaders at the United Nations. He said a time would come when devastating events took place, that we must throw away our indifference, love one another, and live in peace. Maybe that is what he meant by *time*—the time is now."

"Maybe."

The commander in chief continued, "What the world witnessed this past decade has been horrific—the loss of millions of lives due to natural and man-made disasters. Mother Nature slammed our country in February. The violent terrorist attacks, coupled with the economic collapse, the rise of the European Union." Waldron shook his head. "The threats of the FFB and now this—a potential attack on our infrastructure and economy."

"Yep." Giacomo didn't know what else to say.

"Last week, I was informed by Tom's new chief of staff that your father kept a journal. He prophesied events that have come to be. Is that true?"

Giacomo's left eyebrow raised. "You mean to tell me, Mr. President, you *never* read the journal?"

"Never."

"Giacomo, you're surprised?"

"I am, Mr. Maro. The deaths we could have prevented. Now, hundreds of thousands of innocents will be lost when Israel attacks Iran." Giacomo moved his head in disgust. His attention was drawn to the gray headstones in the distance. The gravediggers threw sand on his sister's empty coffin. A shiver traveled through his body.

Both men flashed a look of doubt at Giacomo.

"Israel is going to attack Iran?" Waldron's forehead creased with concern.

"Yes, they will, Mr. President. The attack on our infrastructure will happen as well. I hope you're prepared."

Waldron glanced at Maro. Giacomo didn't let them answer.

"What happened to the journal?"

"Last week, President Stalworth's widow called me. She read his diary. He mentioned the journal and how he lost it. He was distraught at the events that occurred on February 14 and 17. From what she said, he was troubled when he realized the truth after doing nothing. He died several days later." He paused. "Colonel, can you send us a copy of the journal?"

"You'll have my father's writing by the end of the day."

"Good. I heard Stalworth made life difficult for you."

"Yes, he did. I was silenced—but it took heroic efforts to keep my sister quiet."

"That must've been a challenge."

"You got that right, Tom."

"I wish you hadn't retired."

"No choice, Mr. President. Any idea why Stalworth didn't say anything?"

"I think he was embarrassed that he'd misplaced the journal. Most of all, pride. He wouldn't allow anyone to tell him what to do. I call it the curse of the presidency. Pride can easily overcome you. I've been there."

Giacomo's patience was waning. He needed to get back and find those responsible for the attempt on Rio's life. His mind failed to register how Tom's chief of staff knew about the journal.

"Can I ask why you're here together? This is unusual. You're running against each other."

"We need your help, Giacomo."

"*My* help? Seems a little odd. I'm listening."

Waldron drew a sigh.

"I will not be reelected. As the French say, it's a fait accompli. I'm finished."

"Why don't you drop out of the race?" Giacomo's words caught Waldron off guard.

"I don't have faith that our party will do what's best for our people. I trust Tom. We've been friends for many years. He's the better man."

"You can still win, Arthur. This is not a given."

"Believe me, I'm done. Nothing will pass in Congress as long as I'm in the Oval Office. Another four years of my administration won't accomplish a thing."

"Arthur and I have been meeting secretly to discuss strategies to help save the nation."

Waldron swallowed. "When Stalworth's widow informed me of your father's journal, and then when we received this letter, it was evident that we had to meet with you."

"Why?"

"Outside of the obvious, your father mentioned your name. Damn, it doesn't take a rocket scientist to know that the three of us need to work together."

"I can buy that. What are you proposing?"

"We agreed that if I win, you should become part of the transition team."

"I'm honored. What is it you want me to do?"

"First, we need to discuss your sister," Maro said.

"What does Rio have to do with anything? She's dead."

"Our intel sources tell us otherwise."

Arthur Waldron held out his hands. "We don't need the details. To be honest, her views are what this country needs." He smiled. "The way she blasted the leadership—what did that TV commercial used to say? *Priceless.*"

Giacomo laughed. *Can I trust these two?* His gut said yes.

"Yes, Rio is alive, though in a coma. She's safe."

"I'm glad. Induced coma?" Maro asked.

"No."

"Earlier, you mentioned your father wrote you a letter. Can you share it with us?"

Without hesitation, Giacomo informed the two about what his father wrote and about the robbery at his sister's house.

"Do you know what was in the journal?" Maro asked.

"No."

"We have a proposition for you," President Waldron said. "I want to reinstate you as commander of BOET."

"I'm not sure I want that responsibility again."

"Colonel, this is what I propose. Your replacement—Colonel Jason Vandercliff—will be your number-two man. Jason will run the day-to-day operations. You report only to me and no one else."

Giacomo hid a faint smile. He and Jason were friends. Four years earlier, he had recommended him for his job. BOET with its five hundred soldiers became an extension of the executive branch. Its commander reported directly to the president.

"I believe that your father's predictions will happen. Giacomo, our country needs you to uncover the enemy, find out who they are. Now that there's a second journal . . ." Waldron hesitated. "Giacomo, reinstating you would allow you to have more leeway in your search for those responsible for the assassination attempt on your sister *and* help you find the journal. The resources of the American government would be at your beck and call as you tracked those who wish to destroy our democracy."

"Well, it would help—"

The warbled sound of a satellite phone interrupted them. Waldron answered. "Yes, I understand. How many dead? *Damn*—what?" He hung up the phone. Two squad cars raced into the cemetery, and the Secret Service agents jumped into the SUV. Sirens blared on the way to the New Haven airport. Giacomo locked eyes with Tom Maro.

Giacomo said, "I told you it would happen."

Waldron squinted at Maro, then touched Giacomo's arm. "The Golden Gate Bridge collapsed. At least a thousand dead. Plus, the North Koreans hacked our financial institutions' computers." Waldron's anger surfaced, his face a crimson red. "Every American's bank account is frozen. Our economy no longer functions. The stock market just crashed. The Dow dropped five thousand points in the last fifteen minutes."

"The safeguards on the computers?"

"They worked. The banks will cease operations for three hours. I'll address the people when we arrive at the airport. Colonel, your father was right again. Are you on board, son?"

"Yes, Mr. President." Giacomo didn't understand why he said yes. Was it a commitment to country and freedom or fear of the unknown?

"Very well, General."

"General?"

"Yes. I promoted you."

The cars swept into Tweed Airport. An aged F-22 Raptor leapt off the runway to circle the airspace as it waited to escort Air Force One back to Washington. A podium with the presidential seal was positioned in front of the stairs of the government's aging Gulfstream G550. Television cameras and reporters were corralled to the side. The SUV parked. Waldron took a deep breath before he addressed the crowd—his presidency and nation struck with yet another death blow.

Chapter 20

THE FOLLOWING MORNING, the Chinese ambassador to the United States, Xiao Chin, sat alone in a booth at a McLean, Virginia, diner. The morning sun rose. Rays of light traveled across the eatery, lingering at the doorway. The air conditioner groaned as it struggled to cool the sweltering summer air. Xiao's jet-black hair highlighted his round face that reflected his no-nonsense personality as he waited for his guest to arrive. The clandestine meeting had been arranged outside of the normal diplomatic channels.

Xiao had been educated in China, Hong Kong, and America. His father, an influential Communist Party leader, had overseen the governmental transfer of Hong Kong from England to the Chinese in 2000. He'd insisted his son attend a university in the States. He stressed the importance of understanding life in America—it would be of benefit to Xiao in the future. And so, he graduated from Dartmouth with a degree in economics. Now, at fifty-two, he longed to be home in the city where he was raised—Hong Kong. The diplomat had grown tired of the political wrangling among the countries of the world, but even so, today's discussion would be interesting.

The sunlight hid the face of a thin man entering the restaurant. Secretary of State Clifton Webb wore a blue pin-striped gabardine suit. His polished black Italian leather shoes scuffed the floor as he passed an old white-and-black Formica counter with round red stools. The smell of bacon and brewed coffee permeated the establishment. Webb sat opposite Xiao.

Their pleasantries were strained. An older waitress, her hair pulled back in a bun, approached the booth with a coffeepot in hand. She poured the brown liquid into the stained ceramic cups. Xiao drank his black. Webb added milk and three sugars, then tapped his spoon against the saucer.

"You understand, Xiao, Waldron will give the order today?"

"Cliff, what your president proposes to do makes no sense. Our government cannot allow this to happen."

"Then your premier needs to step in, or by tomorrow morning there will be a new landscape. There is no choice. The US government is in shambles—you're well aware of that. *Shit* . . . the whole world knows. The political bickering and backstabbing on the Hill is unbelievable. I wish I had never taken this job . . ." His voice trailed off. Webb spun the tabs on the antique jukebox fastened to the wall and changed the subject. "Did you have these in Hong Kong when you grew up?"

"No. I first saw them at Dartmouth."

"Yeah, the good old days. We need to address the North Korea problem. I don't like it, but the United States has reached its tipping point."

"It is not our fault or responsibility that North Korea hacked your computer systems."

"True, but your country has the most to lose."

Xiao sat back and then leaned forward, his hands folded. "Is it China's fault that America continues to borrow from our financial institutions? Or that your electoral college overturned the presidential election four years ago? The indictment of your politicians? America is ripe for a revolution. Your border security is useless. Your attempts to build a wall were a waste of money. You worry that Hispanics are crossing your southern border?" Xiao's dark eyes grew wide, his left eyebrow raised as he said, "For the past twenty years, you ignored the terrorists who infiltrated the US through Canada. That, my friend, will bite you in the ass."

As in a game of chess, Webb's king had been put into check. The secretary of state sat back in astonishment. He had recently read a CIA report that acknowledged the same thing.

Xiao continued his diatribe. "Your new, revised health care initiative and your taxes on imports will lead your administration back to our banks. Like fools, we will continue to extend loans to your failed government. Your country would be better named the United States of China."

Webb's anger was on the cusp of causing a diplomatic incident. He was tired of the rhetoric. "I'm aware of the plight that faces our country, Mr. Ambassador. This is a bigger problem. Action needs to be taken soon. We might not be able to stop the next cyberattack. At that point, it will be a lose-lose proposition for both of our countries." Webb sighed. "At midnight, we will launch three nuclear strikes against North Korea." He registered the shock on the ambassador's face. *Checkmate? I don't think so.*

Xiao sat back. "This is stupid. Why would Waldron do this?"

"For reasons I can't discuss. Only the Chinese can stop this. We can't rely on the Russians." Webb glanced at his watch. "Time for me to go. Thanks for meeting me here." He dropped two dollars by the coffee cup, buttoned his jacket, and left the diner as he dodged checkmate. He left Xiao shaking his head. Webb reached for his cell phone and dialed the vice president of the United States.

"How did it go, Cliff?"

"The ruse of a nuclear strike shocked him."

"It should've. Well, I cleaned up another one of Waldron's messes."

"You realize we can have our asses thrown in jail for what we did?"

"Not my ass, Cliff—yours." The conversation ended.

Chapter 21

ARTHUR WALDRON WAS exhausted as he unbuttoned his white shirt. The weary man had spent the last twenty-four hours in the situation room, followed by a press conference on the financial condition of the country. The New York Stock Exchange had ceased trading. The economy was at a standstill. Waldron couldn't stop the onslaught of consumers who rushed to withdraw their money. Financial institutions locked the doors as panic devoured the nation.

The frustrated American people had been goaded by an antagonistic news media, and they'd reacted. On the night of the cyberattack, angry citizens rioted in the streets. One thousand and three American lives were lost in the hours of seething blackness. Local police, unable to control the mobs, were powerless as they observed the carnage. At the media briefing, Waldron announced banks would reopen within twenty-four hours. There was an underlying sense of doubt and doom—the people were disillusioned. To the surprise of many, according to the newscasters, only a small number of people removed all their money from the banks—if you consider over half a million to be small. Americans wanted revenge on the North Koreans.

The Joint Chiefs of Staff argued vehemently for a military strike against North Korea as a response to the cyberattacks. Waldron weighed the options and rejected their proposal.

Waldron wandered the hallways of his private residence. The house phone chimed.

"Mr. President, the secretary of state." The Secret Service agent handed him the phone.

"Yes, Clifton. *Dead?* How? Cliff, I expect you to represent the country at the funeral."

Waldron handed the phone back to the agent as he said, "Natural causes, I doubt it."

Before his election, the forty-eighth president of the United States had served three terms as a senator from Colorado. He knew how to play the political game. Although a Democrat, he was neither liberal nor conservative and had been praised for his ability to listen to the residents of his state. He cast his ballots per the wishes of the citizens.

Waldron had even overseen the development of a software program that allowed his constituents to vote for any bill before the Senate through computers, cell phones, and personal devices. Colorado was the only state that quantifiably listened to the voice of the people.

Another Secret Service agent escorted Waldron to his bedroom. His wife, Amy, was in bed, watching a movie on the wide-screen television.

"Hello, stranger," she said as she muted the sound. Married for five decades, Amy was the soothing voice that kept him calm.

"I hate this job." Waldron gazed at his spouse. "The North Korean leader is dead."

"Good. You don't need that worry. What a lunatic."

"Is it?"

"What do you mean?"

"Ignore me. How's the new bed?"

"Too hard."

"I'm sure we can replace it."

"I would hope so! You are the president, the most powerful man in the world."

"Yeah, right."

Arthur continued to undress. He sat on the bed as his childhood sweetheart rubbed his back.

"Who attacked the San Francisco Bridge?"

"Per the FBI, it was the Fighters for Freedom Brigade." With his hands, he cupped his face. "Tom Maro can have this job."

"Why do you say that?"

"I should've listened to you and not run again. The electoral college should never have overturned the election. Our country betrayed the founders because I won the popular vote. I can't do it anymore. It's a constant battle with the fools on the Hill." Waldron let out a sigh. "Rio DeLaurentis is right—our government is being run by a group of moronic a-holes. Myself included."

"Not true, Arthur. You're doing the best you can."

"Yeah, sure." He deflected the statement. "You're right about the bed, Amy." The president lay his head on the pillow and wished he could sleep forever.

Chapter 22

Three Days Later

GIACOMO HAD JUST finished a conversation with Rio's physician. Rio was resting comfortably, he'd been told. He sat on a black leather couch in his father's former study and gazed out the bay window. The sun kissed the tall evergreen trees. Their shadows darkened the freshly cut lawn. The yard hadn't changed much in the past forty years. The swimming pool was now covered, the greenish-blue tarp littered with brown leaves. A brick wall surrounded the two-acre property. Things had seemed simple when he was young and oblivious to the problems of the world. Another era, long ago, when life was uncomplicated by cameras on street corners and computer screens and the need for them in the first place.

General DeLaurentis ambled over to his desk where he managed his surveillance company, Remote, LLC. He had an office in Rome, which Sergio managed. Giacomo trusted his dad's longtime friend to oversee the European "theater," as it was called. There were four secret facilities that housed drones and pilot stations—two in the United States, one on the island of Corsica, one in the Italian capital. The lucrative multi-government contracts provided a steady flow of income. Giacomo read a document from his attorney regarding the potential ethical issues if he accepted Waldron's offer.

Across the front of his massive maple desk were five twenty-one-inch monitors. Images flowed from unmanned aircraft to the displays. Giacomo's company had the capabilities to tap into almost any surveillance camera in any town, city, or country. Remote, LLC could be the roving eye of any government that wished to pay for the shadowing services. The computers housed an elaborate array of software that could recognize any individual or vehicle without the aid of tracking devices.

Giacomo set the legal document down and grasped the black remote for the fifty-inch TV monitor mounted on the wall. He pressed the mute button as the news scrolled on the screen. The nation's banks had reopened.

His mind traveled to the words his dad had sent. He wrote the riddle on a piece of paper. *What are you telling me? What did you mean by "Time continues, not like a clock that can stop—time will reveal the prophecy. When the key finds its rightful place, the third trumpet will protect the angels born of man?"* Giacomo twirled his green Waterman pen between his fingers as he studied the words.

"Mon ami?"

"Si, mi amore."

"Dinner at six?"

"Sure."

"What are you staring at?" Emily went to her husband.

"I'm trying to figure out what Dad meant. Why didn't he tell us? Why the secrets? And this prophecy crap . . ." Giacomo shook his head and let out a sigh.

"You'll put the pieces together, love. Remember, your father was never wrong. He had a reason."

"Yeah, sure."

He turned and faced his wife. Emily leaned over and buttoned the second button of Giacomo's yellow shirt.

"Much better now. Did you hear from your mom yet?"

"The report from the Vatican is unchanged. Rio is sleeping, the normal blah, blah, blah." Giacomo changed the subject. "You should go stay with your father in Corsica."

"Why?"

"It'll be safer. Once I delve into the assassinations, the missile strike, and these latest attacks, life might get a little dicey. I would rather you and the boys be—" he rubbed Emily's belly "—safe and out of the country."

"Does my opinion count for anything?"

"Of course it does. A vacation in the warmth of Corsica? Not bad, if you ask me." He tried to make the visit sound inviting.

Emily began to cry.

"Why are you crying?"

"I just am." She started to leave, then turned. "Did you ever consider that the boys and I want a husband and a father?"

"Honey, honey, honey . . ." He walked to Emily and wrapped his arms around her. She sniffled. "I'm going to be all right. Nothing will happen to me. I want to make sure my family is safe while I'm working." He gazed into her eyes and kissed her salty lips. "Please don't worry."

Chapter 23

The Third Week in September

WITH EMILY ON her way to Corsica, Giacomo chartered a Falcon 2000EX EASy to take him to Washington. His meeting with the president and Thomas Maro was scheduled for early afternoon. He drove his Land Rover on Route 67 on his way to Oxford Airport as he listened to the satellite news station.

"In a joint announcement, Eten Trivette, president of the European Union and the Securities Exchange Commission, announced today that the United States would recommence trading as early as tomorrow. Leaders of the financial markets agreed that the collaboration with the EU will stabilize the nation's economy. According to close government sources, Congress is weighing the option of abolishing the dollar standard and replacing it with the euro. The militant group FFB stated that the treasonous Congress will be held accountable for their actions."

Giacomo's secured satellite phone warbled. "Hello, Sergio?"

"*Buongiorno,* my friend. I'm told you are a general now."

"Boy—word travels fast."

"Your wife told me."

"Glad it wasn't a secret. Anything turn up yet?"

"Two dead bodies."

"Let me guess. The helicopter pilots?"

"Yes, but not the ones you are thinking of."

"Really?"

"They were the original pilots; the other two were imposters. The good news. The two who broke into Rio's house are back in Italy."

"How did we find out?"

"Facial recognition program. One of our drones recorded a car accident along the Amalfi coast. The men happened to be in the vehicle. We followed them to the small village of Erchie, where we apprehended them. They're in an isolated location. I spoke with Alessio. He's arranged for you to watch the interrogation."

"Excellent. How is your son? Doing well as head of the AISI?" The AISI was the government intelligence agency equivalent to the CIA in the United States.

"Very well. He and his wife are expecting their third child."

"Great—your sixteenth grandchild, right?"

"Yes. We are happy."

"I take it the two pilots didn't have the journal?"

"Correct. They said it was stolen prior to their return to Italy."

"Sergio, check the drone images from the day of the missile attack. Maybe we can place those two in the vicinity. I'll fly out tonight, meet you in Rome tomorrow."

"Will do. Giacomo?"

"Yeah?"

"How did you know it was me on the phone?"

"I just knew."

"Ciao."

Giacomo unmuted the radio. "The financial markets around the world rose 25 percent with the news of the EU bailout of the American stock exchanges."

Chapter 24

THE TWO MEN sat opposite Vice President Jerry Richardson. Perspiration marks were visible on his blue oxford-cloth shirt. An insider to Washington politics known for his arm-twisting tactics akin to those of a car salesman, people either liked him or hated him.

He had represented the state of Georgia in the Senate for eighteen years. Richardson detested Arthur Waldron and believed *he* was meant to be the leader of the free world. To his dismay, the country continued to fall apart. Although he had distanced himself, he was now associated with the downfall of the American government. The good ol' boy network had collapsed. Jerry Richardson was trapped in a world where right was wrong and wrong was right.

He bellowed through his tobacco-stained yellow teeth at the men, "Damn it, gentlemen." Richardson's southern drawl was raspy from many years of smoking cigars. "What the hell were you thinking?" He coughed. His face reddened, and he shoved his chair into the wall. "Damn. You attempted to kill the Italians? You stupid jackasses."

"But, sir . . . our instructions." The two men winced as the verbal rampage continued.

"I don't care. You work for me, not that troll of a woman. At least you morons were able to steal the journal. Who were they working for?"

"We questioned them but got no answers."

"*Bah*. Where's the journal?"

One of the men reached into his briefcase and handed Richardson the writings of Paolo DeLaurentis.

"What? Why is this sealed? What the hell?" Richardson threw the book on his desk.

The two men grimaced at one another, afraid to speak. Spit erupted out of the balloon-faced politician. "Get the hell out of my office!" The vice president rose from his chair, turned, grabbed a paperweight, and threw it across the room. The object struck a picture of Richardson with Waldron, their hands raised in victory on the day of their election. "Out!"

The office door burst open as two Secret Service agents ran in with guns drawn. "Everything all right, sir?"

"Yes. Everyone out!"

The men did as commanded.

Richardson threw himself into his chair, pulled the blue trash can from underneath his desk, and vomited. A photo of his family toppled from the force. He picked up the framed snapshot and gazed at the picture. A wave of regret swept his being. He touched the face of his wife. They'd been married for twenty-five years when his Georgia peach succumbed to liver disease in April. He'd tried in vain to help her. The onset of her disease had occurred when he was a freshman in the Senate. Involved in a near-tragic car accident, she never forgave herself for almost killing her two children and drank to ease her pain. Now that he had nothing to lose, he would make them pay for what they did to her. Not wanting to revisit the memory, he opened the right top drawer and reached for the secure phone.

"Is *she* there? No? Well, screw her. I have the journal, and it's sealed. What do you mean, you *know*? So I wouldn't read it? Screw you!" Richardson yelled. "You can't use me anymore. Hello? Hello?" *The bastard hung up on me.*

Richardson contemplated removing the seal and taking a peek. *Why not? What are they going to do—kill me? Kill my wife? Well, that option is off the table. I didn't sign up for this—people dying. Now I'm a friggin' traitor. I was to serve another term and then be president. That was the plan. Innocent people are dead. Maybe I should shred the damn thing.* He smirked, vomited again, and then pressed the intercom button.

"Donna, come in here and bring me two aspirin." *They got the first one, but they're not going to get this one. Screw them.*

When the secretary entered the office, Richardson lifted his head. "Where's Donna?"

"Home sick. I'm filling in for her. Anything else, sir?"

"Yes." He reached in his desk drawer and pulled out a red envelope marked SHRED. Richardson took the journal and sealed it inside.

"Make sure this gets taken care of today."

"Yes, Mr. Vice President."

Chapter 25

SEVERAL MILES DOWN the road in the White House residence, Giacomo and Thomas Maro sat in Arthur Waldron's living room. A painting of Abraham Lincoln and pictures of the current first family adorned the walls that were decorated in floral tones. A full-screen TV faced the six-foot couch. The oak door opened as the two men stood.

"Mr. President."

"Mr. President."

"Gentlemen, please sit." They continued to stand. The struggle of the presidency showed on Waldron's face—dark circles under the eyes, creased skin, and the famous smile diminished to a frown. Arthur shook Tom's hand. "I've missed our nightly talks, my friend."

"Me as well. A rough couple of days for you, I'm sure."

"Yes—I hate this job."

Giacomo found the words of the commander in chief disconcerting. A man whose hope had vanished during his sojourn in the institution that fought for freedom and democracy. Nothing had changed in his four years as president. The electoral college voted him into office with the hopes Waldron would shake up the system. The ruling party behind him failed. The animosity and outrage of the opposition party fueled the revolution. He'd been defeated by elected officials who embraced their personal agendas above the needs of the American people.

Waldron shook Giacomo's hand. "Tell me, how's your sister?"

"Still the same, Mr. President. In a coma—but safe. I'll visit her tomorrow. I leave for Rome this afternoon."

"Good. When will you be back? By the way, Giacomo, we're on a first-name basis here—call me Art."

Giacomo nodded in acceptance. "Depends on the investigation."

"Understand . . . please . . ." Waldron motioned with his right hand to a sitting area in the corner of the room. Arthur unbuttoned his navy-blue jacket as he sat in one of the three high-backed upholstered leather chairs. A maplewood coffee table centered between the seats. Three portfolio-style notebooks had been placed in front of the president. Tom Maro's cell phone rang.

"Excuse me, gentlemen. My chief of staff." He spoke into the phone. "Yes, Dean. I need to get back to you. I'm in a meeting. No, it's personal." Maro ended the call and looked at the president. "Sorry, Arthur."

Waldron handed copies of Paolo's journal to Maro and DeLaurentis. "Giacomo, thank you. Your father's predictions were written twenty-nine years ago?"

"Yes, if not longer."

"Tom, what did you think?"

"This is remarkable—still trying to wrap my head around it. We had this information, yet we did nothing?"

Waldron leaned forward as he turned a page. "I'll tell you, Tom— I'm shocked."

Giacomo shook his head in disgust. "Sorry, I relied on the previous administration to take action. Guess that was a mistake. It won't happen again. Remember, gentlemen, hindsight is great."

"You're correct. The journal is in our hands now. We must move forward."

Giacomo studied their questioning faces. "Let's be honest. My financial resources and global connections can circumvent the government if need be. The facts are my sister is in a coma, and the ambassador to the UN and Tom's cousin are dead, as well as twenty-three civilians. There's a trail of bodies, and it leads back to my father's second journal. We need to act now on the remaining predictions. If you can't, I will. Regarding Dad's first journal, well . . . the words you used the other day, Mr. President, sum it up—fait accompli. The final event will happen."

Waldron sat back in his chair, dumbfounded. Maro gazed into Giacomo's eyes and held his stare.

"First, we must stop Israel from attacking Iran," Maro said.

"The secretary of state contacted the Israeli prime minister this morning. I'm deeply troubled by his response."

"What do you mean, Arthur?"

"He didn't deny it, Tom. His comment was 'We can't rely on our allies.' We told him the attack would have dire consequences for the American people. He said, 'My people are just as important.' Then the phone line went dead. Subsequently, the State Department reached out to their ambassador here in DC."

"And?"

"No response, Giacomo."

"Are we prepared if they attack?"

"Yes." Waldron opened the journal to a tabbed page and read aloud. "'When Israel attacks Iran, the enemies of the US will join the disgruntled citizens and attack American cities.'" Waldron took a breath. "I ordered the Joint Chiefs to mobilize our troops throughout the world, should the need arise."

"The need *will* arise, Mr. President. Be assured it will happen," Giacomo said, wishing he wasn't so certain he was right.

Chapter 26

GIACOMO SHOWERED AND dressed after his two-hour workout and martial arts joust with a local military attaché. He wandered the streets of Vatican City. Three stone walls to the north, south, and west bordered the country. St. Peter's Basilica, the pontiff's residence, and the Vatican Museum guarded the east side. The gardens held rows of waist-high green hedges that outlined the brick pathways. The Holy See encompassed 110 acres. Separated by the Tiber River and the city of Rome, the fortress protected him.

"Good morning, Mr. DeLaurentis."

Giacomo returned the greeting to the Swiss Guard as he entered the papal residence. The building housed one thousand rooms, of which two hundred were residences for the pope's staff and, in this case, one for Rio.

"How is she, Mom?" Giacomo walked to his sister's bed as pain and angst tugged his heart. He leaned over and gave his twin a kiss on the forehead.

"The same." Victoria wiped a tear from her eye. With rosary beads clenched in her hand, she asked, "When did you arrive?"

"Couple of hours ago—dropped my bags off at the hotel and had a quick workout. How's your apartment? Any problems?"

"No, everything is fine. Cardinal Andrew visits often. Even the pope came by one night and prayed for her."

"Wow." A tinge of sorrow echoed in his voice.

Rio heard their voices penetrate her comatose state. Unable to move, she called out in her mind: *Mom, is that you? Don't leave me. What's that? Why is it so dark? Where am I? Giacomo, is that you? What happened to me? Oh God, oh God!* No one heard her silent voice.

"Where's Emily?"

"In Corsica with Arnaud."

"What's going on, Giacomo?"

"I wish I knew, Mom. Whatever's in Dad's second journal has people concerned. I'll be working with President Waldron and Tom Maro. The plan is to recover the journal."

"Your father was an amazing man—he never shared with me his . . ."

"*Gift?*"

"Yes, his gift. One time before we were married, he stared at me. I felt his eyes penetrate my soul. It gave me the willies."

"The willies?"

"Freaky."

The brown maple door to Rio's room opened. "Giacomo, my friend."

"Andrew." A smile crossed his face.

"Giacomo! It's 'Your Eminence.'"

"Victoria, we're on a first-name basis. How is Rio today?"

"The same," she said as she moved her finger to the next rosary bead.

"God protects her."

"It's hard to watch my daughter suffer."

The cardinal put his hand on her shoulder. "Just a matter of time."

She bowed her head to continue her prayers. "Yes, a matter of time."

"What brings you back to Rome, Giacomo?"

"The Italian AISI asked for my help in the investigation." It was a partial truth—they did ask. His primary goal was to protect the interests of the United States and find the journal and those responsible for the attempt on Rio's life. Hopefully he would go unscathed.

"Makes sense. Where's your beautiful Emily?"

"In Corsica at her dad's house. She's not happy. I'm going to the island this weekend."

"Dinner tonight at the Piazza Novano?"

"Sure. Should be a comfortable evening. Do you want to walk?"

"Yeah, I could use the exercise. Your mother told me you met America's potential new president."

"Sure did—a nice guy. I'll tell you all about it at dinner."

"Sounds like a plan."

"Are you making any headway with the reunification?"

"Slow, to say the least. If we only thought like Jesus instead of relying on ourselves, there would be no issues. The minds of men destroy the works of God."

Chapter 27

GIACOMO EXITED VATICAN City at the St. Anne's entrance into St. Peter's Square. Tourists strolled with the hopes of glimpsing the humble pontiff, who often came to greet the people of God. Giacomo wandered past the four-thousand-year-old obelisk and Bernini's granite fountain. The pool of water bubbled from the gentle stream that cascaded from its domed top.

An unmarked police car waited for Giacomo. He gazed back into the piazza as he entered the vehicle. Tuscan colonnades topped with giant statues of popes, martyrs, and other religious figures appeared to touch the sky. The dome of St. Peter's Basilica loomed above the massive gathering place, said to hold sixty thousand people. Giacomo shook his head in awe as the car pulled away from the holy site. The ride to the Marriott Flora hotel took twenty minutes. After a hot shower and a cup of espresso, he headed to his Rome office.

Giacomo sat with Sergio in the operations center as the analysts reviewed the attack on Tony's plane. The thirty-by-thirty-foot room resembled a movie theater. Where the stage would have been were six pilot station cubicles. Along the wall above them, six large television screens projected the images of the drone's cameras. Ten feet behind the cubicles, two curved, twenty-foot countertops housed ten computer stations. Each workspace had the capability to access the Italian, French, and United States governments' satellites, as well as their municipal security cameras.

"We had two remote drones in the vicinity. With the satellite images given to us by the US government, we pinpointed the origination and path of the weapon," Ben, the analyst, explained. "Without a doubt, the Gulfstream G750 was the objective. You can see by this projection of its track." One of the screens flashed the track of the missile with a dotted line.

The other analyst, Alyssa, spoke as she typed a string of commands into the computer. "To be more specific, the Tower of Erchie, located close to SS 163."

"That's where we captured the helicopter pilots. Alessio has them locked up at AISI headquarters," Sergio said.

"Good." Giacomo studied the image. "No doubt they were after Tony's airplane?"

"No doubt," both analysts said at the same instant.

"Any intel that suggests my sister was the target?"

"No, not now," Ben replied.

"Keep up the good work," Giacomo said and followed Sergio out of the operations center, heading to Sergio's office. A camera scanned the ex-prime minister's retinas, and the door opened with a hiss. Remote, LLC occupied the top floor of the building on the Via Del Corso, located close to the Tiber River. The modest offices did not announce the wealth of either man.

"When do we meet with Alessio?"

"In two hours. Giacomo, what's going on?"

"I wish I knew. We'll have a better idea after the interrogation of the two pilots. Do we have any information on them?"

Sergio opened a desk drawer, pulled out a manila folder, and handed it to Giacomo.

"Alessio gave this to me."

Giacomo took out the typewritten single-page report stapled to the photos of the two men. "Anything from Interpol?"

"No."

"It says here they are immigrants of Middle Eastern ancestry?"

"Yes. One of the first tasks the AISI does when they bring in a suspect is to do a DNA test as well as a voice analysis. The information is then downloaded into the computer. With an accuracy of 98 percent, the results show they're of Middle Eastern origin."

"That and four dollars will buy me an espresso." Giacomo wasn't impressed.

"What I found interesting is toward the bottom of the page."

Giacomo read the paragraph aloud: "'We entered the Erchie Tower and found a hidden room with three Polish-made Grom handheld rocket launchers, one with its missile discharged.'" Giacomo put the document on Sergio's desk. "The range on these?"

"Seven to ten miles."

"The aircraft was three to five miles from Erchie?"

"Yes."

"I wonder why it didn't explode."

"An angel on Rio's shoulder . . ."

"Yeah, I guess so." Giacomo handed the folder back to Sergio. "I think, my friend . . . the next couple of weeks will be interesting, to say the least."

"I believe you're right, Giacomo. We should step up security."

"Our offices here?"

"Totally secured. Any intrusion—within one minute, our computers will self-destruct. Our paper files will be destroyed as well."

"The gas?"

"The perpetrators will be asleep within sixty seconds of entering the facility."

Chapter 28

The Same Day

THE OVAL OFFICE was one of the most intimidating places in the world, particularly if you provoked the ire of the president. Seated in the room in that wrath were Senator Robert Schwartz and Congressman Arnold Belmont, leaders of Congress. They sat opposite Lou Holtz, Waldron's chief of staff. Each man held a copy of a report. The two politicians fidgeted in their maroon leather chairs.

President Waldron, his back to the politicians, glared out the south-facing windows. The American flag was to his left, the president's flag to his right, separated by a cherry wood hutch topped with framed pictures. The room was impressive—thirty-five feet in length, twenty-nine feet wide, with an eighteen-foot ceiling. There were four doors: the east door opened to the Rose Garden; the west door led to the president's private study and dining room; the northwest and northeast doors opened to the central corridor and Waldron's secretary, respectively.

Waldron adjusted the drapes, turned, and sat in a brown leather chair. He tilted his head up at the presidential seal carved into the ceiling. He held the report for what felt like a long time and then slammed the document on his desk. Congressman Belmont jumped.

"These are the final numbers?"

"Yes, Mr. President," Holtz replied.

"So, what you are saying is two hundred . . ." He shuffled through the papers.

"Forty-three thousand, Mr. President," the chief of staff said.

"Homeless—no place to live. Two hundred and forty-three thousand we can't help?"

Waldron's face erupted; a blood vessel that stretched the length of his forehead puffed out in his anger. "We are the American government, gentlemen! We are here to serve the people, not ourselves. I don't want to hear that so many of our citizens are homeless. Let alone since February!"

"But, Mr. President," the leader of the Senate said. "It could've been worse."

"Are you kidding me? Worse? Why don't we take away your home and throw your scrawny ass into the street? Then you can tell me it could be worse. These people lost everything they had." He picked up the document again. "Maybe you'd have liked to be one of the forty-odd thousand who lost their lives?" He threw the binder at the senator.

Senator Schwartz scrambled to retrieve it. "You've got me all wrong."

Waldron ignored him. "The devastation caused by Mother Nature—five earthquakes, a hurricane, a blizzard, and ninety-eight freakin' tornadoes in two days. February, a disaster for our country. Our infrastructure attacked. Our economy almost destroyed, and you come here because Congress wants funds to repair the Washington Monument while our people are homeless? Not on my watch, gentlemen! Don't think for a moment I'm going to agree to move our dollar to the euro standard. Also, Mr. *Leader*, I want on my desk by this afternoon a list of funds we can stop allocating to other countries. We're finally going to provide for our own. We'll use that money to rebuild the houses that were lost." Waldron wagged his index finger as he continued his admonishment. "If you fail me, I will be on the airwaves tonight explaining your reckless actions to the American people. Rio DeLaurentis was right; you *should* resign. She does far more . . ." He was about to say "for the poor than we do" but instead blurted out, "God rest her soul."

When he'd mentioned the name of DeLaurentis, both leaders cringed.

"Now leave my—" Waldron was interrupted as the northeast door of the Oval Office opened and the secretary of defense hurried into the room.

"I'm sorry, Mr. President."

"Yes, Jim. What's the problem?"

"For your ears only, sir."

"Go ahead, James."

"Yes, sir. Um . . . we've gotten word that Israel launched an airstrike against Iran."

"What? Are you kidding me?"

"Sir . . . we need you downstairs."

"Let's go. Lou, get me the Israeli prime minister on the phone. And track down General DeLaurentis."

"Yes, Mr. President."

*   *   *

Waldron paced around a twenty-five-foot-long conference table in the Situation Room where the chief of staff, SECDEF, chairman of the Joint Chiefs, NSA director, CIA director, and Colonel Jason Vandercliff, commander of BOET, were seated. On one wall hung a series of large-screen monitors; one displayed a satellite view of two fighter-bombers as they entered Iraqi airspace. Their afterburners blazed as they swept across the land.

"How long before they strike?" Waldron demanded.

"We estimate within the next fifteen minutes, they'll initiate the bombing run, Mr. President," SECDEF replied.

"No luck reaching the prime minister or DeLaurentis, sir."

"Damn it, Holtz—I want a conference call with the president of Russia and the Chinese premier. Now!"

"Yes, sir."

Less than thirty seconds passed.

"They're on speaker, sir."

"Hello, gentlemen. I'm sure you're aware of the impending attack on Iran by Israeli air forces. I wish to make it clear the United States had no advance knowledge of this aggressive act. Our attempts to contact the Israeli government have been unsuccessful."

"I understand. Thank you, Mr. President," Mao Chin, the new Chinese premier, said as he ended the conversation.

"Arthur?"

Waldron leaned forward and picked up the phone. "Vladimir, how are you? I saw the pictures of the earthquake's aftermath. How're your people?"

"Many, many deaths, my friend," the Russian said in his deep baritone voice. "What do you think the Israelis are up to?"

The president of Russia—Vladimir Polotny—and Waldron had met thirteen years earlier; they had represented their respective governments during the investigation of Dr. Colin Payne. After the inquiry concluded, the two stayed in contact. They had a unique bond of trust and camaraderie.

"No clue, Vladimir, other than they were dissatisfied with the UN inspection of Iran's nuclear facilities."

"God help us, Arthur."

"God? I hope He's still with us."

"The Israeli fighters have begun their bombing runs."

"Vladimir, are you seeing this?"

"Yes."

"Sir, they launched their missiles."

Waldron checked the clock on the wall as the white contrail of the missiles could be seen on the monitor. "Any idea of the targets, General?"

"Tehran and Shiraz."

"Mr. President, Iran retaliated with two rockets—we believe armed with nuclear warheads—both aimed at Israel."

Arthur put the Russian president on speaker. "General, any assets in the air?"

"Yes, sir."

"Are they capable of intercepting Iran's missiles?"

"Yes."

"Knock them out of the sky. Vladimir, any problems with that?"

"None, Arthur. Our planes are in flight, ready to back you up if needed."

"General, inform command the Russians are with us. Any chance our planes can knock out the Israelis?"

"No, sir . . . oh my God, Arthur! A nuclear detonation over Tehran!"

"Son of a bitch." Waldron banged his fist. "What have they done? Vladimir, I'll talk with you later."

"Iran's rockets are destroyed. We got one. The Russians got the other."

"Thank you, General."

POTUS turned to the chairman of the Joint Chiefs. "General, execute Paolo's Return. Lou, I will address the nation in fifteen minutes."

Chapter 29

THE HEADQUARTERS OF the Agency for Internal Information and Security—AISI—was housed in a nondescript building in the center of Rome. The agency's role was to defend against any subversive, criminal, or terrorist act that would adversely affect the status of the government of Italy. Alessio—Sergio's son—was director of the organization and reported to the Italian minister of defense.

Giacomo and Sergio were escorted to a conference room on the seventh floor.

"Alessio."

Giacomo smiled and held out his arms. The two men hugged, patting each other on the back. The family friends had become colleagues when they sat together on a NATO summit conference in Rome ten years ago. Alessio greeted the American with the customary European kiss on both cheeks.

"Giacomo." The five-foot-nine Italian was dressed impeccably. He wore a dark gray, handmade, matte satin suit and a white shirt, unbuttoned below the neckline, a gold chain showing through. His sleeves were adorned with eighteen-karat gold cufflinks.

"Retirement suits you well." Alessio cleared his throat.

"Thank you, my friend. Retirement? We'll see."

Although the men hadn't seen each other in two years, they'd kept in contact. The AISI and its American CIA counterpart were primary users of Giacomo's drones.

"Papa." Alessio kissed his father and then turned as he spoke. "Giacomo, our government is concerned about your safety. The attack is unprecedented. Our country will bring to justice those involved. And if Rio should die . . . well, I can assure you the perpetrators will never reach the courts."

"Thanks, Alessio."

"In a few minutes, we'll begin the interrogation. You can view the video feed."

Alessio picked up the remote and turned on the TV. A test pattern popped up on the display, followed by the image of a room outfitted with overhead lights and emergency medical equipment. The interrogator viewed an image on the computer monitor, her right hand pointed to a mark on the screen.

Alessio glanced at the time on his gold watch. "I need to meet with the minister of defense. I'll be back soon."

Giacomo and Sergio watched the two helicopter pilots who were shackled to gurneys. Intravenous bags hung on poles above them. One prisoner rubbed the back of his head and right temple. The examiner sat on a rolling stool. She had short chestnut-brown hair and appeared a bit overweight. Black-rimmed glasses rested on the tip of her nose. She wore a white lab coat with blue lettering sewn above the pocket. A stethoscope hung from her neck. Her nametag read "Dr. B."

Giacomo cringed at the sight. Memories of when he was tortured years ago flooded his mind.

"Giacomo, are you . . ."

"Yeah—bad memory."

"Those two . . . they'll feel no pain. The truth serum affects only their memories."

"Interesting. Why is she studying the computer screen?"

"No idea."

"Probably a monitoring system for the heart." Giacomo poured water from a pitcher on the table into a glass. He removed the seeds from a lemon wedge and squeezed the rind. The juice from the fruit clouded the clear liquid. "She's concerned. Hand me the remote, Sergio. Maybe we can change the camera angle—get a close-up?"

Dr. B used her feet to glide her chair between the two detainees. She examined the head of the prisoner to her left. She then turned to the other and did the same.

"She's going back to the monitor."

Giacomo pushed various keys on the control pad. He zoomed in on the computer screen.

"Sergio, why an MRI image of their brains?"

He shrugged and shook his head. "No idea."

A female voice came through the speakers. Giacomo manipulated the keys, and the lens panned out to show the room and the inhabitants.

"I like her voice—soothing," Giacomo said.

"Yes, the drug will confuse the brain. Her voice will merge with their subconscious."

"No pain?" Giacomo rubbed his shoulder.

"No pain."

The doctor's calm tone interrupted their conversation. "Who ordered you to shoot down the airplane?"

"The one with the prophecy."

"Is that your leader?"

"No."

"Who is?"

"The one who knows."

She turned to the other prisoner and asked the same questions. The responses were repeated.

"What prophecy?"

In unison, both prisoners said, "Prophecy of old. The Gemini."

"Gemini?"

Again, they responded in unison. "The two must not meet. Family must be destroyed. One true world order."

"They sound like preprogrammed robots. What the hell is going on, Sergio?" Giacomo queried.

Dr. B strutted to the door and called an orderly. A man dressed in blue scrubs entered the room and removed the second prisoner. The doctor approached the remaining man. She again examined his skull and then folded her arms across her chest as she reexamined the images. Dr. B shook her head as she plopped back on the stool. With a push of her feet, she scooted over to the prisoner.

"Will we be able to speak with her?"

"I'm sure, Giacomo. Alessio will arrange it."

Giacomo manipulated the controls and zoomed in on the MRI. "Sergio, both men have the same image of a white line in their brain. I want a copy of those MRIs."

"Who has the journal?"

The screen went black.

"What the hell?"

*　*　*

A petite, dark-haired woman lingered in the corridor on the third floor of the AISI building. She glimpsed up at the security camera and waved. The guard monitoring the feed smiled at the display. She walked into the women's bathroom as she always did at this time of day. The guard's eyes focused, he waited for her to return and acknowledge him again. His love framed in front of the camera, opened her blouse, blew him a kiss, waved, and fell to the floor. His hand slammed the red alarm button . . .

*　*　*

Giacomo's face betrayed the disappointment he felt. "What the hell happened to the video?" He took the remote and pushed the buttons as he tried to make the screen come alive. "What the—" The sound of an explosion silenced his words. An alarm rang. The concussion of the blast knocked Sergio off his seat.

Pandemonium ensued. Dazed, Giacomo reached for his friend. "Sergio, are you all right?"

"Yeah." Sergio touched his head. Blood dribbled from a cut where he had hit the table.

Giacomo lifted him up off the floor and placed him back on his chair. He reached for the tissues to clean the head wound. The door to the conference room opened with a bang as Alessio, accompanied by two armed men, ran into the room. The alarm ceased.

"Papa?"

"Just a little scratch, son."

"I have to move you two out of here."

"Alessio, what the hell happened?" Giacomo asked as he helped Sergio stand.

"The interrogation room was blown up."

Chapter 30

IN A SECURE area fenced off by police barricades, Giacomo watched the EMT clean Sergio's wounded forehead. His white shirt was spotted with blood, and his now-wrinkled sports jacket served as a pillow while the technician finished. Dark black smoke escaped from the fourteenth floor of the seventeen-story building. The cloud obscured the afternoon sun. Burned debris and body parts were scattered along the narrow street. Two hundred government employees had been evacuated and moved a safe distance away. The news media interviewed eyewitnesses as their telephoto lenses captured the scene. Alessio approached his father.

"Papa, are you sure?" He touched the now-bandaged wound.

"Other than a headache, I'm fine. Help me sit up."

The EMT nodded as he discarded his bloodied latex gloves.

"This is my fault."

"No, Giacomo, our world is crazy. I reviewed the security footage." Alessio turned his head. "One of our own—an office clerk with a bomb strapped to her stomach."

"Suicide bomber?" Giacomo shook his head in disbelief. "How?"

"No idea."

"Did she target the interrogation room?"

"Yes. The explosive force swept downward into the room, killing the interrogator as well as the prisoner." He described the events in the video.

"She *waved* at the camera?"

"Yes, she was the girlfriend of one of our security people."

"Is he involved?"

"No. He set off the alarm. He is, um—how do you say—devastated."

"The other prisoner?"

"Dead."

"How many civilians?"

"Twenty-seven. I need to get both of you out of here. I've arranged an armed security detail—"

"I don't think—"

"Giacomo, you have no choice. As far as the ministry is concerned, you're an Italian national."

Giacomo's cell phone rang.

"What? Yes, Mr. President. Are we prepared? Good luck, sir." Giacomo silenced the call as he lowered his head in disgust.

Alessio's cell phone chimed next. Giacomo saw the color drain from his face. He guessed Alessio was being briefed on the Israeli attack. The Italian moved to the other side of the street as he listened to his earpiece.

"What's going on?" Sergio asked Giacomo.

"Israel nuked Iran."

"Just like your father said."

"Yeah, but who knew it would be a nuclear strike? A shame we couldn't stop Israel."

"Yes, it is. What'll happen next?"

Giacomo's eyes were distant as he said, "The United States will be attacked—but it will end quickly."

"How do you . . ."

"I just do." He didn't feel the need to explain or justify his inner belief.

Alessio returned with a well-dressed man. "I have a meeting with the defense minister. He wants answers. This is Luciano. He'll be your driver and bodyguard."

The men exchanged pleasantries. Alessio hugged his father longer than usual. Both had tears in their eyes as they kissed each other's cheeks.

"Be careful, Alessio."

"You too, Papa."

"What do you say, Sergio? Let's make our way out of here."

Giacomo's cell phone rang again as they entered the black Mercedes. He gazed at the caller ID.

"Yes, dear. I'm fine. I happened to be nearby—nothing more than that, honey. No, I'm not lying. I love you. I'll talk to you tonight."

"*Happened* to be nearby?" Sergio said.

"I stretched the truth a little."

*   *   *

Luciano drove Sergio and Giacomo to the office building. Two more bodyguards met them upon their arrival. Both similar in size, they had square jaws and broad shoulders. The nozzles of their Uzi machine guns hung below their black leather jackets. The men stationed themselves on either side of the car as Giacomo and Sergio exited the vehicle and were escorted to the secured floor of Remote, LLC. Their protectors stayed stationed by the entrance—their automatic weapons exposed for all to view.

Giacomo pulled his sleeve back, revealing a Tissot watch—a gift from Emily. "Six o'clock, and I'm exhausted."

Sergio rubbed his head. "At least we're not dead. I'm too old for this. Do you think the world will be brought into the conflict between Israel and Iran?"

"No. This is an isolated issue. Nobody wants a war."

Giacomo migrated to the window. In the distance, the residual smoke from the explosion wafted across the Roman sky. He turned and leaned against the pane. Sergio sat at his desk rubbing his head.

"The words of the prisoners are haunting me."

"What words, Giacomo?"

"The 'Gemini prophecy.' And we didn't find out what happened to the journal."

"Why don't we give today a rest? My head is killing me. Go visit your mother and your sister. Take a walk, eat. Most of all, call your wife. Keep her calm. We'll meet tomorrow morning."

"I'm gonna call Andrew. Maybe he has office space available."

"Why?"

"Why? Come on, Sergio. Whoever they are, they attacked AISI. Do you think they can't find us here?"

"True."

"I'll call you tonight. We'll be safer there. Who would dare attack the Vatican?"

*   *   *

Giacomo returned to his suite at the Marriott Flora after dinner with his family and Andrew. Tired, he sat in a black office chair at the desk in his room, a writing pad placed to his right. He withdrew his forest-green pen and doodled. Giacomo took a deep breath as he called his wife for the third time. He spoke in French.

"*Bonsoir, m'amor*—good evening, my love."

"Bonsoir." Her voice was cold.

An uncomfortable silence followed for a few moments.

"Come on, Em. It's not that bad." He regretted the words as soon as they came out of his mouth.

"Not that bad? Giacomo, you could have been killed."

"True, but I'm still here." He grimaced. *I should keep my mouth shut.*

Again, a long silence.

"Em, are you there?"

"Yes. When will you arrive?"

"Friday afternoon."

"Be careful and call me tomorrow."

"Em?"

"Yes."

"I love you. It will get better."

"I love you too."

Giacomo pressed the off button on his cell phone. *At least she's safe with Arnaud in Corsica.*

After a hot shower, Giacomo dressed in dark blue briefs and rested on the bed. His mind swirled with images. He closed his eyes and saw the inauguration of Thomas Maro.

A crowd had gathered in front of the Capitol. Thomas Maro, with his wife and two children by his side, stood as the chief justice began the swearing-in ceremony. The new vice president smiled in the chilly January day. The outgoing president was missing. Vice President Richardson's stomach stretched his black cashmere overcoat. His eyes were red, his lips snarled. He held two babies in his arms. Emily stood to his right, her stomach flat, tears in her eyes.

Giacomo woke up in a cold sweat and tried to shake off the dream.

Chapter 31

GIACOMO, REFRESHED FROM his night's sleep and an early workout in the hotel gym, exited the Marriott. The morning air was crisp and refreshing. He wore blue jeans, mahogany-brown cowboy boots, and a yellow buttoned-down oxford shirt. A brown leather jacket was draped over his arm. His eyes darted back and forth as he scanned the surroundings. The attack on AISI had clouded his thinking. *How does this all connect? Who has the journal? Prophecy? Gemini?* A car's horn interrupted his speculation. By the curbside, he spotted a black Mercedes limousine with blackened windows; attached to the front fender were Vatican flags. A member of the Swiss Guard held the right passenger door open for him.

"Good morning, Sergio. How's your head?" Giacomo entered the bulletproof vehicle. He placed his jacket on the seat next to his friend.

"I have a little pain—nothing much. How are you?"

"Fine—a weird dream last night. Can't remember it, though."

"Did you call your beautiful wife?"

"Sure did. She's not talking to me. Concerned about my safety."

"She's got a point. They went after your sister; you could be next."

"Believe me, Sergio, I can take care of myself."

"Maybe so, but . . ."

"We'll see." Holder of a tenth-degree black belt in karate, Giacomo was confident in his abilities to fend off an attacker.

"That's not going to protect you from a bomb. You know you're going to be a dad. I'm sure Alessio can provide you a security detail," Sergio said.

"I'll think about it."

The car crossed the Tiber River on the Via Vittoria Colanna as they made their way to Piazza del Sant' Ufficio. The vehicle came to a stop. They exited the Mercedes. Cardinal Andrew Angeloni met them, dressed in a black cassock.

"Andrew." Giacomo smiled at his friend.

"Your Eminence," Sergio said.

"Thank you, Andrew, for your help."

"No problem, Giacomo. I arranged a conference room for you in the Palazzo del Governatorato."

"The Palazzo—I like that."

The five-story building housed the administrative offices that governed the Vatican.

"How are you feeling?"

Giacomo eyed Sergio. "Our nerves are shot, but what can I say—we're alive."

"I guess I should continue to keep you in my prayers?" The cardinal chuckled.

"Absolutely. We need all the help we can get."

"Your Eminence, not to sound paranoid, but is the room secure?"

"Yes—Sergio, please call me Andrew. I'm so tired of people calling me that. We forget what our names are in this place. I'm just an ordinary guy."

"Well, you're more than ordinary . . . Andrew." Sergio found it difficult to call the man by his first name.

Giacomo put his arm around Sergio. "What? You're saying . . . Andrew is abnormal?"

"No, no, no . . ."

"Padre, our friend here needs you to hear his confession. Calling a cardinal abnormal—what's this world coming to?"

The three men laughed as they traveled the garden along Via delle Fondamenta. Several ilex trees were in the distance.

Andrew's face turned solemn. "The Holy Father is concerned with how the nations will react toward Israel after their foolish attack on Iran. I remember your father predicted this would happen."

Giacomo nodded. "The aftermath will only take place back home. President Waldron is prepared. Planet Earth is safe."

"Safe . . . strong word, my friend?"

"It is. Nobody wants another war. The United States will be blamed because we are Israel's closest ally. We won't be accused by the governments. We'll be indicted by the Islamic fundamentalists who wish to destroy our democracy."

"I hope you're right."

"We'll see. Andrew, how're your negotiations with the orthodoxy?"

"The discussions are fruitful. This afternoon should be the final meeting before the laity and religious vote on the reunification."

"Do you think it will pass?"

"I do."

Puzzled, Sergio asked, "What are you trying to do?"

Andrew remained silent for a moment. "There was a time when only one church existed—founded by St. Andrew in Antioch. Through the early centuries, the Christian community spread throughout the Roman Empire, governed by the bishops in Constantinople. They decided that one of them had to go to Rome and establish a presence. This made sense because the city was the financial and governing power of the world. The leadership agreed that the representative would become the first among equals. What they didn't expect was how powerful he would become." As the cardinal continued to talk, they stopped and sat on a park bench by the Piazza Santo Stefano. The morning light radiated the warmth of the sun on the men. "In the fifth century, Bishop Leo called himself 'pope'—in Greek, *papas,* or in Latin, *papa.*"

"Excuse me, Andrew," Sergio interrupted. "What is 'the first among equals'?"

"The pope had equal power with the additional authority to make certain unilateral decisions without the consensus of the other bishops."

"So, in other words, during that period, men being men, egos took over, and the pope became *the capo di tutti capi*—boss of all bosses," Giacomo said.

"Yep. We'd like to believe it was the guidance of the Holy Spirit. In the sixth and eleventh centuries, disputes occurred between the Western and Eastern churches, rooted in a clash of cultures—the Latin and the Greek. Our Roman Church reflected in a logical and practical way, while the Greek or Eastern Church held close the mystery, the exploration of faith to the theoretical. Then, as we say in America, the shit hit the fan."

"Andrew, your mouth, please. We are on holy ground." Giacomo's humor didn't go unnoticed.

"Giacomo, I told you I'm just an ordinary man."

"Sure you are."

The cardinal laughed. "In the year 1054, the Great Schism occurred; the church split. There were those who opposed the breakup and tried in earnest to stop the divide. Now is the time to heal the splintered church," Andrew said as he pointed in the direction of the administration building.

Chapter 32

GIACOMO ENTERED THE room first, followed by Sergio. A fresco of the Last Supper hung on the white wall opposite the entrance, centered between two windows. One had been cracked open, and a fresh breeze circulated. A flat-screen TV was suspended from the ceiling in the corner. On the far-right wall was a whiteboard with blue, black, and red erasable markers. A small desk was positioned to its left. The maple conference table had been outfitted with electrical outlets for each attendee.

"Sure is big enough," Giacomo said. He moved to the windows to view the Vatican grounds. Sergio opened his suitcase and retrieved a computer switch box. He connected it to his laptop.

"What's the box for?"

"Security. Alessio gave it to me. It prevents hackers from entering the system."

"Like a VPN—virtual private network."

"Yes. Alessio said this is more secure."

"Interesting." Giacomo sat in one of the six brown leather chairs. "Remember the dream I said I forgot?"

"Yes."

"I felt like it happened."

"Your father used to call that a 'real dream' . . . a premonition of what would occur later in time."

"Well then, Tom Maro will be our next president."

"I don't think you need a dream to tell you that."

"Yeah, you're right."

Giacomo's cell phone rang. The caller ID displayed the name.

"Hello, Mr. President."

"Hello, Giacomo. With me is Tom Maro. Can you talk?"

"Yes, sir. I have Sergio Esposto here and would like to bring him into the loop. He's been influential in the investigation. Any concerns?"

There was a muffled exchange. "No problem."

"Sergio, Arthur Waldron here. I'd like to introduce you to our next president, Tom Maro."

"Hello, Mr. President . . . Mr. Maro."

Waldron inhaled and sighed. "Giacomo, how are you?"

"I'm good, Arthur."

"I'm happy you're not dead."

"Me too."

Sergio nodded in agreement.

"Giacomo, any answers?"

"My sister was the target. Still trying to put the pieces together. From what I observed in the interrogation, I believe the perps were brainwashed."

Sergio's puzzled expression caught Giacomo's eye.

"Brainwashed how?" Maro asked.

Waldron interrupted. "I don't understand . . ."

"At one point, both prisoners answered the questions simultaneously."

"You think because of what you heard that they were influenced?"

"Yes, I do. Their statements sounded rehearsed."

"What did you learn?"

Silence ensued for a minute.

"Giacomo, are you there?"

"I am, Arthur. What did we learn? Difficult to explain because it sounds like an old James Bond movie."

"Old James Bond movie?"

"Yep. They were saying things like 'one true world order' and 'the

Gemini prophecy' and 'the two must not meet.' One more thing. Whoever they are, they want my sister and me dead."

"Wow," Maro said.

"Yeah, I agree with Tom—*wow*. Giacomo, one more question— this debacle in the Middle East?"

"Yes."

"Your opinion is the States will be attacked?"

"Yes. Why?"

"The CIA is hearing a lot of chatter coming from there saying we blessed the nuclear strike."

"That's ludicrous, Arthur."

Sergio interrupted the conversation. "Excuse me, gentlemen. My son also acknowledged Italian intelligence sources are hearing the same."

"The pope is also concerned about a worldwide armed conflict."

"I spoke with our allies, as well as the leaders of China and Russia. I assured them we gave no such approval. The only country at risk is the United States."

"How's the troop withdrawal?"

Sergio shot Giacomo a questioning glance.

"Almost completed. The troops will be back within twenty-four hours. Giacomo, this is one time I hope your father was wrong."

"Don't count on it."

"Let's pray this ends quickly."

"Your words to God's ears," Maro said.

"Giacomo, did the prisoners say what happened to the journal?"

"No."

"Any idea what your father might have written?"

"No, Arthur. Whatever it is, our enemies want the damn thing."

"Giacomo, I want you to stay in Europe and continue to track down the terrorist group and find that journal. I believe there is valuable information in it that would help us. We have to recapture your father's writings. Remember, not only did they attack your sister, they also murdered our ambassador to the United Nations and Tom's cousin." Waldron's voice grew angrier. "Justice must be served. We can't allow our passivity against terror to continue."

"Yes, Mr. President."

         *   *   *

That afternoon two men sat opposite one another at a picnic table in Ann Morrison Park in Boise, Idaho. It was the perfect spot, with lots of activity and a multitude of people. They went unnoticed as they talked.

"So that we understand each other, your team will be in place in Washington. Together we initiate the attack. Remember, Tariq, when this is over, your people leave. We will control the government, not you. You can take the credit, but the FFB will run the country."

"I agree—as long as your government crumbles."

"Oh, I assure you, the government of the United States will crumble."

"And the remaining twin *must* die."

In June 2007, a Pakistani sheik named Tariq Kahn began to recruit American Muslims. He financed an organization—Muslims for Peace, or MFP—to work with local city administrations under the umbrella of peace and fellowship. Five years later, the growing group purchased substantial amounts of property throughout America. The land became training camps for homegrown and immigrant terrorists. ISIL, the MFP, and the FFB joined forces in 2014.

Chapter 33

GIACOMO DESCENDED THE steps of the Falcon 8X into the warm Corsican sun. Emily waited with Arnaud by the stairs. He hoped for a weekend of relaxation and food. Deep inside, he knew that wouldn't be the case. How could it be, with his sister in a coma and the world on the verge of World War III? He'd be lucky to get a good night's sleep.

Emily greeted him with a long-awaited hug. He gave her a quick kiss on the lips. Giacomo cupped his hands around her stomach. "How are the boys?"

"Fine, *mon cherie*. Kicking up a storm."

"Hi, Dad." He stretched out his hand to his father-in-law. Arnaud drew him close and embraced him.

"I'm glad you're safe, my son. Did you bring any bags?"

He lifted the suitcase. "Just this one."

"Where's your security?"

"Back in Rome. I figured I'd be safe here with the head of the DGSE."

Arnaud patted him on the back. "Yes, you are."

They entered a silver Mercedes SUV, its windows blackened. Two police vehicles escorted them to Arnaud's estate.

"When do you have to leave?"

"Two days."

The couple sat next to one another, Emily's hand on Giacomo's thigh. Arnaud sat opposite them. A glass barrier separated the armed military driver from the passengers. Giacomo pointed out the window as they drove along the Corsican coast toward Porta Vecchio.

"Why the EU protest signs? My understanding, Trivette is doing an excellent job of stabilizing the economy."

Arnaud gazed out the window as he spoke. "The Corsicans have always wanted autonomy. 'Cut the apron strings with mother France,' they say. The truth, there are those of us who believe Trivette and his puppets are nothing more than gangsters."

"Us?" The word "puppets" struck a chord with Giacomo.

"Did I say us?"

"Dad, why don't we talk about this later." Emily squeezed Giacomo's leg.

"Trivette is doing remarkable things. He restored jobs. The price of gas is cheaper here than in the States. Your economy is booming. What more could you want? Now I understand our government plans to join economic forces with him."

Arnaud threw an angry look at Giacomo. In rapid French, he began his diatribe. "That would be foolish for the Americans. Eten is manipulating the world's economy. Though it appears pleasant on the outside . . . it's ugly on the inside. You Americans are afraid of the Chinese? This guy is worse."

"Come on, really? What's his motivation?"

"To control the world."

"Really, Dad? What's your issue with this guy?"

"He reminds me of someone your father and I knew."

"Yeah . . . who?"

"*Sharif.*" Through clenched teeth, he added, "This conversation is over."

Emily squeezed Giacomo's leg tighter.

"Em, stop." He removed her hand. He noticed her roll her eyes. For the remainder of the drive, she kept her focus on the scenery outside. *Now I have two people pissed off at me.*

∗　∗　∗

They arrived at the villa in Cala Rosa. The driveway was paved with loose white pebbles. An eight-foot-high stone wall surrounded three of the property's boundaries. The back opened to the sea, an infinite swimming pool two hundred steps from the turquoise Mediterranean. Gardeners manicured the ten-acre estate as the automobile circled a fountain with a statue of Napoleon in the center. The driver stopped the vehicle next to the stone-slabbed sidewalk that led to the main house, an imposing ten-bedroom, dark yellow stucco mansion with rust-colored shutters flanked by security and housekeeping personnel accommodations. The coast of Italy lay sixty miles to the east.

Upset, Arnaud exited the car. "Excuse me. I need to make a phone call."

"Why were you squeezing my leg?"

"Oh, you men. The EU is a sore subject with Papa. I was trying to tell you to stop."

"Why?"

"An incident happened years ago between him and Trivette. All he will tell me is that Trivette reminds him of someone."

"Well, I still think the European Union will be an asset to the United States."

"We'll see, *mon cheri*. Wanna go sit by the pool?"

"Sure. Are you still mad at me?"

"I've gotten over it," Emily said.

Gotten over it, my ass. Giacomo helped his wife out of the car.

*   *   *

Ten paramilitary commandos boarded the ship, dressed as tourists. Their cache of assault weapons was hoisted on the port side of the vessel in two lifeboats that would accompany them. Scheduled to sail from Marseille at two o'clock in the afternoon, they would conclude their twelve-hour journey in the moonless night.

The commander laughed to himself as he jumped from the dock to the luxury yacht. It wasn't just that he and his men were traveling in style—it was also the contracts with two separate clients to do the exact same job. He was going to make five million dollars. "Time to retire," he whispered as he gave the signal to the captain to head out to sea.

Chapter 34

THE BREEZE FROM the Mediterranean Sea rustled the curtains, waking Giacomo from a sound sleep. He slipped out of bed and tried not to disturb his wife as he walked on the sand-colored tile to the open window. His cell phone vibrated on the end table.

"Sergio, it's three o'clock in the morning. What's wrong?" he whispered. Emily shifted her body to her side.

"Visitors are soon to arrive."

"What?"

"Two incoming Zodiac boats with ten men. We notified DGSE as well as the Corsican police. You need to get out of there—ETA ten minutes."

The bedroom door swung open, Arnaud in the doorway.

"Sergio called and told me. Emily, wake up."

"What's the matter?"

"We're being attacked. Let's go!" Giacomo handed Emily her robe.

"I'll be downstairs," Arnaud said.

A commotion erupted outside as lights blazed on the beach and helicopters buzzed, searching for their prey. The sound of the rotors broke the dark silence. By the time the family got downstairs, explosions and flashes of light speckled the horizon. Giacomo unlatched the safety on his 9-mm handgun. Arm outstretched, the Beretta now an extension of his hand, he rounded the corner to the foyer. His eyes swept the room for a target as he motioned for Emily to go to the secured bombproof basement. An alarm sounded—a voice over the speaker gave the "stand down" order. Giacomo lowered his arm. Adrenaline pumped through his veins. He ran to his wife, who stood by the door leading to the cellar.

"Giacomo, what's going on?"

Arnaud ran into the room. "Are you two—"

"Yes, we're fine. What happened, Papa?"

"Enemies tried to attack the villa."

"*Enemies?* Where did they come from?" Emily asked.

"We don't know yet."

"Should we stay here?"

"Yes, my Emily—we're protected. The military sent reinforcements. You two try to go back to sleep. We'll figure this out in the morning."

"Come on, *mon cheri*. Let's go upstairs. You need your sleep."

"Papa?" A look of concern emanated from her eyes.

"I'm good, my little one. Go—go back to bed." He kissed his daughter on the cheek. "Thank you, Giacomo."

"No problem, Dad."

* * *

Giacomo and Arnaud huddled over a computer screen. The morning air held on to the repugnant smell of gunpowder. Giacomo gazed at his watch; it was nine thirty. Emily had managed to fall asleep as her husband wrestled with the thoughts of who would want him dead.

"Sergio, what did you find out?"

His voice crackled through the speakerphone. "We tracked the Zodiac boats to a yacht. The Corsican helicopters destroyed them. There were no survivors."

"What happened to the yacht?"

"Demolished by French Mirages. We don't know anything else yet, but we'll have satellite images in a couple of hours. We should be able to determine where she departed from."

"Sergio, see what you can find. I'll call you when I'm back in Rome." Giacomo hung up and then turned to his father-in-law. "Arnaud, I think we should go our separate ways. I'll send Em to Ottati. I spoke with Alessio. He's providing a security detail to protect her. I'll go back to Rome. I want to be close to Rio in case she wakes up. Give some relief to Mom."

"Good idea. I'm going back to Paris."

"Do I have a say in this?" Emily stood in the doorway of Arnaud's library. She was dressed in stretch pants; a bright red maternity shirt covered the tiny bump.

"Em, honey, listen . . ."

"No. You do not," Arnaud said, his voice firm.

Chapter 35

"I DON'T UNDERSTAND, GIACOMO. Why can't I stay with you in Rome?" Emily asked one more time as the helicopter traversed the Italian countryside.

"Em, it's too dangerous. In Ottati, you'll be safe. Alessio sent AISI agents who will guard you, and the Alburni Mountains provide an excellent vantage point for protection."

"Well, I don't like it."

*　*　*

The Italian police drove Giacomo to Vatican City via a circuitous route. He gazed out the window as they passed the Roman Coliseum. Statues of silver-clad gladiators lined the road. A young girl approached a warrior and jumped back in fright when he moved. Her older brother laughed hysterically. Giacomo smiled. His cell phone rang.

"Hello, Sergio."

"How far away are you?"

"Twenty minutes."

"Come to our office, not the Vatican."

"Why?"

"No remote setup for your video conference call."

"Damn it. Ciao."

Giacomo arrived fifteen minutes later. Two armed agents waited outside the building to escort him to his office. Not happy with the presence of the bodyguards, he rationalized, *At least Em will feel better.*

"Sergio, what did you find?"

"The yacht was US registered, owned by a Chloe Bresden."

"I'll bet you she's dead."

"How did you . . ."

"I guessed. How long?"

"Almost a month."

"A month?" Giacomo stretched his legs as he sat in the chair.

"Her real name was Nava Ben-Reuven."

"Israeli?"

"Waiting for confirmation. Here's the shocker."

"I wait with bated breath." Giacomo sensed Sergio's exasperation. "I'm sorry, Sergio. Go ahead."

"She was the reporter killed at Maro's house."

"*Shit.* Are you kidding me?"

"I kid you not, my friend."

Giacomo's mind churned. "Is there a money trail?"

"None we can find."

"I wonder if Maro knows anything. Are we ready for the conference call?"

"Yes."

The screen in the operations center came alive and split three ways: Arthur Waldron on the left, Thomas Maro in the center, and Arnaud Chambery on the right.

"Giacomo, Arnaud, how the hell are you guys? Glad you're still alive."

"Us too, Mr. President." *Too much coffee, Arthur?*

"What did you discover?" Waldron picked up a cloth napkin and wiped his forehead.

"They want me dead. The attack on the villa . . ."

"Why?"

"A good question, Tom. Apparently, I have information no one else does."

"The James Bond theory?"

"That's part of it, Arthur. The pieces just don't seem to fit. The journal, the death of Tom's cousin, the ambassador, my sister. Doesn't make sense."

"You think this is all connected?"

"I'm starting to believe that, Tom."

Again, Waldron wiped beads of sweat. He sputtered, "The answer has got to be in the journal. Whatever your father wrote links us all."

"Possibly," Giacomo said, not bothering to hide his skepticism.

"Could the attack be against you, Arnaud?"

"Of course, I made many enemies, Mr. President."

Giacomo interrupted. "No! They were after me. I feel it in my gut. Tom, the reporter killed at your press conference, was the owner of the yacht. Her real name . . ."

"Nava Ben-Reuven. I found out today—Dean, my new chief of staff, informed me. Any idea who she is?"

"No. We were hoping you might know."

"Not a clue."

"I uncovered information as well—the Mirage fighters were not ours," Arnaud said.

"What do you mean?" Maro leaned forward toward the camera.

"The French government didn't dispatch them."

Waldron interrupted. "Gentlemen, I need to cut this short. I have a meeting with the Joint Chiefs in the Oval Office in ten minutes. Keep me in the loop, Giacomo. Let's catch these bastards."

"Yes, sir."

The president's image vanished from the screen.

Chapter 36

PRESIDENT ARTHUR WALDRON gazed out the south window as the Joint Chiefs of Staff and Esther Boyle, the acting chair of the Senate Intelligence Committee, left the Oval Office. Soon the sun would set and he could retreat to the residence, putting another dreadful day and bad week behind him. The two-hour meeting had ended in frustration for the commander in chief. He had failed to convince his top commanders that an attack on the country was imminent. *"Mr. President, they are the words of a dead man. There is no intelligence to support an immediate threat. We have left our allies defenseless by our troop withdrawal . . ."*

"Mr. President?" Waldron was abruptly jolted back to the present as Secretary of Defense James Bennett entered the room. He turned and motioned for Jim to sit.

"Jim, we're in big trouble here."

"I agree. The Middle East will be an even more dangerous place to be." The lanky man wavered, his voice skeptical. "Do you really believe what DeLaurentis wrote?"

"I do, but the Middle East is not the problem." Arthur opened his desk drawer and withdrew a green folder titled FBI Top Secret. "I kept this from the Joint Chiefs. I'm surprised that bitch Boyle said nothing. She's aware of this." Waldron unclasped the dossier and read the document aloud. "'It is the director's assessment that the FFB will attack our infrastructure within the next thirty days. We have concluded they will more than likely join forces with the Islamic fundamentalists who blame us for the nuclear strike on Iran. This means that—'" He broke off as the doors to the office burst open. "What the hell?"

Eight Secret Service agents entered the room with their guns drawn. Six of them encircled the commander in chief while the other two stood on either side of Bennett.

"What the hell is going on?"

"Mr. President, you and SECDEF need to come with us. Now!"

No explanation was necessary as an explosion shook the White House.

The rotor blades of Marine One could be heard as it touched down on the south lawn. The eight armed agents escorted Waldron and Bennett out of the Oval Office, running to the escape vehicle. One agent collapsed as blood erupted from his forehead. A marine opened fire at the sniper atop the Executive Office Building. Two men lifted Waldron and threw him into the helicopter as Bennett was shoved into the hatch as it became airborne.

"Mr. President, are you injured?" the marine medic asked as he strapped the president into his seat.

"No. What the hell is going on, soldier?"

"We've been attacked."

Waldron shook his head in disbelief as he saw black smoke rising from three buildings near the White House. The nation's capital was under siege. Escorted by two other marine helicopters, they reached Andrews Air Force Base in less than fifteen minutes. Three hundred soldiers awaited them on the tarmac. The servicemen's rifles were aimed at the rooftops of the hangars and buildings. Three F-22 Raptors ascended into the sky, circling the airport. The president's helicopter settled on the taxiway at the end of the runway. Seven armed marines filed out, their bodies rotated, their guns searching for the enemy. Three men ran up the stairs to board Air Force One. The engines were fever pitched at full power. Doors closed, the aircraft started its takeoff run.

"What the hell is going on?" Arthur Waldron demanded.

As the plane lifted off, an orange flash engulfed the Boeing 747. Air Force One seemed to hang momentarily in midflight, and then, with a thunderous explosion, the airplane split in half and crashed to the ground.

Chapter 37

GIACOMO AWOKE TO the sound of banging on the door and the chime of his cell phone. Startled, he jumped out of bed. He fumbled to find his gun. Roused from a sound sleep, he took a moment to gain his senses. He remembered he was in Rome.

"Hello?" he said as he grabbed his pants.

"What? Thank you, Jason."

He zipped up his blue jeans as he unlocked the door to his suite. Sergio and Alessio waited for him.

"Come in. Vandercliff called me. How bad is it?"

"Bad," Sergio said.

Alessio grabbed the remote control. It was eleven in the evening—5:00 p.m. in the States. The three men sat on the couch across from the flat-screen television. They watched in horror as flames engulfed Air Force One. Scenes flashed of cities attacked—Washington, San Antonio, Burbank—buildings spewing out black smoke, bridges and tunnels collapsed, vehicles charred and stranded on the roads.

"Any other country attacked?"

Alessio cleared his throat. "No, as far as we know, just the United States."

"Like you said, Giacomo."

"Yeah. Sorry to be right, Sergio."

"What did Jason say?"

"The president is safe," Alessio interjected.

"Yes. Who told you?"

"The minister of defense." Alessio cleared his throat once more. "He said Waldron spoke with the heads of state."

Giacomo gave the AISI director a meaningful stare. The Italian avoided his gaze. He said nothing.

The facts were plausible. The governments of the world needed the assurance that the commander in chief was alive. A fleeting question crossed Giacomo's mind: *Why are Sergio and Alessio here?*

The television screen flashed to a new image: a podium with the presidential seal. Arthur Waldron, flanked by the Joint Chiefs of Staff, adjusted a microphone. Colonel Jason Vandercliff, the second in command of BOET, stood behind and to his right. Waldron's left hand shook as he took a handkerchief from his pocket and wiped his brow. Giacomo increased the volume on the TV.

"My fellow Americans." Waldron took a deep breath. "It is with deep sadness that I speak to you this evening. Our country, our land has been viciously attacked by homegrown subversives who teamed with Islamic fundamentalists. We, the people, will not tolerate this attack on our Constitution and our democracy!" Anger welled in Waldron's eyes. The cameras clicked.

"To the FFB, we say the American people will hunt you down and bring you to justice. For you fundamentalist bastards . . ." The commander in chief grabbed the podium with both hands. He leaned forward and in an unambiguous voice continued: "There will be no place on earth where you can hide. We will find you—we will destroy you." He sighed as he relaxed his hands. "Our armed forces have been deployed to the attacked cities. Our capital is under martial law, and the citizens here are safe. By tomorrow, our military forces will regain control of our cities. The enemy will be destroyed. People of this great nation, don't take matters into your own hands. On your television screen, you'll see a three-digit telephone number. If you know where any of the insurgents are hiding, call this number to preserve our freedom . . . and yours. This is your country; don't allow these traitors to take our United States—the land of the free and the home of the brave—away from us. May God bless America. Good night."

Giacomo's cell phone warbled. "Hello, Jason. I will." There was a pause. "Mr. President, I'm happy you're safe."

"Me too, Giacomo."

"Can I ask you, sir, how did you know not to board Air Force One?"

"It was a protocol called hide-and-seek, to be used in the event we were attacked. I give tribute to those men who sacrificed their lives that day for Secretary Bennett and myself."

"Amen to that." Giacomo went to the bedroom without glancing at Sergio and Alessio and closed the door.

"General, you're on speaker. With me is your second in command, Colonel Vandercliff, and Tom Maro."

Pleasantries were exchanged. A shudder traveled through Giacomo's body.

"Giacomo . . . no good way to say this. It appears your sister financed the FFB."

"Not true," he said, but a sickening dread overcame him. His hand clenched into a fist. "Impossible. Where's this intel coming from?"

"Senator Boyle says she's got proof. A money trail that implicates Rio," Maro said.

"Did *you* see the proof?"

"No. My new chief of staff brought it to my attention, and I called Arthur."

"They're full of it—totally not true." Giacomo was adamant. "I'll fly back to the States tonight and straighten her ass out."

"Giacomo, calm down. The FBI and CIA intelligence shows no validity in the accusation. The problem is the news media. They're picking up the story, and Rio will become a scapegoat."

"Jason, this is bullshit. I'll handle this." Giacomo tried to lower his voice.

"Giacomo, stay in Rome. Remember, as far as the media is concerned, your sister is dead."

"Mr. President, I understand, but—"

"No buts, General. Like I said, another scenario is being played out. We need you to resolve it. This is all connected—the attack, you, the journal, and the prophecy."

"I understand, sir." Giacomo realized he'd lost this battle, so he changed the subject. "Arthur, how bad is it?"

"We're still waiting for the final numbers. The Joint Chiefs' plan is working."

"How safe is the capital?"

"We're well protected here. Three buildings were destroyed, but luckily not much loss of life. We captured the insurgents. They're being questioned. This will be over within seventy-two hours."

"Your words to God's ears."

"I hope God is listening. Giacomo, your father's words saved our government from being overthrown today. I'm grateful that you shared his journal. The accusations against your sister are painful for you to hear. Over the next couple of days when the news hits the airwaves—well, I don't think I have to tell you to be patient and try not to forget the bigger picture."

"I'll do my best, but I'll prove her innocence."

"I'm sure you will."

"Gentlemen," Maro said, "Congress is furious. They want answers. They don't want to take responsibility. I wouldn't be surprised if one or two members are behind the FFB. This uprising is as much their fault as it is ours."

"I agree, Tom. Political changes need to be made, per our Constitution, but not by violence. You have to win this election."

"The people need to decide, Andrew—not you and me."

"Yeah, you can have this job."

Giacomo interrupted them. "Can we trust anyone in the government? I'm confident the attack on the White House was orchestrated by an insider."

"You're correct. Four members of our staff and one from Secret Service. I suggested that BOET work with the agency to guard POTUS."

"Excellent idea, Jason. Did you vet the agents?"

"Yes. All checked out. I'd feel more comfortable if BOET was in charge."

"Understood. You'll have a battle on your hands separating the powers."

"Power—screw that. I need to protect our country." Waldron abruptly changed the subject. "General, the road appears to be a difficult one. You'll be on your own for a while." Without further elaboration, he said, "Be careful, son." The phone line died.

Giacomo walked out of the bedroom suite—he said nothing. Sergio, by the TV, watched the news reports from around the world. Images of his country being attacked besieged the screen. Alessio, on the other side of the room, stared out the window as he talked on his cell phone.

"Giacomo, what's going on?" Alessio placed his phone in his pocket.

Sergio turned and faced his business partner.

"Sergio, tomorrow we need to work on a new project."

"Anything I can help with?" Alessio asked.

"Prove my sister didn't finance the FFB."

Chapter 38

GIACOMO OFFERED NO further explanation. He shook his head in dismay as they left. *What do I need to do to prove my sister's innocence? More important, how am I going to do it?* In a matter of hours, the family name would be broadcasted across the news media—and not in a good way. He paced the hotel suite.

He gazed out the seventh-story window. The radiance of the Roman lights devoured the black night. The siren of a police car echoed in the distance. At one o'clock, he decided to go for a walk. He assured the AISI agent who was guarding him he would be fine. The air had a chill but not enough for a jacket. Surprised at the amount of traffic, Giacomo placed his hands behind his back and strolled in contemplation. His father knew the attacks would happen. *The country was prepared, yet we couldn't stop it. What's the purpose of knowing if you can't do anything about it?*

He found himself beneath the yellow glow of lights in St. Peter's Square. The basilica was cast in white beams. He scanned the heavens. A sliver of a moon dangled in the midnight velvet sky as the stars radiated their brilliance to the world below. He circled the obelisk to begin his trek back to the Marriott before his bodyguard sent out a search party.

"Mr. DeLaurentis?"

Giacomo had sensed he was being shadowed. He was surprised that the stalker made his presence known.

"Yes. Who are you?" Giacomo lowered his head, his feet firmly planted. He twisted at the waist. His arm outstretched, he grabbed the man by the throat.

"Wait, wait . . ." The stalker threw up his arms in surrender.

Giacomo, who towered over him, released his grip.

"Why are you following me?"

"I can help you."

He was hidden in the shadows of the streetlight, but Giacomo could see his pudgy nose and the dark circles under his eyes. He was Italian, dressed in dark clothes and a thin overcoat. The man brushed his hair out of his eyes.

"How?"

"We don't have much time, Giacomo." His English was hard to understand. The man's eyes swept the road.

"Who are you?"

"Doesn't matter. Just listen. I received a letter from your father."

They crossed the bridge. The sound of the Tiber broke the eerie silence.

"You're being misled. It's not the journal. It's not what it seems."

"What do you mean?"

"A new world beckons."

"Why? What did my father say?"

"Because, there are people other than your father who know the outcome of the prophecy."

"What outcome?"

"Meet me tomorrow at ten at the Piazza Navo—" Suddenly, a four-door Mercedes screeched to a halt, the scent of the burnt rubber permeating the air. The nameless man turned to run.

The rear passenger door opened. A hooded man jumped out of the vehicle, gun in hand. He aimed the pistol at the running man's back— *pop, pop!* He fell face-first. Giacomo reacted but not fast enough. The assailant leaped back into the car as it sped away.

Giacomo crouched next to the victim and rolled him over. He was still breathing. His eyes opened. He mumbled, "Grosseto . . ." and then let out a little gasp. He was dead. Giacomo checked his pockets for identification and his father's letter—nothing.

Chapter 39

AFTER ANSWERING QUESTIONS and making a phone call to Alessio, Giacomo was released. The *polizia* took him back to the Marriott, where two AISI agents stood guard on either side of his hotel room door. He telephoned Jason and left a message. He then called Emily.

"Sorry to wake you, Em."

"Are you all right?"

"Yes and no." He briefed his wife.

"You're lucky you weren't killed." Emily's voice was full of fear.

"True. But I wasn't the target."

"Still, Giacomo, they could've killed you."

He resigned himself to the argument.

"You don't know who the man was?"

"No."

"Grosseto. Could that be the village in Tuscany?"

"I think so. My father used to visit there. Em, this is so discouraging. The attacks . . ."

"I turned on the TV. The fighting appears to be out west, except for DC."

"Yeah, that's my understanding. I dread tomorrow. Rio's face will be all over the media."

"Giacomo, she didn't finance the FFB. Those allegations are ridiculous."

"How do I prove it?"

"You will. I'm coming to Rome tomorrow. We should be together."

"I don't know, Em. I'm concerned about your safety."

"Giacomo, please. I need to be with you."

He heard the whimper in her voice. "Em, you're safer n Ottati." Giacomo's heart broke as she sobbed. "Please stop crying. You're right. I'll let Alessio know to secure the route. I'll see you in the morning."

"I love you, Giacomo."

"Love you too, Em."

Giacomo tried to sleep but to no avail. His eyes focused on the ceiling. *What the hell's happening? Who was the stranger? What was he trying to tell me? A new world . . . Grosseto . . . prophecy . . . not the journal . . . I'm being misled. Not what it seems? Senator Boyle? Rio?* The questions swirled unanswered in his mind. He finally fell asleep at four in the morning—10:00 p.m. on the East Coast of the United States, where fighting raged into the night.

Chapter 40

TWENTY C-17 GLOBEMASTER III military transports circled their targeted areas. Dispatched from Altus, McChord, Travis, and Dover Air Force Bases, the 1,753 paratroopers waited for the green jump light.

First Sergeant Edward Gaines had recently returned to the United States as part of the emergency pullout from Afghanistan and Europe. The African American man took his position as protector of the American people seriously. Now, he stood in the doorway of the cockpit. At four minutes after midnight, he tapped the pilot on the shoulder.

"Any word yet, Zabs?" he asked the aircraft commander.

"We should be there in ten, Hulk."

His nickname, Hulk, was because of his massive, chiseled body. Gaines was respected within the cadre of the Black Operations Elite Team. He was a no-nonsense military man who believed in the fundamentals of the American Constitution and freedom for its people.

"Roger that, Zabs."

Gaines prepared to address his men.

"Attention! First sergeant on deck," the jumpmaster barked over the whine of the engines.

Ninety-eight men stood dressed in paratrooper paraphernalia; each held an M4 carbine. Facing each other, they formed an aisle for Gaines.

"At ease, gentlemen. A new chapter in the history of America is about to be written. Not since the Civil War have citizens been pitted against one another to threaten the solidarity of our government. Our task tonight is to defend our country against our own people who have united with the Islamic Fundamentalists. It is our duty as defenders of this great nation of ours to defeat those who wish to destroy the fabric of freedom."

Gaines marched toward the rear of the plane. He took his snap hook, attached it to the anchor line, and turned to face the soldiers. "Our orders are to infiltrate the headquarters of Tariq Kahn. We are to capture their communications center. This homegrown training facility is the nerve center of their operations. We will hold no prisoners. Godspeed."

The left and right doors opened in the cargo area. The green jump light was followed by a bell to signal the men. They attached their snap hooks to the cable and jumped into the blistering September night twenty miles south of San Antonio, Texas.

Chapter 41

Fifteen Hours after the Initial Attack

SEATED IN THE US Command Center in Washington, DC, were Thomas Maro, SECDEF, the chief of staff, the Joint Chiefs, and the directors of the CIA, FBI, and NSA. The vice president and Secretary of State Webb were noticeably absent. For the rest of the conflict, the president would be isolated from them to protect the secession requirements of the Constitution.

Waldron, dressed in black sweatpants and a zippered navy-blue fleece jacket, was flanked by Jason Vandercliff. BOET men guarded the entrances to the room and continually scanned the participants. Any unnatural move toward the commander in chief would be met with physical—if not deadly—force.

"The plan worked, Mr. President."

"Excellent. How many captured?"

"Last count: 176,323."

"How many enemy dead?"

"Enemy dead, sir: 63,217."

"Ours?"

"We lost 4,986."

"Injured?"

"So far, 1,751," the chief of staff replied. He placed the report on the conference table.

"Civilian causalities?"

"We believe the final number will exceed a hundred thousand."

Waldron turned ashen. He covered his face with his hands. A moment of rage overcame him as he banged the table with a fist. Startled, a BOET man withdrew his pistol. Jason held up his arm. The man stowed the 9-mm.

"Can we expect another attack?"

The FBI director opened a folder, his attention focused on Tom Maro. "Mr. President, should we discuss this in private?"

Waldron's voice was gruff and angry. "Mr. Maro might well be your next president. There is no party line in this room. We are fighting for our freedom, gentlemen. We must stand strong. And if you don't like it . . ." He glared at the seated men. "Then don't let the door hit you in the ass on your way out."

"My apologies, sir."

"I can leave, Andrew."

"No. Now, when I ask a question, I want a damn answer." He banged his fist once again. Snubbing the FBI director, he said, "Mr. Bennett, can you answer the question?"

"Yes, sir. The information gathered from the seized terrorist headquarters suggests we can expect another attack within the next twelve hours." The lanky man used a laser pointer, the red dot focused on a map of the United States. "Mr. President, these circles denote the training camps of the terrorist cells that we have not yet captured." SECDEF eyed the twenty-four-hour clock above Waldron's head. "With your approval, in eighteen minutes, air force bombers will attack these twenty-three sites."

"Are they still active?" Tom Maro interjected.

"Yes. The successful capture of Kahn's headquarters allowed us to intercept their communications. We were able to break their code and issue new orders for the second wave of attacks—delaying it by three days."

"Will it work?"

"We can't take the chance and wait. We need to attack now."

"How many insurgents?" Waldron asked.

"We estimate seventy-five to a hundred *thousand*."

"How could this be?" The president shook his head in disbelief. "Are you sure?"

"Yes, sir," replied Secretary Bennett.

"Can you show me the satellite surveillance?"

The NSA director grabbed a remote control. A fifty-four-inch screen illuminated. "If I may, Mr. Secretary?"

Bennett nodded.

"Mr. President, from these images, it appears there is nothing but farmland and open wilderness. When we add infrared imaging . . ."

"Oh my God!" Waldron's eyes grew wide in astonishment. "All twenty-three sites are like this one?"

"Yes, Mr. President."

"Is that what I think it is? An underground city?"

"Yes, sir."

President Waldron stood and slammed the table with his fist. Leaning forward, he growled at his Joint Chiefs of Staff. "I want them destroyed. I want those bastards dead." Without hesitation, the commander in chief said, "Execute the operation, Mr. Secretary."

"Yes, sir."

Waldron dropped to his seat. "May God have mercy on us."

Chapter 42

FIFTEEN MINUTES LATER, at forty thousand feet over the Texas Hill Country thirty miles north of San Antonio, two B-52 bombers opened their bay doors. Perched inside each aircraft were three twenty-foot-long, thirty-thousand-pound GBU-57A/B Massive Ordinance Penetrator bombs—known as MOP, designed to destroy underground bunkers. Dropped from a high altitude, the projectiles would penetrate two hundred feet of earth before unleashing their wrath of destruction.

"Weapons release in one minute, Captain."

"Roger. Navigator, inform command."

"Will do, sir."

"Command issued the continue code."

"Roger."

"Bombs away."

The tools of destruction laboriously emerged from the planes. As the laws of physics took over, their downward speed increased into a frenzied plummet to their targets.

*   *   *

The American-born terrorist reviewed the video reports from his room seventy feet underground. Shouts of joy from his troops echoed in the halls of the concrete city as they watched the newsfeed. He had dispatched a thousand of his men to attack the city of San Antonio. In every war, there would be a loss of life. He understood that. What he couldn't comprehend was the rapid response of the United States government. He would have his revenge but not today. In a last-minute communiqué from central command, he was told to stand down for seventy-two hours. The remaining five thousand men under his control were given a reprieve.

The murderer of 15,106 Americans opened a manila folder. Inside were his orders: capture the capital—Austin, Texas. He smiled at the notion of a complete mobilization of forces. They hadn't a clue of the onslaught that would occur. The American administration would fall to its knees. The government crumbling in ruins, a new one would grow from the rubble, and he would rise to the top.

Dressed in a green camouflage combat uniform, he entered the corridor and walked toward the mess hall. Cement dust from the ceiling hit his head. He ran his fingers through his hair and frowned at the powder on his hand. Men flowed into the hallway. He tried to understand the screams of his soldiers. *Are we being attacked? Impossible.* A fissure appeared in the solid cement ceiling. *What the hell?* The bunker shook as he fell to the floor. A four-foot piece of concrete landed on top of his legs. He screamed in agony as the left femoral shaft ripped its way through the thigh muscle and exited the skin above the knee.

A hole erupted in the wall followed by five feet of the GBU-57 bomb. He struggled through his pain to free himself. In punishing slow motion, he saw the explosion. First, he felt the flying metal pierce his body, followed by intense heat as the flames engulfed him. In an instant, his flesh was obliterated and his soul sent to hell in retribution for the innocents he'd slaughtered.

Chapter 43

GIACOMO AWOKE TO the sound of the door opening. Startled, he jumped out of bed.

"Hello, handsome."

"Em . . . what time is it?"

"That's the best you can say?"

"Sorry." He walked to his wife, the mother-to-be, and tried to kiss her, but she turned her cheek at his advance.

"No kisses until you brush your teeth."

"Turn on the TV, will ya?"

A few minutes later, Emily appeared in the bathroom doorway. Giacomo finished shaving and wiped his face with a white hand towel. "What's going on?"

"You need to see this."

He placed the cloth by the sink, grabbed his cell phone, and followed his wife. It was three o'clock in the afternoon—nine in the morning in the States. He had four voicemails.

The headlines sped across the bottom of the screen: *Thousands die as American bombers thrash the US countryside.* The video images showed massive explosions as aerial bombs destroyed the landscape. Husband and wife held hands as they sat on the couch.

"This is unbelievable, Giacomo. The size of those craters?"

Giacomo recognized them right away. "Bunker buster bombs."

"What are they?"

"They destroy underground facilities. That hole—two miles in diameter. This is surreal . . ."

"How could this happen?"

"I don't know, Em. I mean . . ." Giacomo was shocked by the carnage, the destruction. His mind filled with theories. He heard Emily's mumbled words, but his brain was unable to process them. Instead, he floated in and out of reality. He tried to recall what his father had said. *Who can I trust? How am I being deceived? Could Rio really be behind this?* Emily punched his arm; Giacomo turned with a stern gaze and said, "What? What? Damn it, Em."

"Giacomo, what is wrong with you?"

"What do you mean, what's wrong?" He pounded his fist on the wall. "What's wrong? What's wrong? I'll tell you what's wrong. The dead, the hurt, the pain. Em . . . what have we done?" Giacomo noticed her puzzled, distraught expression.

"Calm down, Giacomo." She rose from the couch and approached him. "I don't understand. What have we done?"

His hands covered his face as he drew them to his chin and then folded his arms across his chest.

"My father knew. Hell, so did I . . . but I didn't do enough."

"What could you do?" She reached over and turned the television off. "Your father's words always came true. You can't stop what's inevitable."

"So, we sit here and do nothing?"

"No. You'll figure out what to do. Your father said it wouldn't be easy—hard choices to make."

"Do you realize our government attacked its own people, Em?"

"I'm sure the president had no choice. Giacomo, the terrorists are trying to destroy the country. What options did he have?"

The cell phone rang.

"Pronto," Giacomo answered. "Hi, Andrew. Yeah, I'm fine. Little shaken up over what's going on in the States. What?" He beckoned his wife with a wave. "The news reports are saying Rio financed the FFB."

Emily switched the TV back on.

His cell phone chirped. "Andrew, got another call. We'll talk later."

The TV screen came alive with his sister's picture in the upper right corner. "Yes, Alessio . . . thanks for the heads-up." He hung up and stared at the TV for a moment, incensed.

"I can't watch this. Boyle, that bitch, may she rot in hell."

"Giacomo, calm down. You and I both know Rio was not involved."

He turned his back and walked to the windows. "Honey, come on. Let's take a walk. You need some fresh air."

Giacomo felt the touch of his wife's hand on his back and jerked away from her.

"Yeah, sure. Let's go. I can't take this anymore."

Husband and wife took the elevator to the hotel lobby. They entered the reception area, where they were met by Alessio and two of his men.

"Giacomo." Alessio gave Emily the customary European kiss on either cheek.

"Alessio, what are you doing here?"

"Thought you might need my help with . . . the problem outside."

"Damn. I forgot you even called." Giacomo answered Emily's questioning face. "News media."

"They're waiting for you in front of the hotel."

"Damn it. How did they find out I was here?"

"Your guess is as good as mine," Alessio responded.

"Emily, you up for this?"

"Up for what?"

"We're not gonna run away from this. Let's go meet the press."

Alessio's men stood on either side of Giacomo. Emily was behind her husband. Major news networks from around the world had positioned their cameras outside the hotel. The reporters shouted their questions as they moved closer. The polizia tried their best to keep them back.

"Mr. DeLaurentis, are you involved in the attempt to overthrow your government?"

"Did your sister finance the FFB?"

"As a general in the American military, why aren't you home defending your country?"

The questions continued to pound Giacomo. He listened without answering. How he wished he was anywhere but Rome. But where could he hide? "Keep a low profile," his father had always said. *Damn it, Rio. Why didn't you keep your mouth shut?* His anger surged. Emily touched his shoulder. He held up his hands. The questions stopped. The silence was interrupted only by the sound of the digital camera shutters.

"I love my country and am saddened at the horrific terrorist attacks on the United States. I unequivocally deny the allegations made against my sister."

"General, Senator Boyle said she has proof your sister, Rio, helped finance the FFB," an Italian reporter shouted.

"Where's the proof?"

"So, you deny it?"

"How easy it is to blame the dead."

"Sir, are you afraid to go back to your country?"

"Why should I be afraid? I did nothing wrong. The president and I spoke on the day of the attack. There are no issues."

"So, why do you remain in Italy?"

"This is where *our* president wants me to be. Thank you for your time."

A wedge of eight body-armored police officers made a pathway to the car. The doors shut. The vehicle inched forward through the crowd. Giacomo's face flexed in anger. He tried to control his irritation as his heart pounded. He pulled his cell phone from his pocket. "Hello, Andrew . . . yeah, yeah, I'm fine. I need your help. Do you have an empty apartment in Vatican City?"

Emily whispered, "What are you doing?"

Giacomo held up his hand for her to be quiet. "Thanks, Andrew. Em and I will see you soon."

Chapter 44

Two Days Later

THE WORLD WAS in shock. Condolences from around the globe poured in at the loss of American lives. In joint statements, the leaders of all the religious faiths united in condemning the deplorable actions of the terrorists and called for peace and unity. Countries that were once enemies extended helping hands.

After the capture of Kahn's headquarters, First Sergeant Edward Gaines and his men were dispatched to San Antonio and stationed at what was once the River Walk. Three days earlier a thriving tourist area, it was now a mass of rubble. Their mission was to protect the people while they sought out the enemy. Gaines traversed the darkened streets. Another half hour and the sun would begin to rise. An aerial drone circled overhead.

Daylight began to cast its shadows. Crumbled hotels with blown-out windows highlighted the horizon. Black soot lingered on nearby rocks. To his right, he saw a cordoned-off section and a memorial of flowers with candles, the melted wax spread across the pavement as if frozen in time. All lay tribute to the 15,106 Americans who died in the three-block area he patrolled.

Gaines spotted two men escaping the dark cover of a half-destroyed building. They carried a blue cooler with a white top. The BOET member used the infrared monocle over his left eye to scan the container. He came to a sudden stop.

"Freeze, gentlemen!" Gaines held his M-16 carbine at his shoulder, the red laser light focused on the forehead of one of the men.

An expletive erupted from the other man as he reached for a gun. With a quick motion to his right, the rifle popped—the insurgent left for dead. The sergeant refocused his sight on the chest of the other man, who urinated in his pants.

"I won't run, I promise—please don't shoot me."

"Gaines at section four-one-seven. One insurgent dead, one captured. Explosive response team needed."

His headset squawked. "On the way."

Fifteen minutes later, Gaines and his commander, Captain Haysmith, met outside the operations center. "That's the forty-fifth American traitor we've captured since yesterday, Hulk. Excellent job."

"Thank you, sir."

The ground rumbled. The side of an office building crumbled. Dust flew into the air.

"What the hell?"

"Relax, First Sergeant. One of ours—a GBU-57. We're still cleaning up north."

"We're not going through that again, are we?"

"No." Captain Haysmith pulled his phone out of his pocket. He clicked on the gallery app.

Gaines swiped through the photos. His eyes opened wide in astonishment. "Looks like an asteroid impact. No wonder the buildings shook. How many sites?"

"Twenty-three underground cities."

Gaines shook his head. "May I ask a question, sir?"

The captain nodded.

"What's happened to our country? Our own people are attacking us."

"I don't know, Sergeant. We were the land of the free. Now? *Shit*—I don't know what the hell we are. That bastard over there and his friends—they think they can run the government better."

"They should live in Afghanistan. A friend told me once that the reason the grass is greener on the other side is because it is fertilized with bullshit."

The captain made an unintelligible remark and then said, "Well, First Sergeant, headquarters verified that we have either captured or killed these bastards. The intelligence you gathered provided the names of the enemy. Those two are the last of the San Antonio Fighters for Freedom Brigade. You'll be transferred to a BOET base in Virginia. Washington reports we eradicated the Islamic fundamentalists. Our job is finished here."

*   *   *

Vatican City

"Are you still mad at me?"

"Giacomo, I'm not mad at you. It just drives me crazy when you make decisions without discussing them."

"We need a place where we'll be protected. What better place than here in Vatican City?"

"Well, you're right on that account. Remember, the pope will be our neighbor."

"Why are you laughing?"

"Come on, Giacomo. It's funny. And you'd better watch your language and forget about making love."

"Really?"

"I'm going to visit with your mother. Are you going to the office?"

"Yes, the computer wiring and satellite hookup was completed yesterday. I'm totally operational here."

"Operational? Sounds like the military. Remember where you are, Giacomo."

"Yes, dear. The pope *blah, blah, blah.*"

"Giacomo!"

"Sorry."

"You should visit your sister. You haven't seen her since we moved in here."

"I will. I promise."

Giacomo loved his wife's smile, but not only was the world going to hell, he also needed to make sure he could keep her safe while he focused on exonerating his sister. He was convinced that Senator Boyle was involved in the smear campaign against Rio. His gut told him the legislator was corrupt. *What did Dad say? "Trust your instincts."* He needed Waldron's permission to pursue Boyle. It would be a hard sell. The plan firmly formed in his mind, he would discuss it with the president today.

Chapter 45

GIACOMO OPENED THE conference room door. Sergio sat in the corner by the fresco of the Last Supper. The former Italian prime minister connected the satellite cables through the black VPN box provided by Alessio.

"How're we doing, Sergio?"

"All done."

Giacomo sat in one of the brown leather chairs. He reached for the secure satellite phone. He reviewed his notes as he dialed the access code for Waldron.

"Mr. President."

"Hello, Giacomo. I got your email. Tom and I were just discussing your plan."

"Good morning, Tom."

"Giacomo, I'm concerned about your course of action."

"I understand, Tom. Mr. President?"

"I appreciate where Tom is coming from. I don't care whose personal privacy we invade." Giacomo heard Waldron pound his fist. "I want these bastards out of here."

"Arthur, if you authorize this and it fails, your presidency is doomed."

"I don't care, Tom. My presidency was doomed from the start. We need proof, and we need it today. This betrayal of our Constitution has got to stop."

Giacomo moved the satellite phone from his ear as the president yelled. He visualized Waldron's red face and the protruding vein on his forehead as he continued his angry discourse.

"Boyle is involved. I guarantee you the senator is not the only one. She's a traitor to the American people. Am I correct, General?"

"Yes, sir. I believe she is. With your approval, I can investigate her without the eyes of the government looking over my shoulder. I'd do this on my own if we weren't at war."

"Strong statement, Giacomo."

"I don't care." Giacomo tried to stay calm. No use in two angry people screaming. "There are two issues: our government nearly collapsed, and my sister has been accused of financing the FFB. I cannot accept that. Neither should you. Boyle is behind the overthrow."

"Giacomo, I too am troubled that our congressional leaders could be a part of this. But the laws of this country protect our citizens from having their privacy invaded without due process."

"Due process? Was there any due process given to the thousands of American citizens who lost their lives this week? We must find these sons of bitches, and if Giacomo can catch these traitors with his drones, then let it happen. Let me be very clear—when we find them and discover the truth, I will cut them off at the knees."

"Giacomo, when are you going to start?"

"As soon as Arthur says yes."

"Permission granted, General. How much time do you need?"

"A couple of days."

The phone line went dead.

Giacomo adjusted the white louvered shade on the window, peeking through the slats to peruse the Vatican Gardens. He was anxious for the intel report from Jason. *Any moment now.*

"How was the conversation?"

"Loud and angry. The pressure is getting to him. Kinda surprised at Maro's privacy comments. He's probably right." Giacomo didn't elaborate. His cell phone chimed to alert him that the email from Jason had arrived.

"Sergio, is the drone in place?"

"Yes. Your BOET men are with it now."

The quadrotor reconnaissance vehicle was new to Giacomo's arsenal. The flying machine measured five feet square by two feet high. On its base, a translucent domed apparatus housed an array of surveillance gear. A transmitter issued discreet signals from the pilot station to a geosynchronous satellite back to the remote-controlled aircraft. What set this drone apart from the others was the equipment it carried, its software, and its ability to silently hover in one place for seventy-two hours.

Giacomo transferred Jason's email to the computer. The captured list of ninety-two telephone numbers appeared on the screen. He typed a command, tapped the enter key, and the figures were downloaded to the server. Next, Giacomo uploaded the individual photos of the congressional body, their staff, and assistants. He had only one shot. He hoped his plan would work.

Chapter 46

THE SPEAKERPHONE CRACKLED as the five men and five women waited for the conversation to begin. Three fiddled with their expensive pens. Another tapped his finger. Two of the women examined their manicures as if unconcerned about the thousands of Americans who had died over the past couple of days. Their arrogant attitudes outweighed any beliefs they were wrong in their actions. They said nothing to one another. A beep followed by another echoed through the room. Two more individuals joined the conference. One of the callers cleared their throat.

"Our idea of a new America has been destroyed. We knew this could happen, and another contingency will be discussed later. We must place the blame on DeLaurentis and Waldron." The caller signaled to the other man to end the call. Dean Essex promptly disconnected the transmission. A dial tone crackled over the speaker.

One of the women picked up her pocketbook as she stood and crossed her spindly arms. "Let's start the impeachment process."

"Esther, do you think that's a good idea?"

With contempt in her eyes, Senator Boyle admonished the woman. "How can you be so stupid as to speak my name?" She walked over to the congresswoman and slapped her face.

* * *

Vatican City

Giacomo smiled at the mention of Boyle's name. "I got you now, you bitch." He adjusted his seat at the piloting station. His drone had been aloft for thirty-three hours. He was exhausted as he stood and repeated, "I got you now, bitch." The facial recognition software had tracked Esther Boyle as she entered the Eisenhower Executive Office Building through a side entrance. The electronic array housed within the RPV—remote pilotless vehicle—streamed digital signals to and from her person. The encrypted frequency hacked her cell phone—or, in the case of the senator, the three that she carried. Through a series of software commands, the phones became eavesdropping devices.

The first twenty-four hours that Boyle had been under surveillance yielded no information. His conversations with Waldron were tense— he needed answers; they both did. Fighting had ceased except in a few outlying areas of Wyoming, but the country was in a panic. The commander in chief needed to capture and bring to justice everyone who had betrayed the land of the free.

"Arthur, we have her. I'm sending the information to Jason, who will hand-deliver it to you. Be prepared."

"Oh, I will. Word is I will be impeached."

"I heard the same. *Boyle* is pushing for it."

"I will publicly annihilate them."

"How?"

Giacomo's question was ignored.

"Any other accomplices?"

"We pinged the phone numbers and identified eight of them. The rest appear to be dead."

"Giacomo, can you manipulate those remaining phones?"

"Absolutely."

"Be ready." The president ended the call.

Giacomo sat back. "What the hell does that mean?" He put the computer in sleep mode. He left the building to go visit his sister and wished that he could tell her he had proof that she was not involved. *Will she recover? If she does, she will be one pissed-off lady when she hears about this.*

Chapter 47

September 31, Two Weeks after the Attack on the United States

THE SWISS GUARD exited the Vatican administrative building after delivering Giacomo a diplomatic pouch from the White House. Inside was a single sheet of paper with Arthur's handwritten words: *Congress meeting today. I hope you're ready—let's catch these bastards.* Giacomo expected the communiqué. It was the seventh in a week. Waldron refused to speak via phone; he had become paranoid that factions in the government were listening in on his conversations. The general tried to ease his concerns, but the president rejected his arguments.

Giacomo was prepared. The idea in theory was simple. He had instructed his software engineers to develop a program that bypassed the failsafe circuitry of cell phone batteries. The result was a thermal runaway that caused the lithium-ion battery to smoke, catch fire, and explode.

Giacomo turned on the TV and punched a series of commands on the keyboard. A black, blue, and green test pattern appeared on the screen. Two seconds passed, and then an image of the House of Representatives chamber flashed on the monitor. He looked up when his office door swung open. It was Sergio, carrying two cups of coffee that he placed on the conference table.

"Thanks, Sergio. Can you double-check the satellite relays? I ran the diagnostics on the drone—all systems good."

"Will do."

"I inputted the latitudinal and longitudinal coordinates in the flight management system as well. We need to be airborne in five."

Sergio acknowledged Giacomo. Four minutes later, the drone was aloft. The aircraft ascended to four hundred feet and hovered. The surveillance camera showed Washington, DC, in organized confusion. Helicopters patrolled the skies; the National Guard guarded the streets with M16 rifles across their chests; army tanks surrounded the White House and the Capitol. Giacomo reached for the remote control and increased the volume on the TV.

The House of Representatives and the Senate sat in emergency session. Reporters flooded the Capitol. Speaker of the House Arnold Belmont was handed a note as a congresswoman from Alabama finished her statement in support of the president. Applause and jeers erupted as she returned to her seat. Belmont grabbed the wooden gavel. With three quick bangs, the opponents fell silent.

"The chair recognizes the senator from Texas, Esther Boyle."

Protests erupted from both sides of the aisle. The Lone Star State politician approached the microphone to address her fellow politicians. She wasn't afraid of being obnoxious; she'd dictate and cajole until she got what she wanted.

"I apologize for my intrusion. I thank you, Mr. Speaker, for allowing me to express the Senate's opinion on this sad day." She paused, looking left, then right, to gather the attention of the audience. "My friends, what's happened to our country? Our government almost overthrown because of our inadequate, ineffective President Arthur Waldron. The loss of countless lives in my great state of Texas is sickening." She bowed her head for a moment and continued to play the crowd. "We have a commander in chief who under his own authority attacked our country, with catastrophic results. Without congressional approval, he recalled our troops from the European theater, leaving our allies to defend themselves. He provided no proof other than the writings of a dead man who's purported to have had the ability to know the future. Now, one of his trusted advisers is the brother of Rio DeLaurentis, who financed the FFB." She paused for dramatic effect as her dark brown eyes penetrated the tension-filled room.

"It is time we demand the resignation of the so-called commander in chief. Should he not resign, I call on my colleagues in the House of Representatives to impeach Arthur Waldron so he may stand trial before the Senate. The charge? Treason. Our nation is on the precipice of collapse. We do not have the time or the luxury to be complacent. I ask you, my compatriots in the House, to indict Arthur Waldron today."

The Speaker pounded the gavel over the applause and boos of the congressional body as he called for order. "Thank you, Senator." He glanced at his watch. "We will take a thirty-minute recess."

The partisan arguments would lay the foundation for the case of impeachment. The best-case scenario: a vote to oust Arthur later that day. In private meetings, Boyle incited party members. Her premise: immediate action would ward off their own losses in the election six weeks away. Would the party be able to put forth another viable candidate in the time remaining?

* * *

Giacomo muted the television. "The day is full of surprises."

"Why?"

He rose from the console. The drone hovered on autopilot. "From what I understand, the protocol for impeachment excludes the Senate during the congressional vote."

"I thought I would never see the day that the US government would collapse."

"Believe me, Sergio, the United States will not collapse. We won't allow traitors to steal our freedom." Giacomo pointed to the monitor. "Showtime."

The camera on the PRV zoomed in on Waldron's armed motorcade as it drove down Pennsylvania Avenue. Meanwhile, inside the Capitol, Senator Boyle emerged from the south chamber to face a storm of reporters' questions.

"Senator Boyle, what prompted you to address the House of Representatives?"

"It's my duty as an American citizen to bring the facts to the House members. Waldron has got to go . . ." Her aide tapped her on the shoulder. Esther ignored the poke. The aide whispered in her ear. Surprised, she exclaimed, "What the hell is he . . ." The politician composed herself and then spoke into the assorted microphones. "Well, ladies and gentlemen, our president is on his way to the Capitol. Maybe he'll resign." The arrogant senator turned her back, walking away from the media as they scrambled to greet Arthur Waldron.

Chapter 48

TWO HOURS LATER, the sergeant at arms made the announcement. "Ladies and gentlemen, the commander in chief, the president of these great United States . . . Arthur Waldron."

Cheers interspersed with hisses greeted the president. His head held high, he entered the room with authority. The vice president, who had arrived five minutes earlier, and the Speaker of the House leaned forward. Waldron shook their hands. The Joint Chiefs of Staff, Supreme Court justices, and all the members of the House were in attendance. In the visitors' section sat Thomas Maro and, in an unusual precedent, the ambassadors from Russia, China, England, France, Italy, Germany, Saudi Arabia, Egypt, and the UN. Noticeably absent were the diplomats from Israel and Iran.

Waldron was tired as he approached the podium. He perused the legislative body. A gavel sounded. The applause ceased, and the spectators settled into their seats.

"Once again, we face what many would say is an insurmountable event in the history of our nation. Some of our own people—American citizens—have joined forces with the enemy to destroy the fabric of democracy. And we—you and I—allowed this to occur by not listening to the people."

His statement was met with boos from the floor.

"The battle for our western states has ended. I'm proud to announce our military forces have captured the leaders of both the

FFB and the Islamic fundamentalist group. Our swift action saved our democracy."

Applause surged, accompanied by a partial standing ovation. As the sergeant at arms banged his gavel, the president reached inside his jacket pocket. He pulled out a sheet of paper. His demeanor changed.

"I have here," he waved the paper violently at the group, "a report from the FBI and Homeland Security written twenty years ago, warning us of this threat. Against the wishes of the people, our Intelligence Oversight Committee, chaired by Senator Boyle, withdrew the funding for further investigation."

He had their attention. All eyes focused on the commander in chief. He rolled the paper into a ball and threw it at Congress. "This is what happens when we don't listen to the people." He shook his head, repeating, "We knew this twenty years ago, and we did nothing."

He again reached into his pocket. "This one? You know what this says?" His face ballooned to a bright red. His hands shook as he unfolded the sheet. "This is a list of names of those senators and congressmen who have committed treason against our country. In a few moments, those traitors will be identified."

The congressional body murmured.

"It's been claimed by Senator Esther Boyle that the late Rio DeLaurentis financed the FFB." His eyes targeted Boyle. "I can tell you unequivocally that that claim is false."

The senior politician from Texas rose from her seat. "Mr. President, you are delusional."

Waldron said nothing as his eyes flashed to the ceiling. Five seconds later, several cell phones rang in different areas of the room, then ceased as suddenly as they began.

*　　*　　*

Vatican Conference Room, Moments Earlier

Giacomo typed in the string of computer commands that would beam instructions to the synchronous satellite positioned overhead, which in turn would bounce the signal to the drone that hovered over the

US Capitol. He knew he had just one chance to release the frequency to the cell phones of the traitors. The energy required would deplete the battery that kept the quadcopter aloft. In a controlled descent, the RPV would crash. One million dollars down the drain but a country saved.

Giacomo hit enter. The rings of the traitors' phones crackled through the speakers. A red warning sign illuminated the flight control panel.

"Only 15 percent power left. We're losing altitude," Sergio reported.

"Damn." Giacomo typed in another command.

*   *   *

Inside the Capitol

Waldron waited in anticipation as anxiety crept over his face. His fingers danced on the podium.

"You're nuts," said the ex-governor of Connecticut, now a senator from New York. The president frowned at the man. The failed policies of the politician had caused his affluent state to declare bankruptcy. Waldron despised him and in his first presidential campaign had lobbied for the governor to be impeached. One of Waldron's first acts in the Oval Office was to help restore Connecticut's failed economy.

The president's nervousness showed. He glanced left, then right, several times at the assembled crowd. Then, the first traitor leaped from his seat: a congressman from Texas. Other conspirators jumped from their chairs. In an unusual sight, dense white smoke encircled the eight turncoats as an acrid smell pervaded the room. The legislator from Idaho's pants erupted in flames. Boyle's head swiveled. Giacomo's plan had worked; the cell phones' batteries had overheated.

The commander in chief grinned. "I got you now, you bastards!" he yelled. Arms held wide, he pointed at the traitors. "My fellow legislators, these are the ones who have betrayed our democracy."

Confusion ensued. The representative from New York grabbed

his phone as it smoldered. Hissing sounds emitted from the device. Too hot to hold, it dropped to the marble floor with a clatter. He tried to flee and was met with a blow to the face by the senator from Maine. With a thunderous clap, the doors to the room opened, and an array of military police charged in. The armed men flooded the aisle as a group of BOET surrounded the president, vice president, and Speaker of the House.

Boyle tried to escape but tripped and fell on the floor. She struggled to stand, only to be stopped by a combat boot firmly pressed on her back. A soldier grabbed her arms and handcuffed her. Her last words before he forced her out the door were, "This is not the end. We will defeat you."

The remaining conspirators were apprehended under the protest of their innocence.

Later that afternoon, the Speaker of the House, with the consensus of Congress, withdrew the call for the impeachment of President Arthur Waldron.

Chapter 49

Three Days after the Failed Impeachment Hearings

PRESIDENT WALDRON STRAIGHTENED his tie. Exhausted, he sat on a blue velvet couch in his residence. His wife, Amy, massaged his shoulders.

"How are you doing?"

"Better. At least I slept last night." He placed his hand on hers.

"Terrible news coming out of India."

"Yeah, I saw the photos . . . horrific destruction." The president shook his head in dismay. "Our world is in a state of chaos waiting for the next catastrophe. Will we ever enjoy peace?"

"Your press conference is in a few minutes."

"I can't wait." Waldron's voice was heavy with sarcasm.

"It won't be that bad."

"I've heard that one before."

A Secret Service agent entered the room. "Sir, time to go."

Waldron rose, gave his wife a kiss, and left.

*   *   *

Waldron's face was drawn as he approached the podium that displayed the presidential seal. The White House pressroom overflowed, and with the air conditioner out of service, reporters fanned themselves with sheets of paper.

"Mr. President, we're happy you're still in office, sir. How are you?"

The commander in chief took a deep breath and answered the

ABC reporter. "I'm tired, just like everyone, Henry. These last couple of weeks have taken a toll on us all."

"Mr. President?"

"Yes, Marta."

"Senator Boyle and the other traitors—how soon will they be brought to trial?"

"Not soon enough." The anger on Waldron's face began to surge. "With that said, I will allow our justice system to take the necessary steps to ensure they're given a fair trial under the laws and provisions of our government. Yes, Louis?"

The *New York Times* correspondent loosened his necktie. "Mr. President, has the Fighters for Freedom Brigade been destroyed?"

"Yes. We captured the militant revolutionary leaders and destroyed their forty-two training camps." Arthur reached for a glass of water.

"What about the group MFP, sponsored by Tariq Kahn and ISIL?" The journalist scratched off the question on her pad.

"The government of Pakistan captured and executed Kahn. The MFP is no longer a threat. However, we should always be aware there could be other attacks." Waldron pointed to a man in the back of the room.

"Mr. President, can you confirm for us how many Americans died?"

Waldron took a deep breath. With a handkerchief, he wiped the sweat from his forehead. An aide offered him a statistics report; he waved him away.

"Seventy thousand Americans died. Another forty thousand injured." The numbers etched in his brain, never to disappear. He would be haunted until the day he died.

A simultaneous gasp from the press corps silenced the room.

"Mr. President?"

"Yes, Becky?"

"Mr. President, how many terrorists were involved?"

"At least half a million, of which two-thirds were from other parts of the world; the rest were American citizens. This number does not include the ninety thousand plus from the FFB."

"How did they enter the country?"

"Here's the irony." Waldron's tone was bitter. "These murderers entered our country through our Mexican, Canadian, and southern Florida borders. We allowed the intrusion of the enemy into our nation while we high and mighty politicians argued over the rights of illegal immigrants. Guess what, my friends?" POTUS grasped the front of the podium, leaned forward, and sneered. "The terrorists laughed and danced as they waited for their moment." He stopped suddenly, took a gulp of air. "Our investigation proved that these monsters have lived here for the last twenty years, if not longer. They had the time and the money; all they had to do was wait for the right moment—when Israel attacked Iran. Yes, Rachael?"

"Since the Mexican wall didn't work, are you able to share with the American people how we are protected from further intrusion?"

One of the corner fans squealed to a stop. A technician tried in earnest to repair it as Waldron undid his collar. Arthur removed his arms from the podium. "The northern and southern borders of the country are closed. They are monitored using high-tech satellites with remote-controlled armed drones. We can now prevent any unauthorized interdiction within minutes. I say this to anyone who contemplates crossing into the United States: There will be no questions asked. You enter our nation illegally, you will be apprehended."

"Mr. President? What about their rights?"

He squinted at the reporter with disdain. "What about the rights of our dead, our injured, our people? I refuse to allow our people to become the victims of these murderous acts."

Another reporter raised his hand.

"Yes, Cameron."

"Mr. President, India was struck by two of the largest cyclones ever recorded. The newswires are now reporting a magnitude 9.2 earthquake has destroyed Delhi. Do you have any information?"

Arthur Waldron exhaled a deep sigh as he stared out at the gallery. He noticed a change in the faces of the press corps—a look of despair, a lack of hope. He had seen the look before in the eyes of many Americans. A troubling contentious feeling between spirit and self. Were hope and faith gone from the American character? Sadness gripped the president's heart. His gaze moved to the ceiling as he composed himself. "The devastation is horrific. I spoke with Prime Minister Rasva. The loss of life is expected to top seventy million people."

Another gasp erupted from the crowd. A reporter from the *Times of India* exited the room and could be heard retching in the hallway. Waldron waved over his chief of staff. "Send the doctor to him."

"Mr. President?"

"Yes, Rene."

"The presidential election is five weeks away, and the United Nations has recommended financial sanctions against Israel. Should we leave it up to the voters to decide?"

"First, let me say I deplore the action of the Israelis and the attempted retaliation by Iran. Over two hundred thousand innocent Iranian lives perished in an instant. World War III beckons, so if the sanctions prevent the deaths of innocent people, then yes, I agree. I don't believe we should vote on this issue."

"In an interview, you were asked . . ." The reporter flipped through his notes. "Had you ever read the writings of Paolo DeLaurentis? You answered no and that you wished you had. Why is it you wish you had?"

"I wish I had read what he wrote earlier than a month ago. For if I had, we wouldn't be talking about the enormous loss of life today." Waldron studied the reporters. "Years ago, Paolo spoke before the UN and said our world had gone to hell and a time would come when events such as what we are witnessing now would happen. A reporter from *Time* magazine asked if he was a messenger from God. Today I wonder where God has gone. There is a hell—because we are living in it today."

"Are you saying there is no hope?"

Waldron pondered for a moment. "We must have hope; we are the people of America, the home of the brave, a hodgepodge of immigrants who built this great nation. We lost our way as a society, as a country, and as a people. I pray and hope Americans fall on their knees tonight and pray to our God for mercy."

A reporter chuckled and then apologized when he saw the fury in the president's eyes.

*　*　*

That night, the president exited his private residence to read a congressional brief at the Oval Office. Two Secret Service agents followed him. He walked along the west colonnade, the lights casting an eerie shadow across the Rose Garden. The White House had been unscathed in the attack, although Pennsylvania Avenue was pockmarked with blackened buildings. In time, the private sector would repair them.

One of the agents stepped forward as Waldron approached the entrance to the Oval Office. The other removed a syringe from his pocket and jabbed the president in the neck. Waldron collapsed into the arms of the waiting man.

A cocktail of drugs entered POTUS's bloodstream. When he awoke, he'd remember nothing of the assault. His rational thought process would be destroyed.

Chapter 50

GIACOMO AWOKE TO the first light of dawn. The rays of the Roman sun swept the room. Emily slept with her arm wrapped around his waist. After the president's news conference, the two had gone to bed. The attack on the United States was over; Waldron was still in office. The issues that remained continued to cause Giacomo consternation: Rio's coma, the people who wanted him dead, and the status of his father's writings.

Emily stirred; she rolled to the other side. The father-to-be smiled for a moment. The anticipation of being a dad excited his heart. He crept out of bed so as not to wake her. Unclasping the band, he removed his wristwatch as he entered the bathroom—six fifteen. The warm, soothing shower relaxed his body. He allowed the water to flow down his neck. He pictured what life would be like with his two sons. A brilliant white flash forced him to close his eyes. He froze, his senses suspended.

"Dad, Dad . . ." Giacomo heard the voices of two young boys—but they were nowhere to be seen. His mind's eye saw blue, red, yellow, and green. A scene developed—a dark gray cloud rolled overhead, and the day turned to night. Light rain began to fall—small drops of water made their imprint on a portico. The intensity of the rain amplified to a pelting downpour. Giacomo was unable to move as the water ran down his face, his hair flattened to his head. The wind howled through the trees. The crackle of thunder, then a flash of lightning—the sound almost unbearable. He stood steady as the winds churned around him.

"Giacomo—Giacomo, are you asleep?"

He felt his wife's hands and was confused more than startled by the touch. His eyes opened.

"I hope you don't mind me taking a shower with you?"

He turned and faced her. "Of course not."

"Were you sleeping?"

"I must've been because I was dreaming."

"When did you come in here?"

"Six fifteen."

"Really? It's seven thirty!"

"No . . ."

After they dressed, he checked his watch. *Puzzling. How could I fall asleep in the shower for over an hour?* Giacomo attributed the loss of time to the stress of the last several weeks. He sat on one of two blue upholstered chairs in the living room of the Vatican apartment.

"Giacomo, breakfast is ready." Emily placed two plates of scrambled eggs on the kitchen table.

"I'll be right there."

The television was on, the sound muted. News of an earthquake in China scrolled across the bottom of the screen. A reporter was interviewing the president of the European Union, Eten Trivette.

Chapter 51

Two Days Later

ETEN TRIVETTE SAT at his desk in a black leather chair and pressed a number on a nine-digit keypad. A monitor rose from the floor, followed by a file cabinet. The New York Stock Exchange had reopened today. Trading had ceased while the United States government stabilized. Trivette had anticipated this day; the businessman expected a substantial profit.

One hour before the opening bell, and Trivette would once again be a hero. He focused on the impending financial calamity in China. Today the Asian superpower would tumble. Three massive magnitude 9.8 earthquakes would destroy the giant's economic center; Hong Kong, decimated by a tsunami, would never recover.

Trivette opened one of the two file drawers. He reached for a red sealed envelope marked SHRED. Placing the envelope on the desk, he said, "I'll open you later." He then pulled out a journal and flipped to a tabbed page. As he read the words of the impending Chinese tragedy, he smiled and said, "Thank you, Paolo DeLaurentis . . . you *schmuck*." Trivette had the confirmation he needed that China's reign as an economic power would now falter.

A sound warbled from the speaker of his computer. The Chinese premier appeared on the screen. Eten laughed at the unassuming man who couldn't see him. Today, Eten Trivette and the European Union would become a tyrannical dominant world power without a country. He pondered the enormity of his realm. He had entire nations in the palm of his hands. No one would keep him from his destiny.

Chapter 52

GIACOMO FINISHED READING the *New York Times*. He shook his head in dismay.

"Sergio, can you believe the EU bailed out the Chinese?"

"They're going to control the world."

"Arnaud must be going out of his mind over the news."

"I'm sure he is. According to Alessio, he dislikes Trivette," Sergio said.

"Really? How would Alessio . . ." Giacomo eyed his partner. "Sorry, I forget who your son works for. *Control the world?* An interesting thought." He stared out the window. Two priests roamed the Vatican Garden. Three caretakers trimmed the hedges. "Could Trivette be responsible for this? The assassinations, the helicopter pilots? Or is he capitalizing on the current state of events?" Giacomo leaned against the wall and crossed his arms.

"Trivette is just taking advantage of the situation. The Frenchman would be stupid to be involved. He'd lose his power base and financial influence."

"Who'd be stupid? I hope you're not referring to me." Alessio stood in the doorway.

"No! Trivette," Giacomo said.

"The China bailout?"

"Yeah but more than that."

"What do you mean?"

"We're making no headway in the investigation into the attempt on Rio's life and the assassinations, plus being followed . . . the pieces don't fit. What am I missing?"

Sergio interrupted the conversation. "Giacomo, you haven't had the time. We've been consumed in defeating those who betrayed your country."

"You're right, Sergio." Giacomo's eyes glanced at the ceiling as he said, "We should investigate Trivette."

"Not a good idea, Giacomo."

"Why, Alessio?"

The AISI agent pulled out a piece of paper from his inside jacket pocket. He unfolded the handwritten document and placed it on the conference table.

"Familiar?"

"My father's note. Where did you find this?"

"In a villa, south of Erchie. The helicopter pilots lived there. Our investigation revealed that the men belonged to a fanatical sect that wanted to destroy the wealthy elite."

"So, what you're telling me is that it was a *random* attack on a one hundred-million-dollar jet?"

"I'm sorry, Giacomo."

"What was all that stuff we heard from the prisoners?" The tone of apprehension in Giacomo's voice grew noticeable. "Those two killers knew certain aspects—"

"Giacomo, the Italian investigation is over. The final report will show they were a terrorist cell with ties to those who wished to destroy the wealthy and powerful."

"Bull! And you know it. You saw the interrogation."

"The video was destroyed in the explosion. I never got the opportunity to review the damn thing."

"Sergio, tell him—"

"Alessio, that's crazy—"

"Papa, enough. The case is closed."

Giacomo, his eyes ablaze with fury, pushed Alessio against the wall. The eyes of the two men locked on each other. "What the hell is going on?"

"Nothing." Alessio grabbed Giacomo's arm, twisting it away from his body. "I'm doing what I'm told."

"What do you mean?"

"Giacomo, don't you understand? The Italian government doesn't want to get involved."

"Fine. I'll do it on my own."

"At your own peril, General."

"Alessio, my son. He's our friend."

"Papa, those are my orders. The defense minister informed me this morning."

Giacomo turned away. His father's words echoed in his mind: "Be careful of who you trust." *Alessio?*

"I'll make a couple of calls."

"Papa, no . . ."

Giacomo turned. "He's following orders. We have the ability. No government or person will stop me from finding the answers."

"Be careful, my friend."

"Yeah, I'll be careful, Alessio. Don't worry. Have a good day, my *friend.*"

The AISI director took the hint and left the office.

"I'm sorry, Giacomo."

"Don't be, Sergio."

"Maybe I shouldn't take my vacation. I'll stay here."

"Don't be foolish. Go enjoy the Italian countryside. I can handle this."

Giacomo moved to the window and rested his arms on the sill. His eyes followed Alessio as he rambled toward the exit of Vatican City, his mobile phone cupped to his ear. He stopped in his tracks and made an about-face, placing his handset in his pocket and striding back toward the administrative building. Giacomo watched Alessio shaking hands with someone, the second person hidden by a tree.

"Giacomo, I'm gonna leave. I'll make those inquiries, and maybe I can get some answers."

"Yeah . . . sure. If I need anything, I'll call you. See you in a couple of weeks. Enjoy your vacation."

Giacomo was more interested in Alessio and who he was speaking with. His friend was no longer in a conversation but an argument. Alessio's hands were flailing, his face contorted with rage.

Giacomo's cell phone rang. The caller ID showed the private number of Arthur Waldron.

"Mr. President."

Chapter 53

THE DOCTOR TURNED the door handle with deliberate caution. His patient rested, still in a coma. He approached Rio's bed. Stethoscope in hand, he listened to her heartbeat, then pulled the chair closer. He was surprised her mother was not here. Victoria seldom left her daughter's side.

"Hello, Rio. I know you can hear me. What a terrible fate for you to be a prisoner in your body. Soon you will awaken and remember nothing of our conversations. Or, I should say, nothing of *me* speaking to you. You must be curious as to why."

The doctor touched Rio's face; with his thumb and forefinger, he opened one of her eyelids. "A shame you can't see me." With a penlight, he tested her pupils. "Very good, my dear." He whistled as he exited the room.

*　*　*

The door to the Vatican administrative conference room squeaked as it opened. Giacomo's back was to the window. His phone call with the president had ended, and he stared at the door as Cardinal Angeloni entered.

"Giacomo."

"Hello, Andrew."

"You seem distracted."

"A little. Come on in. Sit. How are you today?"

"Fine. Anything I can do?"

"No. Do you think God is pissed off?"

"Interesting question. What do you mean?"

"Isn't it evident? The natural disasters, the attacks, the deaths . . ."

"Scripture says that all that you mentioned will happen. Doesn't mean God is admonishing us."

"How can He let this happen?"

"We're not puppets, Giacomo. We have the free will to choose. Mother Nature . . . life runs in cycles."

"*Humph*. Well, I guess our choices suck."

"We do at times make bad ones."

"Yep."

"You need a vacation?"

"The president suggested that as well."

"A couple of days in Ottati might do you good."

"But there are so many unresolved issues. And Rio is still in a coma."

"Your mother is here, and Rio is safe. The issues can't be resolved if your thoughts are muddled."

"You're right. It might do me well to clear my mind."

"Go to Ottati. The world with its problems will still be here."

Chapter 54

The Weekend of the Second Week of October

GIACOMO JOGGED THE curved dirt road from the Church of the Madonna de Cordanato toward his ancestors' village of Ottati. The smell of fresh mountain air filled his lungs. He wore a bright orange T-shirt with dark blue shorts. A pasture was to his left, and to his right an olive grove. The scenery changed as he traversed upward. A stone wall he could step over held back the wild oleander bushes. Cyprus trees were scattered throughout the meadow. Opposite was a rising cliff of granite.

The sky was bright blue, and the sun hung in the east. Rolling meadows with lush green trees calmed his nerves. His daily morning exercise did not ease his troubled mind. Giacomo struggled with the circuitous thoughts. He felt betrayed by Alessio. He assumed his friend would have fought for him more and not just accepted his government's position.

Giacomo questioned, *Is it plausible or a coincidence? Is it possible a group of fanatics are out to kill the wealthy? Maybe it's time to go back to the States, sell my business, retire, and move here. With everything going on in the world, what matters in life? I'm going to be a father. I need to protect my family.*

Giacomo grew warmer as he ran. He and Emily had planned a leisurely day. The mountain town with its orange roofs glistened above him. He gazed up at his house, and Emily waved to him from the portico. Beside her, another person stood. *I wonder who that is?* The individual's face was obscured by a holm oak tree.

Before he could question further, he was distracted by a flash of light as the road he ran on erupted into rubble. His military instincts took over. He reached for his gun—it wasn't there. He was under attack.

He heard the hum of an engine. A drone glided overhead. The pilotless aircraft maneuvered straight up, avoiding the ledge of rock. It made a loop and a diving turn toward him. He leaped over the stone wall. He zigzagged as he tried to avoid the gunfire. The drone pivoted on its left wing for another strafing run.

Giacomo took cover behind an olive tree. He had only seconds before the remote-controlled vehicle would take aim once again. The predator wouldn't be happy until its prey was destroyed.

The propeller wailed as lethal projectiles discharged from the machine. This time a bullet grazed his leg as he dove behind another tree. The hair on the back of his neck stiffened. No doubt now— someone wanted him dead. *But who? And why?* The thoughts of fatherhood escaped him as the act of survival took over. He could return to the church. *No—too far away.* Giacomo analyzed the situation. The adrenaline kicked in as he inspected the injured leg. *Just a scratch.* He ripped his orange shirt off and placed it on top of a bush. The trick worked; the drone's guns destroyed the piece of cloth.

A car horn and a siren began to blare. Tires screeched to a halt, and dust from the road flew into the air. Doors swung open as gunshots reverberated into the sky. A familiar voice shouted his name. The drone exploded above him. Giacomo covered his head with his arms to protect himself from the falling debris.

Chapter 55

THE ITALIAN POLICE assisted Giacomo into his house. Emily met him at the doorway.

"Thank God Alessio was here, Giacomo! You'd be dead if his men hadn't shot down that drone."

Alessio? Giacomo hobbled to the kitchen as Emily pulled a chair from underneath the table. A paramedic elevated his right leg. "Just a scratch," Giacomo said. He couldn't help but notice the concern on his wife's face. "Em, it's no big deal."

Emily said nothing as she left the room.

Alessio arrived a few minutes later. "Are you all right, my friend?"

"Friend? I'm surprised you're here. Not to be rude, but *why* are you here?"

"I have information for you."

The paramedics finished dressing the wound. Alessio gave the men a tilt of his head, and they left to position themselves outside the residence. Emily returned, carrying a tray of bottled water, a plate of lemons, and two glasses. She leaned against the black marble counter.

Giacomo locked eyes with Alessio. "I apologize. You were only following orders. Thank you for today."

"You're welcome. We identified the murdered man."

"Murdered man?"

"The guy who was following you in Rome."

"Oh yeah. So much going on I forgot. Who was he?"

"A Benedictine monk by the name of Brother Marco."

"A *monk*?"

"Yes. We don't have much information other than he was stationed in Grosseto. He was from the religious community of Monte Cassino."

"How the hell is he a part of this?"

Alessio shrugged.

"Monte Cassino? Sounds familiar. Grosseto . . . my father used to go there."

"A beautiful city. You should go—take a holiday."

"Yeah, sure. Does your government still think those fanatics are behind the attack?"

"Yes. I'm sorry."

Giacomo quelled his anger. "Come on, Alessio—with what happened today?"

The AISI man poured water into a glass, reached for a lemon, and squeezed. Four seeds plopped into the water.

"Giacomo, I have no choice." He cleared his throat. "In light of the recent events, I can offer you protection. You're going to be a father. Maybe the time has come for you to retire."

"Yeah, twins. How about that?"

"Just like you and Rio."

"Well, not really. We're not identical. Our boys will be a matched set."

"Boys? I hope they resemble your wife and not you." Alessio chuckled.

"Very funny. Did you hear from your father?"

"Last I knew, they were in Venice. Giacomo, you two should go back to the States."

Giacomo gazed over at Emily. The worry on her face could not be ignored.

"I'm on presidential orders—gotta stay. We'll go back to the Vatican. We're safe there."

"I'll arrange for a helicopter."

"Thanks."

Alessio grabbed his phone as he moved to the terrace. Giacomo took Emily's hand and whispered, "I don't trust him."

"Giacomo, he saved your life. He's your friend."

"Why does he want me to go back to the States? Why did he come here?"

"If he hadn't, our sons would be fatherless."

"I understand. Still, this doesn't seem right. Alessio knows more than—"

Alessio returned to the kitchen. "The helicopter is on its way."

*　*　*

Two hours later, Giacomo, Emily, Alessio, and members of the AISI watched as a chopper landed. Giacomo's attention was drawn to the sky where another chopper hovered nearby. A crew member exited to hold the door open for the passengers.

"You'll be safe, my friends."

Distracted, Giacomo asked, "You're not coming with us?"

"No. The defense minister needs me in Genoa."

"Kind of far for a helicopter, isn't it?"

Emily interrupted the conversation by embracing Alessio and giving him a kiss on each cheek. "Thank you for saving my husband's life."

Alessio lowered his head. "Take care of those twins."

Giacomo held out his hand. "Thanks, Alessio. We'll be in touch."

The couple climbed in and fastened their seat belts. The captain steered the aircraft toward Vatican City. Giacomo said nothing on the trip. He tried to pinpoint what bothered him, but he couldn't.

The pilot pitched up the nose of the helicopter to slow the descent, touching down with a thud. As the rotor blades came to a stop, the copilot exited the vehicle and held out his hand to help Emily off. Giacomo jumped. A member of the Swiss Guard carried their bags to a waiting car.

"Appreciate the ride."

"You're welcome, senor."

Giacomo hesitated and then approached the captain. "I forget—where's the other helicopter going?"

"Monte Cassino."

"Right."

Alessio had lied.

Chapter 56

THE MONASTERY OF Monte Cassino sat atop a rocky seventeen-hundred-foot mountain overlooking the Italian village of Cassino. Located eighty miles southeast of Rome, the religious community was the home of Benedict of Nursia, known as the patron saint of Europe and the author of the Benedictine Rule. He founded the abbey in 529, and his tomb in the cathedral was a destination for thousands of tourists every year. The friary had a unique history: razed to its foundation and rebuilt several times, it had originally been the site of a temple to Apollo, the god of prophecy, art, and healing.

Alessio sat in the rear seat of the black Mercedes. He pondered his summons to the isolated community, a consequence of his insolent behavior at the Vatican. The director gazed at the countryside as he tried to overcome the creeping nausea brought on by his automobile traveling the circuitous route up the mountain. The driver stopped the car by the side entrance to the priory. Agitated in so many ways, Alessio slammed the door as he exited the car.

His steps echoed in the stone staircase as he climbed to the third floor. Alessio typed a seven-digit code into the security lock. The latch clicked open. He pulled on the oak door and entered the hallway. On either side were a series of rooms or cells—the bedrooms of the resident monks. For the last ten years, only the leaders of the organization—Alessio among them—had occupied the secluded area. He traipsed to the end of the hall. Drawing in a deep breath, he knocked on the entrance of the corner room.

"Pronto."

Alessio entered the chamber. The walls were constructed of white stone blocks. A wooden shelf held an assortment of religious books. A single bed was positioned under a window in the far-right corner. Opposite, a bearded priest knelt in front of a picture of St. Benedict. The man turned. He pushed himself up off the floor, stood to face Alessio, and plucked his suspenders. He scratched his scraggly beard.

"Why am I here?"

"Communications have to be in person. We can't take the chance that our enemies are listening in on our cell phone conversations. And no one should see you arguing with me in Vatican City."

"I'm sorry." Alessio's eyes were cast down. "What you're doing is wrong. We have the information about who shot down the airplane, so I had to lie to Giacomo."

"He'll recover. We need you for another project."

"I've got my hands full with Giacomo and his sister."

"Rio will soon recover."

"She'd better. What you did to her was wrong. You're a doctor. You're supposed to save lives."

"She's not dead."

"The drone attack on Giacomo—was that us?"

"You saved his life, didn't you?"

"True, but it doesn't answer the question. What about Brother Marco—did we kill him?"

"He betrayed us. No one must stand in our way. We'll use all the resources necessary to carry out the mission of our society. Did you succeed in convincing DeLaurentis to go back to the States?"

"No."

The priest walked to the corner of the room. He pushed aside a tapestry of a dove with the words "Spiritu Sanctus" written underneath the symbolic bird. Behind the cloth was a safe embedded in the stone.

"This is where the original prophecy used to be kept until the year 1054—when the church split in two."

The priest whistled as he dialed the combination. The tumblers locked in place, and he pulled on the handle. Inside was a tattered brown sheet of parchment encased in a glass frame. He took the document and carried it to Alessio.

"This is a portion of the prophecy," he said.

"What happened to the rest of it?"

"Destroyed when the abbey was demolished in World War II."

"So, if this is the prophecy, what does DeLaurentis have?"

"The original. The traitorous monk Frascati absconded with it in 1054."

"How did Giacomo get it?"

"From what we understand, he doesn't know he has the damn thing. His father had the original."

Alessio admired the hand-scripted words. This was the first time he'd seen the prophecy. He read it aloud. "'From the ancient village will arise a family from an orphaned child. Saved by the light from the murderers who wished to destroy the favor of God. His kin who will foresee future events, whose voice will go unheeded in the New World. The light shall surround him and his heirs. The two from the family of Laurentis will pave the way for the Savior's return. The third trumpet shall . . .'" A section of the paper was torn, the words interrupted. Alessio read the last line. "'His heirs the Gemini will unite the two . . .'"

"You see the words 'third trumpet'?"

"Yes."

"Paolo wrote a letter where he mentions the third trumpet."

"Because of that, you believe Paolo had the original?"

"Yes. We are missing pieces of the prophecy, and he is leaving hints for his children to find it."

"Through a letter?"

"Yes."

"My father received one from Paolo."

"The one the helicopter pilots had?"

"Yes. How did you . . ."

"The eyes and ears of our society cross all borders. We believe Paolo's journals are a small portion of his writings."

"So, everything he wrote is true. He knew the future."

"Yes, he did."

"The letters?"

"They exist. Within them are clues to where the prophecy is hidden and much more. Your failure to convince Giacomo to return to his home thwarts our mission. The Gemini or the twins are the keys to the last attempt to help save humanity. Rio is no longer an issue. Her mind's been successfully altered."

"So, you want Giacomo dead?"

"On the contrary, we want him alive and in the States to lead us to his father's writings. Then we will dispatch him."

"Well, that's not going to happen if his president wants him to stay here."

"We're working on that."

Alessio reread the words. Questions raced through his uneasy mind. *It says, "the favor of God"—if this is true, why would they want to thwart Giacomo and Rio?*

"Why stop him?"

"Because knowing the future is wrong. Our existence must take its natural course."

"That doesn't make any sense. *You're* altering the natural course."

"No, we are not." His voice grew angry. "God gave us the gift as scientists and doctors to help humanity. Paolo DeLaurentis wasn't a gift from God. His children will not be the ones who bring the kindness of God upon humanity! It will be His church—our society." The priest calmed.

Alessio said, "Well, I hate to ruin your plan—Giacomo's wife is expecting twins."

The man sat in a chair. "Good for them."

"What if you're wrong and the prophecy pertains to their twins and not Giacomo and Rio?"

"An interesting theory but impossible. The signs are present now. The unification of the church, the natural disasters, nation against nation. The earth is experiencing the pangs of labor as the beast exits the darkness into the light of the world. Soon the Antichrist will take his position. We're too late. It has begun."

"You believe you can stop it?"

"No, no, my son. Once we have the writings and the original prophecy, we will bring upon the world the blessings of God."

"This is wrong. I don't believe the spirit is—"

"We are not to question the workings of the spirit . . . especially you."

Father Alphonso Adinolfi, physician and priest, took back the glass-encased parchment. He tilted his head toward the ceiling as he returned the prophecy to the safe. When he turned back to Alessio, his hand held a gun with a silencer attached. The priest aimed it at Alessio, pulled the trigger, and shot him between the eyes. "Spiritu Sanctus, my son."

The door opened as four monks appeared with a stretcher.

"Take him to the cryogenic chamber."

"Yes, Doctor."

A fifth man entered the room. His shoulders trembled as if holding back sobs. Adinolfi placed his arms around him. "I'm sorry, Sergio."

Chapter 57

GIACOMO AND EMILY had dinner with his mother and John. Afterward, they left Vatican City with their bodyguards close behind them. Giacomo reached for Emily's hand as the couple walked along the Tiber River. The late summer night cooled. Twilight merged with darkness, and the evening stars shimmered as a half moon rose over the Seven Hills of Rome.

"Does the leg still hurt?" Emily asked.

"No. Well . . . maybe a little."

Giacomo had a slight limp. A week had passed since the drone attack. He avoided the conversation with Emily about the assault on his life. He found himself in a quandary. He needed her close so he could watch over her and protect her and the babies. But was he putting them all in jeopardy by having them near? The question lingered within him.

"Giacomo, we need to talk." Emily spoke to him in French.

"Oui."

"I don't know how much more I can take. I should go stay with Dad in Paris until this blows over."

A lump grew in his throat. Emily's words melted his heart.

"Why? You told me we should be together."

"I know, but I can't watch my husband risk his life, and I am tired of the turmoil."

Giacomo didn't reply, his mind filled with rationalization. She was right. What could he say to ease her fear?

Em tugged on his hand.

Giacomo faced her. "We're husband and wife till death do us part." The words no sooner left his mouth than he realized the mistake. "I mean—"

Emily put her index finger to his lips. "Shush. That's the issue. I don't want to be a widow."

"Emily, you're being foolish. I'm not going anywhere . . ."

"Giacomo, stop talking."

"I guess I'm not known for my oratory prowess."

"You're the one who wanted me to go to Corsica, then to Ottati, so I would be safe. So, what the hell is the difference if I go to Paris?"

Giacomo kept silent for a moment. "I know, I know, and you're right. But we're protected here at the Vatican. The Swiss Guards are equivalent to our SEAL teams back home. Give it a chance, Em. Please."

"I'll think about it. Gelato?"

"Sure."

The conversation ended, but there was more to be said. His father's words came to his mind: *There will be hard choices to make.*

* * *

Washington, DC

Arthur Waldron met with Tom Maro in his private quarters at the White House. Together they reviewed the latest intelligence briefing.

POTUS grabbed a napkin. Wiping his forehead, he said, "I can't rid myself of these cold sweats."

"Did you speak with your doctors?"

"Screw them."

"Any word from General DeLaurentis?"

"I spoke with him last week. Nothing new."

"Why did the NSA increase surveillance on him?"

Waldron ignored the question. "I received another letter from Paolo." He handed a paper to Tom.

Mr. President, by now you have witnessed the devastating attacks on American soil. Your actions have foiled the attempt to overthrow the government. My son holds the key to the survival of our country. Be careful in your pursuit of the truth. Danger lurks on the avenues you wish to travel. Let me warn you: you will not survive.

Allow my son to run the course. Giacomo will not fail. Many roads lead to perdition and only a few to heaven. The path you took will condemn your presidency. It's not good to know the future.

Tom Maro finished reading the letter. He handed it back to the president.

"Your thoughts?"

"I'm puzzled, Arthur. This doesn't sound right. What path are you taking?"

His question was ignored. "He's right. I can't sleep at night. I'm haunted by regret and inaction."

"Arthur you're not making any sense."

"Listen, I appreciate the fact that Paolo's journal helped save thousands of lives. What I don't appreciate is a military figure wielding so much power. Who does he think he is?" Waldron slammed his fist into his leg. "I am the president of the free world, damn it!" He punched his thigh repeatedly.

"Arthur, relax. You're not seeing clearly."

"Don't tell me. Now leave. Get the hell out!"

A Secret Service agent entered the room. "I'll escort you, Mr. Maro. Your chief of staff is waiting for you."

What the hell is Dean doing here?

Chapter 58

THE VICE PRESIDENT sat in the West Wing office of the White House, a bead of sweat on his brow, as he read the document. When he'd arrived, he discovered a folded stapled piece of paper on his desk. He questioned the new secretary. She knew nothing about how it got there.

Jerry, time to pay the piper once again.
We're everywhere, and time is short.

"What the hell is this?" He reread the typewritten lines twice more, rolled the paper into a ball, and threw it into the wastebasket.

Richardson glanced at the clock on the wall. He was due in the Oval Office in forty-five minutes. He dreaded the meeting with Waldron, the incompetent fool. A warble emanated from his desk. Sliding out a drawer, he grabbed the receiver of the high-frequency satellite phone.

"Hello, Jerry."

"Who is this? How did you get this number?"

"Allahu Akbar, my friend."

"What the hell are you talking about? God is good? Enough of the fooling around." Richardson frowned in anger.

"Jerry, you remember me, don't you?" The caller's tone was sarcastic.

A wave of nausea overcame him—he held back the bile. He remembered the voice.

The caller was calm as he spoke in a high-pitched, almost feminine voice with a trailing slur. His tone filled with sarcasm as he said, "Jerry, Jerry, Jerry . . . such a long time since we talked. I see you've been busy."

"What do you want, you piece of shit?"

"Jer . . . Jer . . . you're so hostile."

"Mr. Vice President, to you."

"Ooh! You jackass. Keep your mouth shut and listen. We need your assistance."

"Not interested."

"You don't have a choice. Oh, nice try—shredding the journal."

"What? How do you—"

"Tsk-tsk, Jer. We can't be stopped. I'm your new contact. The she-devil is dead."

"Dead? You'll be next."

"*Hm* . . . doubt it. Did you like what I slipped under your office door?"

"How did—"

"Jer . . . Jer . . . Jer, why do you question? Anyway, I wanted to reintroduce myself. And by the way, you'll be needed soon."

"Go to hell."

"Mr. Vice President. I don't think I need to remind you what will happen if you don't—"

"Good luck. You've already killed my wife."

Richardson slammed the phone on his desk, pulled out the trash basket, and vomited.

Chapter 59

A Week before the Presidential Election

GIACOMO EXITED RIO'S room. Still in a coma, she showed no signs of recovery. His shoes scuffed the hallway floor on his way to a three-way video conference call with Tom Maro and the president. His last conversation with the commander in chief had not been a pleasant one. Waldron wanted answers regarding his father's letters, and he didn't appreciate Giacomo's responses.

"Giacomo."

The voice came from behind. He turned. Rio's doctor came to greet him.

"Dr. Adinolfi."

"Giacomo, I wanted to speak with you alone. If I may?"

"Sure. I have a few minutes."

The physician tucked his hands under his suspenders. His breath smelled of garlic.

"We've seen signs that Rio might be coming out of the coma."

"Wow. Great news."

"It is, and it isn't . . ."

"I don't understand."

"Her mind might not be the same."

"Not the same . . . how?"

"She might experience emotional and psychological issues. You should consider bringing her back to the States to recover."

Giacomo's cell phone alarm beeped. "First, she needs to awaken.

Then we'll deal with the issues. I'm going to be late for a meeting."
Giacomo held out his hand. "Thank you, Dr. Adinolfi, for all your
help."

"You're welcome."

The two men shook hands. Giacomo ambled to the Vatican
administrative building.

He entered the conference room. Surprised by Sergio's absence,
he powered up the computer and a few minutes later typed a string
of commands on the keyboard. The screen split in two: on one side,
the seal of the presidency; on the other, Tom Maro sitting at a desk.

"Morning, Tom. Not with the president today?"

"No. With a week left until the election, he determined it'd be best
if we kept our distance. Be warned, Giacomo. Arthur has been a little
irrat—"

A spirited voice erupted over the speakers. Waldron's face replaced
the insignia.

"Giacomo, Tom, how the hell are you guys? Ready for this election next week?" Waldron didn't pause for either man to respond.
He held a piece of paper to the camera. "Giacomo, can you read
this?"

"Yes, Arthur."

"*Mr. President* next time, General."

Odd, I thought he wanted me to call him Arthur. "I'm sorry, Mr.
President. Yes, I can."

"I received this from your father the other day. Where are these
letters coming from?"

"As I told you, I have no idea. Besides, that letter is not from my
father."

Waldron glared into the camera. He had deep, dark circles under
his eyes and looked like he hadn't shaved for days.

"What's this . . ." Arthur fumbled with the paper and then
read aloud: "'My son holds the key to the survival of our country.'
Remember, General, you work for me."

"I'm sorry, sir, but that was not written by my father."

"Damn it—you're wrong." Waldron was growing visibly angry.

Giacomo was blindsided by the tirade. Tom Maro cringed.

"He didn't sign it, sir. My father always dated and signed his letters."

"Bullshit. General, it says right here."

Giacomo could see him stare at the document. The president pounded his thigh with his fist. Giacomo was surprised at the confusion Arthur exhibited.

"It's here. Right here." He scanned the page.

"Arthur, calm down," Maro said.

"Tom, you saw it. Damn. Come on . . ." Arthur's voice pleaded.

Giacomo sensed a problem. The tone of the commander in chief's voice changed abruptly as he said, "Yes, yes, you're right. This can't be your father."

A visible change occurred in Arthur's face. Red blotches with white specks surfaced on his cheeks. His labored breathing caused Giacomo to stand, although there was nothing he could do from three thousand miles away.

"Mr. President, are you feeling all right?"

"Yeah, yeah, yeah." He sat back and loosened his tie, unbuttoned his shirt. "I'm having a hot flash. What am I turning into? A woman?"

"I don't think so, sir."

"Pretty soon I'll have breasts. Excuse me—I'm so bloated." Waldron laughed uncontrollably.

Giacomo was perplexed. Maro's eyebrows rose. After a couple of tortuous minutes, the laughter stopped.

"Gentlemen, soon I will vacate the presidency, and my dear friend Tom here will sit in this chair."

"A little presumptuous, Arthur," Tom said.

"It is not! I will lose the election, damn it." The president punched his leg. "Tom, I will lose. It is important, my friend, that you protect our democracy . . . our freedom."

Tom listened to the beleaguered Waldron's contradictions in astonishment and then replied, "Yes, Arthur, I will."

In a moment of clarity, Waldron said, "We still have unanswered questions. Who assassinated Tom's cousin, Ambassador Tarmac, and who made the attempt on your sister's life? The CIA assessment concluded the attacks were coordinated out of France and Italy."

"Italy? The government here is insisting a group of socialist fanatics are behind the attack. I think they're wrong."

"I agree with you, Giacomo. The CIA . . ." Tom Maro hesitated. "Arthur, can we discuss this?" His voice was tentative.

"Of course. He's a freaking general of the United States military."

Maro continued, "Do you know Brother Marco Lamberti?"

"Why?"

"You were with him when he died."

"Died? He was murdered. Am I under surveillance?"

The president chimed in, "Of course, you are. Giacomo, you're an asset to this country, and we protect our own."

Giacomo was furious. *This is bullshit.* He recognized this was not the time for venting his anger and pulled himself together. Tom's glance reaffirmed his instincts. He replied, "I understand."

"According to our report, the monk is associated with a religious group called the Followers of the Holy Spirit."

"I'll do some research."

"All right, gentlemen. I have a country to run. General, plan on a conference call next Wednesday to discuss the transition to your new commander in chief."

"We'll discuss this *next week*," said Maro.

Giacomo understood—there'd be no private communication between him and Maro.

* * *

Dean Essex placed the headset back in his desk drawer. The speakerphone buzzed.

"Dean, can you come in here for a minute?"

"I'll be right there, Mr. Maro."

Dean cleared his mind of the odd conversation as he locked the desk and went into his boss's office to see what he wanted.

Chapter 60

"WHAT THE HELL was that?" Giacomo pushed the brown leather chair back from the Vatican conference table. *Has the president lost his mind? What's happening? Why am I being shadowed?* He bombarded himself with questions he couldn't answer.

Followers of the Holy Spirit? Really? Giacomo turned to the computer. He typed the name of the organization into the browser. The search revealed no information other than the religious doctrine and definition of the Holy Spirit. *What did Alessio say after Marco was killed? Monte Cassino and Grosseto?* More questions filled his thoughts. *What am I doing this for? Can I change anything? Maybe life is already predetermined, so who cares? Time to retire and be with my wife, my children.*

Giacomo's thoughts clouded over, and his heart raced. His inner being was overcome with joy and peace. Two Earths appeared in his mind as a vision overtook him. *In one, the land was scorched, the oceans boiled, and volcanoes erupted in flames. Dark black ash spewed into the sky. The second Earth was in decay, but as the planet revolved, a rebirth occurred until the land turned lush green with oceans of turquoise blue.* A booming surreal voice overtook his mind, its origin unknown. *"Every choice, every decision molds a pathway of peace or destruction. Sacrifice of self will give life."*

"Giacomo? Giacomo?" He could feel a tap on his shoulder.

"Huh? What?"

Giacomo's eyes focused on the blurred face. He shrugged off the vision.

"Andrew . . . I guess I fell asleep."

"Couple of tough days?"

"Yeah, you got that right." Giacomo rubbed his forehead. "What's up?"

"I saw Emily. She's with your sister."

"Oh, that must've gone well."

"She's concerned."

"I know. What am I gonna do?"

"Retire. Enjoy your life. Go back to the States."

"I wish I could, but I'm being led in another direction." Giacomo touched his chest. "This desire is within me. I need to take it to fruition."

"Why?"

Giacomo shook his head. "No idea. At first, it was finding out who shot down Rio's airplane. The picture changed when I got pulled back into BOET. Now I'm involved in a complicated mess with no answers."

"Often the answers are in front of us—so close we can't see them. Perhaps you should step back."

"I wish I could, but how? The election is next week. Maro will probably win. To top it off, I agreed to help with the transition. Besides that, I'm still investigating the assassinations and the attempt on my sister's life."

"Have you considered praying?"

As he spoke, the door to the conference room burst open and a disheveled, clearly traumatized Sergio entered. Giacomo was shaken by Sergio's appearance. He hesitated and then asked, "What's wrong, my friend?"

"Alessio . . . he's dead."

Giacomo was dumbfounded. Andrew made the sign of the cross. Sergio appeared old and frail—face pale, eyes red. The loss of his son had devastated him.

"What happened?"

"Murdered in Genoa."

"*Genoa*? I thought . . ." Giacomo grew uneasy, a sick feeling in his stomach.

"Alessio was robbed—shot dead."

"I'm so sorry, Sergio." The cardinal placed his hand on the grieving man's shoulder.

"Did the police catch the attacker?" Giacomo folded his arms across his chest.

"No. It appears to be nothing more than a robbery."

Andrew spoke up. "What can I do for you?"

"Pray for me, Your Eminence."

Giacomo perceived a truth was being withheld. He didn't believe the robbery scenario; there was something more. He shrugged it off. At some point, Sergio would tell him. For now, his friend hurt, and it was more important to tend to his needs.

"Sergio, why are you here? You should be home with your family."

Sergio's head bowed as he whimpered, "What have I done? This ache in my heart . . ."

"Sergio, this is not your fault," Giacomo said. "Life sucks."

"My wife is devastated. The pain on her face . . . and Alessio's children . . . what have I done?"

Giacomo exchanged a glance with Andrew, who rose, reached for his cell phone, and dialed as he left the room.

"Sergio, I'll take you home. You shouldn't be here."

Andrew returned with a box of tissues and placed them on the conference table. Sergio took one and wiped his eyes.

"I left a message with the doctor. Maybe he can give you something to help you relax."

Anxiety crept into Sergio's voice. "No, no, no . . . I'll be fine. I need nothing." He shot an odd glance at Andrew and then collapsed in the chair.

Chapter 61

GIACOMO WAS IN the apartment, looking out the window. The Vatican City streetlamps emitted an orange glow and cast shadows on the sidewalks. A moonless night highlighted the stars in the evening sky. Emily came up behind him and wrapped her arms around his waist.

"How are you doing?"

"Tough couple of days." His voice sounded skeptical. "These last three days with Sergio's family were difficult."

"Do you think?"

"Yeah." Giacomo faced Emily. He touched her stomach. "I can't imagine losing one of our children."

"Oui, the heartache."

"Yep. Nice of Andrew to officiate at the funeral."

"Yes, it was. Do you think Sergio will come back to work?"

"I'm sure he will. I told him to take his time. Sergio was helping me with the investigation, but I think I need to go on my own. Things seem a little dicey at the White House."

"What do you mean?"

"I told you, Em—Waldron is off his rocker."

"No, you didn't."

"I'm sorry. The president's conversations have been erratic. He's convinced he's going to lose the election. He *wants* to lose."

"Even after he saved the country?"

"There's no doubt the American people want change. No matter what he did to protect our democracy, he's still blamed for the attack."

"You're probably right."

"*Probably*?"

"All right, Mr. Bigshot." Emily punched him in the chest and then leaned forward and kissed him on the cheek. "I love you, Giacomo."

"I love you too, Em."

*   *   *

Giacomo kissed his wife, turned off the lamp on the end table, and fell asleep. An hour later when he awoke, his spirit was troubled. His mind and body were conflicted with an unknown anxiety. A heaviness enveloped him. It was a struggle to move as he mustered the strength to plod his way to the small living room.

Is life taking its toll on me or is something more going on? Giacomo wondered as he sat in a maroon upholstered chair by the window. His hands covered his face. He rested his elbows on his bare thighs. He felt a buzzing sensation in his head. *Am I fainting?* A vision replaced the rambled confusion of his mind.

Two Earths. In one, the land was scorched, the oceans boiled, and volcanoes erupted in flames. Dark black ash spewed into the sky. The second Earth was in decay, but as the planet revolved, a rebirth occurred until the land turned lush green with oceans of turquoise blue. The surreal voice once again invaded his thoughts. "*Every choice, every decision molds a pathway of peace or destruction. Sacrifice of self will give life.*"

Another vision came into his mind. *Three men, their faces clouded by a haze: two in white robes, one with a frayed and discolored red hem, and the other with a black collar. Each held an Earth in the palm of his hand. The third in sackcloth.* Giacomo strained to see who they were.

The man in tattered robes began to squeeze the planet. As his grip strengthened, his fingers morphed into vices. The screams of humanity erupted. In slow motion, the malformed sphere dripped blood, the life force splattered on the floor. *The man in sackcloth appeared with a mop and cleaned the stained ground.*

Giacomo's inner gaze turned to the man with the black collar and the planet he held. The vision grew three-dimensional; he saw the stars, the planet's place in the universe. The lights of the nations sparkled, and then one country after another grew dark. The man in sackcloth took the sphere. It was heavy; he struggled to embrace it. He fell to his knees, careful not to let it drop, the cities illuminated with a flicker. The man in frayed robes glowered with fierce, seething rage. In his wrath, he squashed the orb into nonexistence. Then he moved to antagonize the man in sackcloth who was writhing with the heaviness of the new earth.

The collared man, his eyes full of fury, struck the aggressor. He grew, towering over the other two men. He reached down, picked up the assailant by his neck, and threw him into a dark chasm. The man's excruciating groans traveled throughout creation. The black-collared man closed the abyss and began to shrink. His robe became a dazzling white. He took the remaining Earth.

Once more, Giacomo heard his name spoken. The three men stood in front of him, but he couldn't discern who was who. He was filled with fear, then anger, and finally peace as a new image formed—a meadow, a distant tree overshadowing a field of bright green grass. Its leaves changed color to the orange and red hues of fall. A young boy sat nestled between two overgrown oak roots that stretched to the horizon. Knees to his chest, he gazed out over the meadow. Another young boy—his twin—approached. He whispered in his brother's ear, and together they climbed the tree and sat on one of the thick, sturdy branches. They waved to Giacomo, who returned the gesture and moved toward the boys. But he heard the wind howl, and the bottom of his coat fluttered behind him. The three men reappeared, standing behind the tree. He tried to run, but the force against him was unyielding. The two boys vanished. He was alone—empty and bereft.

Chapter 62

GIACOMO AWOKE IN an empty bed. He couldn't remember how he got there. The light of the morning seeped through the curtains. A remnant of his vision nagged his subconsciousness—three men he knew but couldn't recall . . .

"Good morning," Emily said.

"Morning. You're up early."

"Early? It's ten thirty."

"Wow, guess I was tired."

Giacomo sat on the edge of the bed and rubbed his face. Emily sat next to him, placing her hand on his thigh.

"Giacomo, you were talking in your sleep."

"What did I say?"

"No idea. Some mumbo jumbo."

"I had a weird dream."

"About what?"

Giacomo's cell phone rang. He picked it up from the night table and rolled his eyes.

"Morning, Mr. President."

Emily turned away as she mouthed the words "Be nice." Giacomo nodded as he walked to a chair in the corner of the living room.

"I'm sorry, Mr. President, what did you say?"

"Giacomo, I wanted to offer my condolences for Alessio."

"Thank you, Mr. President."

"I hope you don't mind me asking—were you able to find any information? I'd like to end my presidency with answers."

"Nothing yet, I'm sorry to say." Giacomo felt an overwhelming compassion for the man. "What's on your mind, Arthur?"

"Your father—who was he?"

"I don't understand the question, sir."

"Was he a messenger from God?"

"Dad had a gift. He always questioned the origin. For him, the gift was a burden. A messenger from God? No idea."

"His letters?"

Oh boy, here we go. "Sir?"

"His letters. If we find them, can they help us?"

"Providing there are more."

"Any way of finding out?"

"No."

"The second journal . . . any idea what he wrote?"

"No idea, sir. I can tell you whatever he jotted down is important."

"Important enough to kill the ambassador, Tom's cousin, and almost Rio?"

"Strong possibility, Arthur. There's more to the story than that."

"The prophecy?"

"Exactly."

"Well, General, tomorrow Tom will be elected, and I can finally sleep."

"Mr. President, the vote could swing your way."

"We don't need your father for this one. The American people will cast me out; I will lose by a landslide.

"I'm sorry, sir."

"Don't be, Giacomo. This is for the good of the people. Besides, I'm still commander in chief for a couple of months." Waldron chuckled.

"True, sir."

"I spoke with Tom this morning. We'd like to have a video conference call with you on Thursday. With the election over, he wants to amp up the investigation to find his cousin's murderer."

Chapter 63

The Day after the Election

THE AMERICAN PEOPLE rose from their beds to a new day filled with hope. The polls closed, the ballots were counted. As Waldron had predicted, Thomas Maro was chosen president of the United States. The populace had swarmed the polling stations. Eighty-three percent of the eligible voters made their choice. The power of the American people reached the depths of the nation's capital. In national races, all but three incumbents lost the election. President Arthur Waldron was on top of that list.

A newscaster spoke of how the failed policies of the Waldron administration coupled with the president's lack of congressional support had destroyed the nation. The propaganda machine was running at full force. A continuous montage of video clips flashed across the airwaves, cataloging the failures of the government. They never mentioned that Waldron had saved the country. The media labeled him a loser, a failure to the citizens. Giacomo was disgusted by the rhetoric and silenced the television. *What happened to America? Hate embodied the people. Rio is right—time to move to Italy.*

Giacomo left the Vatican administrative building to go visit his sister. He walked through the gardens and admired the hedges trimmed to perfection. Two Swiss Guards dressed in black suits followed him. He shook his head. *I need to tell Andrew that this security detail has gotta go.* Giacomo faced the two men.

"Gentlemen, I'm only going to visit my sister."

"We have orders."

Giacomo shrugged. *I should run—see if they can keep up with me.* He laughed aloud as a picture developed in his mind of the two chasing him. The door to the papal apartment building opened.

"Cardinal Angeloni," Giacomo said.

"*Cardinal Angeloni—really?*"

"Well, I don't want to be disrespectful in front of my bodyguards. Might give the wrong impression."

"Oh, I understand. You don't like it, do you?"

"No, I don't. Come on, Andrew. No one will attack me here."

The cardinal dismissed the men. "Are you happy now?"

"Yes."

"How's Sergio?"

"I don't know. I called him but had to leave a message."

"Very sad. Our world is changing and changing fast, Giacomo."

"More than we realize. We've become a society of judgment with no respect for one another."

"I agree with you on that one."

"It's our own fault; our culture allowed it. Where are you off to?"

"A meeting with the Russian Orthodoxy."

"Reunification?"

"Yeah."

"Sounds like fun. You up for dinner later?"

"Yeah, sounds good. Call me."

Giacomo headed down the hall and opened the door to a staircase. He climbed to his sister's fifth-story room, avoiding the elevator in favor of some exercise. As he trotted past the third-floor landing, he paused at a window that overlooked the gardens. Leaning on the sill, he observed Sergio and Andrew speaking to one another. Sergio's head bowed low as Andrew blessed him. The cardinal comforted his friend. Giacomo's eyes tracked the men as they walked to the Vatican City executive offices, stopped, and turned. Another person joined them. Giacomo squinted. *A priest . . .*

"Who's that?" he said aloud.

Giacomo resumed his ascent. The priest seemed familiar. *Was it the beard? Maybe it was Rio's doctor.* His spirit became troubled, but before he could sort his thoughts, he approached the door to Rio's room and heard his mother scream.

Chapter 64

GIACOMO RUSHED INTO the room. His mother and Emily were at Rio's bedside.

"Rio spoke!"

A nurse entered and began to examine Rio.

"What did she say, Mom?"

"Her eyes opened . . . she said 'Mom." Tears welled in Victoria's eyes. "And that was it."

"That's good news."

"Why didn't she stay awake?"

Giacomo shrugged as the nurse adjusted the IV drip. Rio trembled; her body shook and bounced. Her limbs thrashed as a seizure overtook her. A team of medical personnel hurried into the room. The nurse escorted the family to the hallway where Giacomo comforted his mother.

"What's going on, Giacomo?"

Giacomo glanced at Emily. Frightened for his sister, his heart pounded as anxiety swept his mind. It lasted only a moment. He swallowed.

"She'll be fine, Mom. Right, Em?" His eyebrows raised.

"Yes, she will."

A tall, lanky doctor with wavy brown hair exited Rio's room.

"How's my sister?"

"Resting."

The door opened as an aide pushed Rio's bed toward the elevator doors.

"Where are you taking her?" Victoria asked.

"For a CAT scan."

"Why?"

"To make sure she has no brain damage."

Victoria began to sob. Giacomo placed his arm around her.

"Is my sister still in a coma?"

"Yes. Is your sister a fighter?"

"Nothing stops her."

*   *   *

Rio lay unconscious on the gurney as the machine scanned her brain. Three men gathered around the monitor to analyze the images that emerged.

"No damage?"

"There appears to be some type of abnormality that is not consistent with the kind of injury she sustained." The physician scrutinized the picture. "*Hmm* . . . nothing mentioned in the medical record. I'll ask the family."

"That won't be necessary. I will talk to them. You can leave now, Doctor. We can manage from here."

The lanky man left the room. The other two men pulled the patient out from underneath the CAT scan device. Adinolfi extracted a syringe and an ampoule filled with a yellow liquid from his pocket. He inserted the needle into the vial and withdrew the fluid.

"What will that do?"

"Move things along."

Adinolfi plunged the syringe. The drug traveled through the intravenous tube into Rio's arm.

Her eyes opened. Adinolfi recognized the shock on her face as she struggled to move, but she said nothing—the paralytic drug kept her mute.

"Not time for you to wake up just yet," Adinolfi said.

Rio forced words past her dry lips. *"Screw . . . you . . . bastard."*

The doctor patted her forehead. "Yes, yes, my dear. You'll thank me later. Go to sleep."

With his fingers, he closed Rio's eyelids as she slipped back into the induced coma.

Chapter 65

GIACOMO AWOKE AS the door to Rio's room opened.

"Giacomo . . . Giacomo . . ."

He leaned forward and rubbed his face. "Hey, Sergio. What are you doing here?" He noted the time. "Almost nine." Giacomo had spent the night in a chair at his sister's bedside after receiving a call that her body temperature had risen to an abnormal high of 105 degrees. When he arrived, Rio had had a seizure. Not wanting to leave her alone or disturb his mother, he spent the night with his twin.

"How's she doing?"

"Better. She's trying to wake up. Rio's a fighter."

"That she is."

"How are *you*?" Giacomo stretched.

"I've been better. I've been going through Alessio's computer, and I found a file you should know about . . ."

"Yeah, what is it?"

"A video of the interrogation."

"He told us it was destroyed."

"Guess not. The video feed had a thirty-second delay."

"Really?"

"You need to see this." Sergio held up a thumb drive. "Just before to the explosion, the prisoner mentions a name."

"What question was he asked?"

"'Who has the journal?'"

* * *

Twenty minutes later, Sergio and Giacomo were in their office at the Vatican executive building. Sergio queued the video. He forwarded it to the point where the prisoner said, "The traitor in the United States—Richardson. That won't stop us . . . it will soon be in the hands of . . ."

Sergio paused the video as the explosion ripped through the room. Giacomo sat stunned.

"The vice president? Holy shit. I can't believe it." His voice turned to anger. "Why didn't Alessio share this with us?" Out of respect for Sergio, he controlled his irritation. Alessio was dead; no point taking it out on his father.

Sergio lowered his head.

"I'm sorry, my friend." Giacomo placed his hand on Sergio's shoulder. "I'm sure Alessio had a reason."

"According to the prisoner, the journal wasn't in his possession for long."

"Should I mention it to President Waldron?"

"You should."

"Problem is no evidence. But, Sergio, are you sure you're ready to come back to work?"

"Yes, I *need* to be working."

"Let's start with phone and email records. Maybe Richardson spoke to one of the prisoners. I have a conference call with Arthur in seven hours. Can we have the info by then?"

"I'll try. I'm going to our office."

"Be back here by four." Giacomo pushed a button on his cell phone.

Sergio got to the door. "Giacomo . . ."

"Yeah." He put his hand up and said into the cell phone, "Sorry to wake you, Jason—hold on one sec. Yeah, Sergio?"

"We'll talk later."

Giacomo nodded and continued his conversation. "Sorry, Jason. There's a problem."

His next call was to his father-in-law, Arnaud.

Chapter 66

GIACOMO SAT AT the conference table perusing Jason's email on his cell phone. It was 4:00 p.m. in Vatican City—11:00 a.m. in Washington, DC. His right hand twirled the hair behind his earlobe as he read. The vice president's emails and telephone were clean. The colonel had dispatched a new Secret Service BOET detail to the VP's residence to do clandestine work. *Why would Richardson want the journal? If he doesn't have it, who does? And why?*

"Giacomo, coffee?"

"Hey, Sergio! I didn't hear you come in. Sure."

Sergio looked unkempt and had a three-day-old beard. Deep, dark circles enhanced the grief in his eyes.

"Sergio . . ." The concern on Giacomo's face asked the question.

"I never imagined I would bury a child. My heart breaks. I'm at fault."

"Nonsense, Sergio. A lunatic shot Alessio."

"Yeah, you're right about that."

"Any luck in finding the killer?"

Sergio's gaze shifted out of focus, and his eyes watered as he stared into the distance.

"What can I do for you, my friend?"

The ex-Italian prime minister shook his head as he blinked. "I'm fine. I got the telephone numbers. We discovered eleven calls between the prisoners and the United States. Our analysts traced them to Washington."

"That's good news."

"Yes, but . . ."

"But what?"

"The numbers are masked."

"What the hell does that mean?"

"Another name for call forwarding. We have no way of tracing the calls. There were several coded satellite transmissions."

"Satellite—Jason can scan the broadcasts. We can triangulate and pinpoint the broadcast and receiving locations."

A warble emitted from the computer. Giacomo positioned himself before the camera and opened the video conference call. Arnaud's face appeared.

"Bonjour, Papa."

"Hello, Giacomo. How are my grandsons?"

"Fine. Kicking up a storm. How are things in Paris?"

"Hectic. I'm involved in a major investigation. I got the information for you."

"Great."

"Our people here examined the video. We isolated the sounds of the explosion. Through facial analysis, we determined the prisoner's mouth formed the letter S. The sound *Sha*—"

"*Sh*—? Probably realized he was going to die and was saying 'shit.' Thanks, Dad. I wish it could've provided a better clue."

"Don't lose hope. I'm still working on a few leads. Give Emily a hug and a kiss for me."

"Will do." The transmission ended.

Giacomo clicked on the videoconference number for the White House residence. On the monitor, Arthur Waldron sat next to Thomas Maro.

"I told you I'd lose." Waldron slapped Tom Maro's back. "Now the country is his problem. Shit—I can't wait to leave this city." The president's eyes recognized Sergio.

"Mr. Prime Minister, my condolences to you and your family. What the hell is happening to our world? Shit, life sucks."

Waldron was abrasive and loud. Sergio nodded. Appalled, Tom shook his head. Giacomo whispered, "Here we go."

"What did you say, General?"

"Nothing, sir."

Tom smiled.

"Congratulations on the election, Tom."

"Thank you, Giacomo. Sergio, I'm sorry for your loss."

"Thank you, Mr. Maro. Congratulations to you. I hope your presidency is successful."

"Successful presidency? Shit. He will need a lot of luck. This is a thankless job."

The president laughed. Tom rolled his eyes as he absorbed another blow to the back.

To say Arthur was overjoyed at losing the election was an understatement. He leaned forward into the camera, blotting out Tom. His face was white, his mouth open and ready to speak, when his head collapsed on the table with a thud.

"*Art?* I need help in here now!" Maro screamed.

Giacomo and Sergio watched in horror as the Secret Service ran into the room.

"I think he's had a heart attack. Quick—put him on the floor."

The two agents lifted the president off his chair. Maro rushed over and began CPR. The video feed cut off. The last image was of Tom Maro kneeling by his lifeless friend's side as he pumped Arthur Waldron's chest.

Chapter 67

ETEN TRIVETTE RUBBED his cold hands together. The heating system was still not up to par in the new headquarters of the European Union. Outside, the overcast sky muted the City of Lights. Heavy rain pelted the mirrored glass. Twenty floors below, floral umbrellas covered the heads of those who strolled the soaked streets. Was his plan coming to fruition? *The financial domination of the infidel.* He reminisced about the days when his belief in violence consumed his mind. "Destroy the nonbeliever"— that was what he had been taught at a young age. Death to the pagan. His soul darkened long ago, groomed to hate all who didn't believe in the truth. The words of his father echoed in his mind. *"The only truth is the truth of the Qur'an."* How wrong his father was; there were many "truths" fabricated by men. Their God materialized for the good of themselves. Violence begets violence, so Trivette had discovered another way: destroy the soul of the infidel and their belief in God by preying on their greed.

Trivette lauded himself in the successful move of the EU from Brussels to Paris. Granted, the writings of Paolo DeLaurentis helped pave the way. And with a little help from Trivette's sister, the transition moved quicker. Trivette had the last laugh as he manipulated her like he did the world's economy. He grinned, took a puff on his Gitane, and exhaled the caustic smoke as it swirled upward. *The American president is dead. Soon I will pull the strings, and the world's nations will dance as my puppets.*

Trivette stared at the drops of water that slid past the windowpane and reassured himself. *How stupid the violence that existed in the world. The terrorists and fanatics have it wrong. The way to defeat the infidels is to build on their greed and selfishness; slowly they will condemn their own souls.*

The world was different now, the economies of the nations in shambles. The planet seemed to exorcise its inhabitants as Mother Nature swarmed the land with violent upheavals. Chaos erupted. Societies were at risk of anarchy, and the people wanted a savior to minister to their gluttony.

What was the truth? Trivette was shackled by power, by the enjoyment of seeing despair and lack of hope in the eyes of humankind. *God? Well, who really knows of his existence and might. Today was today—tomorrow only a dream.* Eten Trivette knew that when death encapsulated his being, he wouldn't be sent to heaven and seventy-five virgins. No, he'd disintegrate into the earth; his flesh would become fodder to the creatures that would continue to survive beyond the existence of humanity.

His reflections were interrupted by the buzz of his intercom. He smashed the hot ember of his cigarette in the ashtray.

"Oui?"

* * *

Arnaud Chambery, head of security for the DGSE, examined the photograph. The haunting blue eyes, the cynical smile, the arrogant expression—the face the same as Sharif's, except for the nose. His driver stopped in front of the European Union headquarters. Arnaud stepped out of the rear seat of the black Peugeot sedan and left the photo in the vehicle. The two front doors of the car opened. His bodyguards jumped out to escort him to the twenty-story building. One opened an umbrella and held it over Arnaud's head. Tourists, unafraid of the pelting rain, swarmed the city. Thunderstorms with heavy precipitation had been forecasted for the rest of the day.

"François, Jacques, I'll meet with Trivette by myself. Wait for me here."

"Oui, Director, but . . ."

"No." He angled his head skyward at the building. "You'll stay here."

The two men nodded in compliance.

After passing through a security area at the entrance, Arnaud crossed the three-story glass foyer and presented his credentials to the receptionist. In an angry voice, he announced, "Trivette."

She made a phone call. "Oui." She put the phone back in its cradle. "Monsieur, President Trivette is waiting for you. Take the elevators to your left. He's on the twentieth floor."

"Merci."

Arnaud pressed the button that carried him to Trivette's suite. He glared at the cameras positioned in the corner and then composed himself to mask the anger that brewed within him. The doors opened into a secured reception area. Armed guards stood on either side.

"Good morning, Director." A plump secretary whose clothes adhered to her body rose from her desk. "Please come with me. Monsieur Trivette will see you now."

"Merci."

She swiped a badge across a key reader as the door slid open to the right. Tall windows offered a picturesque panoramic view of Paris. The top of the Eiffel Tower was obscured by rain clouds. Glimmering car lights on the Champs-Élysées circled around the Arc de Triumph. Arnaud entered the plush office. Trivette was standing at his desk—a liver-shaped sheet of glass with stainless steel legs. A hum echoed in the room as two file cabinets on either side of the desk sank into the hardwood floor. Two white leather couches were positioned opposite each other, spaced evenly on a multicolored Persian rug.

"Director, a pleasure to meet you." He smiled.

"Trivette, nice name." The intensity of Trivette's eyes penetrated Arnaud, who felt sick to his stomach.

"I am sorry. I do not understand."

"Yes you do, Sharif."

Trivette's demeanor changed; his voice grew arrogant, his eyes threatening. "So, we meet again, Monsieur Chambery. Your life changed as well. Arms dealer to director of security for the DGSE. What brings you here today?"

Arnaud scrutinized the egotistical bastard. With his pudgy forefinger, he pointed at the man whose soul was pure evil. "Watch your back, Monsieur President, because one day . . ."

"One day?" Trivette's lip curled.

"You'll pay, and I'll be there to spit on your grave."

"My, my . . . Director, is that any way to speak to your employer?"

"You're not my employer. I work for the French government."

"Now you do—but in the near future, you'll work for me." He chuckled. "As you can see, I have done well for myself. All that violence back then—how foolish."

"Yeah, foolish. You're up to no good, *Sharif*."

"Sharif? You must have me confused with another person."

Sarcasm surged through Arnaud. "Sure, I do."

"Is there anything I can do for you? I'm busy."

"You can't do anything for me. I wanted you to know . . . I know who you are."

"And I know who you are." Trivette's eyebrows rose as he said, "If there is nothing else?"

"Nothing else."

As Arnaud reached the door, Trivette smirked and asked, "By the way, Director, how is your Emily? It's been quite a few years."

Arnaud turned and strode back into the room. "What do you mean by that?"

"Well, when Payne and I arranged for your daughter to stay with us those couple of days in Paris . . ."

"*Payne* . . . you—you no-good son of a bitch."

Arnaud jumped across the desk and grabbed Trivette by the collar. With a quick, reflexive action, Trivette removed Arnaud's hand from his shirt. Two armed guards barged into the room. Trivette held up his hands.

"The director tripped. Everything is fine. Anything else, Monsieur Arnaud?"

Arnaud said nothing as he followed the men out of the office. Trivette's file cabinet rose from the floor and settled with a clunk. He withdrew the journal, whispering, "Messenger from God? My ass. *I* have the power."

Chapter 68

GIACOMO AND SERGIO leaned back in their chairs, still stunned. An hour passed by as they watched all the major news networks report on the death of President Waldron. Giacomo sensed the tide change; an uneasiness gnawed at his subconscious.

The phone beeped, and Giacomo activated the speaker mode. "Hello?"

"Giacomo—Tom Maro. I'm being transported to my house in Baltimore under heavy armed guard. Richardson's been sworn into office. Giacomo, listen. Be careful of Richardson. When we met, the conversation revolved around you. I said nothing. I think . . ."

The phone went dead.

"Giacomo, what does this mean?"

"Simple. I have a new boss. Richardson will call me back to Washington."

"Giacomo." Sergio pointed to the television.

The presidential podium centered on the screen. In the upper-right corner, a video played as Supreme Court Justice Harold Lin administered the oath of office. President Jerry Richardson turned to the cameras and addressed the nation and the world.

"My fellow Americans, it is with a deep sadness I must inform you that my friend President Arthur Waldron passed away earlier today. The FBI is investigating the circumstances behind this awful tragedy. I promise you that if there was foul play, the United States government will hold those accountable to the greatest extent of the law.

"I assure you that, as president, I will continue to follow the example of my friend and adhere to his policies. Although my sojourn in this office will be brief, I vow to lead us through this difficult period as our nation grieves over the death of our commander in chief and the many tragedies of the past weeks. May God bless America." As the news commentators began their analysis, Giacomo pressed the mute button.

"He didn't seem that upset."

"He wasn't, Sergio. Rumor is they disliked each other."

Giacomo's cell phone rang.

"General DeLaurentis?"

"Yes."

"Please hold the line for the president."

"General DeLaurentis, President Richardson here."

"Hello, Mr. President."

"General, may I ask where you are?"

"I'm in Europe, sir."

"Where?"

"Italy, sir."

"General, I need you back in Washington."

"Sir, I am—"

"I don't care if you're having open heart surgery. I want you in the White House no later than nine tomorrow morning. Do I need to remind you the commander of BOET reports directly to me? Do you understand, General?"

"Yes, sir."

"I want a complete briefing on your activities. Any problem with that?"

Giacomo responded, "No, sir." The president ended the phone call before Giacomo had a chance to comment: "Go to hell."

"Shit, shit—I have to go back to the States."

"Giacomo, you should stay here. It could be dangerous for you, my friend. The time is not right for you to go home."

Giacomo stood silently. His mind flooded with scenes that he cared not to remember. Yes, it was unsafe to go back. His patriotism overcame his anxiety of the potential danger that was before him. At least he knew Emily and the babies would be safe at the Vatican.

"Thanks, Sergio, but I can't. My responsibility is to my country. Richardson is not our only problem. There are others involved; we must find out who they are. This goes beyond the United States—this includes all of us. I have to go back."

"Are you sure, Giacomo?"

"Yes, Sergio—I am." Giacomo looked at his Tag Heuer. "Three hours. Then I head back to Washington." He scanned the timepiece once more. "Damn. If I'm going to risk my life, I want one of our drones to cover me."

"That won't be an issue."

"Include Tom Maro and his people. Let's not take any chances. Make sure they're equipped with the new listening capability."

"Yes, and if you want, we could arm the drone."

"Well, let's not go that far. I'll speak with Andrew about increasing Vatican security for my wife and sister."

"Let me handle that. I'll arrange for her protection."

"Thanks. I gotta go pack and tell Em."

Chapter 69

NEWLY SWORN-IN POTUS Jerry Richardson ended the call with Giacomo. He slammed the receiver down, and the speaker from his satellite phone crackled.

"Now was that so bad, Jer—was it?"

"Screw you, Essex." Richardson threw the device across the Oval Office.

As he sat behind an antique cherry wood desk, the interim president familiarized himself with his surroundings. It felt bittersweet to hold office for only two and a half months.

His cell rang, and Richardson listened to the caller. Agitated, he responded, "I guess you were right. Don't tell me what to do. I'm the president of the most powerful country in the worl—" The hair on the back of his neck stood, and all he could do was listen. Richardson held down the bile in his throat as the phone conversation ended.

His secretary entered the executive suite.

"Mr. President, I thought you would like to see this." She turned on the television.

He grunted. "We have any aspirin? I have a headache."

"Yes, Mr. President."

Richardson sat on one of the couches, seething as he watched President Tom Maro speak. "That should be me! Not him." He searched the room for a bottle of scotch. There was none.

The November day began with a dark, gloomy sky. A rainstorm gave way to a bright cold afternoon; a slight breeze whistled through the leafless trees. Thomas Maro, standing in front of his house, prepared to address the press. Dean Essen, his chief of staff, stood to his right. Cameras clicked as Maro stepped forward to the array of microphones.

Maro held up his hands. "Please, no questions." His eyes filled with tears. "President Arthur Waldron and I—although we were competitors in the political arena . . . we were great friends. He was not only a friend but also a man who loved the United States and all that our wonderful country stands for. Art and I forged a friendship during the campaign. We'd often talk and share dinner together when our schedules didn't conflict. Arthur told me he would lose the reelection—that the time had come for real change."

Maro surveyed the gathered journalists. "After the election, to smooth my transition into the presidency, we met daily for lunch; today was no different." His lower lip trembled as he continued. "As we talked, my friend Art Waldron was stricken with a heart attack. I knelt beside him and heard his last words: 'Save our country.' As we, as a nation, grieve over these next several days, let us not forget this man who treasured America."

"Did you speak with President Richardson?"

"Yes."

"What did he say?"

"I suggest you ask him." Maro stepped away from the microphones.

Chapter 70

THE GRAY AIR force C-141 Starlifter landed at Andrews Air Force base at seven fifteen in the morning. A nearby airman directed General Giacomo DeLaurentis to the VIP suite where he showered and dressed in his uniform. Prepared for his meeting with Jerry Richardson, he knew giving his resignation was a no-brainer.

"Giacomo."

He turned his head toward the voice. "Jason, thanks for meeting me here."

Colonel Jason Vandercliff, the number-two man in BOET, stood in an office doorway. The handsome, square-jawed officer turned. Giacomo followed him.

"We don't have much time. You were right. You're in danger."

"What's going on?"

"You're not going to make it to the White House."

"Doesn't surprise me. You have the chip?"

"Yes. We have a new protocol." Jason pulled out a syringe. "Inside is a Nano tracking device as well as a voice transmitter. It will be active for seventy-two hours. Our men will never be far behind. This is going to hurt a bit." He inserted the needle under Giacomo's skin near his shoulder.

"That wasn't too bad." Giacomo rubbed the area. "Jason, call Sergio, and he'll launch a drone."

"Will do. Giacomo, you don't have to do this. You're taking a risk. What about your family?"

"Jason, I appreciate the concern. But we need to catch these bastards. You've got my back—right, Colonel?"

"I do, General. Trust me—I've got your back. You'd better get going."

As Giacomo entered the hallway, he moved his head to the left and then right. Two military police waited at the security door of the building.

"General DeLaurentis, sir." They saluted.

Giacomo's eyes darted as he scanned the area behind the men. He returned their salute. The adrenaline pumped through his veins. Every sense activated on high alert. A picture of Emily flashed in his mind. Would he ever see his wife and children?

"Gentlemen, are you my escorts to the White House?"

"Yes, sir. Please, follow us."

They exited the private terminal to a black SUV parked at the curb. One man entered the driver's side while the other held open the back door for the commander of BOET.

"How long until we arrive?"

"Thirty minutes, General."

"Thank you." Giacomo rubbed his shoulder.

The driver turned on Route 4 and merged with Pennsylvania Avenue. The SUV crept by Muhammad Mosque #4, then came to a stop. *Maybe I should escape now. I don't need this shit. I wonder how fast I can leave the country. No, I can't do that . . .*

Giacomo's attention was drawn to the windshield. A helicopter swept low over the oncoming traffic. Suddenly, three masked men jumped out of a nearby car. Armed with assault rifles, they surrounded the vehicle. The two MPs pulled their 9-mm semiautomatic handguns from their holsters—too late. The kidnappers opened the forward doors, their rifles raised as they fired an onslaught of bullets. The back door opened.

"Out now, General!" An M-16 carbine was shoved into Giacomo's face. "Now, General!" The six-foot-four, wide-shouldered assailant yelled over the sounds of the helicopter rotors. He threw a zippered vest to Giacomo. "Put this on."

"Are you people crazy? You'll never get away with this."

The man grabbed Giacomo. He then hooked a steel cable from the low-hovering helicopter to the garment. Giacomo became airborne. He spun on his ascent. The 360-degree view showed the pandemonium below. While being pulled on board, he grabbed the jacket of a kidnapper. With a swift jerk, the man sailed through the air to his death. Giacomo couldn't escape what came next—a crushing blow to his face from the butt of an AK-47 rifle. With its cargo loaded, the aircraft tilted forward, departing to the southwest. A moment later, an explosion came from below. The assailants and twenty innocent bystanders were blown to oblivion.

Giacomo awoke as the helicopter touched down on a grassy field. His hands had been tied behind his back. He could feel his legs; they were unrestrained. He squinted and saw three men—two pilots and one other with his back toward him. Giacomo rolled out of the chopper. He fell three feet and tumbled on his side. Still groggy, with a massive headache, he crouched and ran. He moved toward the tail rotor, but another masked kidnapper met him.

"Where do you think you're going, DeLaurentis?" the massive, German-accented man asked. Two men joined the terrorist.

Giacomo faced them. His training in the martial arts and hand-to-hand combat gave him the confidence of a samurai. *I can do this.* With his left leg, he propelled himself upward. His right leg struck the face of the German. A tenth of a second later, his left leg landed on the opposite side. With a twist of the waist, his legs gripped the kidnapper's neck like a vise. The two combatants fell to the ground, the sound of a crack followed by the last breath of life exuded by the extremist. Giacomo set his sights on the second one. The two other men froze in shock at the sight. He rolled to his left and crouched, ready to attack the bastard. The commander of BOET scanned the surroundings. *Shit, a fourth one. Where did he come from? I can't die . . . Emily . . .*

"That will be enough, General," the man screamed as a bullet entered the chamber of his 9-mm Beretta.

Giacomo knew this battle had ended.

"You two take him."

They approached Giacomo with caution. One grabbed his arm. The other punched Giacomo with the butt of the firearm to his midsection, followed by an uppercut to the chin. As he lost consciousness, he heard someone say, "I want to cut off his legs."

"When we have our information, you can cut off his testicles if you want."

"Testicles?"

The two men dragged Giacomo's body to a waiting vehicle. They left their dead comrade behind.

Chapter 71

JASON AND TEN members of the BOET waited in the operations center in Virginia. On an overhead monitor, a GPS satellite feed tracked their leader. Grounded because of a mechanical problem with their Sikorsky Black Hawk helicopter, the men waited as two mechanics struggled to repair the machine. Each soldier was outfitted with a bulletproof vest and a high-powered M16 carbine. Attached to their outerwear was an assortment of grenades and explosives. Two handheld rocket launchers were stowed in the corner.

"Colonel, the chopper is heading toward the West Virginia border. The general still seems to be unconscious."

"Very well. Gentlemen, this will be quick and easy. Kill the insurgents, gather intel, and rescue our boss. They have a fifteen-minute start."

"Sir, we lost the GPS signal."

"What do you mean—we lost the GPS signal?"

"Sir, he's gone off the grid."

"What does diagnostics say?"

"I'm checking now."

The soldier pounded the keyboard. "Nothing, sir."

"All right. What can you tell me?"

"The copter was descending."

"Show me potential landing sites." The colonel issued more orders. "Contact NSA. Tell them to move one of our satellites. We'll try for a visual. Contact the FAA; they might have reports of low-flying aircraft. Damn it, this is not okay . . ."

The monitor displayed a map of northern Virginia and the West Virginia border. Two men sat at keyboards, typing.

"Sir, we've got a satellite picture. A heat signature detected in a field outside of Winchester, Virginia."

"Sir," another soldier yelled, "the general's GPS shows he's moving again. The patterns suggest he's trying to escape."

Colonel Vandercliff gawked at the satellite monitor. The infrared image displayed the helicopter. Five men could be seen, two in hand-to-hand combat. Four of the men moved methodically as they approached Giacomo.

"The helicopter's position is fixed, sir."

"Damn! They got him. Let's saddle up, men. No time to waste."

∗   ∗   ∗

Forty Minutes Later

Giacomo was strapped to a gurney. He was partially aware of the commotion around him. He tried to move his legs but to no avail. He hurt like hell. Through his clouded consciousness, he could hear explosions. He felt the heat of a blast sweep across his face. Garbled voices echoed in his brain.

"He's down! He's down! We need help in here now."

"Backup ETA five out."

Gunshots ricocheted off the floor, and bullets burst into the walls around the three BOET men. They crouched, waiting for help to arrive. A cinderblock wall exploded in the back of the room. Twenty armed BOET members carrying automatic weapons crashed through the hole. Their red laser beams cut a pathway through the smoke and debris as they searched for the enemy. The rapid *pop-pop* of automatic weapons broke the unnerving silence.

"Four men to your left, behind the wall."

Another explosion! The wall and the men were thrown into the air—dismembered body parts scattered on the floor.

"Secure the general."

"General secured."

"Let's move—insurgents ten minutes away. Let's get the hell out of here, gentlemen."

General Giacomo DeLaurentis was still strapped to the gurney as four men carried him to the waiting BOET troop carrier.

Chapter 72

Three Days after the Kidnapping

RICHARDSON YELLED INTO the satellite phone. "No idea where DeLaurentis is. Your stupid-ass people kidnapped an army general in daylight—using a freakin' helicopter. I told you not to do that. You've caused more problems. With today's technology—did your people really think they wouldn't be seen?" His fat face ballooned with rage. "I am the president of the United States! I am no longer your pawn, you stupid son of a bitch." The commander in chief hung up the phone without waiting for a reply.

*   *   *

Baltimore

"Giacomo. Giacomo."

"He's not waking."

"General DeLaurentis, sir?" The nurse touched Giacomo's shoulder.

"Where the hell am I?" His eyes opened slowly as three people came into focus: Jason, Tom Maro, and a nurse.

"Ann, you can leave us now."

"Yes, sir."

"How long—"

"Almost two days." Jason finished his commanding officer's sentence.

"How many days since I was kidnapped?"

"Three."

"What day is today?"

"Wednesday."

"Am I all right?"

"Yes. The drugs they gave you are flushed out of your system."

"Oh." Giacomo sat up with the president-elect's help. Puzzled, he asked, "Tom, why are you here?"

Jason spoke for Maro. "We're at his house. This was the safest place to come. During your transit from Italy to Washington, one of our men attached to the presidential Secret Service detail overheard an irate Richardson discuss the abduction. He relayed it to me. I called Tom, and he suggested you come here. It was a good thing you asked me to meet you at Andrews."

"I'm happy you did." Giacomo rubbed his chin.

"Still sore?"

"A little. I'd like to take that rifle butt and shove it up that son of a bitch's ass."

"I'm sure you would, but they're all dead."

"Unbelievable. Jason, did we get any intel?"

"A laptop—encrypted."

"Damn. What's our next move?" Giacomo winced as he repositioned himself on the bed.

Tom answered, "I spoke with Sergio. You'll be transported back to Italy."

"Why?"

"You're persona non grata, buddy," Jason said.

"At least until my inauguration."

"Jason, Richardson's gotta know you're involved."

"As far as the president is concerned, I'm out of the country."

"How do you explain my rescue? Richardson must be suspicious."

"I'm sure he is. After the rescue, the BOET team was deployed to Afghanistan. Our troops believe you were kidnapped by foreign terrorists—not by our government."

"What do the news reports say?"

"Your face is all over the media. The FBI is going crazy trying to find you."

"What do you mea . . . oh—nobody knows I've been rescued?"

Both men nodded.

"Does Richardson know?"

"We think he does—but we're not sure. He's making a stink about how we can't even protect our own. He says Waldron allowed America to be infiltrated by terrorists."

"Not true."

"You got that right, Mr. Maro."

"Jason, does my wife . . ."

"We told Emily you're safe. We'll arrange a secure line so you can talk."

"Thanks. Tom—what happened with you and Richardson after Art died?"

"At first, Secret Service suspected me of killing Waldron. Richardson intervened. After he took the oath of office, he met me at the holding area in the White House. He was cordial at first, and then he snapped. He said if he'd been president, the country would not be in ruin. Then he stormed out, mumbling something about his wife. His aide approached me, apologized, and said we can expect no help from the acting administration during the transition in January."

"Wow, not available for the transition? What—are we in grammar school again? Did I leak any information?"

"No. We arrived before the interrogation started."

"Jason, did the search at Richardson's office yield any info?" Giacomo asked.

"Search?"

Giacomo reached for a glass of water and took a sip.

"Sorry, Tom. I meant to tell you during our last call before Arthur . . . Sergio found the video of the interrogation of the helicopter pilots. They implicated Richardson, who had the stolen journal."

"So, you took it upon yourself to execute an illegal search of his office?"

Giacomo showed no remorse for his actions. "I did." He found it odd that Tom did not question Richardson's involvement.

"We found a non-government-issued satellite phone."

Hesitant, Jason fixed his eyes on Giacomo.

"Colonel, please continue. But, gentlemen, when I'm in office, this has to stop. We need to uphold the Constitution."

Giacomo said nothing.

"Yes, sir. We put a tracer on all future calls. Due to the death of the president, we weren't able to gain access to the communications databases."

"Can we do it now?"

Jason gave a curious glance at Maro, seeking approval.

"I didn't hear anything." Tom smirked.

"I'll have the info for you by the time you return to Italy."

Jason filled Giacomo in on the details of the rescue.

"Thank you, Jason, for saving my life."

"You're welcome. But we had help."

"What do you mean?"

"We're confident one of your drones fired a missile, blowing a hole in the side of the building. That's how we rescued you."

"Really?" The president-elect shook his head, showing his displeasure.

"I'll ask Sergio. My wife?"

Tom and Jason glanced at each other.

"I already asked, didn't I?"

"Yes, you did. By tomorrow, you'll be 100 percent."

"How did you get me here?"

"Your father's suggestion."

"My father? You received one of his notes?"

"Yes. Five days ago."

"Care to tell me what he wrote?"

"He instructed me to contact Danny, and he would arrange for you to get here safely. To be honest, I wasn't going to go against your father's wishes."

Giacomo shook his head in disbelief. "Smart. Jason, when do I leave for Italy?"

"Tomorrow."

"Tom . . . thank you."

"No problem." The president-elect's cell phone rang. "Yes, Dean? Okay, thanks."

"Issues?" Jason asked.

"No, on the contrary, my chief of staff was able to make headway with Richardson's transition team."

"That's good news. Sounds like you have the right man in the position."

"Yeah, I'm lucky, Giacomo. I still miss my cousin, though." He patted the general's shoulder. "You need to rest, my friend."

Giacomo settled back into the bed. He closed his eyes and dreamt of when he and his father used to walk to the Yale Bowl on Chapel Street.

Chapter 73

PRESIDENT-ELECT MARO LED a weary Giacomo into the attached garage of his house. A black Nissan Maxima with dark-tinted windows waited. A BOET driver would take Giacomo to a remote airport in Maryland.

"Sergio made arrangements for you to enter Italy without clearing their customs. Think of it like being in a diplomatic pouch. There will be no record of you traveling out of the States. You'll be flown to Rome where he will meet you. Any idea how we should handle Richardson?"

"Not yet."

Maro withdrew his cell phone from his pants pocket and typed. "Giacomo, I just forwarded you the number for my chief of staff. If for some reason you can't contact me, you can give Dean a call. He'll get the message to me."

Giacomo's cell phone pinged. He looked at the number. "Got it."

"Can I ask you a question?"

"Sure."

"All those notes from your father . . . how . . ."

"How do they reach us?"

"Yes."

Giacomo shrugged. "Not a clue."

The two men shook hands. Giacomo climbed into the car. Tom pressed a code on a keypad, and the garage door opened.

* * *

The eight-hour flight on the Italian-registered Gulfstream V soothed Giacomo's nerves. He looked forward to being with his wife. Her due date was only two months away. The reunion would be difficult, as Emily was tired and had feared she'd be a widow. What drove Giacomo? What was the unseen force that continued to propel him forward, a strength that ignored danger? Why risk his life, his family?

Mystified, Giacomo stared out the oval window into the darkness over the Atlantic Ocean. *Why did they kidnap me? I didn't have the journal. What information do I have that my enemies want? Enemy? Who is my adversary?* A thought occurred to him as the whine and rhythm of the jet engines eased him to sleep. *There must have been a tracking device in Tony's airplane when it was shot down. How else would they have gotten to Rio?*

A hint of light in the distance slipped through the clouds as the sun rose over Europe. Giacomo's mind took him to Paris. Another vision, if that's what these were . . .

He was sitting on a park bench by the river Seine; the Eiffel Tower loomed above him. Tourists climbed aboard sightseeing boats as street vendors sold trinkets. A man sat beside him, but Giacomo realized he was invisible to the man. Another person sat next to the first. They talked. Giacomo recognized the second person . . . but what was his name? The first man opened his briefcase, took out a red envelope marked SHRED, and handed it to his companion. The second man ripped open the packet in anticipation, and paper floated to the ground. Eten Trivette's familiar face materialized. He held the stolen journal!

The seat belt sign chimed.

"Mr. DeLaurentis, we will be landing in fifteen minutes."

He awoke, bothered by what he'd seen. *Could it be? Do I have my father's gift? It feels more like a curse.* Giacomo adjusted his seat in the upright position, fastened his seat belt, and said aloud, "What do I do now?"

*   *   *

The view of the Seven Hills of Rome dazzled Giacomo. A smile came to his face as he descended the steps of the plane—Emily!

"What an excellent surprise, *mon ami*." The two hugged.

Emily's eyes filled with tears. She touched his face. "Does it hurt?"

"No, other than a bruise on the chin. I feel great. I'm glad you're here."

Sergio stood behind her. "Hello, Giacomo." He patted his arm. "I'm happy you're alive."

"Thanks." His eyes darted as he absorbed the surrounding environment.

"What's the matter?"

"Nothing, honey—just a little paranoid."

They entered a black Mercedes SUV with blackened windows. Attached to the fenders were the diplomatic flags of the Vatican.

"Sergio, did you receive Jason's email?"

"Yes."

"Any answers on the satellite telephone numbers?"

"I just got the email."

"Let's get our people on that. Also, I need a telephone log on my sister's phone."

Sergio nodded.

"What's going on, Giacomo? Why did they kidnap you?"

He placed his hand on his wife's knee. "I don't know, Em. Richardson's behind it."

"You mean *President* Richardson?"

"Our evidence suggests he's involved with the disappearance of Dad's journal."

"I guess we're not going back home anytime soon?"

"Not now. Everything will be all right." He tried to use his calmest voice to assure her.

"Yeah, sure."

Emily turned her head to gaze out the window. Giacomo glanced at Sergio and shrugged.

"Let me ask this question. In the last ten years, who has remained unscathed by the tragedies and economic ruin?"

"Us, of course, because we invested in gold."

"Like my father suggested—right?"

"Yes." Emily continued to stare at the Roman scenery as she replied to his questions.

"The first journal was true. All that Dad wrote occurred."

"Yes."

"We gave the journal to the president, who supposedly gave it to his successor. Which didn't happen."

"Where are you going with this, Giacomo?"

"Where is the journal?"

Giacomo recognized Emily's displeasure. "Em, relax. Sergio?"

"No idea?"

"No idea? Or have we known and just didn't recognize it? Who prospered the most during this time?"

The driver honked his horn as they entered the congested Rome traffic and traversed the narrow roads to the Vatican.

"Eten Trivette," Emily replied.

"Of course—Trivette and the EU," Sergio chimed in.

"Exactly. Trivette stole the original *and* the second journal."

"What makes you believe that?"

"Simple. I dreamt it." Giacomo smiled.

Chapter 74

THE MERCEDES SUV arrived at Vatican City. St. Peter's Square was filled with throngs of people. The Swiss Guards, outfitted in bright blue, red, and yellow uniforms, waved the car through St. Anne's entrance.

"Why are all the television trucks here? What's going on, Sergio?"

"One of the most important days in the history of Christianity."

"Don't tell me! Andrew did it?"

"Yes, he did. On Christmas Day, the churches will once again be one. The Holy Father and the patriarchs of the Orthodoxy will make the announcement today."

"I can't believe nobody told me."

A grin lit up Sergio's weary face. "There's been a lot going on."

The car came to a stop in front of the Vatican papal apartments.

*   *   *

Giacomo, Sergio, and Emily entered Rio's room. Victoria sat by her daughter's bedside, her head bent as she prayed the rosary.

"Hi, Mom."

"Giacomo, Emily." Victoria greeted them. She gave her son a hug and touched the bruise on his face.

"I'm fine, Mom."

"You don't seem fine. Does it hurt?"

"A little." Giacomo changed the subject. "How's Rio?"

Victoria ignored the question. "Excuse me. Sergio, how are *you*?" She gave him a long hug.

"I have good days and bad days, Victoria. And Rio?" Sergio's eyes welled with tears.

"I think better. Today she held my hand."

"Rio will wake up, Mom."

"What do you mean, *will* wake up?" a small voice asked. "I'm awake."

*   *   *

Giacomo, Emily, Victoria, and Sergio were overjoyed as a nurse ushered them to the hallway to wait while the Vatican doctor examined Rio.

"I told you, Mom. Dad said she'd wake up."

Victoria wiped her eyes. "Thank God."

"Giacomo, she'll have a lot of questions."

"That she will, Sergio. She's gonna want to jump out of bed and kick ass."

"You got that right, honey."

"Em, between you and Mom, we can keep her here."

"Giacomo, why don't you tell her the truth?"

"Rio will want to go back to the States—that can't happen. Look what they did to me."

Emily touched her husband's forearm. "Giacomo, I'm sure the doctor won't release her for at least a few weeks. She's been in a coma for such a long time. She's going to need rehabilitative care."

"Yeah, you're right."

Dr. Adinolfi emerged from Rio's room. Dressed in black pants with red suspenders over his white shirt, a stethoscope wrapped around his neck, the older man with the peppered gray beard addressed the gathered family.

"It is a miracle." The physician shook his head as he plucked one of the red straps.

Victoria asked, "How is she, Doctor?"

"As expected, she's weak. The muscles in her legs have atrophied, so she will need to learn how to walk again. There is no brain damage. She remembers being on the airplane. After that—how do you say?

Her mind is empty. Rio understands she is in Vatican City. She said she could hear voices while in the coma."

"Wow."

The doctor squinted as he spoke. "Yes. I'm certain it was frightening for her. She might need psychological help. I will arrange for a psychiatrist to speak with her in a couple of days. You can go in now. Keep nothing from her—it could only add to her confusion."

"I guess that answers that question. Thank you, Doctor."

"One added thought . . . you might want to take her back to the States. The familiar surroundings will help her recovery." Adinolfi's eyes connected with Giacomo. "I'm sure you and your wife would like to be home as well."

The words unsettled Giacomo, and he couldn't hide a grimace of displeasure. "Who the hell do—"

Emily interrupted, "Thank you, Doctor."

Giacomo caught the stern look from his wife. "I'm sorry, Adinolfi."

"Giacomo . . ."

"Thank you, *Doctor* Adinolfi." Giacomo stretched his arm out.

The doctor ignored his hand. Instead, he answered his cell phone as he paced the hall.

"There's something about that guy I don't like."

"Giacomo! He can hear you."

"Good."

They entered the room as a nurse held a glass of water with a straw to Rio's mouth. Giacomo could see her eyes brighten when the family entered. She was able to push the nurse's hand away as a tear trickled down her face.

The nurse left. They sat on either side of the bed. Victoria held her hand.

"So, little sister, did you enjoy your sleep? Are you ready to go back to work?" Giacomo chuckled.

Her voice was weak. "Kiss my butt."

"Yep, she's back, Mom—her spunky old self."

"Giacomo, please."

"Giacomo, what is wrong with you today?" Emily chastised her husband.

Giacomo held up his arms. "Sorry, sorry." He retreated to the window.

"Hi, Em. How are the twins?"

Emily touched her stomach. "They're fine . . . waiting for their aunt to speak to them again."

She smiled a weak smile.

"Hi, Sergio."

"Hello, *principessa*." Sergio turned away and grabbed a tissue to wipe his eyes.

As Rio's gaze moved from one to the other, she grew confused. "What's going on? The blackness, the silence within my head . . ." She began to cry.

"You're awake now, Rio." Victoria squeezed her hand.

"Rio, we can talk tomorrow. We're not going anywhere."

His sister's eyes alarmed Giacomo. Frightened, she beckoned him to come closer. He leaned forward.

"What is it, Rio?"

"Be careful who you trust. It's not what it seems."

Rio was agitated. Her eyes once again darted. Her arm shook. Giacomo touched her.

"Try to relax, Rio."

She began to sob.

"What's the matter?"

"Enough, Giacomo. Go, leave us alone. You can talk tomorrow. I want to be with my daughter."

"We'll stop by tomorrow, Mom. Rio, nothing is going to happen today." He kissed his twin on the forehead. Sergio and Emily did the same.

"Mom, can I have a glass of water? Do you know where my cell phone is?"

"What do you need your cell phone for?" Giacomo questioned.

"None of your freakin' business." Rio snarled at her brother.

"I was only joking. Jeez."

"Giacomo, enough with the questions. Go," Victoria said.

They headed for the exit as Sergio lagged behind. Husband and wife held hands as their footsteps echoed in the hallway.

"Giacomo, what did she say?"

"Did you see how angry she got when I asked her about the phone? Damn, she can be nasty."

"You'd be the same. Now tell me, what did she whisper to you?"

"'Be careful who you trust. It's not what it seems.'"

"'Be careful who you trust.' Your dad said that in the letter." Emily mused. "And 'It's not what it seems.' Isn't that what the monk said to you when he was shot in St. Peter's Square?"

"Yes." He looked around. "Where's Sergio?"

"Emily, Giacomo." A voice from behind caused them to stop.

"Cardinal Angeloni."

He trotted up to them as Sergio followed. "What great news—the Holy Father is thrilled."

"Yes, fantastic news, Andrew. Thank you again."

"Please—no big deal."

"Congratulations are in order."

"For . . ."

"The reunification."

"Oh that." He smiled. "Yes, I just came from the joint announcement. The unification will be good for the church and the people of our world. I'm having a dinner party tonight. Could the three of you come? Sergio, please bring your wife. We'll celebrate Rio's recovery as well."

"Thank you, Your Eminence."

"Sergio, his name is Andrew."

"Giacomo!" His wife slapped his arm.

"Fine. Your *Eminence*, at what hour would you like us to attend the sumptuous dinner?"

Emily rolled her eyes.

"Why, my good man, how does seven o'clock sound?"

"Excellent. My wife and I shall see you then."

"*Men . . .*"

Giacomo and Andrew laughed. Sergio's eyes distant, he forced a slight grin.

"I'm going to visit your sister."

"She will appreciate it, Andrew. See you later."

"Giacomo, I'll head to the office. Maybe I can track those satellite numbers."

"Sure. I'll wait for your call. Sergio, are you sure you're up to this?"

"I'm fine."

Sergio's head hung. His shoes dragged across the floor.

"Poor man."

"Yeah, he's having a tough time."

Chapter 75

THE FOURTEENTH-CENTURY VATICAN dining room with its eighteen-foot ceiling evoked another era. Gold-trimmed wood with ornate carvings of cherubs decorated the ceiling. At one end of the room hung a Raphael tapestry of St. Peter. Three Murano chandeliers were suspended over the twenty-seat maple dinner table. The final course of fruits, nuts, and cheeses was served. Giacomo sat to the right of Andrew with Emily by his side. Sergio and his wife were at the opposite end of the table next to the Italian diplomatic envoy to the Vatican.

"Andrew, the food is excellent," Emily said. She took her fork and stabbed Giacomo's remaining piece of cheese.

"My wife, she's always hungry. I have to protect my food, or I'll starve to death."

Everyone around the table laughed as Emily punched her husband in the shoulder. Giacomo sat back. Taking his napkin, he folded the linen in half and placed it on the tablecloth. "Andrew, nice digs."

"Thank you. My office is close by. I'll give you the ninety-nine-cent tour when we're finished."

"About time."

"Giacomo! I'm sorry, Andrew—I can't take him out in public."

"My mother told me the Holy Father visited Rio."

"Yes, he told me."

"We're very grateful."

Giacomo touched the cardinal's arm. "Yes, Andrew, thank you."

"My pleasure."

*　*　*

The dinner guests left. Emily was exhausted, so Sergio and his wife accompanied her back to the apartment. Giacomo and Andrew strolled the halls toward the cardinal's office.

"Giacomo, how've you been holding up?"

"What do you think? You've seen the news."

"Yes—what can you tell me?"

"Long story."

They arrived at a dark oak, arched doorway. "My office." Next to the entrance, a black-and-white stenciled sign read: *Papal Nuncio Cardinal Andrew Angeloni, Camerlengo.*

"Camerlengo? Since when?"

"Two months ago."

"Should I congratulate you?"

"No, it's no big deal."

Giacomo shook his head. "No big deal? If I remember correctly, if the pope dies, you become Vatican City's acting head of state. That's a big deal. In fact, you're the one who pronounces his death."

"Yeah, but it's just a title."

They entered a reception area. A brown leather couch sat against one wall. They circumnavigated a white birch desk. With the key in hand, Andrew opened his office door. An automatic sensor turned on the lights. "Take a seat, Giacomo." He directed him to one of the two chairs and sat opposite him. Strewn on a coffee table were papers and books on Christendom.

"Welcome to my sanctuary. Would you like a drink?"

"No thanks."

"So, tell me, my friend, what's going on?"

Giacomo told him about the abduction, and when he was finally finished, thirty minutes later, he said, "Andrew, can I ask a question?"

"Sure."

"After everything I told you—based on your knowledge of my

father's writings, do you think, as *Time* magazine stated, he was a messenger from God?"

"Hard question to answer, Giacomo. Your father was insightful; that is indisputable. A gift from God?" He leaned back in the chair. "You and I'll be dead before we find out."

Giacomo rose and walked behind the cardinal's desk as he picked up a picture. "You and your father—"

"Your Eminence? Your Eminence!" One of the Swiss Guards entered the office, his face distraught.

"Yes, Roberto. What is it?"

"Your Eminence, come—the Holy Father!"

"Roberto, what happened?"

"He collapsed."

"Is he dead?"

"You're the camerlengo. Only you can pronounce his death—but I think so."

Chapter 76

THE AMERICAN HOLIDAY of Thanksgiving arrived and was celebrated quietly in Rio's room. The family was so grateful she was alive and on her way to recovery. Sergio seemed withdrawn; Giacomo had met with him twice in the past three weeks and understood the grieving man's heart. Meanwhile, the trace on Richardson's satellite phone had yielded no results.

Rome and the world were in a tizzy. The news of the unexpected death of the beloved pope shocked everyone. The camerlengo, Cardinal Andrew Angeloni, was busy arranging the funeral and the conclave to choose a new Holy Father. Rumors circulated that African Cardinal Adadayo would be the man to sit in St. Peter's chair—the first African in papal history.

In the United States, President Jerry Richardson was pushing Congress to pass the bill moving the monetary standard from the American dollar to the euro before Christmas recess—a week away. With 75 percent of the House and thirty-three senators being replaced in January, the bill passed Congress. This piece of legislation would increase the wealth of several bipartisan senators who traded on the financial markets in secret. Thomas Maro, the president-elect, took to the airwaves denouncing the move as un-American.

* * *

The Day after Thanksgiving

"Tom, is the shit hitting the fan back home?"

"Sure is. Richardson won't even take my phone calls."

"Unbelievable. What's going on with the European Union?"

"A nightmare. My administration asked the court for an injunction until the swearing-in of the new Congress."

"Will it work?"

"I hope."

"What a crazy world."

"How is everything in Rome?"

"Nuts—the city's packed. News was that the election of the pope would wait until after Christmas. My understanding now is that the conclave will begin in three days, on the nineteenth."

"How's your sister?"

"Rio came out of her coma the day the Holy Father died."

"Interesting. What about her recovery?"

"With rehab, she'll walk again. Most days, her mind is sharp."

"Any brain damage?"

"No—she experiences confusion, though. The doctor says it will disappear in time."

"Excellent. I hope we can work together. I believe she can be an asset to my administration."

"Really?"

"We often spoke on the phone."

"You did?"

"Yes, her ideas for our country were remarkable. Did you know Dean Essex, my chief of staff, had a date with her back in New Haven?"

"No. That seems like such a long time ago. How did you find out?"

"This past Tuesday, we discussed cabinet nominees, and I mentioned I would have considered Rio for a post if she were still alive. Long story short, Dean said he'd dated her. He told me they had coffee on the morning she departed for Italy."

"Wow—small world."

"Right? Now, what information did you discover concerning Richardson?"

"Nothing yet. Sergio's been working with AISI and his contacts to track down information. Tom, any word from Jason?"

"Not since the day you left. Giacomo, when you have some evidence, call me on my secure phone."

"Will do, Mr. President."

"Not yet, Giacomo. I have another month to go. Please, make sure you tell your sister I said hello."

"I will, *Tom*."

Giacomo ended the secured satellite phone call. As he sat at his desk in his makeshift office, he shook his head in bewilderment. *Where is this world heading?* He stared at the three computer screens of images from two remote drones flying over the pontifical city.

As he waited, his gaze faltered, and his mind's eye took him to the base of the Eiffel Tower. *He was standing underneath the imposing structure; its four steel girders surrounded him like a giant spider waiting to ensnare him in its web. People milled around. Out of the corner of his eye, a man with a cane . . . Is that . . . ?*

"Giacomo! Giacomo!"

He snapped back to reality. "Hi, Andrew." Giacomo's stare was distant.

"Are you okay?"

"Yeah, daydreaming. Weird, I saw Arnaud at the Eiffel Tow . . ." The questioning look on Andrew's face caused him to change the subject. "What are you doing here?"

"I needed a break, a place to hide. You don't mind, do you?"

"Mind? No. Sit—please. From what I understand, you're the boss."

"Name only."

"You're too modest, Andrew. It's more than a title."

"You could be right."

"Mom told me the funeral was magnificent. I wish I could've attended. Thank you for arranging for her to go."

"No problem. I understand your remote drones are covering the Vatican."

"Yes—everyone will be safe. When do you go into hiding?"

"Hiding?"

"Yeah, the conclave thing."

Andrew laughed. "You have such a way with words. Three days—it will be a short conclave. My brother cardinals and I agree that Adadayo will be the next pope. He'll do an excellent job."

"I thought . . ."

"You thought it had to be done in secret?"

"Yes."

"It will be. We cardinals will pray for the Holy Spirit to move us. When all is said and done, the outcome will be the same. For you see, my friend, we've been praying."

"Praying or politicking?"

"Sorry to say, a little of both."

"Were you shocked at the death of the Holy Father?"

"Yes and no. He's been sick for a while—he had heart disease. Just a matter of time. Giacomo, we never know when death will knock on our door."

"You're right, and then he knocks, and we don't let him in."

"Yes—the fighting spirit of man or maybe the fear of the unknown."

"The fear of the unknown? Never thought of it that way."

"We become so comfortable in this life we forget what our faith tells us."

"What's that?"

"That our Father in heaven has a mansion for each one of us. That he longs for us to be with him and that he allowed his only son to die on the cross for the forgiveness of our sins."

"Whoa, Andrew, you're getting deep now." He leaned forward.

"What is it, Giacomo?"

"My life as a soldier . . ."

"How can you be forgiven for the sins you committed as a soldier?"

"Yes."

"All things are possible with God."

Sergio walked through the doorway. "Your Eminence."

Giacomo smiled. He hugged Sergio.

"Good to see you, my friend."

"Thank you, Giacomo."

"Sergio, how are you?" The cardinal put his hand on the grieving man's shoulder.

"Good days and bad days. How are you? You must be busy."

"I am. I came here to hide." Andrew chuckled. "You two have a lot to do—so I'll be on my way."

Chapter 77

THE CARDINAL EXITED the office. Giacomo watched Sergio place his briefcase by the computer monitor. With a click of the clasps, the black leather attaché case opened.

"Sergio, what's the matter?"

The Italian shook his head. "I'll be fine."

"What do you have?"

"Richardson's phone numbers—incoming and outgoing calls." He set the document down.

"Great. Were we able to trace any of the numbers?"

"Not yet. I received a phone call from the AISI. The Italian inquiry into the plane crash revealed that the missile had homing capabilities."

"Are you serious? I had that same thought the other day. How else could the airplane be shot down?"

"You were right. When the investigators dismantled the device, they discovered a tracking chip."

"Did they find the transmitter on the airplane?"

"Not yet."

"Umph."

"What are you thinking?"

"Tony keeps his airplane under tight security. His pilots are ex-Secret Service and intelligence agents. I wonder how the transmitter got aboard the aircraft." Possibilities swirled in his mind.

"Do you believe Trivette is behind this?"

With an authoritative, uncompromising voice, Giacomo replied,

"I do. Trivette acquired the second journal." He took a deep breath. "Sergio, I have to tell you something—I have my father's gift."

"Your father's gift?"

"Yes."

"Why? How?"

Giacomo noticed the intensity of interest in his friend's eyes. "The real dreams . . ."

"Like your father?"

"Yes but more."

"More?"

Uncertain, Giacomo said, "Yeah . . ."

"Trivette was in your dream with the journal, and you trust this to be true?"

"Yes, I do."

"Eten Trivette? You're drinking too much Italian wine, my friend."

"Glad to see your sense of humor is back."

Sergio's reaction perplexed Giacomo.

Sergio gave a slight laugh. "How are you going to prove Trivette's involvement?"

"I'm going to talk with my father-in-law. He can't stand the man. He'll help us."

"One of the most influential men in the world, who saved more economies and soon the United States, is involved? You're crazy."

"Listen, Sergio, outside of us, who prospered the most? Well?"

"You're right. The European Union."

"Who runs the EU?"

"Eten Trivette. Your reasoning behind his complicity?"

"Speculation, really."

"Speculation?" Sergio shook his head.

Giacomo sat back, pondered for a moment. "Let's initiate a financial investigation into Trivette. Compare the events in my father's journal with his economic successes. If we can couple Richardson's phone calls with the dates and times of the attacks, we might find our answers." He sensed his friend's uneasiness. "What's your issue, Sergio?"

"Giacomo, what good is our investigation going to do? He's one of the most influential men in the world."

"So are we. If this guy's involved, I want him to hang. We'll make the dominos fall, and we're starting with Trivette."

"Now I need a drink."

"One other issue—I meant to ask Andrew. Can priests be doctors?"

Sergio seemed to stumble on his reply. "Why do you ask?"

"I saw a priest who could've been Rio's doctor."

"Oh . . . I think they can."

"Interesting . . ."

Later that night, two men sat next to each other and whispered in the darkness. The red glow of votive candles flickered in the distance.

"He has his father's gift?"

"Yes."

"He's pursuing Trivette?"

"Yes."

"Good. That will keep him off our backs."

"Only for a short time."

"Long enough." As the man rose and exited the pew, he spoke his parting words: "Et Tu Spiritu Sanctus."

Chapter 78

GIACOMO AWOKE WITH a sudden tremble, the nightmare fresh in his mind. He gasped for air. Not able to breathe, he sat up and threw the white sheets off his body.

"Giacomo, what is it?"

"Bad dream."

Emily rubbed his back. "Try to relax, honey." Her voice was soothing. "Do you want to talk about it?"

"I . . . I . . ." Befuddled, Giacomo considered for a moment. "It was so real—I was there."

"Where?"

"Washington. What time is it?"

"Ten after twelve."

"Six o'clock in the States?"

"Yes, ten after six. Why?"

"In my dream, a clock on a wall read six o'clock."

"Who was in the dream?"

"President Richardson and another man were discussing Rio. The other person said Rio was alive. They had to find her and kill her. She's a danger to them. Richardson said no, he wouldn't allow it. The man admonished him. Richardson's face turned red—he yelled. The man slapped Richardson. He shook his finger at him and said, 'The DeLaurentis family must die. If we don't kill them, they will topple us. Start with the Frenchman.' The president said no—and threw the man out of his office."

"I'm sure it's nothing, honey. Try to go back to sleep."

"I can't."

"Why?"

"Because it happened."

"Only a bad dream, honey—nothing more."

Giacomo placed his head on the pillow. His mind struggled. *This must have been what my father referred to as a "real" dream. Like the one I had on the airplane. I really do have my father's gift. Do I want it? Do I have a choice? How do they know Rio is alive?*

Giacomo waited until Emily fell asleep, then dressed and left a note on the kitchen table. The clock on the wall read one thirty. Bundled up in a blue jacket, he headed to the Vatican administrative building. He yawned, and a cold shiver traveled his spine. Was it the chilly air or the reality of the dream? The winter stars sparkled overhead. He strolled past two Swiss Guards. They nodded, acknowledging the friend of the camerlengo.

Giacomo's footsteps reverberated in the empty hallway. The whirls of a floor polisher hummed in the distance. The lights flickered for a moment. He entered the office. Perplexed, he sat in one of the chairs at the conference table, his jacket still on, and let his mind take him on another journey.

Giacomo viewed the valley of colors in Ottati as he grasped the black wrought iron fence. The crisp air swept across his face. In the blue sky, the wispy white clouds played hide-and-seek with the tips of the Alburni Mountains. "Dad, Dad . . ." The voices of two young boys— but they were nowhere to be seen. A dark gray cloud rolled overhead as day turned to night. A light rain began as small drops of water made their imprint on the portico. The shower increased to a pelting deluge. Unable to move, Giacomo let the water cascade over his face. His hair flattened to his scalp. The wind howled through the trees. The crackles of thunder, a flash of lightning—the sound was unbearable. He stayed steady as the winds churned around him and whisked him away from the mountain village. Giacomo was brought to a room with two doors. He opened the one on the left—an enormous elm tree shaded a deep meadow. Branches clothed with massive leaves of golden yellow, red, and orange touched the sky. In front of him. an endless row of crosses with the Star of David over each. Giacomo walked among the graves, stopping at each one. There were no names, just the same inscription again and again: "The truth never changes." He went back to the room and opened the door on the right. Before him the elm tree; beyond it rolling green pastures with bright, colorful flowers of yellow, red, and purple under a magnificent blue sky. He stood in the meadow as peace swept his being.

Giacomo's office door swung open with a crash. Startled, he jumped out of the chair, his hands ready for battle.

"*Mi scusi, signore*—excuse me."

Giacomo squinted at the janitor. "No problem."

The man closed the office door and continued to buff the hallway. Giacomo shook his head. His heart still pounded. The clock on the wall read two thirty. *What a crazy dream. Was it a dream?* He turned on one of the four computers. Grabbing the keyboard, he typed a string of commands. The screen came alive with video images of the current drones that traveled the skies. He inputted more programming language. A few more commands, and he'd isolated the ones flying around Washington, DC. Again, he instructed the computer and called up a video of the White House.

Dawn crept through the office window. He sat back, stunned. He knew now that he had his father's gift of remote viewing. In his dream, he'd discovered who slapped Richardson . . . the person who was really in charge. Now he had to prove it, and when he did, someone might die.

*   *   *

Washington, DC

Filled with angst, the appointed president found himself in a predicament. Awake at three in the morning, Richardson fumed over the literal bitch-slapping he'd received the previous night from Dean Essex. A mix of sadness, dread, and anger strengthened his resolve for revenge. His decision was clear in his mind. *Screw 'em.* He strolled the halls of his private residence on his way to the Oval Office. A Secret Service agent walked four steps behind him as the marine guard saluted.

Richardson sat behind the desk and picked up the photograph of his family. A tear slid down his face, splattering the legislative bill. The signing of this document would change the dollar to the euro. The ceremony was to take place at ten that morning. He reached forward, grabbed a pen, paused for a moment, and then etched his name underneath his nine-word rationale of why he refused to sign the bill. As he wrote, he said, "Screw you, you little pissant."

Chapter 79

GIACOMO ENTERED THE Vatican apartment—it was beginning to feel like home. Emily sat at the kitchen table drinking a glass of orange juice.

"Morning, *mi amore.*" Giacomo kissed Emily on the forehead.

"*Bonjour, mon ami.* You're up early today."

"After the dream, I couldn't sleep, so I went to the office." Giacomo pulled out a chair, sat down, and placed his left hand on Emily's arm. "I inherited my father's gift."

"Are you hungry? Do you want breakfast?"

"No comment?"

"What would you like me to say, Giacomo? 'Whoopee' as I jump up and down with joy?"

Giacomo leaned back, withdrew his hand. "I didn't expect that."

"I'm sorry. Our life is far from normal . . . and now this."

"Maybe I shouldn't have said anything." Giacomo lowered his head.

"Why do you think you inherited this gift . . . or should I say curse?"

Giacomo told her of what he'd discovered.

"Oh." Emily's voice was cold.

"Honey, don't you realize? Good can come from this. Not like Dad—who didn't know what to do, except mail letters to arrive after he'd been dead for so many years."

"Eggs?"

"Em . . ."

"Giacomo, I'm afraid."

"Of what?"

"Of what? That you're going to disappear—or worse. It's not just you and me." The expectant mother rubbed her belly. "The boys—what about them? If the government discovers this gift? Our life will no longer be our own."

Giacomo faced Emily and spoke in French. "*Mon amour,* there is nothing to fear. As to the government, I promise I will only tell the people whom I trust. Should the gift be like Dad's . . . I'll write letters like he did."

"So they can be used after *you're* dead?" Emily's tone of voice cascaded up and down when she said, "I don't want you to be a picture on the mantel. A memory faded away by time."

Giacomo saw the anger in his wife's face. "Why do you say that? I'm not going to die."

"Do you even care about us?" A tear welled in the corner of her eye.

"What a crazy question. Of course, I do. I love you with all my heart. You mean more to me than my life." *That was a stupid thing to say.* "I mean I'd do anything for you and the boys."

"Then quit. Let's go back home."

Giacomo said nothing.

"See? You can't."

Emily turned and walked into the bedroom.

Giacomo gazed out the window. He touched the cold pane. *Emily's right. This is nonsense. What do I do? I have no control. Do I ignore it? How can I?*

"Giacomo, I'm sorry," Emily said as she leaned against the entranceway to the kitchen.

Giacomo didn't turn around; he continued to stare out the window. "You're right, Em—this life is not for us. We don't need this aggravation; I should say, *you* don't need it. We can retire, live comfortably for the rest of our lives. What will be will be. This is not up to me."

Emily rubbed his back. He turned to face her.

"What's the matter—you can't wrap your arms around me?"

"You're such a jerk."

"Thank you very much." Giacomo smiled.

"Were you serious when you said you'd retire?"

"Yep. I hope you understand . . ."

"You need to finish this job."

He lowered his head. "I'm sorry . . ."

"I understand."

"Why don't I take off the next day or two? We can shop for a Christmas tree. What do you say?"

"Christmas tree and presents?"

"Yeah."

"Do you think . . ."

"We'll be safe?"

"Don't worry. All is well."

Chapter 80

TWO DAYS HAD passed since Giacomo's real dream and the argument with Emily. Together they explored the streets of Rome, Vatican security never far behind. The weather was fresh and crisp with a bright blue sky.

"Em, how's this one?" Giacomo pointed to a five-foot-tall evergreen spruce.

"Nice pick, honey."

Giacomo motioned to the two bodyguards. "Do you think this will fit, Angelo?"

"Yes, Giacomo."

The men placed the Christmas tree in the trunk. The thoroughfare was busy—three scooters zoomed by the vehicle.

"Em, why don't you stay in the car. You must be tired. I want to buy a bottle of aged balsamic vinegar for Tony D."

"He'd like that. You're right; I'm tired, and my feet are killing me."

"Angelo, stay here with Emily. Rico, come with me."

The two men trotted to the corner.

"Do you want me to call for a backup, General?"

"No, let's handle this on our own."

As the two men crossed the street, they approached a thin, short man. A camera hung from his shoulder. Rico circled to the left, positioning himself in front. Giacomo, a head taller, placed his right leg between the photographer's, and with a quick kick, the cameraman dropped to the pavement.

"I'm so sorry," Giacomo said with sarcasm. He put his knee on the back of the photographer as he held the man's face against the sidewalk. "Stay right where you are. Don't move."

Rico showed his credentials to the onlookers, who quickly dispersed.

"Why were you taking pictures of me?" Giacomo whispered with a growl.

"Please . . . let me explain."

The security agent took the camera.

"What do we have, Rico?"

Rico leaned over and showed Giacomo the digital screen. He lifted the man by the collar of his jacket. "Why are you following me?"

The man reached inside his coat. Rico grabbed the man's arm.

"I'm unarmed. I only did what I was told." He pulled out an envelope. "Here."

Giacomo shook his head and grabbed the sealed envelope with his father's initials. He crumbled the note and placed it in his pants pocket. "Let him go. I'm sorry." Giacomo counted out ten large bills and handed the money to the photographer. "I'm sorry."

"Yeah, sure, no problem, mister."

"Who gave you the envelope?"

The man rotated his head, pointing. "That guy over there."

The two men turned, but it was too late—the person had escaped into the crowd. Giacomo apologized again and touched Rico's shoulder. "Let's go."

"What did you do to that man? I am disappointed in you. People do have rights. You just can't do what you did." Emily scowled as Giacomo entered the car.

"My paranoia got the best of me. I thought he was taking pictures of you."

"Was he?"

"No."

Giacomo placed his hand in his pants pocket. The envelope from his father crinkled to his touch. The husband and angry wife focused their attention outside their respective car windows. The silence was disrupted by Angelo as he cursed the driver of a speeding Vespa that came close to tearing off the side mirror. When they arrived at the Vatican, Giacomo elected to take a walk to give his wife time to calm down.

The papal conclave was the next day. Giacomo noticed workers tidying up the grounds around the Sistine Chapel. He moseyed along the Via del Seminario Etopico, and when he reached the seminary, he took a right toward the western part of Vatican City. The doubt in his mind overcame him. He recalled the words his father once told him: "*I see the pictures in my mind, and within my being, I'm convinced they are true—yet I'm held back by fear, a dread I can't describe.*" So very true. Giacomo was a soldier, a warrior, who had escaped the clutches of numerous enemies, and yet he was afraid.

"Giacomo."

He stopped. Cardinal Angeloni and another cardinal stood near the Fountain of the Eagle. Giacomo greeted the men of the cloth.

"Your Eminence."

"Eminence?"

"I'm sorry, *Andrew.*"

"Giacomo, I'd like you to meet Cardinal Adadayo."

"Your Eminence."

"Hello, Giacomo." They shook hands. Adadayo said, "Andrew, we'll talk later. I must go pray."

"Sounds good, Dayo."

The regal man who was soon to be the first African pope bowed his head in acknowledgment and went on his way.

"Andrew, can we talk?"

"Let's sit. What's on your mind, my friend?"

Giacomo joined his friend in the afternoon sun on a park bench near St. Peter's Basilica. He explained his dream and what he'd discovered. Andrew listened, his right elbow resting on his leg as his hand covered a part of his face.

"I'm filled with fear, Andrew. Why?"

"If you have a gift like your father, fear might be attributed to the fact he believed he could do nothing with his visions. You said your father considered himself a failure for not speaking out more."

"True."

"And you?"

Giacomo stared past the cardinal. "I'm afraid that the lives of innocent people rest in my hands, and I don't want to fail them."

"Hasn't that always been the case with you, especially during your military service?"

Giacomo considered the comment. "Yes, but everything was black and white—no gray areas. This . . . this . . . whatever it is, it occurs in my mind."

"Remember one thing, Giacomo. You proved that your dream happened."

"Well, partly. I confirmed the two men met. I'll have a transcript of their conversation later today—when I'm able to analyze the laser sound recording."

"Laser sound recording?"

"A listening device. Sergio and our team set it up. The beam is focused on the window. The modulating frequency picks up the noise vibration, which in turn is analyzed. If a conversation took place, the words are recorded to my computer. Then I can compare the written text with what I heard in the dream."

"Amazing how technology and the mystical intersect. I'm glad you're my friend, not my enemy." He paused. "Maybe your fear is based on the unknown. That by itself is scary. Should the vision occur again, embrace the knowledge imparted to you. I caution you, Giacomo, don't act. You must discern or prove the reality, then take action. Don't be afraid—God will guide you as he did your father."

Giacomo pondered the statement. "I guess you're right, Andrew. Thanks. Speaking of my father . . ." He pulled an envelope from his back pocket. "I got this yesterday." He handed the message to Andrew.

"You didn't open it?"

"No." Giacomo changed the subject. "Em and I had an argument the other day. I told her I have my father's gift. She's not happy."

"The pressure?"

"Yeah. She thinks I'll end up like Dad—or worse, I'll be a pawn for the government. We decided I should retire after we've gotten some resolution on the attacks as well as everything else that's going on with the president pro tempore and the president-elect. She's right. I need to spend time with my family, not try to save the world, not put my unborn children at risk."

"You're correct; family is important." The cardinal waved at the envelope. "Are you going to open it?"

"No, you can."

"Me?"

"Welcome to my world. I'm tired of hearing how bad our future will be. Please, you open it."

Andrew looked at the envelope. It was dated December 25, 1999. He took the sheet of paper out and smiled. "Here, this is for your eyes." He handed Paolo's note back to Giacomo.

Hello, Andrew.

Giacomo, I love you. Be strong, my son.

"This is amazing, Giacomo. Your father knew I would read the letter. We should all be as blessed as you to have a father who can tell you that he loves you from beyond the grave."

Giacomo smiled. "Yeah, I wish I knew how he did this . . . this envelope thing."

"I'm sure you'll find out in time."

Giacomo sat back, more relaxed as he said, "In time. Are you ready for the conclave?"

"As ready as I'll ever be. It should only be a couple of days. Did you see the news coming in from the States?"

"No, what happened?"

"The House and the Senate approved the euro bill."

"Not a surprise."

"Well, this is: Richardson *vetoed* the bill."

"I wonder why."

"Your guess is as good as mine. The reports say that his veto will be overridden. Congress has enough votes to do so."

"He wants to distance himself."

Cardinal Angeloni tilted his head and frowned. "Maybe . . . do not fret, my friend."

The two men embraced. "Thanks for listening."

"No problem."

Giacomo continued his stroll through the Vatican Gardens. A dove cooed in the distance. Three of the white birds jumped from their perch. They circled the Sistine Chapel, and together they landed on the dome.

Chapter 81

GIACOMO ENTERED HIS sister's room. The window was open; a cool breeze ruffled the curtains as he entered. Her bed was made, and Rio sat in an armchair. She wore a black sweater with blue jeans. A walker had been stowed in the corner. Giacomo surprised Rio as she talked on her cell phone.

"I need to go now. No, I'll call you. Bye."

"Who were you talking to?"

"You sound annoyed. I can't speak to people now?"

"Rio, you have to be careful." Out of nowhere, the thought entered his mind. *Was she talking to Dean?*

"Careful of what? Why am I here?" She froze, a blank stare on her face. "Hi, Giacomo. Did you just get here?"

Concerned, he said, "Rio, where's Mom?"

"She decided to go with Emily. Our mother is driving me crazy. Watch this."

"Rio, what are you doing?" He rushed over to her.

"Standing, you fool—what does it look like?"

"Are you supposed to be doing that?"

"Why not? Giacomo, this place—I need to go back home."

"Rio, you aren't going anywhere."

"Bullshit. I want to go to Ottati."

"That can't happen. Everyone still thinks you're dead. Well, almost everyone, except for Dean Essex."

"Dean Essex is none of your business. If you haven't noticed, I'm not dead; I'm very much alive. And speaking of my life—stay out of it!"

Giacomo was taken aback by his sister's outburst. He watched as Rio took two steps and started to fall. Giacomo rushed to catch her, then guided her back to the chair. "You're gonna hurt yourself."

"Big deal. Did you find out who shot down the airplane?"

"We're getting close."

"Close? When are we going to talk?"

"We'll discuss this tomorrow with Sergio. Any problem waiting?"

"Do I have a choice?"

"No. When you came out of the coma, you said, 'Be careful of who you trust. It's not what it seems.' What did you mean by that?"

Rio looked confused and then smirked. "I . . . we'll discuss this tomorrow. Any problem?"

"Oh. Kind of sarcastic, baby sister."

"If I can wait, so can you."

"You gonna stick your tongue out at me now?"

"No, you ass."

"Ah, my wonderful little sister is back. Rumor has it you had a date with Dean Essex." Giacomo waited for the onslaught of anger, but instead Rio blushed.

"How did you find out?"

"I have my ways." Giacomo headed to the doorway.

With a smug smile, Rio repeated, "*You're* an ass."

"I love you too."

Giacomo entered the hallway, reached for his cell phone, and called Rio's doctor. He leaned against the wall as he explained his sister's confusion and lack of lucidity. Adinolfi assured Giacomo he would check on her.

As he placed the phone in his pocket, he received another call.

"Sergio, what's going on?"

"They found the transmitter on the plane. A heart-shaped charm on a necklace."

"Interesting. Do we know who it belonged to?"

"No."

"I'll have Tony check with his flight crew. Anything else?"

"We've traced the numbers from Richardson's satellite phone."

"Excellent. What took so long?"

"A computer malfunction with the uplink."

"Let's meet tomorrow. Rio will be there. She wants some answers."

"Ten?"

"I'll be there."

Giacomo found a small chapel behind St. Peter's Basilica. He entered the centuries-old church. A musty smell of age permeated the air. Statues depicting the stations of the cross were lined in sequence between the rows of blue-and-red stained glass windows. A gold tabernacle was tucked in a vestibule to the right of the altar. A life-size cross with a sculpture of the crucified Christ hung on the far wall. Red votive candles flickered in front of a statue of St. Peter. In the sanctuary, two cardinals prostrated in prayer.

Giacomo chose an empty pew in the middle of the church. The military man sat on the hard wood, blessed himself, reached down for the padded kneeler, and knelt in the quiet of God's house. Raised a Catholic, Giacomo had stopped going to Sunday Mass when he left West Point. His conversation with God was a daily Lord's Prayer.

A cardinal strode the center aisle, stopped, put his hand on Giacomo's shoulder, and said in Italian, "Talk to Him as you would speak to your father."

Dad. He started to chuckle. *Damn, what do I say? Oh, sorry, didn't mean to swear.* Giacomo's mind was empty; sorrow gripped his heart. *Please forgive me. I've lost it.* He sat back on the brown-varnished wood—and as he closed his eyes, the vision arose.

The air is cold—a light snow descends from the white-gray clouds. The flakes hang in the sky before they drift to the ground. Tens of thousands of people are gathered. The Capitol is behind me—Tom Maro and President Richardson smile. Fighter jets fly overhead in tight formation. The afterburners emit a bright orange glow as the engines roar . . . A commotion begins. I can't reach Tom—Emily squeezes my hand, and then she's gone. People scream in fear. The scene changes.

Three people stand before me—two men and a woman. Their faces are hidden. One man is dressed in white, the other in a blue silk suit. The woman is clothed in black. The flesh of her brain is exposed. Again, the backdrop changes, and the sunlight is blinding, then plunges into the blackness of night. Bright green auras high on the horizon highlight the heavens. The scene shifts to Paris. Commotion and disorder roam the streets; darkness envelops the City of Lights.

"*Giacomo . . . Giacomo.*"

Cardinal Angeloni touched his shoulder, gave it a shake.

"Giacomo?"

Giacomo's eyes focused. "Andrew, twice in one day?"

"What's going on with you?"

"Yeah . . . I was . . . I don't know, I don't know . . . so real."

"What, Giacomo?" Andrew sat in the pew in front of him.

"I guess I fell asleep."

"Do you sleep with your eyes open?"

"No."

"I thought you were having a seizure—it was freaky."

"Did you say 'freaky'?"

"Don't change the subject."

Giacomo sat quietly as Andrew glowered.

"I'm sorry, Andrew. My mind takes me to another place. I can't control when the vision occurs. A gift my father had as well—but unlike my dad, I'll take action."

"What do you mean?"

"I thought about our conversation. I'm not going to stand by like Dad did. I need to walk through the door and believe there is a reason why I'm having these visions."

"What did you see?"

Giacomo shared the vision with him and then sat back with a sense of relief. A burden lifted from his shoulders.

"Usually a vision or dream is nothing more than symbols. The meaning correlates with the individual's consciousness—aspects of their life."

"You're wrong. I need to be prepared for that day."

"What else did the vision show?"

Giacomo was miffed at Andrew's comment about symbols. He shrugged off the remark. "People . . . but I didn't recognize them."

The cardinal said nothing for a moment. "Remember what I told you—to think and discern. Promise me, Giacomo, you'll ask for God's help. You've entered a realm where few have been. Don't be deceived by this knowledge. Remember—in God's time." The cardinal's eyes traveled upward as he said, "Maybe, Giacomo, you're being given glimpses of the future to be prepared—not necessarily to prevent it from happening."

Giacomo nodded. "You might be right, Andrew. That's what Dad didn't understand. You can't prevent what is meant to be."

"No, we can't. Although we'd like to, it's all ultimately up to God."

Chapter 82

GIACOMO CLOSED THE door of the Vatican apartment as he was leaving with a quiet click of the lock. Emily was still asleep at a few minutes before eight. Giacomo revisited the cardinal's words from the day before as he walked to the office. *You can't prevent what is meant to be.* He added a thought: *You can sure as hell try.* An hour earlier amid paparazzi and television cameras, 120 cardinals in pairs had entered the Sistine Chapel. The conclave to select a new pope had begun.

Giacomo reached for his satellite phone and called the next president of the United States.

"Morning, Tom."

"Morning, Giacomo." He yawned. "Excuse me."

"No problem. I'm not getting much sleep either."

"Yeah, I understand. I received your email last night. I'm having a difficult time with what you said. Can we trust *anyone*?"

"Tom, it never feels good when a person close to you is a traitor."

"Giacomo, I want to throw up."

"I understand. Did you find the listening devices?"

"Yes, downstairs in my office. I followed your instructions; I left them alone. How did you discover them?"

"The remote drone that kept an eye on you and your staff captured a high-frequency transmission originating from your study. The range of the frequency is similar to what we use in clandestine operations."

"Any idea who planted the devices?"

"We have our suspicions. Not to change the subject, but the Italian investigators found the tracking device on the airplane. Hopefully, we'll be able to connect the dots."

"That's good news. Who bugged my house?"

"I want to be positive before I mention names. Tom, we'll need your help in catching these bastards."

"I'll do whatever needs to be done."

"And, Tom, I need to discuss another topic with you."

"Sure. Go ahead."

Giacomo said, "I have my father's gifts."

"What do you mean?"

Giacomo shared with Tom his vision.

"I'm speechless . . . and it just happens?"

"Yes, I have no control over it."

"No control?"

"None."

"Your vision is poignant."

"Why?"

"The green aura."

"Why?"

"Two days ago, my science advisors discussed with me the recent increases in solar flare activity—the intensity of the northern lights."

"Solar flares, the aurora borealis—the vision." He paused. "The darkness . . . so, what did they say?"

"They're concerned our country's power grids are vulnerable to either a massive solar outbreak or a nuclear detonation. They said we should protect ourselves from potential EMPs. Of course, the warmongers are concerned about the bomb."

"Yes, electromagnetic pulses. I studied what would occur if there were a high-altitude atomic detonation. We did an explosion analysis of different magnitudes at various altitudes. For example, let's say a ten-kiloton weapon exploded over Omaha. At the right altitude, the radius of the EMP would be fourteen hundred miles— the entire US power grid would collapse. If you consider our dependency on computers, electronic circuits . . . let's just say the devastation of the country's infrastructure and economy would be insurmountable."

"You said Paris would go dark—a tactical nuclear explosion?"

"Could be, but I doubt it. Years ago, our country worked on a defensive system that would protect us from an EMP attack."

"Yes, we discussed it, but the project was never finished due to budget cuts. The program was named Surge Protector. Stalworth's administration stopped the funding."

"Unbelievable. How long before Surge is online?"

"Three to six months."

"I hope we have that long."

"What do you mean?"

"If the vision is true, then the electrical networks will be destroyed, and no one is prepared. Do you remember the failure in India in 2012?"

"Sure do—three hundred million people were without power. Their grids failed."

"Do you know how they failed?"

"No."

"A terrorist EMP attack."

"Wow. Your vision is forewarning us of an impending power grid failure?"

"Yes. Let's hope the cause is a solar flare and not an EMP or worse . . . a nuclear explosion."

"This is frightening, Giacomo. The blackout in Paris—power grid?"

"More than likely."

"Should we inform the French government?"

"I'll speak to Arnaud, and he can pass the info to their president. It won't help, though. Paris will go dark—it's meant to be."

"Giacomo, will this happen to us as well?"

"Let's hope not. Tom, if I were you, as soon as I entered the Oval Office, I'd make sure Surge Protector is up and running . . ."

"I agree. Any idea what happens at the inauguration?"

"No, but we should be prepared."

"Better to be safe than sorry. The world will be watching."

"Yep. How's the transition going? Any better?"

"A little. My chief of staff, Dean Essex, has a relationship with the White House. We're able to carry out many of the tasks—a tedious process."

There was a long pause. Giacomo's subconscious wrestled with the name of Dean Essex. *What was the connection and why? Coincidental—Rio and him?*

"Giacomo, are you there?"

"Sorry, Tom." A church bell clanged. "No pope."

"What did you say, Giacomo?"

"The church bell rang at St. Peter's, indicating the cardinals cast their first vote. They didn't elect a pope."

"How would you know if a new pope was elected?"

"White smoke will emanate from the chimney, and all the church bells of Rome will sound."

"The Catholic Church always had a special meaning for me. My stepfather was a Coptic Christian, my mom a Muslim. The concept of Catholicism interests me . . . I guess I'm part of it now since the unification of the Christian Church . . ." His voice trailed.

"I'm sure, Tom, when you're president, you'll meet the pope. Maybe he'll convert you."

"I doubt that, my friend, but I do believe in the one true God. Rumor here in the States is that Adadayo from Africa will be the next pope."

"I heard the same."

"Listen, I need to go back to bed. I've got a busy day tomorrow. Goodbye, Giacomo."

Chapter 83

GIACOMO REACHED THE Vatican office. He was troubled by Rio's inconsistent behavior—it was as if her personality had changed. *Why did she call Dean Essex? Now that he knows she's alive, should I add more security?* His thoughts rambled, and then he was plagued by the vision of Essex slapping Richardson. *How involved was Tom Maro's chief of staff and why?*

Giacomo looked at his Rolex—it was ten in the morning. *Rio should be here soon. Am I ready for this? I need to be prepared. No matter what the risk or sacrifice, we will . . .*

"Good morning, big brother."

"I didn't hear you enter. Morning, sis. Hi, Sergio."

"Hi, Giacomo." Sergio pushed Rio's wheelchair into the room.

"With all the money you have, this is the best you could do?"

"It suits our purpose." Giacomo removed a chair from the conference table to accommodate the wheelchair.

"What are you doing?"

"Making room for the wheelchair."

"Sergio, help me?"

Sergio took hold of Rio's outstretched arms. With painstaking slowness, she baby-stepped to the table.

"Well, are you going to stand there, or are you going to get me a seat?"

"Boy, you're tough." Giacomo rolled the chair over and placed it behind her.

"I'm a lawyer, so what do you expect?"

Giacomo rolled his eyes. *She's in a bad mood.*

"I made a fresh pot of coffee."

"Sure—black, please. Do you have my cell phone?"

"No. Why would I have it?"

"Because you're spying on me."

"Don't be ridiculous, little sister."

"Damn it, Giacomo, stop calling me little sister. My name is . . . is . . ."

"Rio, are you okay?"

"Shut up, Sergio, and get me a cup of coffee."

Giacomo glanced at Sergio. Both men were wide-eyed at Rio's strange rantings. Giacomo ignored her outburst and opened the window to let some cool fresh air sweep into the room.

"Rio, I hope you don't mind. The heat is unbearable—no thermostat."

"The temperature is fine. So, Giacomo, what the f is going on?"

"You understand, we are in Vatican City. You should mind your language." *She's never acted like this.*

"What are you, a holy roller now?"

Giacomo said nothing. He lifted the silver pot, pouring the coffee into three white mugs imprinted with the gold-and-red crest of the Vatican. He sat opposite Sergio and Rio.

"Start from the beginning?" Sergio asked.

"How's that sound, Rio?"

"Sure, let's hurry up." She fidgeted in her chair.

Giacomo's eyebrows rose as he reviewed the assassinations of the UN ambassador, Tom Maro's chief of staff, Saleem, and Nava Ben-Reuven. He recounted the downing of Tony's plane, the attack in Corsica, the odd communication from the murdered monk, Alessio's untimely death, and his own abduction when he went to the States. Twenty minutes later, he finished.

"Giacomo, who's behind all this?"

Giacomo rubbed his chin. "Sergio, start with what you found. I'll follow up with what I discovered. What we do next—that'll be the problem."

Sergio opened his black leather briefcase and took out one of two thick, stapled documents. He handed the first to Giacomo. "This is a financial spreadsheet of the European Union as well as Trivette's investments for the last fourteen years."

"*Eten?*" Rio snapped.

"Yes, why?"

"We were scheduled to meet in Paris after I left Ottati. What does he have to do with anything?"

"We think he's involved."

"Don't be stupid, Giacomo."

"Rio, I thought the same thing." Sergio turned toward her. "Let me show you what we found."

"Fine, Sergio—but Eten Trivette?" She shook her head in disbelief. "That man will help rebuild America to the financial world power it once was."

"What do you mean, Rio? I thought you didn't like Trivette." Giacomo's brow furrowed.

"I like him . . . I've talked with him several times."

"You have?"

"Yes. The US is run by a bunch of buffoons who are greedy and corrupt—they care about themselves and not the American people." Rio's voice rose. "Another four years of Waldron, shit . . . we're doomed." Giacomo and Sergio exchanged glances, but Rio didn't stop. "We need Trivette's economic help to secure our . . . our . . . What the hell are you talking about, Giacomo?" Rio began to slap her hands on the table. "What the hell are you talking about? Damn it, are you stupid? Didn't you hear what I said? Another four years of Waldron." Her face was pale, her expression stony, and her eyes blank.

Giacomo frowned at his sister's words and behavior. "Rio, did you watch the news?"

"Of course. Why?" Her voice was terse.

"What month is this?" Giacomo saw uncertainty cross Rio's face.

"November, stupid."

Giacomo's voice stayed calm. "Rio, it's almost Christmas, and President Waldron is dead."

"Don't lie! I know damn well this is November." Her hands went to her neck as she pulled on the skin. "Where is it, Giacomo? What did you do with it? I know you stole it. My necklace, where's my necklace? Dean gave it to me . . . I need to call him." Rio tried to stand.

"Relax. Listen for a moment."

She stared at her brother. "I think . . ." Rio slumped back in her seat.

"Should we do this another day, sis?"

She grabbed the paper out of Sergio's hand and read the headlines. A tear trickled down her cheek. "Giacomo . . ." Her voice fell silent as her eyes rolled back and she collapsed on the table.

Chapter 84

"**G**IACOMO, WHAT YOUR sister experienced is common. We've sedated her, and in a couple of days, she'll be back to her feisty old self."

"She thought it was *November*."

The Vatican doctor—Francesco Ciccone—gave an exasperated sigh. "She was in a coma for weeks. We don't have an accurate understanding of what happens in a patient's brain when they're in that state. I informed Dr. Adinolfi, who said the confusion is understandable. Rio will recover. The medication should help keep her calm."

"Where is Adinolfi? He should've been here."

"I'm taking over for him."

"When's he due back?"

"Sorry to say, he's not coming back. He's headed to Monte Cassino."

Giacomo pondered the words "Monte Cassino" for a moment and then asked, "How long do you think Rio will be this way?"

"A year . . . maybe more. Your family should be aware that in cases like this, recovery is slow, not only for the body but also for the mind."

"I see. A tough road ahead."

Giacomo shook the doctor's hand as Victoria waved goodbye from Rio's bedside. He couldn't wait to get outside and talk with Sergio.

As they walked back to the Vatican office, a church bell sounded. The men glanced at each other. "No pope." The second vote of the morning session ended.

"Sergio, the necklace—did you hear what Rio said? *She* was carrying the transmitter. I knew it. Essex . . . that bastard."

"Could that be?"

"Yes. Why not? I spoke with Tony. He checked with his flight attendant. She doesn't wear jewelry—some kind of metals allergy." Giacomo was excited; at the same time, an inner anger brewed within him. He relaxed as they walked. He needed more evidence. "What did you find out?"

"We inputted the events of your father's journal into the computer. With the derived data, we compared the EU and Trivette's investments."

"And?"

"Just as you suspected—Trivette capitalized on every disaster. For example, the European Union was Iran's largest importer of oil. Further information showed Eten bought the pipeline to the refinery in Tabriz from Tehran. Of course, this did not go unnoticed. The purchase was widely reported by the media but ignored by world leaders. It was only a matter of time before Israel attacked Iran."

"You're right. The Israelis grew tired of Iran's nuclear threats to wipe out their homeland. It's a shame that the United States took the blame."

The two men entered the office building. Their voices resonated in the hallway.

"It is. The fact that Trivette knew this would happen allowed him to stockpile enough oil reserves for thirty years."

"Are you serious?"

"Yes. The EU also purchased a pipeline in Russia."

"That's why gasoline is cheaper in Europe than in the States."

"Yes, the EU controls the pricing. There's more."

"What do you mean?"

"The catastrophes that occurred in India . . ."

Giacomo put the key in the lock, turned it, and they entered the office.

"Yes, 10 percent of their population was killed. The labor force was literally decimated. Their economy was ruined, and their cities destroyed."

"Correct. Trivette acquired the businesses that were the prime outsources for American and European companies. Within days of the catastrophes, he transferred the work to the member states of the EU. He became a lifesaver, a hero to the jobless. In the process, the unemployment rate in the surrounding countries dropped to 2 percent. He's positioned the EU in every major industry with most of their investments in computer manufacturers and software companies."

"Wow. How did they make their money? We're talking vast amounts."

"One guess."

"Gold."

"Correct again. Trivette controls 80 percent of the gold mines outside of the United States."

"Shit—this is unbelievable. It can't be true—no way this could happen. It sounds like a James Bond movie." The logic in his brain erupted as he repeated, "No way this could happen. It can't be true. Sergio, this is unrealistic."

"Not if he got his hands on your father's journal. Trivette capitalized on the prognostications. Now he's manipulating the economies of the world."

"The only issue is we lack proof."

"Come on, Giacomo, even I am convinced—no other way he could do this without your father's writings."

"Damn it. I should've never turned the journal over to Stalworth. We had the resources, and we did nothing. Damn, damn..." Giacomo moved to the window and took a deep breath, sucking the fresh air into his lungs. "What else?"

"Richardson's phone—the last three months of numbers." He gave Giacomo the list.

"Winston Tarmac on the day he died—they were good friends, so nothing unusual there." Giacomo browsed through the papers. "Humph." He reached inside his coat pocket that hung over a chair, pulled out his cell phone, and scrolled until he found a number. "Why would he speak with Dean Essex?"

"What?"

Giacomo ignored the question. "Are the analysts in the office today?"

"Yes."

"I want them to cross-check Dean Essex's phone calls with the assassinations of Saleem, Tarmac, Ben-Reuven, and the attack on Tony's plane. Oh, let's not forget the attack in Corsica. Can you do that while I review these numbers? I need to go to the bathroom—be right back."

Sergio nodded and reached for the phone on Giacomo's desk. Five minutes later, Giacomo returned.

"It might take a few hours—tomorrow morning at the latest. The cell Essex is using is a high frequency like Richardson's. The software program we developed should be able to cut through the codes."

"Great. There are several incoming numbers here. Can we find out where they originated?"

"No. We tried—no success."

Giacomo was quiet for a moment as he processed events and information. The dream of Essex slapping Richardson filled his mind. The necklace he gave Rio. He wondered . . . *What was Essex's motive? Is he connected to Trivette?* Giacomo's inner sense convinced him. He said firmly, "Even without the info, I can assure you Dean is a bad guy. That bastard is the one responsible for bugging Tom's home office. I'll see him rot in hell for what he did to my sister. Much more than that—he controls Richardson."

"What do you mean?"

Giacomo sat across from Sergio and leaned forward. "You're not going to believe this."

Sergio's eyes were wide open, shocked. Giacomo shared with him the real dream. How he proved Dean Essex slapped the president of the United States with the drone's video images and listening devices.

"Now the question is: what is Dean's involvement with Trivette? I'll lay odds he reports to him."

"Trivette? I think you're wrong, my friend. Yes, the journal . . . but the assassinations? That might be hard to prove."

Giacomo glared at Sergio. "I'll get that bastard, put him in the grave along with anyone else who's involved."

Chapter 85

THE WEATHER IN Paris was overcast with snow flurries. The white frozen fluff melted as it kissed the cement, leaving tiny wet spots. Eten Trivette stood by an elevator under the awning of the Jules Verne restaurant at the base of the Eiffel Tower. The area fenced off by police barricades, his security detail of five men hunkered next to the wooden structures as they scanned the area. Trivette tried to erase the recurrent dream of a doctor opening his eyelids and the terrifying emotion that followed. He waited for his driver to return with the car. It had been twenty minutes. Annoyed, he began to pace.

Suddenly, a cascade of bullets whizzed through the air and ricocheted off the steel beam next to him. An innocent passerby was struck in the leg. The crowd of tourists dispersed in a panic. His bodyguards fell to the ground as Trivette found protection behind the steel girder; Arnaud emerged from the shadows. He placed the tip of his walking stick on Trivette's shoulder. "Next time, we won't miss," he said. He disappeared into the crowd as the cowering leader huddled behind the iron leg of the iconic tower.

*   *   *

Giacomo's consciousness morphed, for a moment, the Eiffel Tower flashed in his mind's eye. The sound of the bells of St. Peter's suspended the vision. Giacomo said to Sergio, "No papa—no pope." The third vote yielded no consensus for a new Holy Father. He noticed the strange, questioning look on Sergio's face.

"What?"

"You had a blank expression on your face."

"I'm fine."

"So, where do we go from here?"

"I'll hold off telling Tom about Essex until we can come up with a plan. We must surprise the bastard and bring him back here. The Italian government can prosecute him. The problem is, what do we do with Richardson?"

"What's Dean's motive?"

"No clue, and I don't care."

"Will your country allow us to take him back to Rome?"

Giacomo twirled his green Waterman pen. "I'll talk with Jason."

"This is not going to go well with your sister."

"I know. She's got a thing for Essex. I caught her speaking with him the other day."

"How are you going to stop that?"

"I'm not. I don't want him to find out we're on to him. Rio is well protected here. No one will harm her in Vatican City."

Sergio hung his head. Giacomo noticed his eyes tear up.

"Sergio, she'll be fine."

"I know."

Giacomo gazed at his friend. For a moment, he felt conflicted. He shook off the sense. "I believe Essex will lead us to Trivette."

"Maybe. Why would Rio speak with Trivette?"

"No idea. She also talked to Tom Maro. He said he would consider her for a cabinet position. Rio's relationship with Eten is concerning."

"Why?"

"Rio's idea that Trivette's style of government will benefit the States is flawed."

"The troubling issue is that your government signed on to the euro standard. Let's not forget, Trivette was only able to advance the EU status by stealing your father's journal."

"True."

Giacomo scanned the room and then said, "I've got an idea." He typed in a series of numbers on the keyboard and hit the enter key. He turned the screen around for Sergio.

"Is that the conversation between the president and Essex?"

"Yep. Do you think Richardson is fond of Essex?"

"Not after he slapped him. Why didn't he have him arrested?"

"Good question. Why don't we ask him?"

"What?"

"Richardson's ego is the size of Texas. He hates Essex—so let's turn him around."

"Do you think we can?"

"Yes. With the information we gathered, we can play them against each other."

"It might backfire."

"I doubt it."

Together the two friends worked out a strategy. Two hours later, Sergio's phone rang. "Pronto—hello. When? Ciao."

"What's going on?

"They tried to assassinate Trivette!"

"The Eiffel Tower?"

"Yes. How did you know?"

Giacomo turned on the TV.

The Eiffel Tower provided a backdrop for the Italian newscaster. A picture of Arnaud Chambery was in the corner of the screen. Words scrolled across the bottom. *Arnaud Chambery, director of the DGSE, is accused of arranging an assassination attempt on Eten Trivette.*

"Sergio! *Arnaud.*" A video clip from a security camera showed his father-in-law shove a cane into Trivette's shoulder. "What the hell is going on?" He reached for his phone. "Damn. Emily's not answering. She must be with Rio." He stood. "I need to find my wife. I'll call you later."

The bells of St. Peter's rang as he ran out the door. The final session of the day concluded with no pope.

Chapter 86

GIACOMO RAN OUT of the Vatican City government building. As he hurried to the residence, he noticed Cardinal Andrew walking in the garden. Their eyes met. Giacomo saw sadness in his face. Vatican rules allowed the cardinals in conclave to wander within the city, but they had to maintain strict standards of silence and have no verbal contact with anyone.

He entered Rio's room. Victoria sat on a blue upholstered chair as she read one of Tony's books—*The Considerate Man*. His mother glanced upward.

"Giacomo, what's wrong?"

"Mom, where's Emily?"

"*Hush*. Be quiet. Your sister is sleeping."

Again, louder, "Mom, where the hell is Em?"

"Giacomo, calm down. She got a phone call and left the room."

"How long ago?"

"Maybe an hour. What's going on?"

"Turn on the TV." He exited the room as his mother's voice echoed in the hallway, calling his name.

Giacomo arrived at their apartment a few minutes later. A plate with a half-eaten sandwich and a half glass of milk were on the kitchen table. Emily sat on the loveseat, her eyes fixed on the television as she followed the news reports about her father. She clicked the remote as tears trickled from her red eyes down her chin, splattering her blue shirt. Giacomo watched her feverishly change channels. He sat next to her and slowly took the remote from Emily's hands. He wrapped his arms around her. She placed her head on his chest and wept. Giacomo kissed her forehead.

"Mon amour, please find him," Emily said in a whimper. She sat straight, wiping her eyes with the palm of her hands.

"I will. Em, your father will be all right."

"Yeah." She stood and went to the bathroom.

Giacomo tore out of the building, followed by two Swiss Guards in blue suits.

"Mr. DeLaurentis! Mr. DeLaurentis, please stop."

Giacomo abided by the command and stopped short of the steps of the administrative building. With the arrogance of a general, he said, "Yes. What is it?"

"Is everything all right, sir?"

"Yes—fine. I need to get back to the administrative building."

He was barely out of breath, while the two younger Swiss Guards were huffing and puffing from trying to keep up with him. He stormed into the office.

"Sergio, we have to find Arnaud. Emily's distraught. Start with the drone footage of the Eiffel Tower."

"We had no coverage today."

"Let's tap into the satellites and the French street cameras."

Giacomo peered over Sergio's right shoulder as he watched the video stream come to life. Thirty minutes passed. "Damn it, where is he?"

"Giacomo, look! I got him on a street camera."

The two men watched as Arnaud hurried into the back of a black Mercedes sedan with tinted windows. The car careened down the Avenue des Champs-Élysées. The vehicle exited to the right on Rue de Berri. Making a sudden stop, the doors flew open. Surrounded by armed men, Arnaud entered a white van, but before he did, he looked up into the street camera and gave a wave. The picture went blank.

"Sergio, what the hell happened?"

"We lost the signal. I think one of the men shot the camera."

"What is my father-in-law doing?"

"Giacomo, Arnaud is not stupid. He's been around the intelligence field for most of his life. Believe me—he'll be fine."

Chapter 87

GIACOMO AND SERGIO tracked Arnaud's four-hour circuitous route to a small airport outside of Paris. The evening evolved as the director of the DGSE boarded a helicopter that took him to a field near the small village of Roussillon. Giacomo tapped into a US Army infrared satellite camera that showed Arnaud enter what appeared to be a military truck. At around three a.m., they lost contact as the vehicle entered the mountainous terrain near Nice, France.

Giacomo was exhausted. He did his best to get some sleep on the floor of the Vatican office. The sunlight moved across the room until the warmth settled on his face. He rolled over and opened his bloodshot eyes to see Sergio asleep on top of the conference table.

Startled, he jumped up. "What the hell?"

Behind his desk sat Arnaud Chambery.

"Dad, are you all right?"

"What! What?" Sergio sat upright.

Giacomo walked over to his father-in-law. "What's going on?"

"How do you say it . . . the poop is hitting the fan."

"I'll say. How did you get in here?"

"The Swiss Guards let me in."

"Emily is worried sick."

"I know. I called her when I arrived in Rome. She told me you and Sergio tracked me into the mountains."

"We did."

The two men sat at the conference table, Sergio opposite them. Giacomo stared at his father-in-law.

"Fill you in?"

"Yeah, that would be a good idea, Dad."

"This is not what you think."

"I hope not."

"I and many others in France, Italy, and Spain know Eten Trivette is not who he says he is. Twenty years ago, Eten Trivette's name was . . . Sharif Laden."

"A Muslim?"

"No. He lives by another belief."

"What do you mean?"

"I wish I knew, Giacomo. Before I met your father, I traded in firearms—working with the French government. A Saudi Arabian national approached me to acquire a cache of weapons. In our meetings, a young man with haunting blue eyes stood by his father. Long story short, the transaction was interrupted."

"What do you mean, *interrupted*?"

"We were ambushed by American and English forces. The Saudi turned out to be the young man's father."

"Let me guess—the young man was Eten Trivette?"

"Correct. At that point, I decided to leave the business. Sharif, aka Eten, blamed me for the death of his father. He vanished. Several years later, he kidnapped Emily. What you're not aware of is that Doctor Colin Payne and Eten were—how do you say? Partners."

"Are you kidding me?"

"No. Why would I tell a joke now?"

"Sorry—a figure of speech."

Arnaud shrugged. Giacomo ignored him.

"How did you find out?"

"I recently paid him a visit."

"Why?"

"Because of what your prisoner said in the interrogation."

"I don't understand. He didn't mention Trivette."

"He kind of did."

Giacomo, frustrated, said, "Come on, Dad. Get to the point."

"The prisoners last word was 'Sha . . .'"

It took a moment, and then Giacomo understood.

"*Sharif* is what the prisoner tried to say?"

"Yes."

The bell at St. Peter's Basilica rang. Giacomo and Sergio in unison said, "No papa."

Sergio's phone rang, and he checked its screen. "You guys want some coffee?" he asked.

"Sure," replied Arnaud.

"Holy shit, Dad! He admitted that he kidnapped Emily?"

"Yes. That investigation I told you—"

"Trivette and the EU?"

"Yes, everything legal in their business transactions. We tried to put the pieces together, with no success and plenty of questions. How did an extremist become the leader of the European Union? How did he rise to power? Who else was involved? Then we infiltrated his organization."

"A person close to Trivette?"

"No, too risky—a janitor."

"A janitor?"

Sergio returned with a coffeepot in hand. Giacomo noticed a hurried glance from Sergio.

"Everything okay?"

"Yeah, sure."

"The janitor?"

"He's not your everyday janitor. Let's say he has an extraordinary talent for acquiring information."

"In other words, he's a computer expert and well versed in eavesdropping techniques."

"Exactly, my son. What puzzled us was how Eten knew when to make investments that always coincided with a major world event."

"We discovered the same thing. We traced it to my father's first journal."

"So did we."

"How? Do you have a copy?"

"Yes. Our man found two journals in Trivette's office."

"*Two?*"

"Yes, one your father's. The other one was written by a different person."

"How did you determine it was Dad's?" Anger welled up in Giacomo.

"I have old letters from your father. Besides, who else could it be other than your Paolo?"

"True. The other one, did you read it?"

"Yes. It was like your father's."

"Really? And there was only one journal of my father's?"

"Yes. We believe Trivette does have the stolen journal. We're searching for it."

They were silent for a moment. Giacomo paced the room. The gaze of the men followed him. Sergio's cell phone beeped.

"He needs to know the future, and my father's second journal will give Trivette that information. Without that, he'll become powerless," Giacomo said.

"Providing the second one is like the first."

"Good point."

"Here—look at this."

Sergio gave his smartphone to Giacomo, whose face changed color as he read. His anger escalated as he gripped the instrument. His knuckles turned white.

"Please don't throw it," Sergio said.

Giacomo's eyes blazed. *Why now?* And something else about the email bothered him. He scrolled through it again until he saw it: message sent from cell phone origin Monte Cassino. He gathered his thoughts and handed the phone back to Sergio.

"Who sent you this email?"

"A friend in the government."

"Really?" Giacomo gave Sergio a hard look, and he lowered his head.

"What did the email say?"

Giacomo snapped back from his thoughts and turned to Arnaud. "Eten is behind the assassinations of Tarmac and Tom's cousin Saleem. The shooting down of Tony's airplane and probably my kidnapping."

Giacomo walked over to the window, turned, and leaned against the pane. Troubled by the email, more uneasiness settled over him. "No doubt about where the stolen journal is now." He gave a stern glare at his father-in-law. "The Eiffel Tower business?"

"The incident in Paris is a setup, and we're trying to push—how do you say?" He tilted his head. "Trivette's buttons."

"A setup?"

"Oui. We had no intention of assassinating him. Our plan is to put him in a corner."

"Rats don't do well in corners."

"That's why we must act now."

"When you say 'we,' I understand the governments of Spain, Italy, and France—but how far does this reach?"

"As you are close to President-elect Maro, I am with the three heads of state. Giacomo, we need your help—your technology."

"Technology?"

"Yes. Trivette's phone uses a high-frequency satellite transmitter. Our problem is we can't decrypt it. I believe you can."

Giacomo rubbed his belly as he ambled to the conference table. He grabbed the back of a chair. "Yes, we can. Sergio, fill him in. I need to go to the bathroom again." He glanced at his father-in-law. "Bad stomach day."

"You should eat more French food, my son."

"Funny, Dad."

As Giacomo walked the hallway to the bathroom, his mind became a frenzy of anxiety. He staggered as he made his way to the restroom. His thoughts were overtaken by a video image of the scene with Arnaud and Sergio. *Giacomo watched the passage of time. He saw himself. He saw Sergio leave the room and return with the coffee. Sergio's eyes were worried. What did Sergio know? He thought of Arnaud's words: "Providing the second one is like the first." Giacomo saw himself read the email, and the words "Monte Cassino" caused a cold sweat.*

"Senor DeLaurentis, are you okay?"

Giacomo shook off his nausea. The picture in his mind disappeared. Giacomo gazed at the Swiss Guard, his eyes focused on the opposite wall. He inhaled deeply.

"Yeah, I'm okay. Thank you."

Giacomo entered the restroom under the careful watch of the security man.

Chapter 88

GIACOMO ARRANGED FOR an apartment in Vatican City for Arnaud. With Cardinal Andrew in conclave, he relied on Sergio's government contacts to help facilitate the housing request. The father-daughter reunion was tearful.

That night, Emily sat opposite her husband as she ate pasta fagiole. The expectant woman placed her spoon on the plate.

"Thank you."

"For what?"

"Helping Dad."

Giacomo tilted his head and shrugged. "You understand that your father was—or still is—being hunted by every law enforcement agency in Europe. Except maybe here in Italy."

"I know. Now I have to worry about two people that I love."

"There's nothing to worry about, Em. It's a setup. Your father is undercover."

"Ha! Nothing to worry about? Undercover? Come on, Giacomo. Whoever they are, they want you dead. And now they want my father dead or arrested. Damn it—I just don't understand you." Emily shoved the bowl of food toward him. She pushed the chair with her foot and walked into the bedroom as tears streamed down her face.

"Em, come on, sit."

"No—you're such a jerk."

Giacomo went to the bedroom where Emily rested on her side.

Giacomo sat by his wife and placed his hand on her arm. "I'm sorry, Em. You're right. I didn't mean to . . ."

Emily sobbed, "I . . . I . . . love you, Giacomo. I don't want to be a widow."

"You're not going to be a widow. I'm not going anywhere. This will end soon. We must be patient. After the inauguration in January, all will be normal; we'll be back home in New Haven. I'll sell the business and retire."

"Yeah, sure."

"I promise, honey."

"Will you nap with me? I'm exhausted."

"Sure." Giacomo curled up next to Emily, placing his arm on her stomach. He could feel the flutter of his two sons in her belly. He kissed her neck. "Love you, Em."

*　*　*

Giacomo awoke to the sound of banging on the apartment door. He mumbled the words "Monte Cassino." He was in a dead sleep. "Yes, hold on. I'm coming." He reached for the cell phone. "We've been asleep for two hours."

"Mr. DeLaurentis?" the Swiss Guard asked.

"Yes, Roberto?"

"*Bene.* General, I need you to come with me, please."

"Sure. Where are we going?"

"Please, follow me, sir."

"Give me a minute." Giacomo went back to the bedroom. Emily was still asleep. He wrote a note and placed it on the table. "Let's go. Is everything all right?"

"No, a problem with Cardinal Angeloni."

"What happened?"

"He's very ill and asked for you."

Giacomo grabbed his jacket. Andrew had become the older brother that he never had. His heart palpitated in dread at the thought: *My sister . . . and now Andrew.* The two men hurried out of the residence and took a left along the Piazza del Forno. The guard escorted him to the Sistine Chapel. They entered a dim hallway. Giacomo's anxiety grew. The man stopped at a door, unlocked it, and opened the entrance.

"Mr. DeLaurentis, someone will be here shortly to take you to the cardinal."

"Yeah." Giacomo entered. The room was small, the walls red with an arching white ceiling. A kneeler was positioned in front of a crucifix. Priestly vestments hung on a rack in the corner. The military man felt awkward. He glanced at his watch. To the right, another entrance. On the left, a painting of St. Peter. As he waited, he recalled the conversation with Arnaud and Sergio. The email Sergio received with the words "Monte Cassino" visited his thoughts. *Eten is the leader . . . Essex . . . Trivette . . . Who else is involved?* The nagging questions ended with the sound of the door behind him creaking open.

"They call this place the Room of Tears."

"Andrew, what . . ." As he turned, his mouth fell open in shock. "Your Holiness." His eyes filled with tears. "I thought you were sick."

"Only a ruse, my brother."

"I . . . I . . ." Giacomo was speechless.

"I am just an ordinary man, Giacomo."

Giacomo stared at Andrew, who was dressed in the pontifical white outfit. The man chosen to sit in St. Peter's chair walked over to him. In the distance, the church bells of Rome rang out. The people cheered in the square. The words "Papa! Papa!" echoed from the pilgrims. The two men hugged.

"I wanted you, my brother, to be the first. I'll explain later. You and your family will join the celebration tonight?"

Giacomo was still in shock. "Yeah, sure . . . whatever you say."

"Giacomo, I'm just an ordinary man. I must go." The pope turned. With his white cassock flowing, he exited the Room of Tears.

Chapter 89

THE NEWS TRAVELED around the globe in a flash. The first pope from the United States—His Holiness Peter Andrew I, the man responsible for uniting the Christian churches.

To the dismay of the voting cardinals, the new pope chose to have his first dinner with a few close friends, including Giacomo and his family, Arnaud, and Sergio and his wife, Carmella, dressed in black, still mourning her son.

Andrew sat next to Giacomo, who tapped his wine glass with a spoon. He stood. "To my friend, my brother. By the way, what do I call you *now*? Pete, Andy, what?"

"Giacomo DeLaurentis, where on earth did you come from? He is the pope."

Andrew laughed at Victoria's admonition.

Emily rolled her eyes. "I can't take him anywhere."

"I am just an ordinary man. You are my family. However, Giacomo, you cannot call me Andrew in public. I don't know if the title Your Holiness is suitable, for who in this world is truly holy?"

"May I continue?" Giacomo lifted his glass. "To our brother Andrew. May God our Father in heaven fill you with His wisdom and His love for His people. May you guide our church and world in peace, love, and happiness."

Everyone ogled Giacomo and said almost in unison, "Where did that come from?"

"What?" He shrugged his shoulders.

"Thank you, Giacomo, for the kind words."

"You're welcome, Andrew." Giacomo addressed the dinner guests. "For your information, I do pray. In fact, I was in the chapel the other day. Right, Andrew?"

"Yes, you were, my friend."

"Your Holiness . . ."

"Sergio, will you ever learn? His name is Andrew."

Everyone laughed.

"Yes, Sergio."

"The rumor was Cardinal Adadayo would be the next pope. What happened?"

"Apparently, 119 cardinals didn't think so."

"How many cardinals voted?"

"One hundred twenty. I voted for Adadayo."

"Wow, a landslide. Is that why the first seven votes yielded no pope?"

"Not really, Giacomo. I turned it down seven times."

"What do you mean, turned it down?" Rio said.

"After the votes are counted, the elected is asked if he wants to be pope. I said no. Every time we voted, I was elected. So, after the seventh time, I said yes."

"Why did you say no?"

"Victoria, I'm just an ordinary man. I'm not infallible. I make mistakes, as we all do. How can I be the pope? Then I came to realize that, for whatever reason, God wants me on Peter's throne—so what am I to do?"

"How did you pick your name?"

"The cardinals were adamant that my name be Peter, representing the first pope, and Andrew, who established the first church. So, I agreed to be called Peter Andrew."

"Well, congratulations, Peter Andrew. You'll be a great pope."

"Thank you, Giacomo." He picked up a glass of water and took a sip. "Rio, how are you feeling?"

Rio rubbed the back of her head and then her right temple. "Much better now. I had a meltdown the other day. I was confused. I'm doing better, I think."

"Rio, believe me, you'll be back to your spunky self. Like the doctor said, it will take a while."

His sister lowered her head. Three nuns with seven staff members carried trays with dishes of food.

"Sisters, would you care to join us for dinner?"

Shocked at the pope's invitation, they each turned down his kind offer.

"Nice try," Giacomo said.

They finished their dinner of fresh pasta and baked Tuscan chicken. The dishes were cleared and replaced with fresh fruit, assorted cheeses, and nuts.

The pope wiped his mouth with a white monogrammed cloth napkin. "Being locked up in the conclave the last couple of days has kept me from the news. Arnaud?"

"Yes, Your Holiness?"

Andrew accepted the formality. "I understand you're a wanted man."

"Sorry to say, yes. We made arrangements with the Italian government to keep me in hiding."

"Well, you're protected here in Vatican City as well. Can you share what is going on?"

Giacomo, Sergio, and Arnaud eyed one another. "Emily, why don't you take Mom, John, and Carmella back to our place. We'll update Andrew."

"Giacomo, I'm going to go with them. I'm tired."

"No problem, Rio. Sleep well, feel better."

"Feel better? I'm fine, you jackass," Rio snarled through clenched teeth.

Giacomo lowered his head at his sister's admonition. He glanced at Andrew and mouthed an apologetic, "I'm sorry."

Escorted by two Swiss Guards, the group exited the dining room as the remaining men moved closer to the pope.

Chapter 90

GIACOMO, SERGIO, AND Arnaud explained to the new pope what had occurred over the past week. They kept nothing from him. There was no reason to—as a guest of Vatican City, Giacomo believed he had an obligation to be forthright. Forty minutes passed. Orange peels and cracked nutshells lay on the white tablecloth.

"You think Dean Essex is involved with Trivette?"

"I believe so," Giacomo responded to Andrew's question.

"Arnaud, what's Trivette's motive?"

"Rule the world."

"Rule the world? How does that connect him to wanting Rio dead?"

Giacomo pushed back from the table and walked to the opposite end. He leaned on a chair, stretched his back. "I don't know."

The men sat silently; only the sound of a cracking nutshell broke the quiet. The pope poured sparkling water into a glass and took a sip.

Sergio spoke first. "I had a conversation with our prime minister today. He confirmed the three heads of state for France, Italy, and Spain are concerned about Trivette. His ability to manipulate the world's currency has them worried. Reports are that he wants to change the name from European Union to World Union. One true world order. Sound familiar, Giacomo?"

"Shit—sorry, Andrew. The two helicopter pilots?"

"Two helicopter pilots?"

"The two men who shot Tony's airplane out of the sky. When they were interrogated, they mentioned 'one true world order.'" Giacomo returned to his seat next to Andrew.

"Don't forget the prophecy," Sergio said.

Andrew sat back. "Prophecy? World order? It sounds biblical."

"More like a James Bond movie." Giacomo's vision blurred. An image rose in his mind and then faded.

"Giacomo, are you with us?"

He shook off the vivid image of a world that had gone dark. "Sorry, Andrew. I believe somebody is manipulating Eten Trivette." Giacomo was struck by his own words. His mind was being opened to another possibility. *How could that be? And why?* What was occurring? He left the questions unanswered for the time being.

"I disagree," Arnaud chimed in. "This is all Eten. Trivette is evil. His one wish is to control the world. Guess what, gentlemen? He's almost there. We need to stop him."

"How do we stop him, Dad?"

"Other than killing the bastard . . . no idea."

"We can't kill him."

"I understand, Your Holiness, but what else can we do? Before I left France, the chatter between our intelligence agencies was just that—assassination."

"We can't allow that to happen." Andrew's voice was stern.

Giacomo caught the disturbed glare from his friend and returned the look with a questioning face as if to ask, *What can I do?*

"I have a bad feeling with regard to Trivette—but what if his idea is right? It could help the world."

"Sergio, an evil person can do good as well. Right, Andrew?"

The pope said nothing as he listened.

"Maybe he's redeemed himself."

"Come on, Sergio. That's a bunch of baloney."

"Everyone needs redemption, Arnaud. None of us is perfect. Does he believe in God?" Sergio asked.

"Even the devil believes in God," said Andrew.

"Do you understand the problem now? We feel hopeless."

"Why?"

"We're going up against one of the most powerful men in the world. He can destroy the economies of the nations—or better yet, control them."

"I understand, Giacomo. It sounds dire. However, we should see where the investigation leads us. What about your friend—President-elect Tom Maro?"

"He'll help, but he's not in office yet. Richardson is our only hope, or we wait until January—the inauguration. I need this to end. So does Emily . . . so does the world."

"Trivette used the events in Paolo's journal to capitalize on the tragedies. He realized the terrorist routine was fruitless, as it only unified the people." Arnaud's face was swollen with pent-up anger. The rage seethed from his lips. "I heard him say the way to abolish democracy is to build upon man's greed—his selfishness—then take away their wealth and come back as the savior." Arnaud's voice escalated to a fever pitch. "That is what he will do." With a sweeping arc of his hands, he said, "You'd better be on board and realize the man is evil. He's out to destroy us!"

"Dad, calm down. If what you said is true, then he didn't sanction the assassinations. Believe me, another person is behind this." Giacomo sat back, astonished at his own words. *Another person is behind this.*

"What you're saying, Giacomo, is that he's a puppet."

"Yes."

"He's no puppet."

Arnaud stood in disgust. He mumbled a few words concerning Emily and left the room.

"Excuse my father-in-law. Trivette masterminded Emily's kidnapping. Dad didn't like him to begin with, and now . . ."

"He wants justice."

"You're right, Sergio. I'm sure you can understand that."

Sergio lowered his head. Arnaud came back. An awkward silence filled the room. Giacomo was surprised by his father-in-law's outburst, but it was understandable. What else was bothering him?

He couldn't pinpoint the issue. *Why did I say another person was behind Trivette? Is it just a hunch, or something to do with that brief vision?* He tried to remember.

Arnaud interrupted the contemplation. "Giacomo, tell him your plan against El Diablo."

"The devil . . . a strong term, Arnaud."

"Yes but true, Your Holiness. He is from the devil."

"I hope not."

"Arnaud's theories—to him, Trivette is the Antichrist."

"The book of Revelation."

"Really, Andrew."

"Why not? It's going to happen."

"We've gone on a tangent here. Let's get back on topic." A plan formulated in Giacomo's mind as he glanced at Arnaud. "Dad, if you agree?" Arnaud gave a silent nod. "Okay, you and I are going to Washington right after Christmas . . ." Giacomo explained the strategy. The men listened. "The biggest problem for us is securing safe passage to and from the States."

"Sounds dangerous. Can you implicate Trivette?"

"In time, Andrew. We need Essex to fill in the pieces. He's a threat because he can manipulate Richardson, and we must stop that. I'm confident he knows Rio is alive. I caught her talking to someone the other day on her cell. I'm sure it was him. We tried to trace her calls but failed. To be honest, I haven't figured a way to get her phone without her going ballistic on me. Once we have Essex, we can get some answers. I'm sure his responses will lead us to Trivette." Giacomo paused. His face changed color as his tolerance diminished. "What he did to Rio . . . I can't wait to see him face-to-face."

"Did you tell her about Dean?"

"No. She's still so unstable. You saw how she was tonight. I don't believe she can accept the betrayal. We are taking a risk that she'll continue to speak with him, and that's fine for now. But let's be honest. There's no way he's stupid enough to try anything while she's in Vatican City."

"I hope you're right," Andrew said.

"Our thought, Holiness . . ."

"Arnaud, please, you can call me Andrew."

"Thank you, Your Holiness. Once Tom Maro becomes president, the four countries will unite and work together to get rid of Trivette."

"Providing he isn't assassinated?" Sergio said.

"Yes," Arnaud said.

"You can count on the Vatican's help. Gentlemen, it's been a big day. I'm exhausted and need to go to bed."

The four men embraced Andrew. He blessed them as he called upon the Holy Spirit to guide them.

Chapter 91

The Next Morning

GIACOMO DIALED TOM Maro's private number.

"Good morning, Giacomo."

"Morning, Tom. Sorry for the early call." There was a no-nonsense tone to Giacomo's voice.

"I'm used to it. What is it, ten thirty your time?"

"Yep. Sergio and Arnaud Chambery are here."

The speakerphone crackled. "Good morning, gentlemen. Arnaud, I spoke with your president yesterday. I share their concern. I'm sorry that you're the scapegoat."

"Merci, Monsieur Maro. We must stop this."

"We will." Maro yawned. "Sorry. I didn't sleep much after I read Giacomo's email last night."

"Neither did we."

"Who's the traitor?"

Giacomo took a deep breath. "Dean Essex."

"What? Can't be. Are you sure?"

"Yes—he's collaborating with Richardson."

"*Richardson?* I . . . I don't understand. I'll have him arrested."

"No, Tom, you can't. What about due process?"

"What do you mean?" Maro's voice filled with anger. "Him—Richardson—why, damn it? Tell me."

"Essex is blackmailing Richardson. He's able to manipulate the president. Tom, we're confident he's behind the assassination and the shooting down of Rio's plane."

"The bastard killed my cousin."

"Tom, listen . . ."

"Son of a bitch! I could kill him."

"I understand, Tom, but you gotta relax. Please listen. We have a plan."

"Give me a moment."

"Sure."

The three men eyed one another. Giacomo sat back in the chair.

"What's he doing?"

"Let's hope he's not making any phone calls. If he is . . ."

A knock on the door. Two Swiss Guards in business suits entered, followed by Pope Peter Andrew. The three men rose. "Your Holiness."

Andrew addressed his protectors. "You can leave us now." The men left the office and took positions on either side of the door to stand watch outside. The new pope wore the ordinary black clothing that denoted his priestly status.

"Andrew, where's the white outfit?"

"I'm the pope. I decided to wear this." In his hand, he held a nine-by-twelve manila envelope.

The crackling of the speakerphone interrupted the conversation. "I'm sorry, Giacomo."

"No problem, Tom. His Holiness Peter Andrew the First is with us. Andrew, President-elect Thomas Maro."

"Allahu Akbar—God is great, Mr. President."

"The peace of Christ be with you, Your Holiness. Congratulations."

"Thank you. Please call me Andrew, for I am only a man."

"Call me Tom, for I too am only a man."

"Yeah, I'm a man too . . ." Giacomo shook his head as he chuckled. "Sorry, I forget who I'm speaking with."

"That was funny, my friend," Andrew said.

"Tom, I briefed His Holiness on the situation."

"Yes, I'm aware of the danger that exists. I take it, Tom, they told you."

"Yes, I'm disgusted."

"Be strong in your faith, my friend. God will guide us through this."

"I shall, Andrew. This world we live in—I can't put it into words."

"I know what you mean."

Giacomo noticed a gaze of concern on Andrew's face. The pope squinted in concern as he spoke. "Giacomo, I have doubts about you traveling to the States. Why do you need to go?"

Giacomo grimaced for a moment. "I'm confident that when we leave Rome, we will be followed. I'm hoping that our people will be able to trace our pursuers."

"So, you're going to offer yourself up as targets? Or is there something else?"

Giacomo was silent.

"My friend, pride can be a killer . . . and revenge even more destructive—it kills the soul."

"Okay, so you caught me. I want to see Essex face-to-face. This might be my only time before he's handed over to the authorities."

"Promise me you won't cause him harm."

"I won't. I just wanna see his face."

"All right." His Holiness reached inside the envelope and pulled out two booklets. "In my hand are two passports. One for you, Giacomo; the other for you, Arnaud. You both are now citizens of Vatican City with the titles of emissary of the Holy See. This will ensure safe travels in and out of any country without reprisal or arrest. These passports carry complete diplomatic immunity throughout the world."

"Tom, this is the second time that Giacomo has been speechless."

"Truly a miracle. Are you sure he didn't pass out?"

"Very funny, gentlemen. Andrew, I can't believe you did this."

"I did it more for your wife than for you. Emily doesn't need to be a widow."

"Not gonna happen, Andrew."

"Tom, I hope after your inauguration you'll pay me a visit."

"I look forward to it, Andrew."

The door to the conference room opened. A Swiss Guard in a three-piece suit entered. "Your Holiness."

"My time is no longer my own, gentlemen. We'll get together soon."

The three men rose.

"One more thing, Giacomo. Vatican bodyguards will be with you when you travel to the States—standard protocol between our countries."

"Thanks, Andrew."

The Swiss Guards snapped to attention as the pope stood by the door. He exited the makeshift office.

"Tom, you still there?"

"Yes. Appreciate the introduction—his voice sounds so familiar. All right, so what's the plan?"

"Arnaud and I are traveling to the States the day after Christmas."

"Isn't that risky? I share the concern of your friend."

Giacomo didn't want to have another discussion about his reasoning. He simply replied, "Maybe . . ."

"What's your plan?"

"We'll explain when we meet with you."

"What do you want me to do with Essex? I don't want him here."

"You need to act as normal as possible. Tom, can you do that?"

"I can. But why?"

"Trust me, Tom, I'll tell you when we meet. Sorry for the unwelcome news."

"No issues. Essex was getting on my nerves. Giacomo, Merry Christmas to you and your family."

"You as well, Tom."

"Thank you." The phone conversation ended.

"He celebrates Christmas?" Sergio asked.

"Yes. His wife and children are Catholic. He believes in the one true God. Tom is well versed in Judaism, Christianity, and Islam."

Chapter 92

Christmas Eve

FOUR DAYS HAD passed since the conversation with Tom Maro. Security arrangements were being made for Giacomo and Arnaud to travel to the United States as diplomatic envoys of the Vatican See. The family would attend Christmas Eve dinner with the pope and then midnight Mass.

"Giacomo, where's your mother's present?"

"Under the tree," Giacomo yelled from the bedroom. "Dinner in fifteen minutes."

"Yes, my dear."

Giacomo exited the bedroom dressed in a navy-blue suit with a tie adorned with pictures of Santa Claus. His hair had grown, and the mane now covered his ears. With his trimmed beard, he looked more like an Italian national than an American general. Emily was by the Christmas tree—the colored lights reflected off her radiant face. She wore a blue dress with white snowflakes around the hem.

"You're beautiful." Giacomo approached his wife, wrapped his arms around her, and whispered in her ear, "I love you, Em."

"I feel fat, but I love you too. I can't wait for these little guys to come into the world." She gave him a playful push with her tummy and stepped back.

"Em, I want to make sure you don't have a problem with me going to the States."

"Giacomo, I already told you I didn't. Now come on, or we'll be late for dinner."

"We don't want to keep His Holiness waiting."

"Giacomo."

"I know, honey. He's the pope."

The couple gathered their gifts, left the Christmas tree lights on, and walked out of their apartment. The customary Italian dinner of seven fishes was served in the papal dining room. Presents were exchanged. Emily was tired, so husband and wife went back to the apartment and skipped midnight Mass.

*   *   *

Rio's Room, Later That Night

"It was nice, Dean—thanks for asking. What time is dinner at your sister's house tomorrow?... Seven thirty? You should be on your way... I'm exhausted, I need to go to bed... It could be the time zone change, but I doubt it... Rome—I'm not supposed to tell you that, though... Stop, I can't tell you... Yes, Giacomo was at dinner. Why?... You'll meet him when I get back... No, I have to go. We'll chat tomorrow... What?... Oh, I love you too! Bye."

The tracer pinpointed the call—Vatican City.

Chapter 93

GIACOMO LAY AWAKE as his wife slept. His heart filled with dread, he was overcome by fear. He jumped out of bed, not able to breathe. He trotted into the living room barefoot. The cold floor eased his distress.

His heart pounded. Giacomo could feel his blood as the liquid pulsated through his arteries. He plugged in the lights of the yuletide tree and sat in a high-back red upholstered chair. Giacomo tried to calm himself; he placed his hands on his face, trenched in deep sorrow, and wept. A vision erupted in his mind's eye, taking him to an unfamiliar place. *Volcanoes scarred the planet. Earthquakes broke the land masses in two. Cities were darker than black. Throngs of people packed into churches, synagogues, and mosques. The evilness of humanity invaded the synaptic structures of his brain. Thrown back in time and then forward, he witnessed the sin of humankind. His body panicked, convulsed at the horrific images. When he could take no more—peace. The awfulness vanished.*

Chapter 94

"**M**ERRY CHRISTMAS, EM."

Giacomo leaned against the window. The day was cloudy. Throughout Christendom, the birth of Jesus was being celebrated. He gazed outside.

"Up early?" She kissed her husband on the cheek.

Giacomo was distant. "I couldn't sleep."

"How come?"

"I don't know . . . stupid stuff in my head."

"Do you want to share?"

"Our world makes no sense to me. Our life? This is not what I wanted, and this is not what you want. We're hidden away from life." Emily placed her hand on Giacomo's arm as he continued. "I remember Dad told me life should be simple, filled with peace and love. I think he was delusional. Love—yes. Peace—how? Simple—shit, nothing is simple anymore. I don't understand why. Dad had this knowledge, yet why didn't he do anything?"

"He couldn't, mi amore."

"What do you mean?"

"Because no one would believe him. Did you ever consider that maybe this is meant to be?"

"Andrew said the same." Giacomo shook his head. "Meant to be—this craziness?" Giacomo turned to Emily. "Remember when Dad and Sydney got married in Ottati?"

"Of course. It was beautiful."

"Dad and I were standing by the railing. We didn't speak. The smell of the fresh air added to the brilliant hues of the green trees, the orange and red rooftops. He spread his arms out over the valley. 'Giacomo, this happened in God's time.' I was puzzled and asked him what he meant, and he said, 'In God's time, everything is created. God is the ultimate timekeeper, not us. Though we would like to control our lives, we can't. We make the choices, yes, but for us, if it's not in God's plan, we get redirected.' I said, 'So we're puppets?' 'No, we are gifted with unique gifts to be used according to the will of God for the betterment of His people. We can always say no. I happened to say yes.' He grabbed my shoulders, looked me square in the eyes, and said, 'One day, you'll be asked to say yes.' You and Andrew are right, Em. This is meant to be; it's part of the plan." He forced a smile, gave his wife a kiss on the lips. "You're the best."

"Thank you."

"Let's go to the Piazza Navona. What do you say?"

"Do you think it'll be safe? Can we do that?"

"Why not? We'll have a security detail with us."

*   *   *

Giacomo and Emily trudged through the throngs of people in St. Peter's Square. The crowd gathered to listen to the new pope's Christmas message. The clouds swept by as the late-morning sun cast its brightness on Rome. The temperature was mild. The afternoon sun would warm the city of seven hills to a mild sixty-three degrees.

"Do you remember how to get there?"

"Sure. Do you?"

"Barely."

"Em, it feels good to be in the fresh air—free to walk wherever we want."

"Well, almost free." Emily tilted her head behind her.

"Oh, the Swiss Guards. Well, all right—almost free."

Giacomo grabbed Emily's hand as they crossed Corso Vittorio Emanuele II. Their bodyguards followed. As they entered the piazza, they were greeted by a man who sold warm chestnuts. His pan full, they roasted on an open flame. Children played with their new toys. The centuries-old courtyard was surrounded by small restaurants and outdoor cafés. Italian Christmas music filled the air. Life's problems were erased by the merriment of the season.

Chapter 95

December 26

THE GULFSTREAM G750—N7PD—LANDED at Washington National Airport and was directed by air traffic control to the cargo ramp. Airport handlers met the airplane, attached a tow bar, and tugged the jet into the hangar. The forty-foot-high doors clanked shut. With the plane hidden from potential prying eyes, the stair door hummed as it opened. A black SUV with tinted windows and Vatican diplomatic flags pulled up. Arnaud, Giacomo, and the flight crew exited, followed by two Vatican security agents.

"Tell Tony I like the new digs."

"Be careful, Giacomo."

"Will do, Pat."

"Danny, thanks for the gun."

"No worries. We'll be standing at the ready should an issue arise."

"Thank you." Giacomo shook their hands.

The back door of the SUV opened. As he entered the vehicle, his friend Colonel Jason Vandercliff and two other men greeted him.

"Nice to see you're alive."

"Yeah, I'm glad too."

"You remember Captain Dave Carrano and Commander Don Ham?"

"I do. Gentlemen, great to be with you again."

"Same here, General."

"I like the beard and the long hair. You should be on the cover of a magazine."

"Funny, Jason. Are we set for tomorrow?"

"Yes, President-elect Maro has arranged to meet Richardson privately. You'll be part of his security detail."

"And Arnaud?"

"An advisor on foreign intelligence."

"Will Essex be there?"

"No. Tom promised to keep him busy."

"Once you're on the White House grounds, there will be no place for you to escape if you can't convince him to turn on Essex."

Giacomo looked at his father-in-law. "It's the only way it will work, Dad."

"I know."

"How many people are tailing us?"

"We counted three—as expected. The police will escort us to the Vatican embassy."

"Any idea yet how they discovered us?"

"No, not yet."

"Is the plan still the same—making a stop along the way?"

"Yes, the traffic jam will give you and Arnaud two minutes."

"You have our clothes?"

"Right here."

"Arnaud, put these on."

"Here are the full-face masks. You'll be able to communicate with each other through a Bluetooth link. Oxygen tanks are in place."

"How long of a wait?"

"Close to five hours."

"*Five hours?* Are you crazy? It was only supposed to be for an hour at most. Why the change?"

"Sorry, Giacomo. Trust me. Issues cropped up that need to be addressed. We want to make sure our enemies believe you're at the embassy. That way, you can meet with Tom in the cloak of darkness."

"Cloak of darkness? You're reading way too many thrillers. All right, but let's hurry."

The vehicle crossed the Memorial Bridge. To the right, work crews repaired the Lincoln Memorial. The Washington Monument still lay crippled on its side. The iconic structure toppled in 2017, not able to withstand the fifth earthquake in the region in six years.

They turned right and entered Rock Creek Parkway, sandwiched between a police car in front and Vatican security forces. They traveled in the right lane. A car with two teenagers slowed, and they tried to peer through the darkened windows. The squad car sounded its siren. The officer with his hand out the window motioned the car to move ahead.

"We're almost there, Giacomo. Traffic is slowing."

"How are we going to do this?" Arnaud said.

"By good ol' American ingenuity, Dad. Explain it to him, Jason."

Jason opened his laptop, and the screen came alive. "This is where we are. This flashing ring is our drop point. With the traffic, it will take us five minutes. Once we are over it, I will activate the sequence."

"Sequence?"

"Watch your feet."

He pushed a button. The floor of the SUV slid open, revealing a steel plate beneath the base of the chassis. The sound of air and the smell of asphalt filled the Chevy.

"When we're directly over the point, that iron slab will be placed on top of the cover. An electrical current will magnetize the metal. The winch will tuck the manhole cover under the vehicle behind my seat, and both of you will descend into the sewer. Once you're secured, we'll take your stunt doubles—Dave and Don—to the embassy."

"Colonel, we're ready."

"Have fun, gentlemen."

"Yeah, thanks. Don't forget us."

"We won't."

The two men climbed down the ladder into the sewer where they found two oxygen bottles and a flashlight before a clank of the manhole cover sealed them in darkness.

Chapter 96

FOR NEARLY FIVE hours, Giacomo and Arnaud sat in the sewer, neither of them happy.

"Didn't I say this was like a James Bond movie? All these gizmos and gadgets."

"At least we have masks. The real 007 would be dressed in a suit, smoking a cigarette. We're stuck in the bowels of Washington, DC, like the Greeks when they hid in the Trojan horse."

Giacomo chuckled at Arnaud's sense of humor.

"Good analogy, Dad—Trojan horse. Our situation is worse. We're in a sewer with rats and poop. All the Greeks worried about was body odor."

Arnaud laughed. Giacomo considered what his father-in-law said. They sat on a ledge while their feet dangled in two inches of water. The beam of the flashlight cast an eerie glow on the black stained walls. *Trojan horse* whirled in his mind.

"Dad, can this be a Trojan horse?"

"What do you mean?"

"Are we being played?"

"Played? I don't understand?"

"Maybe we're being used to take down Trivette."

"I think the fumes are getting to your brain. Trivette and his people are bad and deserve to die."

"We can't make this personal, Dad."

"Oui," Arnaud said in resignation. "Giacomo, listen—no matter what my feelings are, Trivette dies, and this all stops. You and Emily can live in peace."

"I understand, but there are still unanswered questions. The murdered monk, the email Sergio received, Alessio's death . . ."

"Alessio's death?"

"We had nothing to go on until Alessio died. Then we saw the video of the interrogation, the Richardson satellite phone . . ."

"What email?"

"Sergio received an email from an Italian government source saying Trivette was responsible."

"See, my son? The pieces are coming together, yes?"

"Could be. Why did Alessio keep the video from us?"

"I'm sure he had a reason."

"Exactly, but what didn't he want us to see?"

Giacomo didn't expect an answer, but his gut told him others were involved. More to come, he had no doubt. The scraping noise of the manhole cover being removed roused them. A light shone through the opened drain, a rope ladder dropped, and the men climbed out of the hole. Jason stretched his arm to help them into the SUV. Night had arrived; the bluish light of the car's instrument panel cast a glow on the men. They took their sealed masks off—a red ring imprinted around each of their faces.

"You two stink!"

"Thanks, Jason. I'll never do that again."

"We only have a couple of minutes."

Giacomo and Arnaud took off their outer clothes and threw them into the sewer. A

whirring noise sounded, and the opening in the floor closed. Giacomo rubbed his face. "Boy, that feels better."

Then he noticed there were four people in the vehicle. He tried to adjust his eyes to the darkness to determine who they were.

"Hello, Giacomo," the person in the front passenger seat said.

"What the f . . ." Giacomo tried to exit the car.

"Giacomo, Giacomo . . . relax."

Arnaud pulled his 9-mm handgun from his holster and aimed the muzzle at the president of the United States.

"Calm down, gentlemen, calm down," Jason said as he pointed *his* gun at Arnaud.

Chapter 97

As Giacomo scanned the passengers, a peace settled over him. He took his hand and placed it on Arnaud's arm. His father-in-law lowered the weapon.

"Hello, Tom. Hello, Mr. *President*." He made no effort to hide the disdain in his voice.

"Didn't mean to surprise you like that, Giacomo—but it was necessary."

"Sure, Tom." Giacomo's anger was not quelled. "I can't trust this scumbag."

In the orange glow of the streetlight, Giacomo recognized a change in the eyes of the president, a different intensity—a realization of truth. Richardson lowered his head. Giacomo sensed a deep sorrow, a profound regret. *Damn it, another one of Dad's gifts. Empathy is a soldier's worst enemy.* Richardson had been transformed. Jason tapped the driver on the shoulder, and the car sped forward.

"I'm sorry, Mr. President. I didn't mean . . ."

"No, Giacomo. I'm sorry. I betrayed my country and myself."

Giacomo flooded with emotion as he struggled with the empathic gift.

Tom spoke. "A couple of days ago, Jerry called and asked to meet for lunch. At first, I was skeptical. After we ate, Jerry passed me a note that said he couldn't speak. He gave me a tour around the White House grounds to avoid the listening devices."

"Listening devices?"

"Yes, General. The United States government is infiltrated by those who wish to destroy us. That is why we are meeting in a car and not at the Oval Office. There are few people we can trust."

"Giacomo, we had to sneak the president out of the White House tonight."

"Are we being paranoid, gentlemen?"

Richardson replied with a curt, "No. The FBI notified me today that the Fighters for Freedom Brigade is trying to remobilize. We can't take chances. We don't know who our enemies are. First—and I know you'll agree—we must rid ourselves of Trivette and his cohort."

"Aren't you one of them?"

"I never wanted to destroy the country. I wanted to *restore* the country, but it was too late."

"What do you mean, too late?"

"It started long ago, Giacomo. September 11, 2001. I was in my Senate office with the traitor Dr. Colin Payne, Bil Laden—an Uzbek national you now know as Eten Trivette—and one of the evilest persons I've ever met, an Israeli woman by the name of Nava Ben-Reuven."

"Nava Ben-Reuven?"

"Yes. Why?"

"We tied her to Essex. You're saying she was associated with Trivette?" Giacomo sat back.

"Yes."

"You don't have to worry about her anymore. She's dead," Giacomo said.

"Nava was the reporter who was killed at the press conference at my house," Maro interjected.

"What was she doing there?"

"No idea, Mr. President—other than she tried to discredit Tom," Giacomo replied.

"Did they find the killer?"

"Yeah—dead."

Richardson shook his head. "It should've happened a long time ago. I bet you Essex knows."

"Probably. So, what happened?"

"A relative newcomer to the Senate, I was being courted by various committee chairmen. Of those, Colin Payne, head of the National Security Council, approached me. Payne told me Nava and Bil were undercover operatives. I said nothing as he spoke—astounded by what I heard. The second World Trade Tower was hit when Payne's cell phone rang."

* * *

September 11, 2001

"That was that jackass Paolo DeLaurentis," Payne said.

"I told you he couldn't pinpoint the attack."

"That you did, Nava."

The fit and trim young senator muted the sound on the television. "Who is DeLaurentis? The name sounds familiar."

"A person you should be afraid of, Senator."

"Why is that?"

"When you become president, his son will destroy you."

"President? Please, Miss Ben-Reuven. I have no aspirations."

"You will," the dark-haired woman with slate-blue eyes said.

Richardson stared at the crazy woman. "Not interested."

"Oh, you will be president." Her face was long, out of proportion, with a tiny nose. Five foot eight and thin, Nava wore a black skirt with a white sweater. Her bare legs were as thin as toothpicks, whiter than paper. "Won't he, Bil?"

"As sure as you and I are sitting here."

"Colin, what's this shit?"

Bil pulled out a piece of paper from his coat jacket and handed the report to Richardson.

"What's this?" Richardson grabbed the paper. He started to sweat as he read.

"Relax, Jerry." Ben-Reuven had a Boston accent. "We know your life story from the first detail of your birth to—well, let's say . . ."

"Read the paper, Senator," said Bil.

"I did, and this is bullshit." Richardson threw the document back at Laden.

Nava approached Richardson. The senator was a head taller than she was. The hair on the back of his neck stood. His head began to ache. He tried to move away but couldn't. Her eyes met his.

"How would it appear to the world and your constituents if they discovered you were a sham? If they found out that their great senator is nothing more than a rapist?" She patted him on the shoulder. "Jer— why are you so upset? We can keep your secret. We just want you on our team. What do you say?"

Richardson stumbled for words, the headache gone. "I didn't rape her. Our relationship was consensual. I was seventeen. She was fifteen. We were in love."

"In love, Jer? Do you think the American people will believe that?"

The senator's face bulged with fury as he yelled, "Out of my office—now!"

Nava sat on the brown leather couch. She crossed her toothpick legs. With an impertinent smile and blazing eyes, she said, "Shut the hell up, you piece of donkey dung. You will do as we tell you. You, young man, do not have a choice." The sweetness of her voice was gone, and the words were sharp. Now she spoke with a Middle Eastern accent. "Tell him, Doctor."

Bil glanced at her, mouthing the words *donkey dung?* Nava shrugged.

"Senator Richardson, I apologize for my friends here. You do understand. We want nothing from you other than your cooperation when you're elected vice president and then president."

Nava said, "This will happen."

Richardson sat behind his desk, bewildered and fuming.

"Remember, Jerry, when I asked you to come on board at the NSC, I shared with you the young boy with the unique gifts—he knew things before they would happen."

"Yes, you showed me the video of him."

"His name was Paolo DeLaurentis."

"The billionaire who gave his money away?"

"Yes. Well, Nava here has the same gift but a little bit stronger." He held out his hand as he put a space between his thumb and index finger. "Whether or not you raped the girl doesn't matter. What the public perceives—whether right or wrong—is the issue. I can assure you my colleagues here didn't mean to threaten you. Nava wanted you to understand the implications if the information got into the wrong hands. No matter how innocent. Your career would surely be over. That's what she meant to say." He squinted at Nava with disdain. "We can make sure your story never goes public, and in return for that, we want you on our team. Right, Nava?"

"Yeah, whatever."

Bil chuckled at the admonishment. Nava elbowed him in the ribs.

"Why don't you at least consider the offer? Nava, tell Senator Richardson what will happen."

With contempt in her voice, Nava said, "Your wife and two children will be killed in a car accident this afternoon at four fifteen. They will be declared dead when they arrive at the hospital."

Richardson sat back in stunned disbelief, his face turning red.

"If you agree to be on the team by the time the ambulance reaches the hospital, they will have recovered—if not, then your family will be gone."

"Are you kidding me? You're all a bunch of crackpots." He reached for his phone. "Out of my office now before I call the Capitol police!"

Chapter 98

PRESIDENT RICHARDSON STOPPED his story as the SUV made a turn. Tears dripped on his shirt. Giacomo was shocked by what the president had said. *Another person with my father's gift?*

"Mr. President, what happened?"

"At four twenty, I received a phone call. My family had been in a car accident. Shocked and frightened, to say the least, I called Payne. He answered on the first ring. I agreed—I was scared shitless. And when I arrived at the hospital, they were alive with no scratches."

"So, you became a member of the NSC?"

"Yes."

"What happened next?"

"Nothing until Stalworth got elected. That's when I met the son-of-a-bitch Essex—the little troll. Dean was part of the Stalworth transition team—a minor employee with one mission, which was to acquire your father's journal. His name at the time was Foster Carrington. The arrogance of the piece of shit annoyed me—still does. Essex paid me a visit in my Senate office. He had the journal and threw it on my desk."

*   *   *

November 10, 2004

"That journal, Senator, has to go to Bil. You'll take it with you on your trip to Paris next week."

Richardson stared at the cocky wimp of a man. "Who are you—you little pissant?"

"Oh, I'm sorry, Jer. I thought you knew." Dean's voice squeaked as he spoke. "I'm your boss."

Richardson laughed. "My boss? I work for the American people, not you."

"Interesting. How are your wife and children? Recovered from that accident?"

"You little shit."

"I've been called worse. Senator, you'll be contacted when you're in Paris. Give the contact this book. Notice the seal and don't break it. You understand?"

"Get out of my office."

Essex turned on his heels. "By the way, don't screw up or your family might not be saved next time."

*   *   *

"So, *you* had my father's original journal?"

"Yes. I took it to the economic summit in Paris the following week. The maid at the hotel ended up being the contact. I gave it to her."

"How did you become the VP?"

"No idea. Waldron and I detested each other. We often battled on the Senate floor. Our ideologies were so different. One day, Arthur called and asked me. The chairman of the party recommended it. The next thing you know, I'm his running mate. When I remembered what that bitch told me on September 11—that I would be president of the United States . . ." Richardson lowered his head as a wave of regret swept over him.

"These people are evil, Giacomo. I became their accomplice because I didn't have the guts to fight. My contempt for Trivette and Essex fueled the anger within me. When I commanded you to come back to the States, I wasn't angry with you—I was mad at me. I hated myself. I'm tired of pretending, of always watching my step and making sure that when I speak, I don't betray my true feelings."

"What caused you to change?"

"My wife died . . . she became an alcoholic. She never recovered from the accident. The knowledge that her children almost died destroyed her. I want revenge. One day last week, Essex—"

"Slapped you."

"How did you know?"

"We had Tom's staff under surveillance. One of the drones recorded your conversation with Essex." Giacomo didn't feel the need to tell him he was also under the watchful eye of the remote flying machines.

The SUV made a quick jerk to the left followed by one to the right, throwing the occupants from one side than the other.

"What the . . ."

"Sorry, gentlemen—a deer in the road," the Secret Service agent said.

"Damn. Scared the hell out of me." Arnaud muttered words in French that nobody understood.

They laughed. It released the tension in the vehicle. A moment of intense silence accompanied the purr of the engine. The SUV came to a stop at a red light on Massachusetts Avenue.

"When did you find out Bil changed his name to Trivette?"

"Years later. After Payne died, Bil and Nava vanished. When the EU announced it had purchased the Iranian pipeline and introduced its new president, Eten Trivette, as the master architect . . . well, all I had to do was look at those hideous blue eyes. The rest is history."

"Do you want to make things right, Mr. President?"

"I do. I want to destroy them, but I'm fearful for my children. I'm president of the United States, and I'm scared shitless. I can't be protected forever. I've done enough harm."

"Tom, any objection that when you take office, BOET can protect the president and his family?"

"Not an issue."

Richardson's head bowed. "Thank you, Tom. I'm willing to accept the consequences of my actions. I wanna get these sons of bitches."

"We will. I have an idea." Giacomo explained his plan to Maro and Richardson.

"Will it work, Giacomo?"

"Yes, to a point, Mr. President. Will we be able to stop Trivette and his plans, whatever they are? Possibly. As for Essex—we've got the bastard red-handed."

"We have company, gentlemen," the Secret Service agent informed them as he unclipped his holster and pulled out his gun, placing it on his lap.

A squad car flashed its red, white, and blue lights. An obnoxious siren sounded, stopped, then sounded again. The SUV came to a stop prior to Observatory Circle. The police vehicle parked twenty feet behind.

Chapter 99

THE POLICE OFFICER stepped out of the squad car, his hand on his holster. He approached the right side of the SUV. The president rolled down his window. A second black SUV pulled up behind the police car.

"Yes, Officer?"

"Kindly step out . . ." He recognized the passenger and stepped back. "Are you?"

"Yes, I am."

The officer stuttered, "I'm sorry, Mr. President." He began to run back to his patrol vehicle.

Arnaud opened the left passenger door, his 9-mm drawn, and said something in French. The officer froze and turned, his gun drawn. Arnaud fired five shots into the cop's chest.

"What the hell! Arnaud?"

Giacomo jumped out, followed by Jason. They ran to the downed man. Members of BOET jolted out of the second Chevy. They aimed their automatic rifles with laser sights as they scanned the perimeter. "Stand down, gentlemen."

Arnaud followed "He's not police—he's an imposter."

"I popped the trunk—there are two dead cops inside! Come on, we need to go!" Giacomo said.

The three men ran back to the SUV and jumped in the vehicle.

"Come on, move—move!" Jason shouted to the driver.

The SUV came alive—lights flashed, sirens blared. The second SUV followed in close pursuit.

Arnaud commanded, "Turn those off. He's not here for your president. He's here for us. He's an assassin."

"Turn that off," Jason commanded. "Arnaud, how did you . . ."

"I recognized his face from Interpol."

"As expected, our enemies knew Arnaud and I are in the States, and they want us dead."

"And apparently they know you're not at the Vatican embassy," Maro said.

"True. Jason, call our cleanup team. Keep the bodies hidden until tomorrow after I leave. Our prime responsibility now is to protect the president and Tom. Driver, stop the car. This vehicle is dirty goods. Some type of a GPS tracker must have told them where we were. Tell the backup POTUS is coming on board." Giacomo leaned forward, his hand on Richardson's shoulder. "Don't worry, Jerry. Essex will disappear from your life tomorrow."

"Your words to God's ears, Giacomo."

"Time is short now, gentlemen. Our window of opportunity is closing fast. If Essex finds out that we're alive, we're screwed. How far are we from the Vatican embassy?"

"Less than two minutes, sir."

By the time Richardson cracked the door open, two BOET members were there to escort him to the waiting SUV.

"Jason, did you scan this vehicle for tracking devices?"

"Yes, earlier today."

"Guess that didn't work."

Giacomo pondered for a moment. "Gentlemen, do you feel like taking a walk?"

"Sure. Where to?" Maro asked.

"Vatican embassy."

"Why not? I can use a bit of fresh air," Maro said.

"Tom, when we arrive at the embassy, Vatican security will take you home. Jason, go directly to the maintenance garage and tear this thing apart. Find that tracking device."

"Will do."

"Dave and Don are still in place?"

"Yes. I spoke with them earlier."

"The three of us will meet you back at the base. I want to review the video footage at the facility. Jason, remember, the night's not over. They want us dead."

Giacomo, Tom, and Arnaud exited the SUV. Two BOET soldiers sandwiched the men as they walked. One in front, the other trailed the three. An unmarked military vehicle hugged the curb thirty feet behind. As they trekked up Massachusetts Avenue to the embassy, Giacomo processed the story President Richardson had told.

"Nava had the same gift as my father. That second journal your man discovered is likely hers. Do you think I can get a copy of it, Dad?"

"I'm one step ahead of you. I emailed our janitor friend. Should have it tomorrow."

"Janitor friend?"

"Nothing for you to worry about, Tom."

They arrived five minutes later. President-elect Maro departed in a Vatican diplomatic limousine followed by the BOET military vehicle. Arnaud stayed at the embassy under the protection of the Swiss Guard. Giacomo, Dave, and Don borrowed an embassy car from one of the service people and drove the Subaru to the BOET facility.

Chapter 100

THE MEN ARRIVED at the security gates of the BOET base in McLean, Virginia, at 10:39. The base housed seven buildings. A square-jawed, pug-nosed army sergeant approached the light blue Subaru Outback, an M20 carbine slung over his shoulder—his right index finger rested on the trigger. The muzzle of the gun faced downward. Yellow-orange lights illuminated the parking lot. A bright silver moon played hide-and-seek with the clouds.

The driver's window rolled down, and Giacomo flashed his credentials to the guard.

"General, sir." The sergeant saluted, his voice raspy and emotionless. With his left hand, he unclasped a holster and pulled out a retina scan gun.

"At ease, Sergeant."

"Sir, kindly step out of the car, sir." The no-nonsense soldier stepped back—his rifle loaded and ready.

The men exited the car as a black armored Chevy Trailblazer pulled up to the inside gate. The right passenger door swung open, and Jason exited the vehicle.

"Where are you from, soldier?"

"Sir, step forward."

His name tag was pinned upside down.

"Sergeant, I asked you a question."

"Sorry, sir. I have my orders."

Giacomo leaned forward—his eyes scanned. "So, Sergeant, where are you from?"

"Sir, New York City, sir!"

"You can relax, son."

"Sir, yes, sir!"

"Yankees fan?"

"Yes, sir." The sergeant's eyes surveyed the area.

"They got a new pitcher. His name is Augustine."

"Sorry, sir. His name is Augliera—traded from the Red Sox."

"Correct, Sergeant. Fix your name tag, will ya? For a minute there, I thought you were one of the bad guys."

"Yes, sir. Sorry, sir."

The three men entered the guardhouse while the sergeant inspected the car. Giacomo approached Jason. "What?"

"A little paranoid?"

"Well, maybe a little. Where the hell did you find him?"

"Gaines is an exemplary soldier, explosives expert. Two tours in the Middle East—Purple Heart, Medal of Honor on his last stint. He saved seven men in a border skirmish. He was stationed in San Antonio after the terrorist attacks, where he captured the two remaining members of the brigade. He plays by the rules—takes no chances. Be assured, he will place his life on the line."

"Glad he's on our side. Now if only he knew how to put on his name tag."

"Man—you are so anal retentive."

"Thanks."

The steel and cement-block maintenance building was five hundred feet from the guardhouse. A snowbank lay against one side. The minimum-security structure was isolated from the elite military headquarters by a concrete wall and fortified gate topped with razor barbed wire.

"Surprising . . . it's not cold."

"Outside of the snowstorm we had last week, December's been mild."

"Yeah, the same in Italy. Are we ready for tomorrow?"

"Yeah, I'll be at the White House at three in the morning. The other men by six."

They approached the entrance to the building. Jason punched a series of numbers onto a keypad. A green light illuminated, and the door unlocked. The four men stepped over a jamb into the twenty-thousand-square-foot building. In the center of what could be a warehouse sat the SUV. The vehicle was on jacks. On the back wall, a staircase led to a second-floor office. From there, one could observe the inside of the facility through a picture window. Opposite the door was a group of wooden crates stamped "United States Army." Throughout the structure were security cameras.

"New facility?"

"Nine months old. All incoming materials are delivered here for screening before entering the base. We also do our final staging here prior to mission deployment."

"Great idea. Did you find the tracker?"

"Yes, hidden in the exhaust. It's been destroyed."

"Anybody follow you here?"

"No."

"Any idea how it got there?"

"Not yet."

"Where's your man?"

"Inspecting the scanning equipment to see what went wrong. Come on—we'll go upstairs and review the security video of the last twenty-four hours. Dave, you and Don go help Clovis."

"Yes, sir."

Giacomo and Jason climbed the steps. An orange rotating light came on, followed a few seconds later by a blast of an air horn.

Giacomo jumped. "What the hell was that?"

"A warning. Low-level security personnel just entered the building. It's the cleaning crew. They arrive at twenty-three hundred hours—eleven p.m."

Jason placed his right hand on a fingerprint scanner next to the door. After a few seconds, the office door clicked open. The men entered. The lights came on. Giacomo went to the window. He watched as the maintenance crew swept the floor below. To the left, a woman proceeded to go into the restrooms with mop and bucket.

"How do they gain access to the building?"

"A private entrance on the far side. We came in on the other side."

Jason crouched over a computer monitor, turned it on, and logged in. "We'll be able to access video from here."

"What the hell? Jason, come here."

Jason walked over to the window where Giacomo still stood.

"The second crate. Look!" As the general pointed, three men exited the wooden box.

"Holy shit. How'd they . . ." Jason reached over to sound the alarm.

"No alarm. We'll surprise them. Come on, let's go."

The men ran down the carpeted stairs. They rounded the flight of steps as gunfire erupted. Two assailants met them. Giacomo made a quick assessment, dropped to the floor, and kicked out the legs of one attacker. Jason did the same to the other one. With a sharp turn to his right, he used his forearm to crush the aggressor's esophagus. The man lost consciousness.

"This guy is done."

"Yeah. This guy too. They'll be asleep for a while."

They seized the guns from the enemy as bullets ricocheted off the steel walls.

"How many?"

"At least three more."

There was a muffled explosion, and suddenly a five-foot hole appeared in the side of the building near the SUV. A rapid-fire machine gun opened fire. Tracer bullets could be seen coming through the new emergency exit.

The two men hunkered down by the stairs. "What the hell, Jason?"

"We need to leave—and now. We have to get you out of here."

"No, we'll stay and fight." Giacomo tilted his head to the right. "Don, Dave, and Clovis are pinned down by the car."

"I'll cover you."

Crouching, the two men ran toward the vehicle, Giacomo first as Jason covered his back. Arms outstretched, they shot at the intruders by the wooden boxes. Giacomo dove headfirst while Jason slid feet first as he fired his 9-mm, killing one of the attackers by the crates. Their bodies came to a stop against the side of the truck.

"Gentlemen, how are you doin'?"

"Fine, General. Sir, I found this on one of them."

The soldier handed Giacomo a torn piece of paper. He read the words "Et Tu Spiritu Sanctus, protect the prophecy." He placed it in his pocket as a rapid-fire machine gun released a storm of .50-caliber rounds. A man groaned—then silence.

"General, General!" a loud voice echoed.

Dave peered around the bullet-ridden front bumper. "Shit, General. That's Sergeant Gaines from the guardhouse. Damn, he looks like frickin' Rambo."

"General, the area is safe!" the no-nonsense soldier screamed.

The five men behind the SUV counted seven dead bodies on the floor. Gaines swung around as he scanned for more insurgents. A cell phone rang in the distance.

Gaines shouted. "Bomb! Bomb!"

Giacomo saw the flash, then felt the heat of the incendiary explosive as it swept through the building. A wall of flame cascaded across the ceiling. The sprinkler heads unleashed a torrent of water. Thick black smoke and soot filled the air. Giacomo was stunned; his ears rang from the concussion.

"General, are you hurt?"

A whispered voice reverberated in his head. He yelled, "No!"

The five men coughed and gasped as they escaped. The sirens of fire engines traveled through the air as they approached the base.

"Clovis, go to the guardhouse. Shoot anybody who tries to enter," Jason ordered.

"Yes, sir," said a six-foot soldier with blackened soot on his face.

"Anybody hurt?"

"My leg is burned. Other than that, I'm ready to go, General."

"You, Dave?"

"Just a little ringing in my head—reminds me of when I played football."

"Jason?"

"Yeah, fine."

"Dave, you and Don stay here. Meet with the authorities. The colonel and I were not here."

"Copy that, General."

"Gentlemen, when you find Sergeant Gaines's body, make sure he's given the respect of a hero. He saved our lives tonight."

Giacomo and Jason ran to the car and sped to the Vatican embassy.

*   *   *

"They're both dead. I don't know—it wasn't our team. We couldn't reach them in time. The good news is they're finished." Dean Essex ended the phone conversation. A broad smile crossed his face as he sat at his desk in his study. He couldn't see the amber laser beam bounce on the window as it recorded his words.

Chapter 101

A BREEZE WHIPPED AROUND the fallow White House Rose Garden. The air was crisp; the blue sky sparkled with winter sunlight. Jerry Richardson sat in the Oval Office. Jason had been there earlier, his search revealing six high-frequency listening devices.

The door to the president's sanctuary opened. Giacomo and Arnaud, dressed as utility workers, entered. Richardson said nothing. He shook their hands and accompanied them to his private study. Jason was seated in the corner, and he stood to greet them.

An hour later, the intercom buzzed, "Mr. President, President-elect Maro and his chief of staff are here."

"Please send them in."

Richardson stayed behind his desk.

"Mr. President."

"Please, Tom, call me Jerry." A broad smile crossed his face.

"Mr. President, a new secretary?" Dean Essex said.

Richardson ignored him. He smiled. "Please sit," he said, pointing to one of the two facing couches. He sat opposite Essex.

"With less than a month to go, Tom, I thought I would give you the fifty-cent tour. Sorry it had to be so early in the morning."

"I wish I had known. I would've arranged for Mrs. Maro to be here," Essex said.

Maro's tone was condescending. "When the president and I spoke the other day, he suggested it should be just us men."

Essex was bewildered and shocked. He fidgeted.

"Dean, I don't need to tell you everything. Besides, you've never been in the Oval Office, or have you?"

"Of course I've been here, Tom."

"With me, right?"

"Of course." A bead of sweat on his brow.

"Ever been here without me?"

Richardson smiled as Essex squirmed.

The cockroach tugged at his left ear. "What do you mean, Tom?"

"Well, let's see. I believe the first time was—Jer, do you remember?"

"Oh, do you mean when Stalworth was in office?"

"I think so, Jer. A journal?"

"Yeah—you know the journal, don't you, Dean—or is it *Foster*? I'm confused as to your real name, you little piece of shit."

Essex's right leg bounced. His eyes darted. He unbuttoned the collar of his white shirt, loosened his blue silk tie.

"What's the matter, Dean? Is it hot in here? I'm comfortable—and you, Jer?"

"I'm comfortable, and you, Dean? I can open a window."

The toad squirmed as he tugged on his left ear again. A door opened to his right, and his head swung toward the sound.

"Hello, Dean."

Essex sat on the couch, stunned, as Giacomo approached him.

"Let me introduce myself. I'm Giacomo DeLaurentis."

The chief of staff rose from the couch. "I . . . I . . ."

With his opened right hand, Giacomo slapped Essex in the chest. He fell backward onto Tom. The president-elect shifted and allowed the traitor to sit by himself.

"You're surprised to see me, Mr. Essex?" Giacomo's sarcastic, cold voice shattered the traitor's demeanor. "Could it be that your assassin failed again last night?"

Essex said nothing for a moment but then lashed out with spunky arrogance. "If it'd been my men, you'd be dead. Whatcha gonna do, DeLaurentis—kill me? You stupid moron." He jumped up, eyes ablaze, face red, a bead of sweat dripping from his chin.

"No, I'm going to leave that up to the Italian government."

"I'm an American citizen! You can't take me away!"

"Oh, he can, and he will," President Richardson said. "You're a threat to national security, so by executive order, I have agreed with the Italian government to release you to them."

"By the way, you little shit, how did you know I was in DC?" Giacomo's voice roared.

With contempt, Essex said, "Why, your little sister, of course. She can't keep her mouth shut. What an imbecilic wench."

Giacomo stepped back. He cocked his arm, his clenched fist ready to smash the toad, when he remembered his promise to Andrew not to hurt the man.

Essex snarled at Richardson as he rubbed his left ear. "You can say goodbye to your family—they'll be gone by the end of the day."

"You pissant." Richardson rose and with a quick right punched Dean Essex squarely on the chin. Essex collapsed, falling backward on the couch, unconscious. Blood ran from his mouth, splattering his pristine white shirt.

"Damn, that hurt," Richardson said. He shook his hand as he tried to rid himself of the pain. "But it felt great."

"Damn, Jerry—a hell of a punch."

"It was, wasn't it, Tom?"

Giacomo eyed his father-in-law.

"You didn't break your promise, son. It wasn't by your hand."

"True, Dad. That makes me feel better." He gazed at the collapsed body of Dean Essex. "One kick to the face. Do you think that will be okay?" He answered his own question; he knew better. "All right, let's remove this creep. Jason, let's get on with it."

"Yes, sir." He pulled out a syringe from a small black zippered case.

"Giacomo, roll up his sleeve—will you?"

"Sure. Excellent punch, Mr. President."

"Boxing lessons when I was a kid. I guess they paid off."

"Remind me not to get into a fight with you," Arnaud said.

"Kind of scary for you guys last night?"

"Yeah, we're lucky the fireball never touched us. If it weren't for Sergeant Gaines, we wouldn't be here. In fact, my head is still buzzing from the explosion."

"Who do you think they were?"

"No idea, Mr. President. We'll find out and nail their asses. No one is going to come into my house, kill my people."

The tone of Jason's voice comforted Giacomo. His top man dead, the colonel would have his retaliation. Giacomo had complete confidence in Jason. The nagging question for him was, who couldn't he trust? When he found out, he would take his revenge.

Tom grabbed Dean's legs and threw them on the couch while Jason injected him with an amnesia drug.

"Jason, he won't remember anything?"

"He won't remember a thing, Mr. Maro."

"What's our next step, Giacomo?" Maro walked over to Richardson, and the two leaned against the president's desk—their arms crossed.

"As we agreed, we take him to Italy and hand him over to the Italians for questioning. When we have our answers, he comes back to the States for prosecution. Sergio made the arrangements. If we can't implicate Trivette, at least we've got him."

"They're not going to kill him, right?"

"No. I said that to scare him."

"How are you going to move him out of the White House?"

"In a box. We're gonna fold him like a pretzel and carry this son of a bitch out the front door. A BOET mobile hospital truck is waiting. The doctor will strip him, remove any transmitters that are on or in him."

"*In* him?"

"Yep. Not only is there a GPS transmitter surgically inserted in him, we also discovered a microphone, the receiver implanted behind his left ear. Every move and sound this guy makes is being monitored and recorded."

"Wait—are they monitoring our conversation right now?"

"No, no. After we went our separate ways last night, I contacted Sergio back in Rome. He placed two additional remotes over Dean's house, one equipped with infrared and the other fitted with a high-frequency monitor. The infrared picked up his heat signature. When Sergio analyzed the photo, he noticed another area coming from his ear. The monitor triangulated and confirmed the hidden GPS, microphone, and receiver. This morning, we jammed the frequency, replacing it with a ghost frequency—so whoever is monitoring him will think he's still at home."

"Wow—the White House cameras, the visitors' log?"

"Everything is taken care of, Tom. I had Jason replace my entire staff with BOET members. The cameras? Well, they're turned off."

"Your secretary?"

"BOET as well. The time has come to stop these people. I'll do anything I can to capture these bastards."

"I'm sure red flags are being raised."

"Without a doubt—we must act fast. Remember, every move we make is being watched," Giacomo said.

The Oval Office door opened. A parade of men in work clothes entered, carrying a wooden box. The military elite acknowledged the president and their commanding officer.

"Gentlemen, are the other vehicles ready?" Vandercliff asked.

"Yes, sir, Colonel. The three trucks are at the service entrance."

"Very well—let's place this dirtbag in the box. Gentlemen, don't seal it too tightly; we don't need him to die of suffocation."

"Yes, sir."

As the men put the limp body of Dean Essex in the box and carried him out of the Oval Office, Giacomo received a text from Sergio. "You're cleared back to Italy. Land in Grosseto."

"Grosseto? My father used to visit there. And the man who was killed near the Vatican—he mentioned it. What the . . ."

"What, Giacomo?"

"Nothing important, Mr. President." He paused. "Jerry, you have a country to run. We'll keep Jason abreast of our progress. We'll work silently from this point on."

"Godspeed, son." The two men shook hands.

"Tom, for you as well. All our communication ceases."

"I understand. Good luck, my friend. See you at my inauguration."

"I'll be there."

*   *   *

Eten Trivette sat in his office. Troubled by a headache and a terrifying emotion, he focused his attention on the Eiffel Tower, obscured by fog. Dark clouds rolled across the sky. The EU president filled with anger as he read Nava's final journal entries.

The winter months will be unkind. Your decisions will cause your ruin, your death. Those below you thwart your efforts; your house has become divided. Your wisdom will fail you. You cannot change what is already foretold. The child of long ago survived, now his heirs and theirs can't be stopped. The ancient village holds the key. Destroy the key, and the door can't be opened, the prophecy will never be known. For the two heirs know nothing of the prophecy. Neither do you. Passover will bring darkness as the souls are condemned . . . You cannot escape what you have done, you foolish man.

Trivette threw the journal across the room. "We? Prophecy? You stupid, traitorous bitch. I'll exact my revenge."

*   *   *

From the air vent, a light mist began to fill the room. Eten Trivette fell asleep, his head rested on the desk. A bearded man entered the workspace with two others. He whistled as he monitored Trivette's pulse and then nodded to the other men.

"Clean the desk and lay him on top of it."

"Yes, Doctor."

The physician carried a computer tablet and a wooden box. He whispered as he opened the case and arranged the vials of DNA and stem cells. "This will be the last time you and I shall meet, Mr. Trivette." He picked up the syringe . . .

Chapter 102

December 28

F-35 FIGHTER JETS escorted the Gulfstream from the United States. Midway across the Atlantic, two Italian Euro Typhoon aircraft joined them. They landed at the airbase in Grosseto, Italy, at seven in the morning. Armed vehicles surrounded the plane as it taxied to the military side of the airport.

The ancient city of Grosseto was founded in AD 803. Brick walls filled with mortar protected the original village. In 1574, the Medici family began reconstruction, and nineteen years later, the fortress was completed. Located five miles off the Tuscan coast of the Tyrrhenian Sea, the area was known as Maremma. The land overflowed with vineyards and olive groves, attracting tourists from all over the world. Of the 83,000 inhabitants, only a small percentage lived within the city walls.

Giacomo paused in the doorway of the plane. He was still plagued with the sense that there was another scenario being played. *Two plus two does not add up to four. The notes . . . and what did Essex mean when he said, 'If it'd been my men, you'd be dead.' Whose men were they then? What if Trivette is only part of this . . .*

"I appreciate the ride, Danny. I'll call Tony later."

The cool air refreshed him as he descended the stairs. Giacomo's attention was drawn to the bright blue sky as the two Typhoon fighters roared overhead.

"Glad you made it here, my friend."

"Me too, Sergio." The two men hugged.

At the tail of the aircraft, Arnaud supervised the removal of the wooden crate they'd used to transport Essex. The seven military personnel placed the box onto a waiting military vehicle.

"We need him alive. Sergio, make sure your people understand—don't kill him."

"Don't worry, my friend. Do you want to witness the interrogation?"

"No, the last one almost got me killed. You're going to keep him here?"

"Yes, at the base hospital."

"Excellent." Giacomo scanned the area. He took Sergio to the side, out of earshot. He whispered, "Trivette may not be our only threat. The people who tried to kill Jason and me—they were not his people. And look . . . we found this on the body of one of the attackers."

Giacomo removed the note that he'd hidden in his wallet. Sergio's eyes widened.

"And Sergio, Essex made a remark that is concerning."

"What did he say?"

"He said, 'If it'd been my men, you'd be dead.' So . . . who sent those men?"

Sergio was silent, his head lowered as he reread the note. He looked up at Giacomo. "I'm so sorry."

"What do you have to apologize for?" He looked at the time on his cell phone. "Emily and my family will be here in two hours. We're going to spend New Year's here. Take a couple of days off."

"Time off? Wouldn't you all be safer at the Vatican or back in the States?"

Giacomo didn't answer the question, his mind preoccupied.

"What am I going to do, Sergio? I can't stay hidden in a bubble forever. Essex is in custody. Who could possibly know we're here?"

"The people who tried to kill you."

"As far as they're concerned, I'm dead."

Sergio lowered his head. "Still, you have to be careful. Where are you staying?"

"A hotel within the walls of the Medici fort. And you?"

"With my cousin."

"Good."

"Giacomo, a change of plans," Sergio said as he finished reading an email on his phone.

"What now?"

"Your sister decided to go to Ottati."

"She what?"

"No worries. She has a protective detail. She'll be fine."

"Damn her—she's so independent. Sergio, did you get her cell phone?"

"Yes. Our people are still checking her calls and texts."

"I don't understand what's taking so long." Giacomo shook his head. "You didn't say anything to her about Essex, did you?"

"No. I told her Vatican security needed it. I replaced the phone."

"Excellent. Thanks, Sergio. I need to go to the hotel. Are you ready, Dad?"

"Oui. I need to sleep."

"Me too."

A security detail dropped Giacomo and Arnaud off at the Grand Hotel Bastiani, located within the Medicean walls of Grosseto. Giacomo entered his hotel room—not big but comfortable. He felt relieved that Essex was in custody. He welcomed the three-day respite with his wife, her due date just three weeks away. He hoped he could wash away the beleaguering concerns.

After a much-needed hot shower, Giacomo exited the bathroom.

"Nice abs, soldier."

"Em." A smile crossed Giacomo's face. "When did you get here?"

Emily lay down on the bed as the chiseled body wrapped in a white towel approached.

"Let's just say in time to hear you singing in the shower. Between Puccini's 'Nessun Dorma' and James Taylor's 'You've Got a Friend,' please, honey, don't quit your day job."

"That bad?"

"If you come over here and give me a kiss, I'll lie and say you sounded great."

"Sounds good to me. Should I let my towel drop?"

"You'd better."

Eventually, husband and wife fell asleep, both exhausted.

Chapter 103

New Year's Eve

GIACOMO WOKE AT dawn. The morning sun poked through the opening of the brown curtain. Transfixed by a sunbeam that frolicked across Emily's sleeping face, his mind formed a picture. Out of his body, he watched the vision.

In the distance, a tree overshadowed a meadow of bright green grass. The color of the leaves changed. The orange and red hues of fall had arrived. His hair was long, his black beard trimmed. He wore blue jeans, a button-down shirt, and a long brown leather coat. A young boy sat nestled between two overgrown oak roots that stretched to the horizon. Knees to his chest, the youngster gazed out over the field. Another boy—his twin—approached. He whispered in the brother's ear. Together they climbed the tree and sat on one of the thick, sturdy branches. They waved to Giacomo, who responded in kind. As he moved toward the boys, the wind howled. The bottom of his coat fluttered behind him. Giacomo tried to run, but the force against him was unyielding. In an instant, the two boys vanished. He stood alone—empty and heartbroken.

"Giacomo! Giacomo, are you all right?"

"What?" His eyes focused on the blurred face.

His wife's soft hands stroked his cheeks.

"Yeah—a weird dream."

"You were dreaming?"

"Yeah—why?"

"Your eyes were open."

"No?"

"Yes, they were."

"I'm fine—only a dream."

"Want to tell me?"

"Strange—so real." Giacomo described the dream as he stared into Emily's eyes.

"It's a dream, Giacomo. Come on, let's get up." Emily kissed him on the forehead. "We'll go have breakfast with Dad. I'm starving."

"I'm not that hungry. Why don't you go? I have to make a couple of phone calls."

"Are you sure?"

"Yeah—go bond with your father."

"*Bond?*"

"Yes, bond—be together."

Emily rolled over on her back, and using her arms as leverage, she stood. The bare skin of her puffed belly as she unbuttoned the pajama top caused the father-to-be to smile. He'd soon be a dad.

After Emily left, Giacomo showered and dressed. He sat at a small desk and grabbed the cell phone while he pulled back the curtain and opened the window. A fresh breeze rustled the loose papers on the writing table. He leaned back, placing his left leg on the piece of furniture. Giacomo called his mother and left a message; he tried Rio as well but got no answer.

He looked out of the third-floor window at the café across the street. Sounds of the locals as they drank their espressos drifted into the room. Scenarios whizzed through his mind. It was clear that he had inherited his father's paranormal abilities. *For what purpose? Why not a regular life? Why is it so hard? Being transformed into a God-serving prophet . . . Can't you just leave me alone . . .*

A voice broke his train of thought. "Why do you question?"

Giacomo leaped from the chair and turned around. No one was there. The room was empty. The silence was eerie. He no longer heard the morning patrons of the cafe.

"Why do you question?" The voice repeated, setting off an alarm within his soul. He turned again—no one.

The door of the room opened. Giacomo was baffled as he watched Emily place her pocketbook on the table. The Italian chatter across the cobblestone street drifted back into the room.

"Did I scare you?"

"No, you startled me." Giacomo collected himself. "How's Dad?"

"Exhausted. You look like you've seen a ghost."

"No, no ghost here." *What the hell is happening?* "These last couple of days." He shook his head.

"Dad said the same. I think he's happy he's here, protected."

"You—are you happy?"

"I'm glad we're here. Am I happy? I wish we were home."

"Your words to God's ears. At least we got the guy responsible for the killings." He didn't add that he suspected there were others involved and that Trivette might be just a scapegoat. Giacomo's eyes fixed on an unknown point in the distance.

"You got Trivette?"

"No, we got his right-hand man, Dean Essex—and it's only a matter of time before we get Trivette." He questioned himself. *Should I tell her there were others involved?* He tried to hold it together. He sat on the bed. Emily placed her hand on her husband's forehead.

"You don't have a fever, but you look terrible."

He put his hand on her thigh. "I'm fine."

"At least the color came back to your face."

He smiled.

"Dean Essex? Is that the same person . . ."

"Yep, it sure is."

"Rio is in love with him. She'll be crushed. How much more can she go through?" A tear left a streak on Emily's makeup.

"My sister will be fine—please don't cry." Giacomo leaned over, kissing Emily on the cheek.

"I can't take this anymore—the attempts on your life, my dad living in exile—can't even go home. This paranormal . . ."

Giacomo gently held her face in his hands. "Honey, it will be all right. I told you, when this is over, I'm going to retire." He wiped the tears from her eyes.

"It'll never be over, Giacomo."

He gazed into her brown eyes. Giacomo feared she was right but said nothing. Emily composed herself, grabbed his hands. He kissed her lips.

In a quiet voice, she said, "I need to go pee—the boys are pressing on my bladder."

Ten minutes passed, and Emily reemerged. Her face was clear, the redness gone from her eyes.

"Emily, when did Rio decide to go to Ottati?"

"A couple of days ago. I tried to call you, but you didn't answer."

"Sorry—I was tied up in a firestorm and couldn't call you back."

"Anyway." She rolled her eyes. "It was her idea. She said we needed alone time."

"Isn't that nice of her?" Giacomo's voice filled with sarcasm.

"Don't be angry. When she finds out about Dean, she'll be crushed. Rio's gone through an awful lot."

"Yeah, and the rest of us?"

"Don't be angry now."

"I'm not."

"Yes, you are. Your ears are turning red."

"I can't hide anything from you, can I?"

"Nope. By the way, where are the security people?"

"They're hidden—secretly watching the three of us."

"Rio and Mom?"

"Sergio arranged for the security teams."

"I don't want to talk about this anymore. We're together for a couple of days—right?"

"Yep."

She came close to him, her voice seductive. "What do you say we enjoy ourselves for once?"

"Yes, about time."

Emily held her stomach. "The boys are jumping. They missed their daddy."

"What do you mean?"

"Come, put your hand here. Now talk."

Giacomo placed his hand on the side of her stomach. "Hello, boys. Wow, did you feel that?" Emily nodded. "Of course you did. I love you guys." A broad smile crossed his face. He leaned over and spoke to her distended belly. "Paolo, Arnaud, you behave in there."

"What are they going to do?"

"Well, you never know."

"Stop. Want to explore before we eat?"

"Sure. You're already hungry?"

"No, but I will be."

Giacomo shook his head. "Did I ever mention to you Dad used to come here?"

"No."

"He mediated a merger with a company headquartered here. He came a couple of times. After he died, we discovered he'd donated a lot of money to the church in the piazza here to help restore it."

"Wow, can we go see it?"

"Sure."

"Can we walk the fortress walls too?"

"Yep. The concierge gave me a map of the city. There's a park, and tomorrow we can go on a picnic."

"You're so romantic, honey."

"Oh, yeah, just me."

Chapter 104

THE COUPLE EXITED the Bastiani and took a left on Via Daniele Manin. They walked the short distance hand in hand to the Piazza Dante Alighieri. The day was warm for late December—fifty-eight degrees. It was twenty degrees above the seasonal average, the air still, and the early morning breeze absent.

"Is that the church?"

Giacomo didn't hear his wife ask the question. His mind was still engrossed by the voice that had spoken to him earlier. *Am I going crazy? What does it mean, 'Why do you question?'*

"Giacomo, are you listening? Giacomo?"

"I'm sorry, honey . . . what?"

"Is that the church your father donated the money to?"

"Yes—the Cathedral of San Lorenzo."

"Why are the stones black and white?"

"Ah yes, the Romanesque style—those marble blocks . . ."

"How do you know that?" Her tone was skeptical.

"I read the brochure. I had you fooled, didn't I?"

"No . . . well, maybe a little."

They climbed the ten stone steps. Giacomo held open one of the four oak doors for Emily. They entered the centuries-old church. Several people sat in the wooden pews, while others roamed the aisles of the cathedral, taking pictures.

"Do you mind if I sit down and pray?"

"No, I'm going to walk around. The boys and I can use the exercise."

Giacomo genuflected, blessed himself with the sign of the cross, and sat. Emily went to the statue of St. Lawrence. A kneeler with red-glassed votive candles cast its light on the mother-to-be. The sculpture enclosed by a small black iron fence. Blue-and-red stained glass windows filtered the sun's rays into the church. The colors danced and flickered in the quiet house of God, the silence broken only by the occasional sound of a camera's shutter.

The day is cold—a light snow appears. Tens of thousands of people are gathered. The Capitol before me—Tom Maro gives me a smile. President Richardson shakes my hand. Fighter jets fly overhead in tight formation as the orange of the afterburners glows bright. The engines crackle in the crisp air. A commotion begins. I can't reach Tom—screams erupt from the crowd. The scenery changes. There are two men. I don't know who they are. One dressed in white, the other in a blue silk suit. Again, the backdrop changes, and the sun glares. Then a brilliant flash of light followed by an enormous explosion. Suddenly, I am in Paris. Chaos rules the streets, darkness envelops the City of Lights. I'm swept away to a field. Two young boys run in the distance . . .

"Giacomo . . . Giacomo . . ." Emily rested her hand on his shoulder.

"What, what—hi, honey. Sorry, I dozed off."

"With your eyes open again? I think you need a doctor."

"No, I'm fine." He tried to shrug off the vision. *Why do the images change? What does it mean?*

"Come look at this."

"At what?" Giacomo felt distracted.

"You'll see."

She grabbed his hand. He followed her to the statue of a saint.

"The plaque." Emily pointed.

"I can't read the words." He squinted.

"I'll read it."

"No, I can. I'll climb over the fence."

"You can't do that."

"Yes, I can. Watch."

"You're crazy."

He jumped the fence, nearly falling over. He dusted off the bronze plate.

"'Donated by Paulo DeLaurentis. St. Lawrence, the patron saint of fire, keeper of the treasures of the church.' My father! Wow."

"Buongiorno." A soft voice came from behind them.

Giacomo turned. Embarrassed, he spoke in Italian to the thin, bearded priest with a crooked nose. "Excuse me, Father." He climbed back over the barrier, wiped his dusty hands on his jeans.

The priest glared at Giacomo with curiosity, his gray eyebrows raised.

"I'm so sorry. That's my father."

"San Lorenzo is your father?"

"No, no, I mean the man who donated . . ."

"Ah, Paolo—nice man. Oh my . . . oh my."

"You knew him?"

"A friend of mine did."

"I'm his son, Giacomo. This is my wife, Emily."

"Buongiorno, senora." The priest nodded. "I was told you would visit one day. Please, come with me. We'll discuss your papa in my office."

The couple's eyes met. Giacomo shrugged. In French, he said, "I hope it's not one of his notes."

"No." The priest smiled as he limped ahead of them.

Chapter 105

AN HOUR LATER, Emily and Giacomo exited the church through the back entrance.

"What do you think the key is for?"

"Got me. What did Dad say in the letter? 'When the key finds its rightful place.' Who knows. Did you catch the priest's name?"

"No—I called him 'Father.'"

"Me too. I wanted to ask him if he boxed."

"Why?"

"Did you see the shape of his nose? Crooked to one side. I wonder how he breathes."

"Yeah, what about how he mumbled to himself?"

"What did he say? Wait, I remember. It was 'Oh my, oh my.' Strange, if you ask me."

"Yes, but he's a very nice man."

"True. We'll come back and ask. If not, when we get home, I'll go through Dad's records. I'm sure his name is on a document. Dad donated $700,000. There's got to be a record."

"He said he never met Dad."

"Oh, right." Giacomo put the envelope in his pants pocket.

"When did you say that your father was here?"

"I think it was in the late eighties . . ."

*   *   *

October 27, 1989

Paolo read the *Wall Street Journal*. He placed the paper on the seat opposite him. The billionaire glimpsed at the monitor on the bulk-head of the Gulfstream V. The screen showed the aircraft's position as they flew across the Atlantic Ocean to Rome. He was scheduled to meet the Italian prime minister—his friend Sergio—that afternoon.

"Paolo, Pepsi?" his flight attendant Jayne asked.

He loved her Australian accent. "Sure, Jayne." Paolo reached into his pocket and pulled out a piece of paper. "Please give this to Pat and Danny. I want to go to Grosseto after Rome and spend a couple of days there."

"Grosseto. We've been there—last year, we took Mike Quinn."

"Yes, you did, Miss Jayne. I remember the pictures of the walled city, and since I don't want to drive to Ottati, I figured why not? Victoria and I are not getting along. She can use a break."

"She?"

"All right, me too. Where's that Pepsi?"

"Coming right up, Mr. DeLaurentis."

Paolo chuckled, picked up the paper, and continued to read.

Three days later, Paolo sauntered through the entrance of the Medicean walled village of Grosseto. The Hotel Bastiani to his left, he strode further toward the piazza. The Cathedral of San Lorenzo was outfitted with scaffolding as men restored the marble.

"Buongiorno," Paolo said to the heavyset priest with a slight hint of gray across his temples.

"Buongiorno."

The men stood next to each other and watched the workers fifty feet above the ground on a platform.

"Father Luccati?"

"Yes." The priest continued to gaze skyward. "Vincenzo! To the left, to the left!" the priest yelled and gestured. Still not looking at Paolo, he asked, "What can I do for you?"

"My name is Paolo DeLaurentis. I understand you need help?"

"Help—*basta, basta*—enough, enough, Vincenzo."

The worker squinted at the priest and shrugged.

"Ugh!" The priest shook his head. He turned toward Paolo. "If only I had the funds to hire good employees. My nephew Vincenzo—ugh! You are American?"

Paolo chuckled. "Yes."

"Your name again?"

"Paolo DeLaurentis."

"Yes—what can I do for you, Paolo?"

"I understand you need help. Can I buy you lunch?"

Father Luccati's eyes met Paolo's. He couldn't say no.

The two men walked away from the church into the neighboring Piazza Dante Alighieri, where they sat at an outdoor café.

"Father Luccati, as I said, I understand you need help."

The priest picked up the white espresso cup and took a sip. "I need more than help—I need a miracle. The cathedral is falling to pieces, and there is not enough money to pay for experienced workers. I have no staff except for my secretary, who happens to be Vincenzo's mother—my sister. You're not a priest, are you?"

Paolo laughed. "I'm sorry, Father. I can't help you there."

"Oh." He rolled his eyes.

"I *can* help with a donation."

Father Luccati's eyes brightened.

"But I need a favor in return."

The priest pushed back his chair to leave. Paolo handed him an envelope.

"My son, Giacomo, will be visiting here. When he arrives, I need the priest in charge to give this envelope to him." Paolo recognized the suspicion in the priest's eyes. Paolo smiled. "No need for concern, Father. You can open it if you like."

Father Luccati peeked inside the small manila envelope.

Paolo reached into his left jacket pocket and withdrew his checkbook. "How much do you need, Father?"

The priest eyed Paolo with suspicion as his pen wavered over the checkbook.

Paolo's forehead creased as their eyes met. "Father?"

"Whatever you wish to give."

Paolo gazed at the cathedral. He filled in an amount and gave the check to the priest. "That should cover your costs and give you a little extra to hire a staff."

Father Luccati held the bluish-green paper with both hands in shock. "I . . . I . . . thank you! Thank you."

"You're welcome, Gennaro."

The priest's eyes opened wide. "How do you know my first name?"

"I just know . . . I just know." Paolo stood and reached out his hand. "Father, it has been a pleasure. Remember when my son comes to make sure he receives the envelope."

"I will, Senor DeLaurentis. May God bless you."

Paolo and the priest exited the piazza. When they reached the Via Daniele Manin, Paolo stopped to sit on a stone bench. His mind took him to a place that caused him to grieve.

"Paolo, do you need anything?"

He stared at the priest. "No, Father Luccati. I guess I'm a little tired." Paolo wiped the tears from his eyes and departed the ancient city.

Chapter 106

"THAT WAS SPECTACULAR. The gnocchi light, the sauce fantastic." Giacomo gazed into Emily's eyes and held her hand. "I love you, Em. Everything will be fine."

"I hope so."

The couple ate at Vinecia Osteria on Via Vinzaglio—a cobblestoned street that was little more than a car width wide. The owners lived above the eatery. On either side of the road were apartment buildings with small shops on the ground floors. Overhead, the stone walls were painted orange, yellow, and pink, highlighting the living space. The windows were covered with green-slatted shutters.

"Giacomo, I love this place—nice and quiet. It reminds me of Ottati."

"Ottati is peaceful, an oasis of tranquility."

"You like the silence and the breezes from the mountains."

"Yeah, the clear air. It's fresh, untouched compared to the world we live in." He placed his hand on hers. "I can't wait for all this stuff to be over. No matter what you believe, when this is finished, I'm done."

"How can you say that, Giacomo?"

"Because inside me I know this is wrong. Our life is crazy."

"You don't mean our life like you and me?"

"No, no, the world—the chaos. Dad was right about simplicity of life and love—that's the key. It's clear to me—maybe because our boys will soon be born. This life—this world—is too crazy."

"Hmm. Giacomo, there are good people in the world. Not all are bad."

"True. Still, do we have it wrong? I mean life in general. When we were in the cathedral earlier, and you left so I could pray, only the echoes of my thoughts were in my mind."

"The echoes of your thoughts? Do you have a fever?"

"No. Can I continue?"

"Yes, mon amour. I'm sorry."

"I forgive you. This sense of peace came over me. I looked up, and there was the crucifix. I wondered why anyone would give up their life for us—what sacrifice we as a people have to give up for our own salvation."

"You're starting to scare me."

"Why?"

"You've never talked this way. Your life has always been a fight for justice. What's right and what's wrong—an eye for an eye. Why now?"

"I don't know—this, this . . ."

"This *what*, honey?"

"It's hard to explain. My mind is conflicted. I've done terrible things."

"What do you mean, Giacomo—terrible things?"

"I killed wounded people as a soldier. All the bad . . . my involvement—damn. The evilness that surrounds us. I'm afraid of being drawn further into it. I need to retire. Two weeks ago, I was in one of the chapels in Vatican City. This cardinal came up to me and said, 'Talk to Him the way you would speak to your father.'"

"God?"

"Yeah. At first I felt foolish—I giggled. Then, in the quiet of my thoughts, I talked to Him. A sense of peace came over me—as it did this morning. Then I had this concern. What will I need to sacrifice in my life for the good of us?"

"Very deep, Giacomo. Perhaps God is going to use you."

The waiter placed the check on their table as they continued to chat.

"That's what I'm afraid of. I talked to Andrew about my past as a soldier. I asked if God would forgive me. He said all things are possible with God. We sat and talked. I should say I confessed, and he gave me absolution—forgiveness of my sins. Then you know what he said?"

"What?"

"'Forgive *yourself*. We as a people are hindered by our lack of forgiving each other. Most of all ourselves.'"

"Isn't that what your father said?"

"Yep." Giacomo reached into his pants pocket. He pulled out two twenty-euro notes along with the small manila envelope. He slipped the money under his plate. "Wanna take a stroll? I'm tired of talking."

Emily pointed to the envelope. "Where do you think the key goes?"

"No clue." He placed it back in his pants pocket.

"Let's go sit in the piazza."

They arrived at the large circular area of the Piazza Dante Alighieri. There was a statue in the center with seven stone benches around its perimeter. The afternoon sun warmed the western wall. Its orange-yellow brilliance infused the ancient village. The temperature dropped to a mild fifty degrees. They sat next to an outdoor cafe. The cathedral was to their left. Residents and tourists promenaded the piazza. The New Year's Eve celebration had started, with libations and laughter.

"The hotel receptionist told me the fireworks for tonight are spectacular. The best viewing point is on top of the walls of the city. Do you think we can go, Giacomo?"

"Why not? We'll celebrate the new year on the Medici fort. Do you think you can ..." Giacomo jumped—startled by a movement he'd seen from the corner of his eye.

"What's the matter?"

"I guess I'm hypervigilant."

"Relax, honey. Nothing can happen to us here. Oh, look. Here's my dad ..."

"Why don't we go? I have an uneasy feeling."

"Sure."

Giacomo detected the hesitation in her eyes. He took her hands as he helped her stand. The married couple's eyes fixed on each other, and they kissed. A man rushed out of a nearby store and pushed Giacomo and his pregnant wife with so much force they toppled over. A bullet ricocheted off the stone bench as it struck an unsuspecting tourist. Three armed men surrounded the couple, their guns drawn. They scanned the sky for the sniper. A fourth man knelt beside Giacomo.

"Are you all right, General?"

Dazed, he asked, "What?"

"Are you all right, sir?"

"Yes—Em, Em?" He rolled on his side to see his wife.

"What happened, Giacomo?"

Time slowed for the husband and wife. Love radiated from their eyes; no words were spoken as sorrow overwhelmed the couple.

More shots echoed through the air. People in the piazza fled into stores and restaurants as they scurried for a place of refuge. A passerby was shot; his body lay on the cold stone. One of the men took aim, fired at where he thought the gunman hid. They scanned the walls in their quest to find the marksman. A flash caught their eye from the bell tower of the church. The bodyguards unleashed a torrent of gunfire at the killer, who fired two shots in turn—one whizzed by Giacomo, lodging itself in a piece of wood. In a matter of minutes, a SWAT team encircled the house of God. They hand-signaled each other. With precision, the elite soldiers entered in pursuit of the slaughterer.

From the south wall of the city came a series of thuds as a volley of mortar shells escaped their launchers. The deadly rockets struck targets in and around the piazza. The sacristy at the rear of the cathedral collapsed. White dust from the destroyed stone exploded into the sky and coated those who were screaming in fright as they tried to escape the horror. Tourists and citizens were strewn about on the sidewalks, injured or dead. Within moments, Italian Air Force helicopters flew over the once-fortified village as they tracked the terrorists. Members of the elite forces were tethered to the choppers' landing skids. Armed with the Beretta ARX 160 assault rifles, they scanned the southern wall. With pinpoint accuracy, they killed the assailants without causing any civilian casualties. In the distance, sirens blared from emergency vehicles as they sped to the scene of pandemonium and sadness. Flames exploded from a restaurant. The attack ended. People cautiously rose from the rubble and moved as they helped others.

Giacomo covered his wife with his body and wiped the white dust from his head—his ears still rang from the concussion of the explosions. Emily's hand clung to his shirt. Arnaud turned the corner. Then he stopped—he knew.

"Em, you can let go." Her face was covered with pulverized stone. A tear left a trail through the dust—her eyes open. Blood trickled from her ear. "Em—Emily, can you hear me? Damn it, Emily." He spoke louder, and grabbing her shoulders, he shook the lifeless body. Her hand fell to her side. The wedding band that united the two in this world slipped off her finger. The sound of the ring hitting the cobbled stone rang in his ears. "Emily DeLaurentis, talk to me! Em— no! Em—no!" He sat back on his haunches. His hands covered his face as he shook his head. His father-in-law touched his shoulder. Arnaud knelt beside him, tears in his eyes.

"She's dead, Giacomo."

"No, Dad, no! It can't be ... Em ... Em ..." He touched her stomach. "My boys ... I'll never see my boys."

An ambulance pulled up. The attendants jumped out of the vehicle and rushed over to Emily. The leader of the security forces tried to stop them. With a resigned shake of his head, he indicated that a life had been lost. They pushed him aside and tended to the pregnant woman.

"Come on, son—nothing more we can do." Arnaud's lip quivered. His chin wobbled. He wiped a tear from the corner of his eye. He gasped at the sight of his only child as she lay dead with her swollen belly that nourished his grandchildren—Giacomo's two sons.

Giacomo struggled to his feet, his grief overtaken for a moment by anger. He shouted at one of the guards. "Give me your gun." He threw out his hand. "Now!"

The man protected the pistol.

"Giacomo, what are you going to do?" a voice from behind him asked.

"I'm going to kill the son of a bitch."

The piazza filled with military, the local police tended to the wounded and placed towels over the heads of those who had perished. With agonizing strength, the residents gathered to help the injured. The SWAT team trotted out of the cathedral. They dragged the sniper behind them.

"I'm going to kill him! I want the gun now!"

Arnaud stepped away as Sergio came closer. With the wave of his hand, Sergio whisked the security man away.

The Italian, handkerchief in hand, wiped his eyes at the sight. "Giacomo, let the police do their job. The sniper is in custody."

"I want him dead. He killed my wife . . . my children. I want him dead!"

"I understand, but that will not erase your pain." Sergio wrapped his arms around Giacomo. He tried to pull away; Sergio tightened his grip. "Your father would not agree. You'll get your justice but not today."

The dreaded *pop-pop* of a gun was followed by a crack that resounded in the piazza. Everyone ducked, running for shelter—then there was silence. Giacomo ran to the doors of the church. Sergio trailed behind him. The SWAT team aimed their rifles at the two as they approached.

"It's all right," a voice shouted. The men stepped back. The lifeless sniper was on his back from a gunshot to the head. A few feet away, his face to the sky, was the corpse of Arnaud Chambery. A priest knelt beside him, closed his eyelids, and administered last rites. Furious over the death of his daughter, the leader of the DGSE with his gun drawn shot the sniper as a member of the SWAT team in return killed Arnaud.

Giacomo was in shock. He said nothing, for nothing could be said. Sadness swept his heart. A military helicopter approached the piazza. White dust swirled from the downwash. The aircraft hovered over its landing spot.

"Giacomo, come on. I have to get you out of here."

With a simple acknowledgment, Sergio and a security guard escorted Giacomo to the waiting helicopter. The airship lifted. The damaged village, the destroyed sacristy at the back of the church, the bodies scattered about, the scores of military police with their guns drawn—the scene was nothing more than surreal. The sound of the rotor blades transfixed Giacomo's attention on the ambulance that carried the dead body of his wife, Emily DeLaurentis, pregnant with their two unborn sons. He watched the vehicle as it traversed the streets of the ancient city en route to the morgue.

* * *

Rio walked the road from her father's house in Ottati to the Church of Cordanato, nestled in the fields below the ancient village. Dust from the dirt road rose into the sky. An old orange Fiat approached her. The car stopped, and the driver rolled down the window.

"Senora, the prophecy has been destroyed."

"Grazia." For a moment, she was confused. *Prophesy destroyed . . . what does that mean?* Then her confusion vanished. She smiled as the car drove back to the village.

Chapter 107

THE PERSON ON the other side of the phone line spoke in Italian. "The priest is dead. The key has been destroyed. DeLaurentis, his wife, and your nemesis Chambery are dead as well. Where is Essex?"

"I haven't spoken to him in weeks."

"Essex knows nothing about us?"

"Correct—nothing." Trivette stumbled on his words as he spoke.

"We don't need another problem like your sister Nava caused. Et Tu Spiritus Sanctus."

Trivette was confused as he rubbed his head. "Et Tu Spiritus Sanctus—what the hell does that mean?" As he sat in his office and admired the view of Paris, the memory of the conversation dissolved. Two months had passed since the fateful day of Nava's death. Now her last journal entry haunted him. He'd grown sick of listening to his sister—Colin Payne's other child prodigy.

He muttered to himself. *What did they know? Both foolish, idiotic—their plans—their ability to see the future. Thwarted by Paolo DeLaurentis—another idiot who did not realize what he had. We were always one step ahead of him—but the so-called messenger of God had the genuine gift. DeLaurentis waited until now—with his warrior son and his ideological idiot daughter—to defeat me.* The pain in Trivette's head increased as his mind transformed. Fear overcame him as he yelled out loud, "Not going to happen. I am the most powerful person in the world!"

Trivette's mind swirled with anger and discontent. The Frenchman grimaced. His body contorted, and he thrashed as the evilness of man overtook him. Eten Trivette's soul was black, filled with pride and greed. A flashback of a doctor hovering over him caused him to panic. Eten's mind sought but did not find the hidden truth. As his discomfort increased, the puppet rubbed the back of his neck and right temple. Would he become a device for the one who now controlled him?

Chapter 108

January 4

GIACOMO WAS DISILLUSIONED with life. He returned to Vatican City because he couldn't bear to go back to the States. The coldness of the winter morning wrapped its arms around Rome. The weather had drastically changed since his return. In the three days that had passed, the record-high temperatures had plummeted to record lows.

Giacomo refused to speak with anyone. Rio and Victoria were transported back to the Vatican despite an irrational protest from Rio. Although always under tight surveillance, Giacomo roamed the streets of the city. He traveled the circuitous paths of the gardens. He grieved alone.

An ashen, overcast sky shed its tears of white fluffy snow. The purity of the ice crystals was little antidote to the sadness of Giacomo's family and friends. The funeral of Arnaud Chambery, his daughter, Emily DeLaurentis, and her unborn sons took place in a private chapel within the pontifical city.

"We're gathered today to celebrate the lives of Emily and her father, Arnaud. Although the term *celebrate* is contrary to today's reality. We are filled with sorrow and pain. There is no justification for the tragic deaths of these two beautiful people and the unborn children of Giacomo and Emily. To celebrate is to acknowledge their acceptance into the hands of God and His eternal kingdom of heaven. For this is what faith teaches us. If we believe, and our lives are one with God, then surely we will be one with Him in His kingdom.

"I believe Arnaud, his daughter, Emily, and her two sons—Paolo and Arnaud—are in the loving hands of God, enjoying eternal life with Jesus, Mary, and the saints. The heartache we sense at the loss of our brother and sister is insurmountable. During this trying time, we must, we *must* rely on God. To be angry is understandable. It is what we do with the anger that lies within us that will define who we are and who we become."

Giacomo sat in the last pew at the back of the chapel as he listened to his friend Andrew give the eulogy. His mind was a void. At his request, no one sat next to him, but he felt the presence of an entity. A tear trickled on his cheek as Andrew concluded the tribute.

"For whatever consolation I might give can only come from a man, a father who just maybe was a messenger from God. A man whom I never met but whose memory and words we will never forget. I love you . . ."

A hand touched Giacomo's shoulder, and he knew at once that his father was with him—just as he'd been with him all those years ago when Payne's men tortured him. Although he could not see him, Giacomo realized everything would be better . . . eventually. A weak smile crossed his face. He sobbed as the caskets of his family were wheeled past him. The realization of the sacrifice of his wife and children invigorated him with the will to live, to move forward, to stop the evil that threatened humanity.

Pope Peter Andrew stopped by Giacomo's pew. He reached out his hand and with tears in his eyes said, "Come, my brother."

Giacomo grabbed hold of his hands, and the men embraced. Andrew pulled back. "God is with you. Be not afraid—for your sacrifice is great. He will help you destroy the wicked. Open your heart. He will show you."

With his words, the doors of the chapel blew open, and a sudden wind entered the church. A break in the overcast sky let through a ray of sunlight that illuminated the two men.

Giacomo took a deep breath. His lungs filled with the clean air. He waited for his mother, John, and Rio.

"Giacomo."

"Hi, Mom. Sorry for being so distant these last couple of days."

"I understand, Giacomo."

"Hi, John." The two men shook hands.

Rio wiped the tears from her eyes. Giacomo wrapped his arms around his younger sister. "They're in heaven—a much better place than here."

"Giacomo, I'm so sorry. My . . . my heart hurts so much."

"Mine does too, little sister. We need to move on and give their sacrifice meaning."

Rio's face filled with anger. "Meaning? You need to kill the people who did this. If you won't, I will."

Giacomo listened to his sister's words. *Will she ever recover?* At one point in his life, he would have agreed with her—but not now.

"No, my little sister. God will exact justice. I know who did it. We'll get them—and it will be soon." His voice was strong with the purpose behind his words.

Chapter 109

Vatican City, January 6

GIACOMO ROUNDED A corner. The Church of San Pellegrino was to his right. Hesitant, he climbed the stone steps. The grieving man blessed himself with holy water. In reverence, he genuflected and entered the first pew.

Giacomo's mind was weary. His heart ached. He closed his eyes and let go.

He was in Washington, DC, on the day of the inauguration; Emily absent. He was not far from Tom Maro as he said the oath of office. Outgoing President Richardson smiled; he smiled back. A commotion occurred, and people screamed. His eyes darted back and forth.

His mind whisked him to Paris. Eten Trivette sat behind the desk. The president of the EU on the phone grimaced as he listened. Trivette rubbed the back of his neck and then his right temple. Someone stood over him . . . Trivette's appearance grew disfigured as a black shadow overcame him and evil overtook his soul.

Giacomo watched as Trivette's ghostly face was replaced by images of men and women. He recognized them but could not put names to the people. His heart raced, and he felt full of anxiety and disgust. Paris occupied his mind's eye as the City of Lights flashed with a blaze of blinding luminosity. In an instant, daytime was followed by complete blackness. Images of other cities and villages he recognized flashed through his mind and filled him with fear . . . the words "not what it seems" echoed in his being.

A calmness ensued as Emily, his father, Paolo, and Arnaud materialized before him. They smiled, touched, and hugged him. A sense of love, peace, and immense joy filled him. His mind was swept away in ecstasy.

Giacomo jumped off the pew, shouting, "Whoa, whoa!" His face felt radiant. He couldn't contain the elation within him. His security detail—papal guards—rushed into the church. He stood in the aisle, his head raised to the ceiling, then turned to see the pope and ten cardinals.

Andrew approached him, the cardinals three steps behind. "Giacomo?"

"Andrew . . . how long have you been here?"

"Almost twenty minutes."

"I didn't hear you. I'm sorry."

"Please, don't be. What happened?"

"Andrew. I'm sorry, Your Holiness—the euphoria . . . the joy. I . . . I . . ."

Andrew placed his hand on his shoulder. "Giacomo, relax. For the last twenty minutes, you were surrounded by a globe of white light so bright we had to shield our eyes."

"Really?"

"Yes."

"What does it mean?"

Andrew discharged the cardinals. Four of the red-clothed men left the chapel, while the rest stayed and prayed.

"The bigger question is, what does it mean to you?"

The two men sat on the steps of the sanctuary, the altar behind them.

"I feel I'm loved—an immense love deep within me, and . . . I'm not sad. Emily is fine. There is nothing to worry about . . . everything is good."

"The vision?"

The elation subsided as he tried to recall the disturbing image. "Hmm . . . the last eulogy."

"Last eulogy?"

"Yep—my dad wrote me a note a long time ago. He said, 'The last eulogy of humankind has begun.' I wondered what he meant. I took it to be that we . . ." He contemplated for a moment. "The last eulogy is the final acclamation of God's people. This is the time when we are given the last chance to right the wrongs before darkness falls upon us. The goodness and mercy of God will explode one final time. Then the evilness of humanity will be poured out into the streets. When that happens, God will take a back seat. Then, when all that was foretold comes to fruition, out of the depths of nowhere, with no warning, it will end. The victory will be His."

"Giacomo, do you believe what you just said?"

He closed his eyes. "Yes, I do, Andrew. It's imprinted on my heart. It will happen, and it will happen soon—sooner than you and I think." He stood. "I have work to do."

The two friends walked down the aisle together. The papal guards opened the doors as they emerged into the sunlight.

Chapter 110

LATER THAT NIGHT, Adinolfi—both doctor and priest—navigated the corridor of the military hospital and stopped at the nurses' station. The young woman spoke on her cell phone. The physician stroked his gray-and-white beard and whistled as he waited patiently for the girl to finish her conversation. A Typhoon fighter jet shook the building as it soared overhead.

"I'm sorry, Doctor. How may I help you?"

"The patient in room 840—file please."

"Yes, Doctor." She turned and went to a locked cabinet.

Without hesitation, the doctor reached inside his white jacket, pulled out a dart gun, and fired it at her. With a brief groan, the nurse fell to the floor.

Two people ran down the hall.

"Quickly, there is not much time, Brother. The airplane departs in an hour.

Adinolfi directed the three men to the security ward. He inputted the four-digit code, and the electric door swung open.

"The second room on the left. Be careful—we need to do this fast. Military guards will be making their rounds in thirty minutes. *Spiritus Sanctus Vobis*—the Holy Spirit is with you."

"Yes, Father," they replied in unison.

The two hurried to the room while Adinolfi guarded the doors. His right hand plucked at his red suspenders as he anxiously checked his watch. Five minutes passed. The men exited the room. Each held a newborn baby boy in his arms.

Epilogue

UPON GIACOMO'S RETURN to the United States, his father's old pilot, Danny, a former Secret Service agent, drove him home. As they turned from Chapel Street to Alston, Giacomo said, "We have company." Parked outside his house was a cadre of television cameras and news reporters.

"A couple of phone calls, and I can make them disappear."

"No, need for that, Dan. Guess I'm not staying here tonight. Can you drop me off at the Omni?"

"No problem."

They arrived at the hotel fifteen minutes later.

"Danny, I appreciate the ride. My dad always spoke highly of you."

"No worries, Giacomo. I'm available if you need me."

"Thanks." He opened the car door and stepped out into the cold January day.

Danny opened the center console of the 1968 Pontiac Firebird Trans Am. "Giacomo." In his hand, he held an envelope. "This is for you."

Giacomo shook his head. "From my dad?"

"Yes."

He took the envelope. "Thank you, Danny. I'm sure we'll talk soon."

Danny drove away in the antique car. Giacomo studied his father's signature and the words "October 27, 1989, Grosseto, Italy" that were written across the envelope seal. As he waited in line to check into the hotel, he removed the page and was surprised to see it was torn:

Giacomo, my son, I know your heart aches. I don't understand why but know you are loved. The sacrifice you endured will allow you to move forward. There is still more to do. Betrayal and deceit are in front of you. Then, my son, an extraordinary joy will fill your being. Giacomo, when Paris goes dark, when the two reunite, give them this message: the two brothers will fight for peace among the warmongers of the world. A picture is worth a thousand words. The principalities will now topple. The four horsemen have arrived—the angels' trumpets blare. Do not bear arms; put your weapons down. For God's justice will reign true, and those who heed this word will not falter from God's grace. His justice cannot be stopped!

The key from Grosseto will open the pathway to the prophecy hidden in time. Open your heart and mind, for you are the third trumpet to sound.

Giacomo folded the piece of paper, placing it in his pants pocket. He shook his head as he approached the check-in counter. The woman recognized him. "How may I help you, Mr. DeLaurentis?"

*   *   *

Twenty minutes later, the 1968 Trans Am pulled into a three-story garage and parked next to a 1965 Cobra. The doors closed behind the vehicle. Danny exited the car and walked to a white wooden door. He tilted his head toward a camera while his eyes were scanned. The ex-Secret Service agent entered a ten-foot by four-foot hallway. Sensors examined his body for hidden cameras and recording devices. A humming motor activated the wall as the partition fell into the floor. Danny stepped forward and then waited for the structure to return to its position. Once he heard the final locking pin click into place, he took another step forward. Lights illuminated the two flights of stairs that he took down to the fireproof, bombproof steel vault. He slid his thumb on a fingerprint reader and punched in the combination with his other hand. The door swung open. He turned to his left, flipped on a light switch, and glanced at the rows of shelves. They contained the three thousand documents and more than fourteen hundred sealed envelopes that represented the writings and messages of Paolo DeLaurentis. Danny went to a computer that hung on a wall and typed in "Dropped Giacomo at Omni Hotel." The machine directed him to a labeled shelf. He grabbed three envelopes. Placing them in the shredder, he watched as the machine chewed the written words. A printer began to type. Danny read the letter. Directed to another shelf, he pulled out two envelopes. The message read: "Mail on March 28, 2021."

Danny grabbed his cell phone and hit a number on his speed dial.

"Hello, Danny."

"We're all set here until March."

"Sounds good. We'll talk soon."

Danny left the bunker, changed into his work clothes, and went out to the garage to work on restoring his antique Bugatti motorcycle. He whispered to himself, "A couple of months off."

CPSIA information can be obtained
at www.ICGtesting.com
Printed in the USA
LVHW112316181218
601006LV00002B/179/P